THE
THE
AND
THE WAY THROUGH
THE WOODS

Colin Dexter graduated from Cambridge University in 1953 and has lived in Oxford since 1966. His first novel, *Last Bus to Woodstock*, was published in 1975. There are now thirteen novels in the series, of which *The Remorseful Day* is, sadly, the last.

Colin Dexter has won many awards for his novels, including the CWA Silver Dagger twice, and the CWA Gold Dagger for *The Wench is Dead* and *The Way Through the Woods*. In 1997 he was presented with the CWA Diamond Dagger for outstanding services to crime literature, and in 2000 was awarded the OBE in the Queen's Birthday Honours List.

The Inspector Morse novels have, of course, been adapted for the small screen with huge success by Carlton/Central Television, starring John Thaw and Kevin Whately.

THE INSPECTOR MORSE NOVELS

Last Bus to Woodstock
Last Seen Wearing
The Silent World of Nicholas Quinn
Service of All the Dead
The Dead of Jericho
The Riddle of the Third Mile
The Secret of Annexe 3
The Wench is Dead
The Jewel That Was Ours
The Daughters of Cain
Death is Now My Neighbour
The Remorseful Day

Also available in Pan Books

Morse's Greatest Mystery and other stories
The First Inspector Morse Omnibus
The Second Inspector Morse Omnibus
The Third Inspector Morse Omnibus
The Fourth Inspector Morse Omnibus

COLIN DEXTER

THE RIDDLE OF THE TIIIRD MILE

AND

THE WAY THROUGH THE WOODS

PAN BOOKS

The Riddle of the Third Mile first published 1983 by Macmillan
and first published in paperback 1984 by Pan Books
The Way Through the Woods first published 1992 by Macmillan
and first published in paperback 1993 by Pan Books

This omnibus edition published 2003 by Pan Books
an imprint of Pan Macmillan Ltd
Pan Macmillan, 20 New Wharf Road, London N1 9RR
Basingstoke and Oxford
Associated companies throughout the world
www.panmacmillan.com

ISBN 0 330 42094 1

1 3 5 7 9 8 6 4 2

A CIP catalogue record for this book is available from
the British Library.

Printed and bound in Great Britain by
Mackays of Chatham plc, Chatham, Kent

THE RIDDLE OF
THE THIRD MILE

For My Daughter, Sally

And whosoever shall compel thee to go a mile,
go with him twain.

(Matthew v, 41)

The First Mile

CHAPTER ONE

Monday, 7th July

In which a veteran of the El Alamein offensive finds
cause to recall the most tragic day of his life.

THERE HAD BEEN the three of them – the three
Gilbert brothers: the twins, Alfred and Albert; and the
younger boy, John, who had been killed one day in
North Africa. And it was upon his dead brother that
the thoughts of Albert Gilbert were concentrated as he
sat alone in a North London pub just before closing
time: John, who had always been less sturdy, more
vulnerable, than the formidable, inseparable, and virtually indistinguishable pair known to their schoolmates
as 'Alf 'n' Bert'; John, whom his elder brothers had
always sought to protect; the same John whom they had
not been able to protect that terrible day in 1942.

It was in the early morning of 2nd November that
'Operation Supercharge' had been launched against the
Rahman Track to the west of El Alamein. To Gilbert, it
had always seemed strange that this campaign was
considered by war historians to be such a miraculous

triumph of strategic planning, since from his brief but not unheroic participation in that battle he could remember only the blinding confusions around him during that pre-dawn attack. 'The tanks must go through' had been the previous evening's orders, filtered down from the red-tabbed hierarchy of Armoured Brigade to the field officers and the NCOs of the Royal Wiltshires, into which regiment Alf and Bert had enlisted in October 1939, soon to find themselves grinding over Salisbury Plain in the drivers' seats of antique tanks – both duly promoted to full corporals, and both shipped off to Cairo at the end of 1941. And it had been a happy day for the two of them when brother John had joined them in mid-1942, as each side built up reinforcements for the imminent show-down.

On that morning of 2nd November, at 0105 hours, Alf and Bert moved their tanks forward along the north side of Kidney Ridge, where they came under heavy fire from the German 88s and the Panzers dug in at Tel Aqqaqir. The guns of the Wiltshires' tanks had spat and belched their shells into the enemy lines, and the battle raged furiously. But it was an uneven fight, for the advancing British tanks were open targets for the antitank weapons and, as they nosed forward, they were picked off piecemeal from the German emplacements.

It was a hard and bitter memory, even now; but Gilbert allowed his thoughts full rein. He could do so now. Yes, and it was important that he *should* do so.

About fifty yards ahead of him, one of the leading tanks was burning, the commander's body sprawled across the hatch, the left arm dangling down towards the main turret, the tin-helmeted head spattered with blood. Another tank, to his left, lurched to a crazy standstill as a German shell shattered its left-side track, four men jumping down and sprinting back towards the comparative safety of the boundless, anonymous sands behind them.

The noise of battle was deafening as shrapnel soared and whistled and plunged and dealt its death amidst the desert in that semi-dawn. Men shouted and pleaded and ran – and died; some blessedly swiftly in an instantaneous annihilation, others lingeringly as they lay mortally wounded on the bloody sand. Yet others burned to death inside their tanks as the twisted metal of the hatches jammed, or shot-up limbs could find no final, desperate leverage.

Then it was the turn of the tank immediately to Gilbert's right – an officer leaping down, clutching a hand that spurted blood, and just managing to race clear before the tank exploded into blinding flame.

Gilbert's turret-gunner was shouting down to him.

'Christ! See that, Bert? No wonder they christened these fuckin' things "Tommycookers"!'

'You just keep giving it to the bastards, Wilf!' Gilbert had shouted back.

But he received no reply, for Wilfred Barnes, Private in the Royal Wiltshire Yeomanry, had spoken his last words.

The next thing Gilbert saw was the face of Private Phillips as the latter wrestled with the driver's hatch and helped him out.

'Run like hell, corporal! The other two have had it.'

They had struggled only some forty yards before flinging themselves down as another shell kicked up the sand just ahead of them, spewing its steel fragments in a shower of jagged metal. And when Gilbert finally looked up, he found that Private Phillips, too, was dead – a lump of twisted steel embedded in his lower back. For several minutes after that, Gilbert sat where he was, severely shocked but apparently uninjured. His eyes looked down at his legs, then at his arms; he felt his face and his chest; then he tried to wriggle his toes in his army boots. Just thirty seconds ago there had been four men. And now there was only one – *him.* His first conscious thought (which he could recall so vividly) was a feeling of ineffable anger; but almost immediately his heart rejoiced as he saw a fresh wave of 8th Armoured Brigade tanks moving up through the gaps between the broken or blazing hulks of the first assault formation. Only gradually did a sense of vast relief surge through him – relief that he had survived, and he said a brief prayer to his God in gratitude for coming through.

Then he heard the voice.

'For Christ's sake, get out of here, corporal!' It was the officer with the bleeding hand, a lieutenant in the Wiltshires – a man who was known as a stickler for discipline, and a bit pompous with it; but not an unpopular officer, and indeed the one who the night before had relayed to his men the Montgomery memorandum.

'You a'right, sir?' Gilbert asked.

'Not too bad.' He looked down at his hand, the right

index finger hanging only by a tissue of flesh to the rest of his hand. 'What about you?'

'I'm fine, sir.'

'We'll get back to Kidney Ridge – that's about all we *can* do.' Even here, amid the horrifying scenes of carnage, the voice was that of a pre-war wireless announcer, clipped and precise – what they called an 'Oxford' accent.

The two men scrambled through the soft sand for a few hundred yards before Gilbert collapsed.

'Come *on*! What's the matter with you, man?'

'I dunno, sir. I just don't seem...' He looked down at his left trouser-leg, where he had felt the fire of some intense pain; and he saw that blood had oozed copiously through the rough khaki. Then he put his left hand to the back of his leg and felt the sticky morass of bleeding flesh where half his calf had been shot away. He grinned ruefully:

'You go on, sir. I'll bring up the rear.'

But already the focus had changed. A tank which had seemed to be bearing down upon them suddenly slewed round upon its tracks so that now it faced backwards, its top completely sheared away. Its engine, however, still throbbed and growled, the gears grinding like the gnashing of tortured teeth in hell. But Gilbert heard more than that. He heard the voice of a man crying out in the agony of some godforsaken despair, and he found himself staggering towards the tank as it lurched round yet again in a spurting spray of sand. The man in the driver's seat was alive! Thereafter Gilbert forgot himself completely: forgot his leg-wound, forgot his fear, forgot his relief, forgot his anger. He thought only of Private Phillips from Devizes . . .

The hatch was a shattered weld of hot steel that just would not open – not yet. *Almost* it came; and the sweat showered down Gilbert's face as he swore and wrenched and whimpered at his task. The petrol-tank ignited with a soft, almost apologetic 'whush', and Gilbert knew it was a matter only of seconds before another man was doomed to death inside a Tommycooker.

'For Chrissake!' he yelled to the officer behind him. 'Help! Please! I've – nearly – ' He wrenched for the last time at the hatch, and the sweat poured again on to his bulging, vein-ridged forearms.

'Can't you fuckin' well see? Can't you – ' His voice tailed off in desperation, and he fell to the sand, overwhelmed by failure and exhaustion.

'Leave it, corporal! Come away! That's an *order*!'

So Gilbert crawled away across the sand and wept in frenetic despair, his grimed face looking up to see through his tears the glaze in the officer's eyes . . . the glaze of frozen cowardice. But he remembered little else except the screaming of that burning fellow soldier. And it was only later that he thought he'd recognized the voice – for he hadn't seen the face.

He was picked up (so they told him) soon after this by an army truck, and the next thing he could remember was lying comfortably in very white sheets and red blankets in a military hospital. They didn't tell him until two weeks later that his brother John, tank driver with the 8th Armoured Brigade, had been killed in the second-phase offensive.

Then Albert Gilbert had been almost sure; but even now, he wasn't *quite* sure. He knew one thing, though, for nothing could erase from his cerebral cortex the name of the officer who, one morning in the desert, in the battle for the ridge at Tel Aqqaqir, had been tried in the balance of courage – and been found wanting. Lieutenant Browne-Smith, that was the name. Funny name, really, with an 'e' in the middle. A name he'd never seen again, until recently.

Until very recently indeed.

CHAPTER TWO

Wednesday, 9th July

We are in the University of Oxford, at the marks-meeting of the seven examiners appointed for 'Greats'.

'HE WOULD HAVE walked a first otherwise,' said the Chairman. He looked down again at the six separate assessments, all of them liberally sprinkled with alphas and beta plusses except for the one opposite Greek History, where stood a feeble-looking beta double minus/delta. Not, this last, the category of the finest minds.

'Well, what do you think, gentlemen? Worth a viva, surely, isn't he?'

With minimal effort, five of the other six men, seated at a large table bestrewn with scripts and lists and mark-sheets, raised the palms of their hands in agreement.

'*You* don't think so?' The Chairman had turned towards the seventh member of the examining panel.

'No, Chairman. He's not worth it – not on this evidence.' He flicked the script in front of him. 'He's proved quite conclusively to me that he knows next to nothing outside fifth-century Athens. I'm sorry. If he wanted a first, he ought to have done a bit more work than *this*.' Again he flicked the script, an expression of disgust further disfiguring a face that had probably been sour from birth. Yet, as all those present knew, no one else in the University could award a delicate grading like B+/B+?+ with such confident aplomb, or justify it with such fierce conviction.

'We all know, though, don't we,' (it was one of the other members) 'that sometimes it's a bit hit-and-miss, the questions we set, I mean – especially in Greek History.'

'I set the questions,' interrupted the dissident, with some heat. 'There's never been a fairer spread.'

The Chairman looked very tired. 'Gentlemen. We've had a long, hard day, and we're almost at the finishing-post. Let's just—'

'Of course he's worth a viva,' said one of the others with a quiet, clinching authority. 'I marked his Logic paper – it's brilliant in places.'

'I'm sure you're right,' said the Chairman. 'We fully take your point about the history paper, Dr Browne-Smith, but . . .'

'So be it – you're the Chairman.'

'Yes, you're quite right. I *am* the Chairman and this man's going to get his viva!'

It was a nasty little exchange, and the Logic examiner immediately stepped in with a peace proposal. 'Perhaps, Dr Browne-Smith, you might agree to viva him yourself?'

But Browne-Smith shook his aching head. 'No! I'm biased against the fellow – and all this marking – it's been quite enough for me. I'm doing nothing else.'

The Chairman, too, was anxious to end the meeting on a happier note: 'What about asking Andrews? Would *he* be prepared to take it on?'

Browne-Smith shrugged. 'He's quite a good young man.'

So the Chairman wrote his final note: 'To be vivaed by Mr Andrews (Lonsdale), 18th July'; and the others began to collect their papers together.

'Well, thank you all very much gentlemen. Before we finish, though, can we just think about our final meeting? Almost certainly it's got to be Wednesday 23rd or Thursday 24th.'

Browne-Smith was the only one of the panel who hadn't taken out his diary; and when the meeting was finally fixed for 10 a.m. on Wednesday the 23rd, he appeared to take no notice whatsoever.

The Chairman had observed this. 'All right with you, Dr Browne-Smith?'

'I was just about to say, Chairman, that I'm afraid I probably shan't be with you for the final meeting. I should very much like to be, of course, but I – I've got to be . . . Well, I probably shan't be in Oxford.'

The Chairman nodded a vague, uneasy understanding. 'Well, we'll try to do our best without you. Thank you, anyway, for all the help you've been – as ever.' He closed the thick, black volume in front of him, and looked at his wrist-watch: 8.35 p.m. Yes, it had been a long, hard day. No wonder, perhaps, that he'd become a little snappy at the end.

Six members of the panel agreed to repair to the King's Arms in Broad Street; but the seventh member,

Dr Browne-Smith, begged leave to be excused. Instead, he left the Examination Schools, walked slowly along the High, and let himself through the back-door ('Senior Fellows Only') into Lonsdale College. Once in his rooms, he swallowed six Paracetamol tablets, and lay down fully-clothed upon his bed, where for the next hour his brain blundered around uncontrollably in his head. Then he fell asleep.

On the morning of the next day, Thursday, 10th July, he received a letter. A very strange and rather exciting letter.

CHAPTER THREE

Friday, 11th July

In which we learn of an Oxford don's invitation to view
the vice and viciousness of life in a notorious area of the
metropolis.

NEVER THROUGHOUT HIS life – almost sixty-seven
years of it now – had Oliver Maximilian Alexander
Browne-Smith (with an 'e' and with hyphenation) MC,
MA, D.Phil., really come to terms with his inordinately
ponderous names. Predictably, in his prep-school days
he had been nicknamed 'Omar'; and now, with only
one year before his University appointment was due to
be statutorily terminated, he knew that amongst the
undergraduates he had acquired the opprobrious sobri-
quet of 'Malaria', which was not so predictable and very
much nastier.

It was some small surprise to him, therefore, to find
how quickly he had managed to bring himself to terms,
in a period of only a few weeks, with the fact that he
would quite certainly be dead well within a twelve-
month ('At the very outside, since you insist on the
truth, Dr Browne-Smith'). What he did not realize,
however, as he walked on to Platform One at Oxford

Station, was that he would be dead within a shorter period than that so confidently predicted by his distinguished and expensive consultant.

A very much shorter period.

As he made his way to the rear end of the platform, he kept his eyes lowered, and looked with distaste at the empty beer cans and litter that bestrewed the 'up' line. A few of his University colleagues, some from Lonsdale, were fairly frequent passengers on the 9.12 a.m. train from Oxford to Paddington, and the truth was that he felt no wish to converse with any of them. Under his left arm he held a copy of *The Times*, just purchased from the station bookstall; and in his right hand he held a brown leather briefcase. For a fine, bright morning in mid-July, it was surprisingly chilly.

The yellow-fronted diesel snaked its slow way punctually through the points just north of the station, and two minutes later he was seated opposite a young couple in a non-smoking compartment. Although an inveterate and incurable smoker himself, one who had dragged his wheezing lungs through cigarettes at the rate of forty-plus a day for fifty years, he had decided to impose upon himself some token abstinence during the hour-long journey that lay ahead of him. It seemed, somehow, appropriate. When the train moved out, he folded *The Times* over and started on the crossword, his mind registering nothing at all on the first three of the clues across. But on the fourth, a hint of a grin formed around his slightly lopsided words: 'First thing in Soho tourist's after? (8).' He quickly wrote in 'stripper'; and with more and more letters thenceforth making their horizontal and vertical inroads into the diagram-grid, the puzzle was finished well before Reading. Then, hoping that the couple opposite had duly noted his cruciverbalistic competence – if not the ugly stump of his right index finger, chopped off at the first joint – he leaned back in his seat as far as his longish legs would allow, closed his eyes, and concentrated his thoughts on the very strange reason that was drawing him to London that day.

At Paddington he was almost the last person to leave the train and, as he walked to the ticket barrier, he saw that it was still only 10.15 a.m. Plenty of time. He collected a Paddington-Reading-Oxford timetable from the Information Bureau, bought a cup of coffee at the buffet, where he lit a cigarette, and looked up the possible trains for his return journey. Curiously enough, he felt relaxed as he lit a second cigarette from the first, and wondered vaguely what times the pubs – and clubs – would be open in London. 11 a.m. perhaps? But that was a matter of no great moment.

It was 10.40 a.m. when he left the station buffet and walked briskly to the Bakerloo line, where, as he queued for his ticket, he realized that he must have left his timetable in the buffet. But that was of no great moment, either. There were plenty of trains to choose from, and he'd made a mental note of some of the times.

He could not have known, of course, that he would not be travelling back to Oxford that night.

On the tube he opened his briefcase and took out two sheets of paper: the first was a letter addressed to himself, amateurishly typed but perfectly literate – a letter that still seemed very strange to him; the second was a more professionally typed sheet (indeed, typed by Browne-Smith himself) comprising a list of students from Oxford University, with the names of their colleges appended in brackets, and the words 'Class One, *Literae Humaniores*' printed across the top in bold, red capitals. But Browne-Smith glanced only cursorily at the two sheets through his bifocal lenses. It appeared that he was merely reassuring himself that both were still in existence. Nothing more.

At Edgware Road he looked up above the carriage-windows, noting that there were only two more stops, and for almost the first time he felt a flutter of excitement somewhere in his diaphragm. It was that letter ... *Very* odd! Even the address had been odd, with the full details carefully stated: Room 4, Staircase T, Second Quad, Lonsdale College, Oxford. Such specificity was rare, and seemed to suggest that whoever had sent the letter was more than usually anxious for it not to go astray – more than a little knowledgeable, too, about the college's geography ... Staircase T, Second Quad ... In his mind's eye, Browne-Smith saw himself climbing those few stairs once more; climbing them, as he had done for the past thirty years, up to the first landing, where his own name, hand-printed in white, Gothic lettering, still stood above the door. And immediately opposite him, Room 3 – where George Westerby, the Geography don, had lived for almost exactly the same time: just one term longer than himself, in fact. Their mutual hatred was intense, the whole college knew that, though it might just have been different if Westerby had ever been prepared to make the feeblest gesture towards some reconciliation. But he had never done so.

Via the ziggurat of steep escalators, Browne-Smith emerged at 11.05 a.m. into the bright sunlight of Piccadilly Circus, crossed over into Shaftesbury Avenue, and immediately plunged into the maze of roads and alleyways that criss-cross the area off Great Windmill Street. Here abounded small cinemas that featured films of hard, uncompromising porn, with stills outside of nudes and semi-nudes, vast-breasted and voluptuous; clubs that promised passers-by the prospects of erotic, non-stop nudity; bookshops that boasted the glossiest, grossest magazines for paedophiles and buffs of bestiality. And it was along these gaudy streets, beneath the orange and the yellow signs, past the inviting doors, that Browne-Smith walked slowly, savouring the uncensored atmosphere, and feeling himself inexorably sucked into the cesspool that is known as Soho.

It was in a narrow lane just off Brewer Street that he spotted it – as he'd known he would: 'The Flamenco Topless Bar: No Membership Fee: Please Walk Straight Down.' The wide, shallow steps that led from the foyer down to the subterranean premises had once been carpeted in heavy crimson, but now the middle of the tread resembled more the trampled sward of a National Trust beauty spot at the height of a glorious summer. He was walking past, but there must have been some tell-tale hesitation in his step, for the acne-faced youth who lounged just inside the doorway had spotted him already.

'Lovely girls in here, sir. Just walk straight down. No membership fee.'

'The bar is open, is it? I only want a drink.'

'Bar's always open here, sir. Just walk straight down.' The young man stepped aside, and Browne-Smith took his fateful step across the entrance and slowly descended to The Flamenco Topless Bar. *Facilis descensus Averno.*

At the foot of the stairs further progress was barred by a velvet drape, and he was wondering what he should do when a seemingly disembodied head poked through a gap in the middle of the curtain – the head of an attractive young girl of no more than nineteen or twenty years, the hazel eyes luridly blued and blackened by harsh mascaras, but the sensuous mouth devoid of any lipstick. A pink tongue completed a slow circuit round the soft-looking mouth, and a pleasant voice asked simply and sweetly for only £1.

'There's no membership fee; it says so outside. And the man on the door said so.'

The face smiled, as it always smiled at the gullible men who'd trodden those broad and easy stairs.

'It's not a membership fee – just admission. You know what I mean?' The eyes held his with simmering sexuality, and the note passed quickly through the crimson curtain.

The Flamenco Bar was a low-ceilinged affair with the seats grouped in *alcôves à deux*, towards one of which the young girl escorted him. She was, herself, fully clothed; and, after handing her client a buff-coloured drinks list, she departed without a further word to her wonted seat behind a poor imitation of a drinking-man's bar, whereat she was soon deeply engrossed in her zodiacal predictions as reported in the *Daily Mirror.*

It seemed to Browne-Smith, as he struggled to interpret the long bill of fare, that the minimum charge for any semi-alcoholic beverage was £3. And he was beginning to suspect that the best value for such an exorbitant charge was probably two (separate) half-glasses of lager – when he heard her voice.

'Can I take your order?'

Over the top of his glasses he looked up at the young woman who stood in front of him. She was leaning forward, completely naked from the waist upwards, her long, pink skirt split widely to the top of her thigh.

'The lager, I think, please.'

She made a note on the pad she held. 'Would you like me to sit with you?'

'Yes, I would.'

'You'd have to buy me a drink.'

'All right.'

She pointed to the very bottom of the card:

Flamenco Revenge – a marriage of green-eyed Chartreuse with aphrodisiac Cointreau.
Soho Wallbanger – a dramatic confrontation of voluptuous Vodka with a tantalizing taste of Tia Maria.
Eastern Ecstasy – an irresistible alchemy of rejuvenating Gin and pulse-quickening Campari.
Price: £6.00

£6.00!

'I'm sorry,' said Browne-Smith, 'but I just can't afford—'

'I can't sit with you if you won't buy me a drink.'

'It's so terribly expensive, though, isn't it? I just can't aff—'

'All right!' The words were clipped and final, and she left his table, to return a few minutes later with his first small glass of lager, setting the meagre measure before him with studied indifference and departing immediately.

From the alcove behind him, Browne-Smith could hear the conversation distinctly:

'Where you from?'

'Ostrighlia.'

'Nice there?'

'Sure is!'

'You'd like me to sit with you?'

'Sure would!'

'You'd have to buy me a drink.'

'Just you nime it, bighby!'

Browne-Smith swallowed a mouthful of his flat and tepid lager and took stock of the situation. Apart from the proximate Australian, he could see only one other customer, a man of indeterminate age (forty? fifty? sixty?) who sat at the bar reading a book. In contrast to his balding pate and the grey-white patches at his temples, the neatly trimmed and black-brown beard was quite devoid of grizzled hairs; and for a few seconds the fanciful notion occurred to Browne-Smith that the

man might be in disguise, this notion being somewhat
reinforced by the fact that he was wearing a pair of
incongruous sunglasses which masked the eyes whilst
not, apparently, blurring the print of the page upon
which he appeared so totally engrossed.

From where Browne-Smith sat, the décor looked
universally cheap. The carpet, a continuation of the
stairway crimson, was dirty and stained, with threadbare
patches beneath most of the plastic tables; the chairs
were flimsy, rickety, wickerwork structures which
seemed barely capable of supporting the weight of any
overfleshed client; the walls and ceiling had clearly
once been painted white, but were now grubby and
stained with the incessant smoke of cigarettes. But there
was one touch of culture – a most surprising one: the
soberly volumed background music was the slow movement of Mozart's 'Elvira Madigan' piano concerto
(played by Barenboim – Browne-Smith could have
sworn it), and this seemed to him almost as incongruous as listening to Shakin' Stevens in St Paul's
Cathedral.

Another man was admitted through the curtain and
was duly visited by the same white-breasted beauty who
had brought his own lager; the man at the bar turned
over another page of his book; the Australian, clearly
audible still, was none too subtly prodding his hostess
into revealing what exactly it was she was selling,
because she'd got what he wanted and his only concern
was the price she might be asking for it; the girl behind
the bar had obviously exhausted whatever the *Daily*

Mirror could prognosticate; and Barenboim had landed lightly upon the final notes of that ethereal movement.

Browne-Smith's glass was now empty, and the only two hostesses on view were happily supping whatever the management had decided were today's ingredients for Soho Wallbangers, Flamenco Revenges, *et al.* So he got up, walked over to the bar and sat himself down on a stool.

'I've got another one paid for, I think.'

'I'll bring it to you.'

'No, don't bother. I'll sit here.'

'I said I'd bring it to you.'

'You don't mind me sitting here, do you?'

'You si' down where you were – you understand English?' All pretence at civility had vanished, and her voice sounded hard and mean.

'All right,' said Browne-Smith quietly. 'I don't want to cause any trouble.' He sat down at a table a few yards from the bar, and watched the girl, and waited.

'You still didn't 'ear wha' I *said,* did you?' The voice was now crudely menacing, but Browne-Smith decided that a few more rounds of small-arms fire could safely be expended; not *quite* time yet for the heavy artillery. He was enjoying himself.

'I *did* hear you, I assure you. But—'

'Look! I told you!' (Which she hadn't.) 'If you want a bloody rub-off there's a sauna right across the road. OK?'

'But I don't—'

'I shan't tell you again, mister.'

Browne-Smith stood up, and stepped slowly to the bar, where the man reading the book flicked over another page, disinterestedly neutral, it appeared, in the outcome of the escalating hostilities.

'I'd like a pint of decent beer, if you have one.' He spoke quietly.

'If you don't want tha' lager—'

Abruptly Browne-Smith crashed his glass on the counter, and fixed the girl with his eyes. 'Lager? Let me tell *you* something, miss! That's not lager – that's horse-piss!'

The battle odds had changed dramatically, and the girl had clearly lost her self-control as she pointed a shaking, carmined finger towards the crimson curtain: 'Get out!'

'Oh no! I've paid for my drinks.'

'You heard what the lady said.' It was the man sitting reading his book by the bar. Although he had neither lifted his eyes one centimetre from the text, nor lifted, it seemed, his flat (West Country?) voice one semitone above its customary pitch, the brief words sounded ominously final.

But Browne-Smith, completely ignoring the man who had just spoken to him, continued to glare at the girl. 'Never speak to me like that again!'

The hissed authority of these words reduced the girl to speechlessness, but the seated man had slowly closed his book, and now at last he raised his eyes. The fingers of his right hand crept across to the upper muscles of his left arm and, although as he eased himself off the bar-stool he stood some two or three inches shorter than Browne-Smith, he looked a dangerous adversary. He said nothing more.

The velvet curtains by which Browne-Smith had entered were only some three yards to his left, and there were several seconds during which a quick, if inglorious, exit could easily have been effected. But no such decision was taken; and before he could consider the situation further he felt his left wrist grasped powerfully, and found himself propelled towards a door marked 'Private'.

Two things he was to remember as his escort knocked quietly upon this door. First, he saw the look on the face of the man from Australia, a look that was three-parts puzzlement and one part panic; second, he observed the title of the book the bearded man was reading: *Know Your Köchel Numbers.*

The anonymous Australian, sitting no more than four or five yards from the door, was destined never to mention this episode to another living soul. And indeed, even had he reason to do so, it seems most improbable that he would have mentioned that enigmatic little moment, just before the door closed behind the two men, when the one of them who seemed to be causing the trouble, the one whose name he would never know, had suddenly looked at his wrist-watch, and said in a voice that sounded inexplicably calm: 'My goodness! I see it's exactly twelve noon.'

For a few seconds after he had crossed the threshold of the office, Browne-Smith experienced that dazzling, zigzag pain again that seemed to saw its way across his brain, momentarily cutting him off from any recollection

of himself and of what he was doing. But then it stopped
– as suddenly as it had started – and he thought he was
in control of things once more.

Looking out over the lawn of Second Quad, George
Westerby had watched the tallish figure (several inches
taller than himself) striding out towards the Porter's
Lodge at 8.15 a.m. that same morning. Uppermost in
his mind at that moment – and he gloried in it – was
the realization that he would be seeing very little more
of his detested colleague, Browne-Smith. He himself,
George Westerby, having recently celebrated his sixty-
eighth birthday, was retiring at last. Indeed, a removal
firm had already been at work on his vast accumulation
of books; and the treasured rows from more than half
his shelves had been removed in blocks, stringed up,
and stacked into the tea-chests that now occupied an
uncomfortably large area of the floor space. And soon,
of course, there would be the wooden crates, and the
lumbering, muscled men who would transfer his
precious possessions to the flat he had purchased in
London. A smaller place, naturally, and one that might
well pose a few storage problems. That could wait
though, certainly until after his forthcoming holiday in
the Aegean Isles ... over to Asia across that azure
sea ...

But even as he stood there by the window, nodding
slowly and contentedly to himself for a few moments, it
was Browne-Smith who still dominated his thoughts. It
had always been 'Browne-Smith' with him – not even

'Malaria' Browne-Smith, as though such familiarity might compromise his eternal antagonism. There would be only a few more nights now when he would have to dine in Hall with that odious man; just a few more lunches, occasionally standing awkwardly proximate over the cold buffets; only one more College meeting, at the beginning of next week – the very last one. For the Trinity Term was almost over now; his last term, and very soon his last day and his last hours; and then the moment (when it came) of looking down for the very last time on that immaculate lawn . . .

George Westerby was collectively conscious of all these things as he stood watching from his first-floor window on that chilly early morning of the 11th July. What he did not know at that time – what he could not have known – was that Lonsdale College was never again to welcome Browne-Smith within its quiet quads.

CHAPTER FOUR

Friday, 11th July

In which we have a tantalizing glimpse of high-class harlotry.

THE TAXI-DRIVER KNEW the street, and Browne-Smith settled himself in the back seat with a heightened sense of excitement. He would have wished to savour these moments longer, but in less than five minutes the taxi pulled up at the kerb of Number 29, a large four-storied balconied building in a fashionable terrace just behind Russell Square. In general, although the original brickwork on the lower reaches of the walls had been smutted by traffic-fumes and smoke, the house seemed to have maintained its elegant facade with comparative ease. The black door, with its polished brass knobs and letter-box, was framed by white pillars; and the woodwork of the windows was also painted white, with neatly kept window-boxes adding their splash of greens and reds. Black railings, set in concrete, were stretched along the front; behind which, after a gap of about five feet, the wall of the house continued down to a basement. On these railings a board had been affixed:

Luxury Apartments for Sale or to Let
Please apply: Brooks and Gilbert
(Sole Agents) Tel. 01–483 2307
Viewing by appointment only

Browne-Smith walked up the three shallow steps, and pressed the single bell, apprehensively fingering the blue card that was now in his inside jacket-pocket. He waited. But he had heard no sound of ringing on the other side of the great door, and he could see no sign of life. At this moment, and for the first time, the idea filtered into his mind that he might have been cruelly duped for the silly fool – the silly *old* fool – that he was, in going along with the whole disreputable and dishonourable business. He turned to look at the busy street and saw an aristocratic female disembarking from a taxi only a few doors away. No, it wasn't too late even now! He could just forget it all, hail the taxi . . .

But the door had opened silently behind him.

'Can I help you?' (That West Country intonation again.)

'I'm a friend of Mr Sullivan's.' (Hardly the customary tone of his Mods tutorials – hesitant and slightly croaky.)

'You have an appointment?'

He took out the small, oblong card and handed it to her. The typewritten legend was exceedingly brief, but also (as Browne-Smith saw it) exceedingly significant: 'Please admit bearer' – nothing else, except for that little constellation of asterisks clustered in the top right-hand corner.

The woman stood aside and beckoned him over the threshold, closing the door (again noiselessly) behind them. 'You're an important client, sir, and we welcome you.' She smiled appropriately as they moved through the large entrance hall, carpeted in a light-olive shade, with the same carpeting leading up the wide staircase which faced the front door. She turned to him as she walked on ahead up these stairs, and Browne-Smith noticed her inappropriately ugly teeth as she smiled again. 'All blue cards are on the first floor, sir. I'm afraid we haven't got our full complement of girls just for the moment – it's the evenings usually that we have our busiest time. But I'm sure you won't be disappointed in any way. No one's ever disappointed here.'

On the first landing, she turned to him again, her eyes assessing him shrewdly, like a tailor mentally measuring some wealthy customer. Then, after looking along the corridor to left and right, she appeared to decide where the most appropriate prospects lay, for she opened the door immediately across the landing with a brusqueness which seemed clearly to betoken her mistress-ship of the establishment.

At a table immediately inside the room on the left sat a woman of some forty summers, blonde and big-breasted, wearing a low-cut, full-length purple gown; and, as the lady of the house introduced her client, she stood up and slowly smiled.

'You're free, I think, this afternoon, Yvonne?'

'Thees eevening, also, madame, eef you weesh it.' The blonde smiled bewitchingly again, showing her beautifully even teeth. She was exquisitely made up, a moist lipstick marking the contours of her sensuous mouth, her hair piled immaculately on top of her finely-boned head.

'Is Paula free, too?'

'She weel be, madame. She 'ave a client for lernch, but she weel be free aftair.'

'Well – ' (madame spoke directly to Browne-Smith) ' – if you're happy to stay here with Yvonne, sir?'

He swallowed and nodded his unequivocal assent.

'Good. I'll leave you, then. But you are to have everything you want, sir – I hope you understand that? Absolutely *everything*.'

'I'm most grateful.'

She turned to go. 'You must know Mr – er – Sullivan *very* well, sir?'

'I was just able to do him a little favour, that's all. You know how these things are.'

'Of course. And you promise to let me know if there's anything that Yvonne here can't—'

'I don't think you need worry.'

Then madame was gone, and the back of Browne-Smith's throat felt parched as he fought to stem the flood of erotic imaginings that threatened to swamp him. He had little help from the woman who, briefly resuming her seat in order to make some entry in a red leather-bound diary on the table, leant forward as she did so and revealed even to the most casual glance that beneath her dress she was wearing little else – at least above her rather ample hips.

'I am weeth you now, sir.' She rose from her chair and walked round to him. 'Let me take your coat.'

31

Browne-Smith took off the light brown summer raincoat he had worn continuously since leaving Oxford, and watched her as she folded it neatly over her left arm, slid her right hand under his elbow, and guided him over to a door at the far end of the room.

Compared with the somewhat austere and sparsely furnished room they had just left, this inner room was lavishly and (to Browne-Smith's tastes) rather luridly equipped. Two blood-red lamps, affixed to the inner wall, cast a subdued light around, and thick, yellow curtains, drawn fully across the single window, cut out all but the narrowest chink of natural light. The other furnishings were gaudily provocative with a cohort of multi-coloured cushions covering the long, low settee, and, behind that, bright yellow sheets and pillows on the widely welcoming bed, its coverlet already turned back. Opposite the settee was a tall, well-stocked, drinks cabinet, its doors standing open; and beside it a film projector, pointing a protruding snout towards the white expanse of wall to the left of the curtained casement. Pervading all was the heavy, heady smell of some sweet scent, and Browne-Smith felt a semi-permanent, priapic push between his loins.

'You'd like a dreenk?'

She went over to the cabinet and recited a comprehensive choice: whisky, gin, campari, vodka, rum, martini . . .

'Whisky, please.'

'Glenfeeddich?'

'My favourite.'

'And mine.'

There seemed to be two bottles of each drink, one of them as yet unopened, as though the liquid capacity of even the most dedicated toper had been nobly anticipated. And he watched her (why was he puzzled?) as she ripped the seal off a new bottle, poured out a half-tumbler of the pale malt whisky, and brought it over to him.

'Aren't you going to have one, er—'

'Eevone. Please call me "Eevone". I call you "sir" – because madame, she inseest on eet. But for me – Eevone!'

Even as she spoke, Browne-Smith found himself thinking, albeit vaguely, that her French accent was carefully cultivated and – yes, completely phoney. But why worry about that? More important, for his own fastidious tastes, was the fear that someone else might enter the room. So he took a large gulp of Scotch and voiced his anxiety.

'We shan't be interrupted, shall we?'

'*Non, non!* Madame, you raymember, she say you 'ave everything you want? So? Eef you want me to lock the door, I lock eet. Eef you want Paula, per'aps, you 'ave Paula, OK? But I 'ope you want me, *non?*'

Phew!

She went over to the door and turned the key, went over to the cabinet and poured herself a gin and dry martini, and finally came to sit beside him on the settee, her thigh pressing closely against his own. She clinked their glasses: 'I'm sure we 'ave a good time together, eh? I always like it eef I dreenk.'

Browne-Smith took a further gulp of his Scotch,

sensing even at this early stage that the alcohol was
having an unwontedly powerful effect upon him.

'I feel you up a leetle?'

Momentarily he misunderstood her pronunciation
of that second word; but when she took his glass he
nodded in happy acquiescence, watching her in a
wonderful anticipation as she walked away.

'You like my dress?' She was in front of him now, the
replenished glass in her left hand. 'Eet show off my
figure, *non*?'

'You have a lovely figure.'

'You theenk so? But eet ees so 'ot in 'ere. You take
off your coat, per'aps?' She leaned over him, helping
to remove his jacket, the dress soft against him, her
body soft, the lighting soft; and he sat there passively as
she slid her hands beneath the cuffs of his shirt, and
deftly unfastened the cufflinks (Oxford University)
before pushing the sleeves slowly up the arms. 'Just to
see eef you 'ave a leetle, what you call eet, "tattoo"?'

'No, I haven't, actually.'

'Nor 'ave I. But soon you weel be able to see for
yourself, *non*?' She sat closely beside him again, and
Browne-Smith gulped back another large mouthful of
his drink and willed himself to relax for a while. But
she gave him little chance, taking his right hand and
placing it on the shoulder of her dress.

'You like that?' she asked.

My God! His hand fumbled for a few seconds with
the material of the dress, and then slipped tentatively
beneath it, feeling the soft flesh around her neck.

'Can I—?'

'You can do anytheeng.' Even as she spoke those blissful words her eyes sparkled, and she jumped to her feet, pulling him up in turn with both hands. 'But we 'ave a leetle feelm first, OK?'

Reluctantly, Browne-Smith did as he was bidden, taking his seat in an upright chair in front of the projector, and seeking to prepare himself for the voyeuristic aperitif. Clearly the pattern of events she'd suggested was not an unusual one; she, doubtless, must occasionally feel the need for some erotic stimulus. It was rather sad, this last fact, but he was too intelligent a man to feel surprised.

The scenes now witnessed on the white patch of wall beside the yellow curtaining were wilder by a dozen leagues than the few X-certificated films that Browne-Smith had paid to see at the ABC cinema during the Oxford vacations. It was a pity that the woman wasn't seated close to him; but (as she'd explained) unless she continually made some slight adjustments to the focusing mechanism, the technicolour delineation tended to drift out of true.

It was all so strangely *déjà vu*.

A man, in a smartly cut business suit; a beautiful blonde in a full-length, purple gown; a few intimate drinks on a multi-cushioned settee; the man's hand slipping slowly inside the low-cut bodice and hoisting therefrom a bronzed, globed breast; then a teasingly slow, provocative undress on the part of the blonde, followed by much mutual grasping and gasping – before a finale that was fully orchestrated by climactic groans and an energetic spurting of semen.

The whirring, clicking projector was now switched off, and he felt her hands on his shoulders from behind.

'You like eet again?' She came round and sat on his knees. 'Or would you rather 'ave *me*?'

He swallowed the first '*You!*', but managed the second.

'There ees a long zeep at the back of my dress – that's eet. Just pull down – pull! Yes, that's eet!'

Browne-Smith felt the sinuous movement of her hips pressing down on him as his fingers ventured across her naked back; and then she got up and walked over to the bed.

'Come and let me undress you.'

Her back was turned away from him as she shrugged the dress off her shoulders, bent down to slip off her black, high-heeled shoes, stepped professionally out of her dress, and folded it neatly over the chair at the foot of the bed. Then she turned fully towards him, and he felt an enormously urgent need to take her immediately; but still she teetered on the brink of things, and he thought of the mercilessly tortured Tantalus and the illicit grapes that dangled just above his lips.

'One more leetle drink, per'aps?'

Browne-Smith, now almost in a delirium of anticipation, watched her as she walked over to the cabinet, watched her as she poured the two drinks, watched her as her beautifully formed breasts bounced towards him once more.

'Just lie there a leetle meenite. You can 'ave me very soon.'

She had disappeared through the only other door in

the room, doubtless (judging by the flushing of water) a bathroom. And he, for his part, lay there almost fully clothed upon the yellow sheets, wondering in a hazily distanced sort of way just what was going on. Although his mouth seemed dry as the Sahara, he put down his drink untasted on the bedside-table, and for a while his mind grew clearer. Why had she used the *other* bottle of Glenfiddich? Perhaps . . . perhaps it had been watered down a bit? Just as the Bursar always said at a Gaudy: 'Let them have the good stuff first.'

When, after what seemed an eternity, she returned, he watched her again, leaning half-upright on his right elbow. But his request was the oddest she had ever heard.

'Have you got any sort of *cream*, or something? My lips are awfully dry.'

She fetched her handbag from the settee, opened the flap, and delved around for a few seconds. Then, unscrewing a circular container, she leaned over him, her breasts suspended only inches from his eyes, and smoothly smeared some cream along his lips.

'That ees better, *non*? Dreenk up, darleeng!'

She unfastened his tie; then unfastened the front of his shirt, one button at a time, at each stage her fingers splaying across his chest.

For Browne-Smith these moments were almost unbearably erotic, and he knew that he had little hope of lasting out much longer. Yet he made one further quite extraordinary request. 'Can you open the curtains – just a little bit?'

When the woman returned she saw that the man's

jacket, hitherto folded at the foot of the bed, was now lying beside him; and as she looked down at his motionless body, she saw the tell-tale stain that seeped around the front of his well-cut, dark-blue trousers. His eyes were closed and his breathing steady, the right hand hanging loosely over the side of the bed, the index finger missing below the proximal inter-phalangeal joint. His glass, on the table beside his head, was now empty. She gently took his right arm and lay it alongside his body. Almost, for a moment or so, she felt a pang of tenderness. Then she hurriedly redressed, unlocked the door of the room, went out, and spoke in whispers to a man standing outside – a man who was reading a book entitled *Know Your Köchel Numbers*.

Her duties were done.

CHAPTER FIVE

Friday, 11th July

A woman of somewhat dubious morals seeks to relax, although such is her nature that she recalls too clearly, and too often, the duties she has been paid so handsomely to perform.

IN THE LATISH evening of the day on which the events described in the previous chapter took place, a woman was seated alone in an upstairs flat, bedsitter-cum-bathroom-cum-kitchen, of a house situated in one of the many residential streets that lead south off the Richmond Road. Half an hour earlier she had walked from East Putney tube station, and now she felt tired. Piccadilly to Earls Court, change trains, across the Thames to Putney – how many times had she made that tiresome journey? It would have been so much easier to live in Soho, and there had been no lack of opportunity on that score! But she enjoyed her two lives – her two spheres of existence which intersected at (almost) no single point. Here, in soberly bourgeois suburbia, she was a middle-aged woman with a job in the city. Here, she kept herself very much to herself, quietly, pleasantly, comfortably, dealing with rent and rates and household bills, and furnishing her few rooms at lavish expense. Yet these rooms were for *her* enjoyment only, since she had never invited another person into them, except for the cleaning woman (two hours per week). Except, too, for the man who had come to see her only four days ago.

The woman we are describing looked to be about forty, but was in fact some ten years older. Yet one could readily be forgiven for such misjudgement. She was a large-breasted woman, with hips that had put on several inches over recent years, but her legs were finely graceful still, her ankles slim and firm. There were, certainly, a few tell-tale lines at the corners of her mouth, and again at the sides of her eyes; but the mouth itself was as delicately, deliciously sensitive as it had always been, and the eyes were normally as clear and bright as a summer's noon in the Swedish hills.

Tonight, however, those selfsame eyes were dull and sombre. Seated in an armchair, she crossed her nyloned legs, rested her blonde head upon her left arm, and stared down for many minutes at the richly patterned Wilton carpet. She still felt that residual sense of triumph and achievement; but she felt, too, a certain tension and concern which, over the last few hours, had been growing inexorably into a sense of guilt-ridden remorse.

It had all had its beginnings early on the previous Monday morning, almost immediately after the Sauna Select (just off Brewer Street) had opened its doors to the men who frequented that establishment. There was nothing common, nothing mean about it all; just a gentlemanly and a ladylike understanding that with little fuss and large finance the whole gamut of erotic refinements was readily available. Many of the steady if unspectacular clients were men of middle or late-middle age; some of them were undisguisedly and indisputably ancient. But all were wealthy, since that was the *sine qua non* of the business. How else could the management afford the princessly salaries of its four assorted hostesses? For (as the woman so often reminded herself) it *was* a big salary – far better than her former wages as a popular stripper in the Soho clubs, commuting with her bulky case of costumes from one cramped dais to another.

It had been 10.35 a.m. when the man had come in. He'd wanted a sauna, he said; he wanted nothing else. That's what they all said; but soon the moisture and the heat and the inhibitions slowly dissipating in a world of steam and relaxation would almost always lead to something else. And this man? He had assessed the four of them with an almost embarrassing thoroughness – their figures, their complexions, their eyes – and he had chosen *her*; thereafter being escorted to the steam-room, and thence to one of the private massage parlours (£20 extra) in which the expertly fingered and minimally clad girls would exercise their skills.

He was sweating profusely under the belted white towelling that reached down to mid-thigh. She, for her part, cool and elegant, was dressed in the regulation white-cotton housecoat, with only the thinly transparent bra and pants beneath.

'Would you like to lie down on the couch, sir? On your back, please.'

He had said nothing at that stage, obeying her suggestions mechanically and closing his eyes as she stood behind him, her fingers gently massaging the muscles round his neck.

'Nice?'

'Lovely!'

'Just relax!' She insinuated her hands beneath the towelling and massaged his shoulders with the tips of her strong and beautifully manicured fingers, working down from the neck towards the armpits – repeatedly, gently, sensually. And then, as she'd done a thousand times before, she walked round the couch and stood at his side, leaning over him, the top two buttons of her tunic already unfastened.

'Would you like me to undress while I massage you?' Wonderful question! And almost invariably an offer that couldn't be refused, even when the price of such an optional extra was clearly stated in advance.

It was a surprise to the woman, therefore, when her apparently pliable and co-operative client had slowly sat up, swung his legs off the couch, leaned forward to fasten the buttons of her tunic, pulled the white towelling back over his shoulders, and said 'No'.

But there followed an even bigger surprise.

'Look! I think I know you, and I certainly knew your father. Is it safe to talk here?'

*

Her father! Yes, she could still remember him. Those interminable rows she had heard so often from her lonely bedroom when the amiable drunkard had finally reached home from the local – rows apparently forgotten by the following dawns, when the household moved about its normal business. Then, in 1939, he had been called up in the army, when she had been only eight years old; and his death, three years later, had seemed to her little more than the indefinite prolongation of an already lengthy period of absence from her life. There had been many reminders of him, of course: photographs, letters, clothes, shoes. But, truth to tell, the death of her father had been an event that was less than tragic and only dimly comprehended. But it had been otherwise for her mother, who had wept so often through those first few weeks and months. And it was largely to try to compensate for such an uneven burden of things that the young girl had tried so very hard with her schoolwork, helped so regularly with the housework, and even (later on) kept in check those symptoms of teenage rebelliousness that had threatened to swamp all sense of filial piety. As the years went by, she had gradually taken over everything from an increasingly neurotic and feckless mother, who had sunk into premature senility by her early fifties, and into her grave before reaching her sixtieth year.

When the man had fastened up her buttons, she had felt belittled and cheap – on the wrong side of the habitual transaction. But she also felt deeply interested.

'Yes, it's safe,' she said, finally answering his question.

'No microphones? No two-way mirrors?'

She shook her head. 'About my father—'

'You don't remember me, do you?'

She looked at him: a man over sixty, perhaps; fairly well-preserved by the look of him; head balding, teeth nicotined, jowls blue, chin somewhat sagging, but the mouth still firm and not without some sensitivity. No, she couldn't remember him.

'I called at your house once, but that was a long time ago. You were, I don't know, fifteen or sixteen – still at school, anyway, because your mother asked you to go and do your homework in the kitchen. It was the year after the war was over, and I'd known your father – we were in the same mob together. In fact, I was with him when he died.'

'What do you want?' she asked abruptly.

'I want you to do something for me – something you'll be paid for doing – paid very well.'

'What—?'

But he held up his hand. 'Not now! You're living at 23A Colebourne Road – is that right?'

'Yes.'

'I'd like to come and see you, if I may.'

He had come the next evening, and talked whilst she listened. And, when she'd expressed her willingness to do what he asked, a deal was done, a partial payment made. And now, this very day, she had acted the role that he had asked of her, and the final payment had been made. A lot of easy money for a little easy work, and yet . . .

Yes, it was that little 'and yet' that caused her mind to fill with nagging doubts as she sat and sipped her China tea. She knew *enough*, of course – she'd insisted on that. But perhaps she should have insisted on knowing more, especially about the sequel to her own performance in the drama. They couldn't – they wouldn't, surely – have . . . *killed* him?

Her lips felt dry, and she reached for her handbag, opened the flap, and delved around for a few seconds before unscrewing a circular container – for the second time that day.

CHAPTER SIX

Wednesday, 16th July

In which the Master of Lonsdale is somewhat indiscreet to a police inspector, and discusses his concern for one of his colleagues, and for the niceties of English grammar.

ON THE FIFTH morning after the events described in the preceding chapter, Detective Chief Inspector Morse, of the Thames Valley Constabulary, was seated in his office at Kidlington, Oxon. One half of him was semi-satisfied with the vagaries of his present existence; the other half was semi-depressed. Earlier that very morning he had sworn himself a solemn vow that the day ahead would be quite different. His recent consumption of food, tobacco, and alcohol had varied only within the higher degrees of addictive excess; and now, at the age of fifty-two, he had once again decided that a few days of virtually total abstinence was urgently demanded by stomach, lungs, and liver alike. He had arrived at his office, therefore, unbreakfasted, having already thrown away a half-full packet of cigarettes, and having left his half-empty wallet on the bedside-table. Get thou behind me, Satan! And, indeed, things had gone surprisingly well until about 11.30 a.m., when the Master of Lonsdale had rung through to HQ and invited Morse down to lunch with him.

'Half-past twelve – in my rooms – all right? We can have a couple of snifters first.'

'I'd like that,' Morse heard himself saying.

As he walked towards the Master's rooms in the first quad, Morse passed two young female students chattering to each other like a pair of monkeys.

'But surely *Rosemary*'s expecting a first, isn't she? If she doesn't get one—'

'No. She told me that she'd made a *terrible* mess of the General Paper.'

'So did I.'

'And *me*!'

'She'll be awfully disappointed, though . . .'

Yes, life was full of disappointments, Morse knew that better than most; and, as he half-turned, he watched the two young, lovely ladies as they walked out through the Porter's Lodge. They must be members of the college – two outward and happily visible signs of the fundamental change of heart that had resulted in the admission of women to these erstwhile wholly masculine precincts. Now when he himself had been up at St John's . . . But, abruptly, he switched off the memories of those dark, disastrous days.

'What'll it be, Morse? No beer, I'm afraid but – gin and tonic – gin and French?'

'Gin and French – lovely!' Morse reached over and

took a cigarette from the well-stocked open box on the table.

The Master beamed in avuncular fashion as he poured his mixtures with a practised hand. He had changed little in the ten years or so that Morse had known him: going to fat a little, but as distinguished-looking a man now, in his late fifties, as he had been in his late forties; a tall man, with that luxuriant grey hair still framing the large head; the suits (famed throughout the University) as flamboyant as ever they were, and today eye-catchingly complemented by a waistcoat of green velvet. A successful man, and a proud man. A Head of a House.

'You've got women here now, I see,' said Morse.

'Yes, old boy. We were almost the last to give in – but, well, it's been a good thing on the whole. Very good, some of them.'

'Good-looking, you mean?'

The Master smiled. 'A few.'

'They sleep in?'

'Some of them. Still, some of them always did, didn't they?'

'I suppose so,' said Morse; and his mind drifted back to those distant days just after the war, when he had come up to Oxford with an exhibition in Classics from one of the Midland grammar schools.

'Couple of firsts this year – among the girls, I mean. One in Greats, one in Geography. Not bad, eh? In fact the Classics girl, Jane—' Suddenly the Master stopped and leaned forward earnestly, awkwardly twiddling the large, onyx dress-ring on the little finger of his left hand. 'Look Morse! I shouldn't have said – what I just said. The class-lists won't be out for another week or ten days—'

Morse waved his right hand across the space between them, as though any mental recollection of the indiscretion had already been expunged. 'I didn't hear a word you said, Master. I know what you were going to tell me, though.'

'Oh?'

'She's got the top first in the University, and she'll soon get a summons for a congratulatory viva. Right?'

The Master nodded. 'Super girl – bit of a honey, too, Morse. You'd have liked her.'

'Still would, I shouldn't wonder.'

The Master's eyes were twinkling with merriment now. How he enjoyed Morse's company!

'She'll probably marry some lecherous sod,' continued Morse, 'and end up with half a dozen whining infants.'

'You're not exactly full of the joys of summer.'

'Just envious. Still there are more important things in life than getting a first in Greats.'

'Such as?'

Morse considered the question a few moments before shaking his head. 'I dunno.'

'I'll tell you one thing. There's not likely to be anything much more important for *her*. We shall probably offer her a junior fellowship here.'

'You mean you've already offered her one.'

'Please don't forget, will you, that I – er – I shouldn't have said anything about all this. I'm normally very discreet.'

'Must be the drink,' said Morse, looking down into his empty glass.

'Same again? Mixture about right?'

'Fraction more gin, perhaps?' Morse reached for another cigarette as the Master refilled the glasses. 'I suppose she could take her pick of all the undergrads?'

'*And* the dons!'

'You never married, did you, Master.'

'Nor did you!'

For some minutes the two of them sat silently sipping. Then Morse asked: 'Has she got a mother?'

'Jane Summers, you mean?'

'You didn't mention her surname before.'

'Odd question! I don't know. I expect so. She's only, what, twenty-two, twenty-three. Why do you ask?'

But Morse was hardly listening. In the quad outside it had been comparatively easy to pull the curtain across the painful memories. But now? Not so! His eyes seemed on the point of shedding a gin-soaked tear as he thought again of his own sad days at Oxford . . .

'You listening?'

'Pardon?' said Morse.

'You don't seem to be paying much attention to what I'm saying.'

'Sorry! Must be the booze.' His glass was empty again and the Master needed no prompting.

'Will you keep a gentle eye on things for me, then?

You see, I'm probably off myself this weekend for a few days.'

'Few weeks, do you mean?'

'I'm not sure yet. But if you could just, as I say, keep an eye on things – you'd put my mind at rest.'

'Keep an eye on *what*?'

'Well, it's just – so *unlike* Browne-Smith, that's all. He's the most pedantic and pernickity fellow in the University. It's – it's odd. No arrangements, none. Just this note left at the Lodge. No apology for absence from the college meeting; nothing to the couple of students he'd arranged to see.'

'You've got the note?'

The Master took a folded sheet from his dove-grey jacket and handed it over:

Please keep any mail for me here. I shall be away for several days. Sudden irresistable offer – quite out of the blue. Tell my scout to look after my effects, i.e. to keep the rooms well dusted, put the laundry through and cancel all meals until further notice.

B-S

Morse felt a tingle in his veins as he read through the brief, typewritten message. But he said nothing.

'You see,' said the Master, 'I just don't think he wrote that.'

'No?'

'No, I don't.'

'When did the Lodge get this?'

'Monday morning – two days ago.'

'And when was he last seen here?'

'Last Friday. In the morning, it was. He left college at about quarter-past eight, to catch the London train. One of the fellows here saw him at the station.'

'Did this note come through the post?'

'No. The porter says it was just left there.'

'Why are you so sure he didn't write it?'

'He just *couldn't* have written it. Look, Morse, I've known him for twenty-odd years, and there was never a man, apart from Housman, who was so contemptuous about any solecism in English usage. He was almost paranoiac about things like that. You see, he always used to draft the minutes of the college meetings, and even a comma out of place in the final version would bring down the wrath of the gods on the college secretary. He even used to type a draft before he'd have put a bloody notice on the board!'

Morse looked at the letter again. 'You mean he'd have put commas after "sudden" – and "through"?'

'By Jove, yes! He'd *always* use commas there. But there's something else. Browne-Smith was the *only* man in England, I should think, who invariably argued for a comma after "i.e.".'

'Mm.'

'You don't sound very impressed.'

'Ah! But I am. I think you may be right.'

'Really?'

'You think he's got a bird somewhere?'

'He's never had a "bird", as you put it.'

'Is Jane Summers still in residence?'

The Master laughed aloud with genuine amusement. 'I saw her this morning, Morse, if you must know.'

'Did you tell her she'd got a first?' A smile was playing slowly around Morse's mouth, and the Master's shrewd eyes were again upon him.

'Not much point pretending with you, is there? But no! No, I *didn't* tell her that. But I did tell her that perhaps she had every reason to be – er, let's say, optimistic about her – ah, future. Anyway, it's time we went down for lunch. You ready to eat?'

'Can I keep this?' Morse held up the single sheet, and the Master nodded.

'Seriously, I'm just a fraction worried. And you just said, didn't you, that I might be right?'

'You *are* right. At least, you're almost certainly right in suggesting that he didn't *type* it. He could have dictated it, of course.'

'Why are you so sure?'

'Well,' said Morse, as the Master locked the door behind them, 'he was a literary pedant for a good many years before *you* met him. He was one of my "Mods" tutors, you see; and even then he'd bark away at the most trivial sort of spelling mistake as if it were the sin against the Holy Ghost. At the time, of course, it didn't seem to matter two farts in the universe; but in an odd sort of way I came to respect his views – and I still do. I'd never let a spelling mistake go through *my* secretary – not if I could help it.'

'Never?'

'*Never!*' said Morse, his grey-blue eyes sober and serious as the two men lingered on the landing outside the Master's rooms. 'And you can be absolutely sure of one thing, Master. Browne-Smith would have died sooner than misspelt "irresistible".'

'You don't think – you don't think he *is* dead?'

''Course he's not!' said Morse, as the two old friends walked down the stairs.

CHAPTER SEVEN

Week beginning Wednesday, 16th July

In which those readers impatiently waiting to encounter the first corpse will not be disappointed, and in which interesting light is thrown on the character of the detective, Morse.

IT HAD BEEN 2.30 p.m. when Morse finally left Lonsdale; and after stocking himself up from a tobacconist's shop just along the High, he was back in his Kidlington office just before three o'clock, where nothing much appeared to have happened during his absence.

On leaving Lonsdale, he had promised the Master to 'keep an eye on things' (a quite meaningless phrase, as Morse saw it) should any aspect of Browne-Smith's sudden departure take on a slightly more sinister connotation.

To an observer, Morse's eyes would have appeared slightly 'set', as Shakespeare has it, and his mood was mellowly maudlin. And as he sat there, his freely winged imagination glided easily back to the fateful days of his time at Oxford . . .

*

After eighteen months as a National Serviceman in the Royal Signals Regiment, Morse had come up to St John's College, where his first two years were the happiest and most purposeful of his life. He had worked hard at his texts, attended lectures regularly, been prompt with unseens and compositions; and it had been no surprise to his tutors when such an informed and intelligent young man had duly gained a first in Classical Moderations. With two years ahead of him – two years in which to study for Greats – the future seemed to loom as sure as the sun-bright day that would follow the rosy-fingered dawn – particularly so, since the slant of Morse's mind was ideally suited to the work ahead of him in History, Logic, and Philosophy. But in the middle of his third year he had met the girl who matched the joy of all his wildest dreams.

She was already a graduate of Leicester University, whence a series of glowing testimonials had proved sufficiently impressive for her application to take a D.Phil. at Oxford to be accepted by St Hilda's. For her first term, she had been allotted digs way out in the distances of Cowley Road. But amidst the horsehair sofas and the sombre, dark-brown furnishings, she had been unhappy and had jumped at the opportunity of a smaller flat in Number 22 St John Street (just off St Giles') at the start of the Hilary Term. It was so much brighter, so much nearer the heart of things, and only a short walk from the Bodleian Library, where she spent so much of her time. She felt happy in her new room. Life was good.

At this same time it was customary for the Dean of St

John's to farm out most of his third-year undergraduates to some of the nearby College property and, from
the start of the Michaelmas term, Morse had moved
into St John's Road: Number 24.

They first met one night in late February, during the
interval of the OUDS' production of *Doctor Faustus* at
the New Theatre, only some fifty yards or so away, in
Beaumont Street. Morse had finally managed to order
a pint of beer at the crowded bar when he felt a lightly
laid hand upon his shoulder – and turned round to
find a pale face, the blonde hair high upswept, the
hazel eyes looking into his with an air of pleading
diffidence.

'Have you just ordered?'

'Yes – I'll soon be out of your way.'

'You wouldn't mind, would you, ordering a drink for
me as well?'

'Pleasure!'

'Two gins and tonics, please.' She pushed a pound
note into his hand – and was gone.

She was seated in a far corner of the bar, next to a
dark-haired dowdy-looking young woman; and Morse,
after negotiating his way slowly through the throng,
carefully placed the drinks on the table.

'You didn't mind, did you?'

It was the blonde who had spoken, looking up at
him with widely innocent eyes; and Morse found himself looking at her keenly – noting her small and thinly
nostrilled nose, noting the tiny dimples in her cheeks,
and the lips that parted (almost mischievously now)
over the rather large but geometrically regular teeth.

'Course not! It's a bit of a squash in here, isn't it?'

'You enjoying the play?'

'Yes. Are you?'

'Oh yes! I'm a great Marlowe fan. So's Sheila, here. Er – I'm sorry. Perhaps you don't know each other?'

'I don't know *you*, either!' said Morse.

'There you are! What did I tell you?' It was the dark girl who had taken up the conversation. She smiled at Morse: 'Wendy here said she recognized *you*. She says you live next door to her.'

'Really?' Morse stood there, gaping ineffectually.

A bell sounded in the bar, signalling the start of the last act; and Morse, calling upon all his courage, asked the two girls if they might perhaps like to have a drink with him after the performance.

'Why not?' It was the saturnine Sheila who had answered. 'We'd love to, Wendy, wouldn't we!'

It was agreed that the trio should meet up again in the cocktail-bar of the Randolph, a stone's throw away, just along the street.

For Morse, the last act seemed to drag its slow length interminably along, and he left the theatre well before the end. The name 'Wendy' was re-echoing through his mind as once the woods had welcomed 'Amaryllis'. With the bar virtually deserted, he sat and waited expectantly. Ten minutes. Fifteen minutes. The bar was filling up now, and twice, with some embarrassment, Morse had assured other customers that, yes, there *was* someone sitting in each of the empty seats at his table.

She came at last – Sheila, that is – looking around for him, coming across, and accepting his offer of a drink.

'What will – er – Wendy have?'

'She won't be coming, I'm afraid. She says she's sorry but she suddenly remembered—'

But Morse was no longer listening, for now the night seemed drear and desolate. He bought the girl a second drink; then a third. She left at ten-thirty to catch her bus, and Morse watched with relief as she waved half-heartedly to him from the bar entrance.

It was trying to snow as Morse walked slowly back to St John Street, but he stopped where he knew he would stop. On the right of the door of Number 22, he saw four names, typed and slotted into folders, a plastic bell-push beside each one of them. The first name was 'Miss W. Spencer (Top Floor)', but no light shone at the highest window, and Morse was soon climbing the stairs to his cold bed-sitter.

For the next three days he spent much of the time hanging about in the vicinity of St John Street, missing lectures, missing meals, and missing, too, any sight of the woman he was aching to see once more. Had she been called away? Was she ill? The whole gamut of tragic forebodings presented itself to his mind as he frittered away his hours and his energies in fruitless and futile imaginings. On the fourth evening he walked over to the Randolph, drank two double Scotches, walked back to St John Street, and with a thumping heart rang the bell at the top of the panel. And, when the door opened, she was standing there, a smile of gentle recognition in her eyes.

'You've been a long time,' she said.

'I didn't quite know—'

'You knew where to find me – I told you that.'
'I—'
'It wasn't *you* who made the first move, was it?'
'I—'
'Would you like to come in?'

Impetuously – even that first night – Morse told her that he loved her; and she, for her part, told him how very glad she was that they had met. After that, their days and weeks and months were spent in long, idyllic happiness: they walked together across the Oxford-shire countryside; went to theatres, cinemas, concerts, museums; spent much time in pubs and restaurants; and, after a while, much time in bed together, too. But, during those halcyon days, both were neglecting the academic work that was expected of them. At the end of the Trinity term, Morse was gently reminded by his tutor that he might be in danger of failing to satisfy the examiners the following year unless he decided to mount a forceful assault upon the works of Plato during the coming vacation. After a similar interview with her own supervisor, Wendy Spencer was firmly informed that unless her thesis began to show more obvious signs of progress, her grant – and therewith her doctorate – would be in serious jeopardy.

Surprisingly, perhaps, it was Morse who saw the more clearly the importance of some academic success – and who sought the more anxiously to promote it. But such success was not to be. Just before the Christmas vac a tearful Wendy announced that her doctorate was terminated; her grant, w.e.f. January 1st, withheld. Yet the two of them lived on very much as before: Wendy stayed on in her digs, and almost immediately got a job as a waitress in the Randolph; Morse tried hard to curb his beer consumption and occasionally read the odd chapter of Plato's *Republic*.

Ironically, it was one day before the anniversary of their first, wonderful evening together that Wendy received the telegram, informing her that her widowed mother had suffered a stroke, and that help was urgently required. So she had gone home – and stayed there. Scores of letters passed between the lovers during the dark months that followed; and twice Morse had made the journey to the West Country to see her. But he was very short of money now; and slowly he was learning to assimilate the truth that (for some reason) her mother was a more important figure in Wendy's life than he was. His performances for his tutors were now so pathetically poor that his college exhibition was rescinded, and he had the humiliating task of writing to beg his county authority to make up the deficit. Then, three weeks before Greats, he had received his last letter from her: she could not see him again; she had almost ruined his life already; she had a duty to stay with her mother, and had irrevocably decided to do so; she had loved him – she had loved him desperately – but now they had come to the end; she implored him not to reply to her letter; she urged him to do himself some semblance of justice in his imminent examination; *that* would always be important for her. Morse had immediately sent a telegram, begging her to meet him once more. But he received no reply – and had no money for a further journey. In his despair, he did nothing – absolutely nothing.

Two months later he learned that he had failed Greats; and, although the news was no surprise, he departed from Oxford a withdrawn and silent young man, bitterly belittled, yet not completely broken in spirit. It had been his sadly disappointed old father, a month or so before his death, who suggested that his only son might find a niche somewhere in the police force.

Morse's attractive young secretary came into the office and handed over his letters for signature.

'Do you want to dictate the others, sir?'

'A little later. I'll give you a ring.'

After she had gone, he continued his earlier train of thought – but not for long. In any case, there was nothing more to recall. Of Wendy Spencer he had never heard another word. She would still be alive, though, surely? Even at that minute – that very second – she'd be *somewhere*. He repeated to himself the line from *Wessex Heights*: 'But time cures hearts of tenderness – and now I can let her go.' It was a lie, of course. But so it had been for Hardy.

Nor had Morse ever met any of his Greats examiners since he had first come down from Oxford. Yet even now he could remember with dramatic clarity the six names that were subscribed to the class-list on that bleak day some thirty years ago:

Wells (Chairman)
Styler
Stockton
Sherwin-White
Austin
Browne-Smith.

During the following week Morse did nothing about his tenuous promise to the Master. Well, virtually nothing. He *had* rung Lonsdale early on the Monday morning, but neither the Master, nor the Vice-Master, nor the Senior Fellow, nor the Bursar, was on the premises. Everyone had either gone or was about to be gone. With the heavy work over for another academic year, the corporate body of the University appeared to be taking a collective siesta. The thought suddenly occurred to Morse that this would be a marvellous time to murder a few of the doddery old bachelor dons. No wives to worry about their whereabouts; no families to ring their fathers from railway stations; no landladies to whine about the unpaid rents. In fact, nobody would miss most of them *at all* – not, that is, until the middle of October.

It was on Wednesday, 23rd July, two days after his abortive phone-call to Lonsdale, that Morse himself, in mid-afternoon, received the news, recognizing Sergeant Lewis's voice immediately.

'We've got a body, sir – or at least part—'

'Where are you?'

'Thrupp, sir. You know the—'

''Course I know it!'

63

'I think you'd better come.'

'I've got a lot of correspondence to get on with – *you* can handle things, can't you?'

'We fished it out of the canal.'

'Lots of people chuck 'emselves into—'

'I don't think this one drowned himself, sir,' said Lewis quietly.

So Morse got the Lancia out of the yard, and drove the few miles out to Thrupp.

CHAPTER EIGHT

Wednesday, 23rd July

The necrophobic Morse reluctantly surveys a corpse, and converses with a cynical and ageing police surgeon.

TWO MILES NORTH of police headquarters in Kidlington, on the main A423 road to Banbury, an elbow turn to the right leads, after only three hundred yards or so, to the Boat Inn, which, together with about twenty cottages, a farm, and a depot of the Inland Waterways Executive, comprises the tiny hamlet of Thrupp. The inn itself, only some thirty yards from the waters of the Oxford Canal, has served generations of boatmen, past and present. But the working barges of earlier times, which brought down coal from the Midlands and shipped up beer from the Oxford breweries, have now yielded place to the privately owned long-boats and pleasure-cruisers which ply their way placidly along the present waterway.

Chief Inspector Morse turned right at the inn, then left along the narrow road stretching between the canal and a row of small, grey-stoned, terraced cottages, their doors and multi-paned windows painted a clean and universal white. At almost any other time, Thrupp

65

would have seemed a snugly secluded little spot; but already Morse could see the two white police cars pulled over on to the tow-path, beside a sturdy-looking drawbridge; and an ambulance, its blue light flashing, parked a little further ahead, where the road petered out into a track of grass-grown gravel. It is strange to relate (for a man in his profession) that in addition to incurable acrophobia, arachnophobia, myophobia, and ornithophobia, Morse also suffered from necrophobia; and had he known what awaited him now, it is doubtful whether he would have dared to view the horridly disfigured corpse at all.

A knot of thirty or so people, most of them from the gaudily painted houseboats moored along the water-way, stood at a respectful distance from the centre of activities; and Morse, pushing his way somewhat officiously through, came face to face immediately with a grim-looking Lewis.

'Nasty business, sir!'

'Know who it is?'

'Not much chance.'

'What? You can *always* tell who they are – doesn't matter how long they've been in the water. You know that, surely? Teeth, hair, finger-nails, toe-nails—'

'You'd better come and look at him, sir.'

'Ha! Know it's a "him" do we? Well, that's something. Reduces the population by about 50 per cent at a stroke, that does.'

'You'd better come and look at him,' repeated Lewis quietly.

A uniformed police constable and two ambulance

men moved aside as Morse walked towards the green tarpaulin sheet that covered a body recently fished from the murky-looking water. For a few moments, however, he was more than reluctant to pull back the tarpaulin. Instead, his dark eyebrows contracted to a frown as mentally he traced the odd configuration of the bulge beneath the winding-sheet. Surely the body had to be that of a child, for it appeared to be about three and a half feet long – no more; and Morse's up-curved nostrils betokened an even grislier revulsion. Adult suicide was bad enough. But the death of a child – agh! Accident? *Murder*?

Morse told the four men standing there to shield him from the silent onlookers as he pulled back the tarpaulin and – after only a few seconds – replaced it. His cheeks had grown ashen pale, and his eyes seemed stunned with horror. He managed only two hoarsely spoken words: 'My God!'

He was still standing there, speechless and shaken, when a big, battered old Ford braked sharply beside the ambulance, from it emerging a mournful, hump-backed man who looked as though he should have taken late retirement ten years earlier. He greeted Morse with a voice that matched his lean, lugubrious mien.

'I thought I'd find you in the bar, Morse.'

'They're closed.'

'You don't sound very cheerful, old man?'

Morse pointed vaguely behind him, towards the sheet, and the police surgeon immediately knelt to his calling.

'Phew! *Very* interesting!'

Morse, his back still turned on the corpse, heard himself mutter something that vaguely concurred with such a finding, and thereafter left his sanguine colleague utterly in peace.

Slowly and carefully the surgeon examined the body, methodically entering notes into a black pocket-book. Much of what he wrote would be unintelligible to one unversed in forensic medicine. Yet the first few lines were phrased with frightening simplicity:

First appearances: male (60–65?); Caucasian; torso well nourished (bit too well?); head (missing) severed from shoulders (amateurishly?) at roughly the fourth cervical vertebra; hands l. & r. missing, the wrists cut across the medial ligaments; legs l. & r. also missing, severed from torso about 5–6 inches below hip-joint (more professionally done?); skin – 'washerwoman effect' . . .

Finally, and with some difficulty, the surgeon rose to his feet and stood beside Morse, holding his lumbar regions with both hands as though in chronic agony.

'Know a cure for lumbago, Morse?'

'I thought *you* were the doctor.'

'Me? I'm just a poorly paid pathologist.'

'You get lumbago in mid-*summer*?'

'Mid-*every*-bloody-season!'

'They say a drop of Scotch is good for most things.'

'I thought you said they're closed.'

'Emergency, isn't it?' Morse was beginning to feel slightly better.

One of the ambulance men came up to him. 'All right to take it away?'

'Might as well.'

'No!' It was the surgeon who spoke. 'Not for the moment. I want to have a few words with the chief inspector here first.'

The ambulance man moved away and the surgeon sounded unwontedly sombre. 'You've got a nasty case on your hands here, Morse, and – well, I reckon you ought to have a look at one or two things while we're *in situ*, as it were – you *were* a classicist once, I believe? Any clues going'll pretty certainly be gone by the time I start carving him up.'

'I don't think there's much point in that, Max. You just give him a good going-over – that'll be fine!'

In kindly fashion, Max put a hand on his old friend's shoulder. 'I know! Pretty dreadful sight, isn't it? But I've missed things in the past – you know that! And if—'

'All right. But I need a drink first, Max.'

'*After* Don't worry – I know the landlord.'

'So do I,' said Morse.

'OK, then?'

'OK!'

But, as the surgeon drew back the tarpaulin once more, Morse found himself quite incapable of looking a second time at that crudely jagged neck. Instead he concentrated his narrowed eyes upon the only limbs that someone – *someone* (already the old instincts were quickened again) – had felt it safe to leave intact. The upper part of the man's body was dressed in a formal, dark-blue, pin-striped jacket, matching the material of the truncated trousers below; and, beneath the jacket, in a white shirt, adorned with a plain rust-red tie – rather awkwardly fastened. Morse shuddered as the surgeon peeled off the sodden jacket, and placed the squelching material by the side of the dismembered torso.

'You want the trousers, too? – what's left of 'em?'

Morse shook his head. 'Anything in the pockets?'

The surgeon inserted his hands roughly into the left and right pockets; but his fingers showed through the bottom of each, and Morse felt as sick as some sensitively palated patient in the dentist's chair having a wax impression taken of his upper jaw.

'Back pocket?' he suggested weakly.

'Ah!' The surgeon withdrew a sodden sheet of paper, folded over several times, and handed it to Morse. 'See what I mean? Good job we—'

'You'd have found it, anyway.'

'Think so? Who's the criminologist here, Morse? They pay *me* to look at the bodies – not a lump of pulp like that. I'd have sent the trousers to Oxfam, like as not – better still, the Boy Scouts, eh?'

Morse managed to raise a feeble grin, but he wanted the job over.

'Nothing else?'

Max shook his head; and as Morse (there being nothing less nauseating to contemplate) looked vaguely down along the outstretched arms, the surgeon interrupted his thoughts.

'Not much good, arms, you know. Now if you've got teeth – which in our case we have not got – or—'

But Morse was no longer listening to his colleague's idle commentary. 'Will you pull his shirt-sleeves up for me, Max?'

'Might take a bit of skin with 'em. Depends how long—'

'Shut up!'

The surgeon carefully unfastened the cuff-links and pushed the sleeves slowly up the slender arms. 'Not exactly a weightlifter, was he?'

'No.'

The surgeon looked at Morse curiously. 'You expecting to find a tattoo or something, with the fellow's name stuck next to his sweetheart's?'

'You never know your luck, Max. There might even be a name-tape on his suit somewhere.'

'Somehow I don't reckon you're going to have too much luck in this case,' said the surgeon.

'Perhaps not...' But Morse was hardly listening. He felt the sickness rising to the top of his gullet, but not before he'd noticed the slight contusion on the inner hollow between the left biceps and the forearm. Then he suddenly turned away from the body and retched up violently on the grass.

Sergeant Lewis looked on with a sad and vulnerable concern. Morse was his hero, and always would be. But even heroes had their momentary weaknesses, as Lewis had so often learned.

CHAPTER NINE

Wednesday, 23rd July

> In which Morse's mind drifts elsewhere as the police
> surgeon enunciates some of the scientific principles
> concerning immersion in fluids.

IT WAS LATER that same afternoon that Morse, Lewis,
and the police surgeon presented themselves at the
Boat Inn, where the landlord, sensibly circumspect,
informed the trio that it would of course be wholly
improper for him to serve any alcoholic beverages at
the bar; on the other hand the provision of three chairs
in a back room and a bottle of personally purchased
Glenfiddich might not perhaps be deemed to contrav-
ene the nation's liquor laws.

'How long's he been dead?' was Morse's flatly
spoken, predictable gambit, and the surgeon poured
himself a liberal tumbler before deigning to reply.

'Good question! I'll have a guess at it tomorrow.'

Morse poured himself an equally liberal portion, his
sour expression reflecting a chronic distrust in the
surgeon's calling.

'A week, perhaps?'

The surgeon merely shrugged his shoulders.

'Could be longer, you mean?'

'Or shorter.'

'Oh Christ! Come off it, Max!' Morse banged the bottle down on the table, and Lewis wondered if he himself might be offered a dram. He would have refused, of course, but the gesture would have been gratifying.

The surgeon savoured a few sips with the slow dedication of a man testing a dubious tooth with a mouthwash, before turning to Morse, his ugly face beatified: 'Nectar, old man!'

Morse, likewise, appeared temporarily more interested in the whisky than in any problems a headless, handless, legless corpse might pose to the Kidlington CID. 'They tell me the secret's in the water of those Scottish burns.'

'Nonsense! It's because they manage to get *rid* of the water.'

'Could be!' Morse nodded more happily now. 'But while we're talking of water, I just asked you—'

'You know nothing about water, Morse. Listen! If you find a body immersed in fresh water, you've got the helluva job finding out what happened. In fact, one of the trickiest problems in forensic medicine – about which you know bugger-all, of course – is to prove whether death *was* due to drowning.'

'But this fellow wasn't drowned. He had his head—'

'Shut up, Morse. You asked how long he'd been in the canal, right? You didn't ask me who sawed his head off!'

Morse nodded agreement.

'Well, *listen*, then! There are five questions I'm paid to ask myself when a body's found immersed in water, and in this particular case you wouldn't need a genius like me to answer most of them. First, was the person alive when entering the water? Answer: pretty certainly, no. Second, was death due to immersion? Answer: equally certainly, no. Third, was death rapid? Answer: the question doesn't apply, because death took place elsewhere. Fourth, did any other factors contribute to death? Answer: almost certainly, yes; the poor fellow was likely to have been clinically dead when somebody chopped him up and chucked him in the canal. Fifth, where did the body enter the water? Answer: God knows! Probably where it was found – as most of them are. But it could have drifted a fair way, in certain conditions. With a combination of bodily gases and other internal reactions, you'll often find a corpse floating up to the surface and then—'

But Morse interrupted him, turning to Lewis: 'How *did* we find him?'

'We had a call from a chap who was fishing there, sir. Said he'd seen something looking like a body half-floating under the water, just where we found him.'

'Did you get his name – this fisherman's?' Morse's question was sharp, and to Lewis his eyes seemed to glint with a frightening authority.

'I wasn't there myself, sir. I got the message from Constable Dickson.'

'He took down the name and address, of course?'

'Not quite, sir,' gulped Lewis. 'He got the name all right, but—'

'—the fellow rang off before giving his address!'

'You can't really blame—'

'Who's blaming *anybody*, Lewis? What *was* his name, by the way?'

'Rowbotham. Simon Rowbotham.'

'Christ! That's an unlikely sounding name.'

'But Dickson got it down all right, sir. He asked the fellow to spell it for him – he told me that.'

'I see I shall have to congratulate Constable Dickson the next time I have the misfortune to meet him.'

'We're only talking about a name, sir.' Lewis was feeling that incipient surge of frustrated anger he'd so often experienced with Morse.

'*Only*? What are you talking about? "*Simon*"? With a surname like "*Rowbotham*"? Lew-is! Now *George* Rowbotham – that's fine, that squares with your actual proletarian parentage. Or Simon *Carruthers*, or something – that's what you'd expect from some aristocrat from Saffron Waldon. But *Simon Rowbotham*? Come off it, Lewis. The fellow who rang was making it up as he went along.'

The surgeon, who had remained sipping placidly during this oddly intemperate exchange, now decided it was time to rescue the hapless Lewis. 'You do talk a load of nonsense, Morse. I've never known your first name, and I don't give a sod what it is. For all I know, it's "Eric" or "Ernie" or something. But so bloody *what*?'

Morse, who had ever sought to surround his Christian name in the decent mists of anonymity, made no reply. Instead, he poured himself another measure of the pale-yellow spirit, thereafter lapsing into silent thought.

It was Max who picked up the thread of the earlier discussion. 'At least you're not likely to get bogged down in any doubts about accident or suicide – unless you find some boat-propeller's sliced his head off – and his hands – and his legs.'

'No chance of that?'

'I haven't examined the body yet, have I?'

Morse grunted with frustration. 'I asked you, and I ask you again. How long's he been in the water?'

'I just told you. I haven't—'

'Can't you try a feeble bloody guess?'

'Not all that long – in the water, that is. But he may have been dead a few days before then.'

'Have a guess, for Christ's sake!'

'That's tricky.'

'It's always "tricky" for you, isn't it? You do actually think the fellow's *dead*, I suppose?'

The surgeon finished his whisky, and poured himself more, his lined face creasing into something approaching geniality. 'Time of death? That's always going to play a prominent part in your business, Morse. But it's never been my view that an experienced pathologist – such as myself – can ever really put too much faith in the accuracy of his observations. So many variables, you see—'

'Forget it!'

'Ah! But if someone actually *saw* this fellow being chucked in – well, we'd have a much better idea of things, um?'

Morse nodded slowly and turned his eyes to Lewis; and Lewis, in turn, nodded his own understanding.

'It shouldn't take long, sir. There's only a dozen or so houses along the towpath.'

He prepared to go. Before leaving, however, he asked one question of the surgeon. 'Have you got the slightest idea, sir, when the body might have been put in the canal?'

'Two, three days ago, sergeant.'

'How the hell do you know that?' growled Morse after Lewis had gone.

'I don't really. But he's a polite fellow, your Lewis, isn't he? Deserves a bit of help, as I see it.'

'About two or three days, then . . .'

'Not much more – and probably been dead about a day longer. His skin's gone past the "washerwoman" effect, and that suggests he's certainly been in the water more than twenty-four hours. And I'd guess – guess, mind! – that we're past the "sodden" stage and almost up to the time when the skin gets blanched. Let's say about two, two-and-a-half days.'

'And nobody would be fool enough to dump him in during the hours of daylight, so—'

'Yep. Sunday night – that's about the time I'd suggest, Morse. But if I find a few live fleas on him, it'll mean I'm talking a load of balls; they'd usually be dead after twenty-four hours in the water.'

'He doesn't look much like a fellow who had fleas, does he?'

'Depends where he was before they pushed him in. For all we know, he could have been lying in the boot of a car next to a dead dog.' He looked across and saw the Chief Inspector looking less than happily into his glass.

'I can understand somebody chopping his head off, Max – even his hands. But why in the name of Sweeney Todd should anyone want to slice his *legs*?'

'Same thing. Identification.'

'You mean . . . there was something *below* his knees – couple of wooden legs, or something?'

'"Artificial prostheses", that's what they call 'em now.'

'Or he might have had no toes?'

'Not many of that sort around . . .'

But Morse's mind was far away, the image of the gruesome corpse producing a further spasm in some section of his gut.

'You're right, you know, Morse!' The surgeon happily poured himself another drink. 'He probably wouldn't have *recognized* a flea! Good cut of cloth, that suit. Pretty classy shirt, too. Sort of chap who had a very-nice-job-thank-you: good salary, pleasant conditions of work, carpet all round the office, decent pension . . .' Suddenly the surgeon broke off, and seemed to arrive at one of his few firm conclusions. 'You know what, Morse? I reckon he was probably a bank manager!'

'Or an Oxford don,' added Morse quietly.

CHAPTER TEN

Wednesday, 23rd July

In spite of his toothache, Morse begins his investigations
with the reconstruction of a letter.

IN SPITE OF his unorthodox, intuitive, and seemingly
lazy approach to the solving of crime, Morse was an
extremely competent administrator; and when he sat
down again at his office desk that same evening, all the
procedures called for in a case of murder (and this *was*
murder) had been, or were about to be, put into effect.
Superintendent Strange, to whom Morse had reported
on his return to HQ, knew his chief inspector only too
well.

'You'll want Lewis, of course?'

'Thank you, sir. Couple of frogmen, too.'

'How many extra men?'

'Well – er – none; not for the minute, anyway.'

'Why's that?'

'I wouldn't quite know what to ask them to do, sir,'
had been Morse's simple and honest explanation.

And, indeed, as he looked at his wrist-watch (7.30
p.m. – 'Blast, missed *The Archers*!'), he was not at all
sure what to ask himself, either. On his desk lay the

soddenly promising letter found on the corpse; but his immediate preoccupation was a throbbing toothache which had been getting worse all day. He decided he would do something about it in the morning.

As he sat there, he was conscious that there was a deeper reason for his refusal of the Superintendent's offer of extra personnel. By temperament he was a loner, if only because, although never wholly content in the solitary state, he was almost invariably even more miserable in the company of others. There were a few exceptions, of course, and Lewis was one of them. Exactly why he enjoyed Lewis's company so much, Morse had never really stopped to analyse; but perhaps it was because Lewis was so totally unlike himself. Lewis was placid, good-natured, methodical, honest, unassuming, faithful, and (yes, he might as well come clean about it!) a bit *stolid*, too. Even that afternoon, the good Lewis had been insistently anxious to stay on until whatever hour, if by any chance Morse should consider his availability of any potential value. But Morse had not. As he had pointed out to his sergeant, they *might* pretty soon have a bit of luck and find out who the dead man was; the frogmen *might* just find a few oddments of identifiable limbs in the sludge of the canal waters by Aubrey's Bridge. But Morse doubted it. For, even at this very early stage of the case, he sensed that his major problem would not so much be who the murderer was, *but who exactly had been murdered.* It was Morse's job, though, to find the answer to both these questions; and so he started on his task, alternately stroking his slightly swollen left jaw and prodding down viciously on the offending double-fang. He took the letter lying on the desk in front of him, pressed it very carefully between sheets of blotting-paper, and then removed it. The paper was not so sopped and sodden as he had feared, and with a pair of tweezers he was soon able to unfold a strip about two inches wide and eight inches long. It was immediately apparent that this formed the left-hand side of a typewritten letter; and, furthermore, except for some minor blurring of letters at the torn edge, the message was gladdeningly legible:

Dear Sir,
This is a most unusua
realize. But please re
because what I am pro
both you and me. My wa   5
College has just take
final examinations in G
in about ten or twelve
an old man and I am de
how she has got on ah   10
The reason for my r
ridiculously   impatient
to America in a few
able to be contacte
want to know how J   15
this. I have spent a
education, and she is
I realize that this
only that you should g
to such an impropriet   20

publication of the cl
July.
If you can possibly se
shall be in a positi
unconventionally. You s   25
most select clubs, sa
give you a completely
delights which are as
Please do give me a r
may be, at 01–417 808   30
you feel able to do
result, I shall give
able to enjoy, at no c
the most discreet er
ever imagined.   35
You

Morse sat back and studied the words with great joy. He'd been a lifelong addict of puzzles and of cryptograms, and this was exactly the sort of work his mind could cope with confidently. First he enumerated the lines in 5's (as shown above); then he set his mind to work. It took him ten minutes, and another ten minutes to copy out his first draft. The general drift of the letter required no Aristotelian intellect to decipher – primarily because of the give-away clue in line 7. But it had been none too easy to concoct some continuum over a few of the individual word-breaks, especially 'wa – ' in line 5; 'ah – ' in line 10; 'cl – ' in line 21; and 'sa – ' in line 26.

This is the first draft that Morse wrote out:

Dear Sir,

This is a most unusua | l letter as I know you'll
realize. But please re | ad it with great care
because what I am pro | posing can benefit
both you and me. My wa | strel daughter at _____
College has just take | n (without much hope) her
final examination in G | eography, and will get the result
in about ten or twelve | days' time. Now I am
an old man and I'm de | sperately anxious to know
how she has got on ah | ead of the official lists.
The reason for my r | equest is that I am
ridiculously   impatient, | and in fact I am off
to America in a few | days' time where I may not be
able to be contacted | for some while. All I
want to know is how J | _____ got on, if you can tell me
this. I have spent a | great deal of money on her
education, and she is | the only child I have.
I   realize   that   this | is an improper request. I ask
only that you should g | ive a thought to stooping
to such an impropriet | y. I think the official date for
publication of the cl | ass list is _____ _____
July.

If you can possibly se | e your way to this favour,
I shall be in a positi | on to pay you very well, if
unconventionally. You s | ee I manage some of the
most select clubs, sa | unas and parlours and I will
give you a completely | free access to the sexual
delights which are as | sociated with such places.
Please do give me a r | ing, whatever your decision
may be, at 01–417 808 | _____. If it so happens that
you feel able to do | what I ask about J_____'s

result,   I   shall   give   you details about how you'll be
able to enjoy, at no c   ost at all to yourself,
the   most   discreet   er   otic thrills you can have
ever imagined.

You   rs sincerely,

Morse was reasonably pleased with the draft. It lacked polish here and there, but it wasn't bad at all, really. Three specific problems, of course: the name of the college, the name of the girl, and the last bit of the telephone number. The college would be a bit more a difficult now that almost all of them accepted women, but . . .

Suddenly Morse sat at his desk quite motionless, the blood tingling across his shoulders. Could it be? That 'G – '? It needn't be Geography or Geology or Geophysics or whatever. And it wasn't. It was *Greats*! And that 'J – '? That wasn't Judith or Joanna or Jezebel. It was *Jane* – the girl the Master had indiscreetly mentioned to him! And that would solve the college automatically: it was *Lonsdale*!

Phew!

The telephone number wouldn't be much of a problem, either, since Lewis could soon sort that out. If it was a four-digit group, that would only mean ten possibilities; and if it was five digits, that was only a hundred; and Lewis was a very patient man . . .

But the tooth was jabbing its pain along his jaw once more, and he made his way home, where doubling (as he invariably did) the dosage of all medical nostrums he took six Aspros, washed them down well with whisky, and went to bed. But at 2 a.m. we find him sitting up in bed, his hand caressing his jaw, the pain jumping in his gum like some demented dervish. And at 8 a.m. we find him standing outside a deserted dentist's premises in North Oxford, an inordinately long scarf wrapped round his jaw, waiting desperately for one of the receptionists to arrive.

CHAPTER ELEVEN

Thursday, 24th July

Wherein such diverse activities as dentistry, crossword-solving, and pike-angling make their appropriate contributions to Morse's view of things.

'YOU'VE NOT BEEN looking after these too well, have you, Mr Morse?'

Since at this point, however, the dapperly dressed dentist had his patient's mouth opened to its widest extremities, Morse was able only to produce a strained grunt from his swollen larynx.

'You ought to cut out the sugar,' continued the dentist, surveying so many signs of incipient decay, 'and some dental floss wouldn't come amiss with all this . . . Ah! I reckon that's the little fellow that's been causing you—' He tapped one of the lower-left molars with a blunt instrument, and the recumbent Morse was almost levitated in agony. 'Ye-es, you've got a nasty little infection there . . . does *that* hurt?'

Again Morse's body jumped in agonizing pain, before the chair was raised to a semi-vertical slant and he was ordered to 'rinse out'.

'You've got a nasty little infection there, as I say . . .'

Everything with the dentist appeared to warrant the epithet 'little', and Morse would have been more gratified had it been suggested to him that he was the victim of a massive great bloody infection stemming from an equally massive great bloody tooth that even now was throbbing mightily. He continued to sit in the chair, but the dentist himself was writing something across at his desk.

'Aren't you going to take it out?' asked Morse.

The dentist continued writing. 'We try to preserve as many teeth as we can these days, you know. And it's particularly important for *you* not to lose many more. You haven't got too many left, have you?'

'But it's giving me—'

'Here's a prescription for a little penicillin. Don't worry! It'll soon sort out the infection and get that little swelling down. Then if you come and see me again in – a week, shall we say?'

'A *week?*'

'I can't do anything till then. If I took it out now – well, let's say you'd have to be a brave man, Mr Morse.'

'Would I?' said Morse weakly. He finally rose from the chair, and his eyes wandered to the shelf of plaster-casts of teeth behind the dentist's desk, the upper jaws resting on the lower, a few canines missing here, a few molars there. It all seemed rather obscene to Morse, and reminded him of his junior-school history books, with their drawings of skulls labelled with such memor-able names as *Eoanthropus dawsoni*, *Pithecanthropus erectus*, and the rest.

The dentist saw his interest and reached down a

particularly ugly cast, snapping the jaws apart and together again like a ventriloquist at a dumb-show. 'Remarkable things teeth, you know. No two sets of teeth can ever be the same. Each set – well, it's unique, like fingerprints.' He looked at the squalid lump of plastering with infinite compassion, and it seemed quite obvious that teeth obsessed not only his working life but his private soul as well.

Morse stood beside him, waiting for the prescription; and when the dentist got to his feet Morse became surprisingly aware of how small a man the dentist was. Had it been the white coat that had given him the semblance of being taller? Had it been the fact that the last thing Morse had earlier been interested in was whether the kindly man who'd readily agreed to see one of his most irregular clients was a dwarf or a giant? Yet there was something else, wasn't there?

Morse's mind suddenly grasped it as he stood waiting at the Summertown chemist's. It had been when the dentist had been sitting at his desk – yes. Because the length of his back was that of a man of normal height; and so it must have been *the legs* . . .

'Are you a pensioner, sir?' asked the young assistant as she took his prescription. (My God! Could he really look as old as that?)

After an exhortation to stick religiously to the stated dosage, and also to be sure to complete the course, Morse was soon on his way to Kidlington, quite convinced now of the perfectly obvious fact that whoever had dismembered the corpse had been at desperate pains to conceal its identity.

Teeth? The murderer would have left a means of certain identification – 'unique', as his little torturer had said. Hands? If they had been deformed in any way, or one of them had? It was difficult for fellow humans to forget deformity. Legs? What if that exciting idea that had occurred to him at the chemist's . . .

But he was at HQ now, and the need for instant action was at hand. He swallowed twice the specified dosage of tablets, told himself that the marvellous stuff was already engaged in furious conflict with the 'little infection', and finally greeted Lewis at 9.30 a.m.

'You said you'd be here by eight, sir.'

'You're lucky to see me at all!' Morse snapped, as he unwrapped his scarf and bared his bulging jaw.

'Bad tooth, sir?'

'Not just *bad*, Lewis. It's the worst bloody tooth in England!'

'The missus always swears by – '

'Forget what your missus says! She's not a dentist, is she?'

So Lewis forgot it, and sat down silently.

Soon Morse was feeling better, and for an hour he discussed with Lewis both the letter and the curious thoughts that had been occurring to him.

'Someone certainly seems to be making it difficult for us,' said Lewis; and the sentence did little more than state in simple English the even simpler thought that had gradually dawned on Morse's mind. But for Lewis life was full of surprises, since he now heard Morse ask him to repeat exactly that same sentence. And as he did so, Lewis saw the familiar sight of his chief looking out over the concreted yard, or wherever it was those eyes, unblinking, stared with more than a hint of deeper understanding.

'Or it could be just the opposite,' Lewis heard him mumble enigmatically.

'Pardon, sir?'

'Do you reckon a cup of coffee would upset this tooth of mine?'

'Be all right, unless it's too hot.'

'Nip and get a couple of cups.'

After Lewis had gone, Morse unfolded *The Times* and looked at the crossword. 1 across: 'He lived perched up, mostly in sites around East, shivering (6,8).' Anagram, obviously: 'mostly in sites' round 'e'. Yes! He quickly wrote in 'Simon Stylites' – only to find himself one letter short. Of course! It was *Simeon* Stylites, and he was about to correct the letters, when he stopped.

It *couldn't* be, surely!

He wrote a circle of letters in the bottom margin of the newspaper, crossed off a few letters, then a few more – and stopped again. Not only could it be, it was! What an extraordinary –

'I told her to stick some extra cold milk in, sir.'

'Did you sugar it?'

'You do take sugar, don't you?'

'Bad for the teeth – surely you know that?'

'Shall I go and—'

'No – siddown. I've got something to show you. Oh God! This coffee's cold!'

'You haven't done much of the crossword.'

'Haven't I?' Morse was smiling serenely, and he

thrust the paper across to Lewis who looked down uncomprehendingly at the almost illegible alterations in the top row of squares. But Lewis was happy. The chief was on to something – the chief was always on to something, and that was good. That's why he enjoyed working with Morse. Being on the receiving end of all the unpredictability, all the irascibility, all the unfairness – it was a cheap price to pay for working with him. And now he whistled softly to himself as Morse explained the riddle of the circle of letters he had printed.

'Do you want me to get on to it, sir?'

'No, I'd rather you got on with those telephone numbers.'

'Straight away, you mean?'

Morse gestured gently towards the phone on his desk, a smile spreading lopsidedly across his swollen mouth. 'You said it was Dickson on the desk yesterday when we got the call from Thrupp?'

'Yes.'

'Well, you get on with things here, Lewis. I'm just going to have a little chat with Dickson.'

If Lewis's weakness in life was the smell of freshly fried chips (and fast driving!), with Dickson it was the sight of amply jammed doughnuts, and he sought to swallow his latest mouthful hastily as he saw Morse bearing down on him.

'Fingers a bit sticky this morning, Dickson?'

'Sorry, sir.'

'Sugar is bad for the teeth, didn't you know that?'

'Do you eat a lot yourself, sir?'

For the next few minutes Morse questioned Dickson patiently about the informant who had telephoned HQ about the corpse in the water by Aubrey's Bridge. The facts were clear. The man had not only given his name, he'd spelt it out; he hadn't been absolutely sure that what he had seen was a human body, but it most decidedly looked like one; the call had been made from a phone-box, and after the second lot of 'pip-pips' the line had gone dead.

'*Is* there a phone-box in Thrupp?'

'On the corner, by the pub, sir.'

Morse nodded. 'Did it not occur to you, my lad, that after getting this fellow's name you ought to have got his *address*? In the book of rules, isn't it?'

'Yes, sir, but—'

'Why didn't he want to keep talking, tell me that.'

'Probably ran out of 10p's.'

'He could have rung you again later.'

'Probably thought he'd – he'd already done his duty.'

'More than you did, eh?'

'Yes, sir.'

'Why didn't he stay there at Thrupp?'

'Not everybody like seeing – sort of drowned people.'

Morse conceded the point, and moved on. 'What do they fish for there?'

'They say there's a few biggish pike up by the bridge.'

'Really? Who the hell's "they"?'

'Well, one of my lads, sir. He's been fishing for pike up there a few times.'

'Keen fisherman, is he?'

Dickson was feeling more at ease now. 'Yes, sir, he's joined the Oxford Pike Anglers' Association.'

'I see. Is the fellow who rang you up a member, too?'

Dickson swallowed hard. 'I don't know, sir.'

'Well, bloody well find out, will you!'

Morse walked away a few steps from the flustered Dickson; then he walked back. 'And I'll tell you something else, lad. If your man Rowbotham *is* a member of whatever it's called, I'll buy you every bloody doughnut in the canteen. And that's a promise!'

Morse walked over to the canteen, ordered another cup of coffee with plenty of milk, smoked a cigarette, assessed the virulence of his gnathic bacteria, noted the pile of approximately thirty-five doughnuts on the counter, and returned to his office.

It was Lewis who was beaming with pleasure now. 'Got it, I reckon, sir!' He showed Morse the list he made. 'Only four digits and so there are only the ten numbers. What do you think?'

Morse read the list:

8080 – J. Pettiford, Tobacconist, Piccadilly
8081 – Comprehensive Assurance Co., Shaftesbury Avenue
8082 – ditto
8083 – ditto
8084 – Douglas Schwartz, Reproductions, Old Compton
       Street

8085 – Ping Hong Restaurant, Brewer Street
8086 – Claude & Mathilde, Unisex Hairdressers, Lower Regent Street
8087 – Messrs Levi & Goldstein, Antiquarian Books, Tottenham Court Road
8088 – The Flamenco Topless Bar, Soho Terrace

'There's one missing, Lewis.'

'You want me to—?'

'I told you to try them all, I think.'

But whoever was renting number 8089 was clearly away from base, and Morse told Lewis to forget it.

'We are not, my friend, exactly driving through the trackless wastes of the Sahara with a broken axle, you agree? Now, if you can just make one more call and find out the price of a cheap-day second-class return to Paddington—'

'Are we going there?'

'Well, one of us'll have to, Lewis, and it's important for you to stay here, isn't it, because I've got one or two very interesting little things I want you to look into. So I'll – er – perhaps go myself.'

'It won't do your tooth much good.'

'Ah! That reminds me,' said Morse. 'I think it's about time I took another pill or two.'

CHAPTER TWELVE

Thursday, 24th July

A brief interlude in which Sergeant Lewis takes his first steps into the Examination Schools, the Moloch of Oxford's testing apparatus.

IT WAS LATE morning when, from its frontage on the High, Sergeant Lewis entered the high-roofed, hammer-beamed lobby of the Examination Schools. Never before had there been occasion for him to visit this grove of Academe, and he felt self-conscious as his heavy boots echoed over the mosaics of the marble floor, patterned in green and blue and orange. At intervals, in front of the oak panelling that lined the walls, were stationed the white and less-than-animated busts of former University Chancellors, former loyal servants of the monarchy, and sundry other benefactors. And along the walls themselves was a series of 'faculty' headings: Theology, Philosophy, Oriental Studies, Modern History, and the rest; below which, behind glass, were pinned a line of notices announcing the names of those candidates adjudged to have satisfied, in varying degrees, the appropriate panels of the faculties' examiners.

On the *Literae Humaniores* ('Greats') board (as Morse had assured him he would) Lewis duly found a long list of names, categorized into Class I, Class II, Class III, and Pass Degree. He noticed, too (as Morse had assured him he would), that a young lady by the name of Summers (Jane) of Lonsdale College, had secured a place in the first of these aforesaid categories. Then, doing precisely as he had been told, Lewis looked to the bottom of the list, where he saw the signatures of seven examiners. A few of them were barely legible. But one of them was conspicuously clear: the neatly penned signature of O. M. A. Browne-Smith. So Lewis made a brief entry in his notebook, and wondered why Morse had bothered to send him on this particular errand.

An attendant was seated in an office to the left of the lobby, and Lewis was soon enlisting this man's ready assistance in learning something of the processes involved in the evolution of the class-lists. What happened, it seemed, was this. After candidates had finished their written examinations, mark co-ordination meetings were held by each of the examining panels, where 'classes' were provisionally allotted, and where borderline candidates at each class-boundary were considered for vivas, especially those candidates hovering between a first and a second; finally, but then only the day before the definitive lists were due to be published, the chairman of the examiners (and no one else) was fully in possession of all the facts. At that point it was the duty of the chairman of examiners to summon his colleagues together in order to make a corporate,

meticulous check of the final lists, and then to entrust
the agreed document to one of the senior personnel of
the Schools, whose task it now was to deliver the
document for printing to the Oxford University Press.
Immediately this was done, five copies of the lists were
redelivered to the waiting panel, who would usually be
sitting around drinking tea and eating a few sandwiches
during the hour or so's interval. There would follow
the long and tedious checking of all results, the spell-
ings of names, and the details of index-numbers and
colleges, before the chairman would read aloud to his
colleagues the final version, down to the last diaeresis
and comma. Only then, if all were correct, would the
chairman summon the Clerk of the Schools, in whose
august presence each of the five copies would be signed
in turn by each of the examiners. Then, at long last,
the master-copy would be posted in the lobby of the
Schools.

Lewis thanked the attendant, and clattered out
across the entrance hall, where examinees, parents,
and friends were still clustered eagerly round the
notice-boards. For the first time in his life he felt a little
envy for those white-tied, subfusc-suited students so
happily perched upon the topmost boughs of the tree
of knowledge. But such thoughts were futile. Anyway,
he had his second assignment ahead of him – at the
Churchill Hospital.

Morse was out when he returned, and so for a change
it was Lewis who had some little time in which to

ponder how the case was going. On the whole, he
thought that Morse was probably right. Far from being
stranded in the Sahara, they were following a fairly well-
directed route, with signposts at almost all the early
stages – quite certainly at the Examination Schools; but
not (Lewis reminded himself) at the Churchill, where
his inquiries had yielded nothing, and where Morse's
confident predictions had clearly gone dramatically
askew.

CHAPTER THIRTEEN

Thursday, 24th July

Quite fortuitously, Morse lights upon a set of college rooms which he had no original intention of visiting.

MORSE HIMSELF HAD decided to postpone for a day or two the pleasures of a trip to Soho, and instead to make some more immediate inquiries in Oxford. Thus it is that just before midday he was parking the Lancia in one of the spaces at the back of Lonsdale ('Reserved for Senior Fellows'), walking through the front gate ('No Visitors'), and introducing himself at the Lodge. Here, a bowler-hatted porter, very young but already equipped with the requisite blend of servility and officiousness, was perfectly willing to answer the questions Morse put to him: yes, most of the undergrads had now gone down for the long vac; yes, most of the dons had also departed, amongst their number the Master, the Vice-Master, the Investments Bursar, the Domestic Bursar, the Senior Tutor, the Senior Fellow, the . . .

'Off to the Bahamas, all of them?'

'Continent mostly, sir – and Greece.'

'You think it's all those topless beaches, perhaps?'

For a few seconds the young porter leered as though he were about to produce a dirty postcard from one of the innumerable pigeon-holes, but he quickly resumed his dignity. 'I wouldn't know about that, sir.'

'What about Dr Browne-Smith? Is he still away?'

'I've not seen him in college since we had a note from him . . . and then we had a – just a minute.' He went over to his desk and returned to the 'Enquiries' window with a sheaf of papers. In spite of having to read them upside-down, Morse was able to read some of the messages clearly: 'Professor M. Liebermann – back 6th August. All post to Pension Heimstadt, Friederichstrasse 14, Zurich'; 'Mr G. Westerby – off to Greece until end of August. Keep all mail at the Lodge'; 'Dr Browne-Smith . . .'

'Here we are, sir.'

Morse took the handwritten sheet and read the few words: 'Away untill further notice no forwarding adress.' Mentally deleting an 'l', inserting a 'd', and introducing a major stop into mid-message, Morse handed the sheet back. 'Phone message, was it?'

'Yes, sir. Yesterday, I think it was – or Tuesday.'

'You took it yourself?'

The porter nodded.

'It was Dr Browne-Smith who rang?'

'I think so, yes.'

'You know him well?'

The young man shrugged. 'Pretty well.'

'You'd recognize his voice all right?'

'Well—'

'How long have you been here?'

'More than three months now.'

'Just let me have the key to his rooms, will you?' Morse pointed peremptorily to a bunch of keys hanging beside the pigeon-holes, and the porter did as he was told.

The book-lined room to which Morse admitted himself was shady and silent as the grave. Everywhere there were signs of the academic pursuits to which Browne-Smith had devoted his life: on the desk, a large stack of typescript of what appeared to be a forthcoming opus on Philip, father of Alexander the Great, and scores of photographs, slides, and postcards; on a bookcase beside the desk a marble bust of a sombre-featured Cicero; on the few square yards of the walls still free from books, many black-and-white photographs of temples, vases and statuary. But nothing untoward; nothing out of place.

Leading off this main room were two other rooms: one a bleakish-looking, rather dirty WC; the other a small bedroom, containing a single bed, hundreds more books, a white washbasin and a large mahogany wardrobe. The door of the wardrobe creaked noisily as Morse opened it and looked vaguely along the line of suits and shirts. He told himself he should have brought a tape-measure, but he accepted the fact that usually such forward-planning was quite beyond him. Apart from patting a few pockets, his only other interest appeared to lie in a very large selection of socks, whence he abstracted a brand-new pair and stuffed them in his pocket.

Back in the main room, his eyes wandered along the shelves and into the alcoves (failing to observe the small cooking-ring); but again he seemed mildly satisfied. He picked up a virgin sheet of paper, flicked it into the portable typewriter which stood beside the typescript, and clumsily tapped his way through the leap of the lazy, brown fox over the something or other. Morse couldn't quite remember it all, but he knew he'd got most of the letters included.

As he closed the door behind him (forgetting to re-lock it), he felt a few more sudden jabs in his lower jaw; and, although that unsettled July had at last turned hot and sunny, he pulled his scarf round his throat once more as he stood on the wide, wooden landing. He looked around him, first up the stairs, then down them; then across to the room immediately opposite, where the name G. D. Westerby was printed above the door. Yes! He had seen that name ten minutes ago in the Porters' Lodge; and the owner of that name was, at that very moment, sunning himself on some Aegean island, surely. Yet the door stood slightly open, and Morse stepped silently across the landing and listened.

There was someone there. For a few seconds Morse felt a childlike shudder of fear, but only (he told himself) because of his recent prying in the quiet rooms behind him. Anyway, it would only be some staircase-scout doing a bit of tidying up, dusting . . . But suddenly the rustling noises ceased, succeeded by the more reassuring clean-cut metallic clacks of hammer upon nails; and Morse felt better. Pushing open the door he saw a room very similar to the one he had just left, except that tea-chests and packing crates (most of them with address labels already attached) were bestrewn over almost the whole of the carpet-area, in the midst of which a youth of no more than sixteen or seventeen, dressed in a khaki overall, was inexpertly fixing a lid to one of the wooden crates. As Morse came in, the youth looked up; but only it seemed from curiosity, for he promptly returned to his amateurish bangings.

'Excuse me, is Mr – er – Westerby in?'

'On holiday, I think,' said the spotty-faced youth.

'I'm – er – one of his colleagues. I was very much hoping to catch him before he went.' This explanation appeared unworthy of further comment, for the youth merely nodded and drove yet another nail askew into the wooden lath.

Almost exactly the same layout of rooms as opposite – even the similar positioning of the working desk, with a similar pile of typescript, and exactly the same model of portable typewriter. And Morse knew in a flash what he was about to do, although he had almost no idea of why he did it.

'I'll just leave a note for him, lad, if you'll let me through.'

From his pocket he took out the sheet he had just typed, and put the lazy, brown fox through his faltering paces once more.

'Your firm's moving the old boy, I see.'

'Yeah.'

'Lot of stuff – he always kept a lot of stuff.'

'Books!' (Clearly the youth had as yet no great respect for literature.)

The crate that was in the process of being lidded was doubtless packed with objects that were eminently breakable, since three quarters of its contents appeared to be wrapped in crumpled newspaper. And there was another crate, alongside, presumably designated for a similar purpose, with a battalion of cut-glass objects, still unwrapped, surrounding it on the carpet. But other objects had already been deposited in this second crate – bulkier objects; and one in particular that lay snugly in the middle, swathed in past editions of *The Times*. It was about the shape of a medium-sized goldfish bowl, almost the size of a – yes! – almost the size of a head.

'I'm glad to see you're being careful with the old boy's valuables,' Morse heard himself saying as he knelt down beside this crate and, with a shaking hand, touched the packaged article, where his probing fingers soon felt the configurations of a human nose and a human mouth.

'What's this?' he managed to ask.

The youth looked across at him. 'Mr Gilbert told me to be very careful about that.'

'Who's Mr Gilbert?'

'*I'm* Mr Gilbert!'

Morse almost panicked as he turned to the door and saw a man of about sixty, perhaps – grey-flannelled and shirt-sleeved, with a pair of gold-rimmed, half-glasses on his nose, and a pair of no-nonsense eyes behind them. But there was something else about him – the first thing that anyone would notice: for, like Morse, he wore a scarf that draped his lower jaw.

'Hullo, Mr Gilbert. I'm – ah – one of Westerby's colleagues here. He asked me to look in from time to time to see, you know, that the stuff was being stowed away carefully.'

'We're looking after that all right, sir.'

'He's got some valuable things here—'

'Have no fears, sir! We're looking after everything beautifully.' With agility he picked his way across the room and stood above the still-kneeling Morse. 'You know we get more fusspots in this business, especially with the women—'

'But some of this stuff – well, you just couldn't replace it, could you?'

'No?' Mr Gilbert's tone sounded too knowledgeable for Morse to demur. 'I'll tell you one thing, sir. Almost all my clients would prefer to collect their insurance money.'

'Perhaps so.' Morse rose to his feet, and as he did so Gilbert's shrewd eyes seemed to measure him for crating, like some melancholy undertaker surveying a corpse for coffining. 'It's just that he asked me—'

'Look around and check up, sir! We're only too anxious to give every satisfaction – aren't we, Charlie?'

The young assistant nodded. 'Yes, Mr Gilbert.'

Almost involuntarily Morse's eyes were drawn down once again to the head in the unlidded crate, and Gilbert's eyes were following.

'He's all right. Don't worry about him, sir. Took us a good ten minutes to put him to bed.'

'What is it?' asked Morse weakly.

'You want me to—?' There was annoyance in Gilbert's face.

Morse nodded.

If it had taken ten minutes to put this particular valuable finally to rest, it took less than ten seconds to resurrect it. And it *was* a head, a marble head of Gerardus Mercator, the Flemish geographer – a head chopped off at the neck, like the head of the man who had been dragged from the canal out at Thrupp.

A somewhat foolish-looking Morse now hastened to take his leave, but before doing so he sought briefly to mitigate the awkward little episode. He addressed himself to Gilbert: 'You're a fellow sufferer, I see.'

For a second or two Gilbert's eyes looked puzzled – suspicious almost. 'Ah – the scarf – yes! Abscess. But the dentist won't touch it. What about you, sir?'

So Morse told him, and the two men chatted amiably enough for a couple of minutes. Then Morse departed.

From the window, Gilbert watched Morse as he walked towards the Lodge.

'How the hell did he get in?'

'I must have left the door open.'

'Well, you're going to have to learn to keep doors *shut* in this business – understand? One of the first rules of the trade, that is. Still, you've not been with us long, have you?'

'Month.' The youth looked surly, and Gilbert's tone was deliberately softer as he continued.

'Never mind – no harm done. You don't know who he is, do you?'

'No. But I saw him go into the room opposite, then I heard him come out again.'

'Opposite, eh?' Gilbert opened the door, and looked out. 'Mm. That must be Dr Browne-Smith, then.'

'He said he was a friend o' this fella here.'

'Well, you believed him, didn't you?'

'Yeah – course.'

'As I say, though, we can't be too careful in this job, Charlie. Lots of valuables around. It's always the same.'

'He didn't take anything.'

'No, I'm sure he didn't. He – er – just sort of looked round, you say?'

'Yeah, looked around a bit – said he wanted to leave a message for this fella, that's all.'

'Where's the message?' Gilbert's voice was suddenly sharp.

'I dunno. He just typed—'

'He *what?*'

The unhappy Charlie pointed vaguely to the portable. 'He just typed a little note on that thing, that's all.'

'Ah, I see. Well, if that's all—' Gilbert's face seemed to relax, and his tone was kindly again. 'But look, my lad. If you're going to make a success of this business, you've got to be a bit cagey, like me. When you're moving people, see, it's easy as wink for someone to nip in the property and pretend he's a relative or something. Then he nicks all the silver – and then where are we? Understand?'

'Yeah.'

'So. Let's start being cagey right away, OK? You be a good lad, and just nip down to the Lodge, and see if they know who that fellow was in here. It'll be a bit of good experience for you.'

Without enthusiasm, Charlie went out, and for a second time Gilbert walked over to the window, and waited until the young apprentice was out of sight. Then he put on a pair of working gloves, picked up the portable typewriter and crossed the landing. He knew that the door opposite was unlocked (since he had already tried it on his way up), and very swiftly he entered the room and exchanged the typewriter he carried for the one on Dr Browne-Smith's desk.

Gilbert was kneeling by one of the crates, carefully repacking the head of Gerardus Mercator, when a rather worried-looking Charlie returned.

'It was the *police*.'

'Really?' Gilbert kept his eyes on his work. 'Well, that's good news. Somebody must have seen you here and thought the college had a burglar or something. Yes – that explains it. You see, lad, there aren't many people in the colleges this time of year. They've nearly all gone, so it's a good time for burglars, understand?'

Charlie nodded, and was soon attaching an address label to the recently lidded crate: G. D. Westerby, Esq., Flat 6, 29 Cambridge Way, London, WC1.

CHAPTER FOURTEEN

Thursday, 24th July

Preliminary investigations are now in full swing, and Morse appears unconcerned about the contradictory evidence that emerges.

IT MIGHT PERHAPS appear to the reader that Morse had come off slightly the worse in the exchanges recorded in the previous chapter. But the truth is that after a late pub lunch Morse returned to his office exceedingly satisfied with his morning's work, since fresh ideas were breeding in profusion now.

He was still seated there, deep in thought, when three quarters of an hour later the phone rang. It was the police surgeon.

'Look, I'll cut out the technicalities. You can read 'em in my report – and anyway you wouldn't be able to follow 'em. Adult, male, Caucasian; sixtyish or slightly more; well nourished; no signs of any physical abnormality; pretty healthy except for the lungs, but there's no tumour there – in fact there's no tumour or neoplasm anywhere – we don't call it cancer these days, you know. By the way, you still smoking, Morse?'

'Get on with it!'

'Dead before immersion—'

'You *do* surprise me.'

'—and probably curled up a bit after death.'

'He was carried there, you mean?'

'I said "probably".'

'In the boot of a car?'

'How the hell do I know!'

'Anything else?'

'Dismembered *after* death – pretty certain of that.'

'Brilliant,' mumbled Morse.

'And that's almost it, old man.'

Morse was secretly delighted with these findings, but for the moment he feigned a tone of disappointment. 'But aren't you going to tell me *how* he died? That's what they pay you for, isn't it?'

As ever, the surgeon sounded unperturbed. 'Tricky question, that. No obvious wounds – or unobvious ones for that matter. Somebody could have clobbered him about the head – a common enough cause of death, as well you know. But we haven't *got* a head, remember?'

'Not poisoned?' asked Morse more quietly.

'Don't think so. It's never all that easy to tell when you've got your giblets soaked in water.'

'Didn't you bother to have a look at his guts?'

'Ah, yes. Drop of Scotch there, Morse. But, after all, there's a drop of Scotch in most – By the way, Morse, you still boozing?'

'I've not quite managed to cut it out.'

'And some kippers. You interested in kippers?'

'For breakfast?'

'He'd had some, yes. But whether he'd had 'em for breakfast—'

'You mean he might have had the Scotch for breakfast and the kippers for lunch?'

'We live in a strange world.'

'Nothing else?'

'As I said, that's almost the lot.'

With huge self-gratification, Morse now prepared to launch his Exocet. 'Well, thanks very much, Max. But if I may say so I reckon somebody at your end – I'm sure it isn't you! – deserves a hefty kick up the arse. As you know, I don't pretend to be a pathologist myself but—'

'I said it was "almost" the lot, Morse, and I know what you're going to say. I just thought I'd leave it to the end – you know, just to humour an old friend and all that.'

'It's that bloody *arm* I'm talking about!'

'Yes, yes! I know that. You just hold your horses a minute! I noticed you looking down at that arm, of course, almost as if you thought you'd made some wonderful discovery. Discovery? What? With that bloody great bruise there? You don't honestly think even a part-time hospital porter could have missed that, do you?'

Morse growled his discomfiture down the phone, and the surgeon proceeded placidly.

'Funny thing, Morse. You just *happened* to be right in what you thought – not for the right reasons, though. That contusion on the left arm, it was nothing to do with giving blood. He must have just knocked himself somewhere – or somebody else knocked *him*. But you were right, he *was* a blood donor. Difficult to be certain, but I examined his arms very carefully and I reckon he'd probably had the needle about twenty to twenty-five times in his left arm; about twelve to fifteen in his right.'

'Mm.' For a few seconds Morse was silent. 'Send me the full report over, please, Max.'

'It won't help much.'

'*I'll* decide that, thank you very much.'

'What do I do with the corpse?'

'Put it in the bloody deep-freeze!'

A few minutes later, after slamming down the phone, Morse rang Lonsdale and asked for the college secretary.

'Can I help you?' She had a nice voice, but for once it didn't register with Morse.

'Yes! I want to know whether the college had kippers for breakfast on Friday 11th July.'

'I don't know. I could try to find out, I suppose.'

'Well, *find* out!' snapped Morse.

'Can I ring you back, sir?' She was obviously distressed, but Morse was crudely adamant.

'No! Do it now!'

Morse heard a hectic, whispered conversation at the other end of the line, and eventually a male voice, defensive but quite firm, took over.

'Andrews, here. Perhaps *I* could help you, Inspector.'

And, indeed, he could; for he happened to live

with his family in Kidlington, and professed himself only too glad to call in at police HQ later that same afternoon.

Lewis, who had come in during this latter call, realized immediately that someone had seriously upset the chief, and he was not at all hopeful about how his own two items of information would be received – especially the second. But Morse appeared surprisingly amiable and listened attentively as Lewis recounted what he had learned at the Examination Schools.

'So you see, sir,' he concluded, 'no one, not even the chairman, could be absolutely certain of all the results until just before the final list goes up.'

Morse just nodded, and sat back almost happily.

But Lewis had barely begun his report on his second visit when Morse sat forward and exploded.

'You couldn't have looked carefully enough, Lewis! Of course he's bloody there!'

'But he's not, sir. I checked and rechecked everything – so did the girl.'

'Didn't it occur to you they'd probably put him under "Smith" or something?'

Lewis replied quietly: 'If you really want to know, I looked under "Brown", and "Browne" with an "e"; and "Smith", and "Smithe" with an "e"; and I looked through all the rest of the "B"s and the "S"s just in case his card was out of order. But you'd better face it, sir. Unless they've lost his records, *Dr Browne-Smith isn't a blood donor at all.*'

'Oh!' For some time Morse just sat there, and then he smiled. 'Why didn't you try under the "W"s?'

'Pardon?'

'Forget it! For the minute anyway. Now let me tell you a few interesting facts.'

So Morse, in turn, recounted his own morning's work, and finished up by handing over to Lewis the sheet of paper on which he had typed his two sentences.

'See that second one, Lewis?'

Lewis nodded as he looked down at the version beginning 'The laxy brown fox 13aped . . .'

'Well, that's the same typewriter as the one used for the letter we found on the body!'

Lewis whistled in genuine amazement. 'You're sure you're not mistaken, sir?'

'Lew-is!' (The eyes were almost frighteningly unblinking once more.) 'And there's something else.' He pushed across the desk the note that the Master of Lonsdale had given him earlier – the note supposedly left in the Porters' Lodge by Browne-Smith. '*That* was done on the same typewriter, too!'

'Whew!'

'So your next job—'

'Just a minute, sir. You're quite certain, are you, which typewriter it was?'

'Oh yes, Lewis. *It was Westerby's.*'

He was very happy now, and looked across at Lewis with the satisfaction of a man leaning over the parapet of infallibility.

*

So it was that Lewis was forthwith dispatched to impound the two typewriters, whilst Morse took two more penicillin tablets and waited for the arrival of Mr Andrews, Ancient History Tutor of Lonsdale.

CHAPTER FIFTEEN

Thursday, 24th July

From two sources, Morse gains valuable insight into the workings of the human mind, and specifically into the mind of Dr Browne-Smith of Lonsdale.

ANDREWS ('A GOOD young man', as Browne-Smith had earlier described him) turned out to be about Morse's age – a slim, bespectacled, shrewd-looking man of medium height who gave the immediate impression of not suffering fools at all gladly. For the time being he was (as he told Morse) the senior resident fellow at Lonsdale, in which capacity he was far from happy about the way the college secretary had been telephonically assaulted. But, yes: on Friday, 11th July, the college had breakfasted on kippers. That had been the question – and that was the answer.

So Morse began to like the man, and was soon telling him about the Master's mild anxiety over Browne-Smith, as well as about his own involvement in the matter.

'Let me come clean, Inspector. I know more about this than you think. Before he left, the Master told *me* he was worried about Browne-Smith.'

'If he's got any sense, he's *still* worried.'

'But we had a note from him.'

'Which he didn't write.'

'Can you prove that?' Andrews asked, as if prodding some semi-informed student into producing a piece of textual evidence.

'Browne-Smith's dead, I'm afraid, sir.'

For a few moments Andrews sat silently, his eyes betraying no sense of shock or surprise.

'Was he a blood donor?' asked Morse suddenly.

'I don't know. Not the sort of thing one broadcasts, would you say?'

'Some people have those "Give Blood" stickers on the car windows.'

'I don't remember seeing—'

'Did he have a car?'

'Big, black, thirsty Daimler.'

'Where's that now?'

'I've no idea.'

'What was his favourite tipple in the Common Room?'

'He liked a drop of Scotch, as most of us do, but he wasn't a big drinker. He was an Aristotelian, Inspector; with him it was always the half-way house between the too much and the too little – if you – er – follow what I'm saying.'

'Yes, I think I do.'

'You remember the Cambridge story that Trinity once saw Wordsworth drunk and once saw Porson sober? Well, I can tell you one thing: Lonsdale never once saw Browne-Smith drunk.'

'He was a bore, you mean?'

'I mean nothing of the sort. It's just that he couldn't abide woolly-mindedness, shoddiness, carelessness—'

'He wouldn't have made too many mistakes in English grammar?'

'Over his dead body!'

'Which is precisely where we stand, sir,' said Morse sombrely.

Andrews waited a moment or two. 'You really are quite sure of that?'

'He's dead,' repeated Morse flatly. 'His body was fished out of the canal up at Thrupp yesterday.'

Morse was conscious of the steady, scholarly eyes upon him as Andrews spoke: 'But I only read about that in the *Oxford Mail* this lunchtime. It said the body couldn't be identified.'

'Really?' Morse appeared genuinely surprised. 'Surely you don't believe everything you read in the newspapers, sir?'

'No, but I believe most of it,' replied Andrews simply and tellingly; and Morse abruptly switched his questioning.

'Dr Browne-Smith, sir. Was he a fit man – considering his age, I mean?'

For the first time Andrews appeared less than completely at ease. 'You know something about that?'

'Well, not officially, but . . .'

Andrews stared down at the threadbare carpet. 'Look, Inspector, the only reason the Master mentioned anything to me . . .'

'Go on!'

'. . . Well, it's because I shall be taking over his duties in the College, you see.'

'After he retires?'

'Or before, I'm afraid. You – er – you knew, didn't you, that he'd only a few months to live?'

Morse nodded, quite convincingly.

'Tragic thing, Inspector – cancer of the brain.'

Morse shook his head. 'You're as bad as the Master, sir. "Cancer"? Forget the word! "Tumour", if you like – or "neoplasm". They're the generic terms we use these days for all those nasty things we used to call "cancer".' (He congratulated himself on remembering the gist of what the surgeon had told him earlier that afternoon.)

'I'm not a medical man myself, Inspector.'

'Nor me, really. But, you know, in this job you have to pick up a few things, sometimes. By the way, are you likely yourself to be much better off – financially, I mean – with Dr Browne-Smith out of the way?'

'What the hell's *that* supposed to mean?'

'It means we're dealing with murder, that's all,' said Morse, looking across the table with guileless eyes. 'And that's what they pay me for, sir – trying to find out who murdered people.'

'All right. If you must know, I shall be just over two thousand a year better off.'

'You're gradually shinning up the tree, sir.'

'Not so gradually, either!' Andrews' eyes glinted momentarily with the future prospects of further academic preferment, and momentarily Morse was taken aback by the honesty of his answer.

'But the Master's still got about ten years to go,' objected Morse.

'Eight actually.'

Strangely, this was neither an unpleasant nor an embarrassing moment, as though each man had perfectly understood and perfectly respected the other's thoughts.

'Head of House!' said Morse slowly. 'Great honour, isn't it?'

'For me it's always seemed the greatest honour.'

'Do most of the dons share your view?'

'Most of them – if they're honest.'

'Did Browne-Smith?'

'Oh, quite certainly, yes.'

'So he was a disappointed man?'

'Life's full of disappointments, Inspector.'

Morse nodded. 'Had Browne-Smith any physical abnormalities you can remember?'

'Don't think so – except for his finger, of course. He lost most of his right index finger – accident in the war. But you probably know all about that.'

Morse nodded, again quite convincingly. God, he'd forgotten all about that! And suddenly the hooked atoms were engaging and re-engaging themselves so rapidly in his mind that he was desperately anxious to rid himself of the worthy man seated opposite who had put the fire to so many fuses. So he stood up, expressed his thanks and showed the Lonsdale don to the door.

'There is just one thing,' said Andrews. 'I was meaning to mention it earlier, but you side-tracked me.

Browne-Smith was never down to College breakfast in *my* time at Lonsdale – and that's fifteen years, now.'

'Well, that's very interesting, sir,' said Morse in a light tone that masked a heavy blow. 'You've been extremely helpful, sir, and thank you for coming along. There's just one more thing. Please, if you will, convey my apologies to the College secretary. I'm sorry I was rude to her – I'd like her to know that.'

'I'll certainly see that she does. She was upset, as I told you – and she's a lovely girl.'

'Is she?' said Morse.

As soon as Andrews had gone, Morse reached for the phone to put his query to the curator of the Medical Science Library at the Bodleian, and, a few minutes later, he was listening carefully to the answer.

'It's the definitive work, Inspector – Dr J. P. F. Coole on *Carcinoma in the Brain*. This is what he's got to say – chapter six, by the way: "Tumours are broadly divided into malignant tumours, which invade and destroy surrounding tissues; and benign tumours, which do not. Most malignant tumours have the additional property of giving rise to metastases or secondary tumours in parts of the body remote from the primary growth. A minority of malignant tumours fall into the category of tumours of local malignancy which invade and destroy surrounding tissues, but never metastasize. There are several tumours of local malignancy that occur in or on the head."'

'Bit slower now,' interposed Morse.

' "Many brain tumours are local in their malignancy; for example, the *spongioblastoma multiforme* and the diffuse *astrocytoma*. All tumours inside the skull are potentially fatal, even if they are quite benign – as this term has already been defined in—" '

'Thanks. That's fine. From what you're saying, then, it's possible that a brain-tumour might not spread to somewhere else in the body?'

'That's what this fellow says.'

'Good. Now, one more thing. Would one of these brain-tumours perhaps result in some sort of irrationality? You know, doing things quite out of character?'

'Ah! That's in chapter seven. Just let me—'

'No, no. Just tell me vaguely, that'll be fine.'

'Well, judging from the case-histories, the answer's a pretty definite "yes". *Very* strange things, some of them did.'

'You see, I'm just wondering whether a man who'd got a brain-tumour, a man who'd been sober and meticulous all his life, might suddenly snap and—'

'By Jove, yes! Let me just quote that case of Olive Mainwearing from Manchester. Now, just let me—'

'No! Please don't bother. You've been wonderfully helpful, and I'm most grateful. The beer's on me next time we're together in the King's Arms.'

Morse sat back in his black leather chair, happily ignorant of the aforementioned Olive's extraordinary behaviour, and happily confident that at last he was beginning to see, through the mists, the outline of those further horizons.

CHAPTER SIXTEEN

Thursday, 24th July

Lewis again finds himself the unsuspecting catalyst as
Morse considers the course of the case so far.

WHEN LEWIS CAME in half an hour later, he found
Morse sitting motionless at his desk, staring down
fixedly at his blotting-pad, the orange-and-brown-
striped scarf still round his jaw, and the signature
'On-no-account-disturb-me' written overall.

Yet Lewis shattered the peace enthusiastically. 'It was
Browne-Smith's typewriter, sir! Portable job, like you
said. No doubt about it.'

Morse looked up slowly. 'It was Westerby's typewriter
– I thought I told you that.'

'No, sir. It was *Browne-Smith's*. You must have made a
mistake. Believe me – you can't get two identical
typewriters.'

'I told you it was Westerby's,' repeated Morse calmly.
'Perhaps you didn't hear me properly.'

Lewis felt the anger rising within him: why couldn't
Morse – just for once! – allow a fraction of credit for
what, so conscientiously, he tried to do? 'I *did* hear
what you said. You told me to find the typewriter—'

'I told you no such thing!' snapped Morse. 'I told you to get *Westerby's* typewriter. You *deaf?*'

Lewis breathed deeply, and very slowly shook his head.

'Well? *Did* you get Westerby's typewriter?'

'It wasn't there,' growled Lewis. 'The removal people must have taken it. And don't blame me for that! As I just said, sir, it would do me good just once in a while to get a bit of thanks for—'

'Lew-is!' beamed Morse. 'When – *when* will you begin to understand the value of virtually everything you do for me? Why do you misjudge me all the time? Listen! I remember perfectly well that the first sentence I typed out was done on Browne-Smith's typewriter, and the second on Westerby's. Now, just think! Since it was the *second,* as we know, that matched the letter we found in the dead man's pocket, it was on Westerby's typewriter that someone wrote our letter. Agreed? And now you come and tell me it was typed on Browne-Smith's? Well . . . you see what it all means, don't you?'

Over the years, Lewis had become skilled in situations such as this, knowing that Morse, like some inexperienced schoolmaster, was far more anxious to parade his own cleverness than to elicit any halting answer from his dimmer pupils. So it was that Lewis, with a knowing nod, sat back to listen.

'Of course you do! *Someone changed those typewriters.* And that, Lewis – does it not? – throws a completely new perspective on the whole case. And you know who's given me that new perspective? You!'

Sergeant Lewis sat back helplessly in his chair, feeling like a man just presented with the Wimbledon Challenge Cup after losing the last point of the tennis match. So he bowed towards the royal box, and waited. Not for long either, since Morse seemed excited.

'Tell me how you see this case, Lewis. You know – just in general.'

'Well, I reckon Browne-Smith gets a letter from somebody who's terribly anxious to know how some-one's got on in this examination, and he says if you'll scratch my back I'll scratch yours: just tell me that little bit early and I'll see you get your little reward.'

'And then?'

'Well – like you, sir – this fellow Browne-Smith's a bachelor: he's quite tempted with the proposition put to him, and goes along with it.'

'So?'

'Well, then he finds out that the people who run these sex-places in Soho are pretty hard boys.'

'I wish you wouldn't start off every sentence with "Well".'

'You don't sound very convinced, sir?'

'Well, it all sounds a bit feeble, doesn't it? I mean, going to all that trouble just to get a girl's results a week or so early?'

'But you wouldn't understand these things. You've never had any children yourself, so you can't begin to imagine what it's like. I remember when my girls were expecting their eleven-plus results – then their O-Levels – waiting for the letter-box to rattle and then being scared to open the envelope; just hoping and praying there'd be some good news inside. It sort of gets you, sir – all that waiting. It's always at the back of your mind, and sometimes you'd give anything just to *know*. You realize *somebody* knows – somebody typing out the results and putting them into envelopes and all the rest of it. And I tell you one thing, sir: I'd have given a few quid myself to save me all that waiting and all that worriting.'

Morse appeared temporarily touched by his sergeant's eloquence. 'Look, Lewis. If that's all there is to it, why don't we just ring up this girl's father? You don't honestly think *he* wrote that letter, do you?'

'Jane Summer's dad, you mean?' Lewis shook his head. 'Quite impossible, sir.'

Morse sat upright in his chair. 'Why do you say that?'

'Both her parents were killed in a car-crash six years ago – I rang up the college secretary. Very helpful, she was.'

'Oh, I see.' Morse unwound his scarf and looked a little lost. 'Do you know, Lewis, I think you're a bit ahead of me in this case.'

'No! I'm miles behind, sir – as well you know. But in my opinion we shouldn't rule out the parent angle altogether. She could only have been in her late teens when her parents died, and somebody must have had legal responsibility for her – an uncle or a guardian or something.'

Morse's eyes were suddenly shining; and taking the torn letter from a drawer in his desk, he concentrated his brain upon it once more, his perusal punctuated by 'Yes!', 'Of course!', and finally 'My son, you're a genius!'; whilst Lewis himself sank back in his chair and dropped back a further furlong in the case.

'Very illuminating,' said Morse. 'You say that not even the chairman would know the final results until a few hours before the lists are put up?'

Lewis nodded: 'That's right.'

'But doesn't that cock up just about everything?'

'Unless, sir,' Lewis now felt happy with himself, 'she was way out at the top of the list – the star of the whole show, sort of thing.'

'Mm. We could ring up the chairman?'

'Which I have done, sir.'

It was Morse himself who was happy now. The penicillin was working its wonders, and he felt strangely content. 'And she *was* the top of the list, of course?'

Lewis, too, knew that life was sometimes very good. 'She was, sir. And if you want my opinion—'

'Of course, I do!'

'—if this girl's uncle or whatever turns out to own a sex-club in Soho, we've probably found the key to the case, and the sooner we get up there the better.'

'You've got a good point there, Lewis. On the other hand it's vital for one of us to stay here.'

'Vital for *me*, I suppose?'

But Morse ignored the sarcasm, and adumbrated for the next half-hour to his sergeant a few of the stranger thoughts that had criss-crossed his brain throughout the day.

*

It was getting late now; and, when Lewis left, Morse was free once more to indulge his own thoughts. At one time his mind would leap like a nimble-footed Himalayan goat; at another, it would stick for minutes on end like a leaden-footed diver in a sandbank. It was time to call it a day, that was obvious.

He was not quite finished, however, and before he left his office he did two things.

First, he amended his reconstruction of the fifth line of the torn letter so that it now read:

both you and me. My ward, Jane Summers of Lonsdale

Second, he took a sheet of paper and wrote the following short piece (reproduced below as it appeared in the *Oxford Mail* the following day):

CLUE TO MURDER

Customers of Marks and Spencers in the Oxford area are being asked to join in the hunt for the murderer of a 60-year-old man found in the canal at Thrupp. The bloodstained socks on the body (not yet identified) have been traced as one of just 2,500 pairs distributed around a handful of M & S stores in the Oxford region. The socks were of navy-blue cotton, with two light blue rings round the tops. Anyone who might have any information is asked to ring Kidlington 4343.

Only after dictating this absurd news-item (comma included) did Morse finally leave his office that day to return to his bachelor flat. There he played through the first act of *Die Walküre* and began to make significant inroads into the bottle just purchased from Augustus Barnett. When, at midnight, he looked around for his pyjamas, he couldn't quite remember why he had bothered the newspaper editor; yet he knew that when a man was utterly at a loss about what he should do, it was imperative that he should do *something* – like the motorist stuck in a snowdrift who decided to activate his blinkers alternately.

CHAPTER SEVENTEEN

Friday, 25th July

Discussion of identity, and of death, leads the two detectives gradually nearer to the truth.

LEWIS CAME IN early the next morning (although not so early as Morse), and immediately got down to reading the medical report from the lab.

'Gruesome all this, isn't it, sir?'

'Not read it,' replied Morse.

'You know, chopping a chap's head off.'

'It's one way of killing someone. After all, the experiment has been tried on innumerable occasions and found to be invariably fatal.'

'But the head was cut off *after* he was dead – says so here.'

'I don't give two monkeys *how* he was killed. It's the *why* that we've got to sort out. *Why* did someone chop his head off – just tell me that, for a start.'

'Because we'd have identified him, surely. His teeth would have been there and—'

'Come off it! Helluva job that'd be, hawking some dental chart round a few million dentists—'

'Thousands, you mean.'

'—and perhaps he didn't *have* any teeth, like sometimes I wish I hadn't.'

'It says here that this chap might have been killed somewhere else and taken out to the canal later.'

'So?'

'What do people usually get carried around in?' asked Lewis.

'Cars?' (Morse hardly enjoyed being catechized himself.)

'Exactly! So if the body was too big to get into the boot of the car . . .'

'You cut him down to size.'

'That's it. It's like one of those ghost things, sir. You sort of tuck the head underneath the arm.'

'Where's the head now, then?'

'Somewhere in the canal.'

'The frogmen haven't found it.'

'Heads are pretty heavy, though. It's probably stuck way down in the mud.'

'What about the *hands*, Lewis? You reckon we're going to find them neatly folded next to the head? Or is some poor little beggar going to find them in his fishing-net?'

'You don't seem to think we're going to find them, sir.'

Morse was showing signs of semi-exasperation. 'You're missing the bloody point, Lewis! I'm not asking *where* they are. I'm asking *why* someone chopped them off.'

'Same as before. Must be because someone could have identified them. He may have had a tattoo on the back of his wrist or something.'

Morse sat quite still. He knew even then that Lewis had made a point of quite extraordinary significance, and his mind, like some downhill skier, had suddenly leaped into the air across a ridge and landed neatly upon a track of virgin snow . . .

Lewis's voice seemed to reach his ears as if through a wadge of tightly packed cotton wool. 'And what about the legs, sir. Why do you think *they* were chopped off?'

'You mean *you* know?' Morse heard himself saying.

'Hardly that, sir. But it's child's play these days for the forensic boys to find a hundred-and-one things on clothes, isn't it? Hairs and threads and all that sort of thing—'

'Even if it's been in water for a few days?'

'Well, it might be more difficult then, I agree. But all I'm saying is that if we knew whose the body was—'

'We do, Lewis. You can be sure of that – surer than ever. It's Browne-Smith's.'

'All right. If it's Browne-Smith's body, then we shan't have much trouble in finding out if it's Browne-Smith's *suit*, shall we?'

Morse was frowning in genuine puzzlement. 'You're losing me, Lewis.'

'All I'm trying to say, sir, is that if someone carefully chopped off this fellow's head and his hands to stop us finding out who he was—'

'Yes?'

'—well, I don't reckon he would have left the fellow dressed in his own suit.'

'So someone dressed the corpse in someone else's suit, is that it?'

'Yes. You see, a lot of people could wear each other's jackets. I mean, I could wear yours – you're a bit fatter than I am round the middle, but it'd fit in a way. And with a jacket in the water a few days, it'd probably shrink a bit anyway, so no one's going to notice too much. *But* – ' and here Lewis paused dramatically ' – if people start wearing each other's trousers, sir – well, you could find a few problems, couldn't you? They might be too long, or too short; and it wouldn't be difficult for anyone to see almost immediately that the suit was someone else's. Do you see what I mean? I think the dead man must have been several inches shorter, or several inches taller, than the fellow whose suit he was dressed in! And *that's* why the legs were chopped off. So as I see it, sir, if we can find out whose suit it is, we shall know one thing for certain: the owner of the suit isn't the corpse – he's probably the murderer!'

Morse sat where he was, looking duly impressed and appreciative. As a result of his visit to the dentist he had himself arrived at a very similar conclusion (although by a completely different route), but he felt it proper to congratulate his sergeant.

'You know, they say your eyes begin to deteriorate about the age of seven or eight, and that your brain follows suit about twenty years later. But your brain, Lewis. It seems to get sharper every day.'

Lewis leaned back happily. 'Must be working with you, sir.'

But Morse appeared not to hear him, staring out (as Lewis had so often seen him) across the concreted yard that lay outside his window. And thus he stared for many, many minutes; and Lewis had almost read the medical report through a second time before Morse spoke again.

'It's very sad about life, really, you know. There's only one thing certain about it, and that's death. We all die, sooner or later. Even old Max, with all his laudable caution, would probably accept that. "The boast of heraldry, the pomp of power . . . ".'

'Pardon, sir?'

'We shall all die, Lewis – even you and me – just like that poor fellow we fished out of the pond. There are no exceptions.'

'Wasn't there just the *one*?' asked Lewis, quietly.

'You believe that?'

'Yes.'

'Mm.'

'Why do you mention all this, sir – you know, about dying and so on?'

'I was just thinking about Browne-Smith, that's all. I was just thinking that a man we all thought was dead is probably alive again – that's all.'

That's all. For a little while Lewis had almost convinced himself that he might be a move or two ahead of Morse. Yet now, as he shook his head in customary bewilderment, he knew that Morse's mind was half a dozen moves ahead of all the world. So he sat where he was, like a disciple in the Scriptures at the feet of the Master, wondering why he ever bothered to think about anything himself at all.

CHAPTER EIGHTEEN

Friday, 25th July

Morse decides to enjoy the hospitality of yet another
member of Lonsdale's top brass, whilst Lewis devotes
himself to the donkey work.

IT WAS HIGH time something was done, Morse knew
that. There was the dead man's suit to start with, for
surely Lewis had been right in maintaining that the
minutest detritus of living would still be lingering
somewhere in the most improbable crannies of pockets
and sleeves. Then there was the mysterious man
Gilbert, who had been given free (and official) access
to the room in which the two letters had probably been
typed: Gilbert the furniture-man, who might at that
very minute be shifting the last of the crates and the
crockery ... Yes, it was high time the pair of them
actually *did* something. *Necesse erat digitos extrahere.*

Morse was (as almost always when in a car) a morose
and uncommunicative passenger as Lewis drove down
to Lonsdale via St Giles' and the Cornmarket, then left
at Carfax and into the High. At the Lodge, it was the
same young porter on duty. But this time he refused to
hand over the keys to any room before consulting

higher authority; and Morse was still trying to get through to the Bursar when a man walked into the Lodge whom he had seen several times when he had dined at Lonsdale. It was the Vice-Master.

Ten minutes later, Lewis, with two keys in his hand, was climbing up the steps of Staircase T, whilst Morse was seating himself comfortably in a deep armchair in the Vice-Master's suite, and agreeing that although it was rather early in the day a glass of something might not be totally unwelcome.

'So you see, Inspector' (it was several minutes later) 'it's not a very happy story at all – not an unusual one, though. That pair could never have got on together, whatever happened; but there were no signs of open animosity – not, as I say, until five years ago.'

'Since when they've never even spoken to each other?'

'That's it.'

'And the reason for all this?'

'Oh, there's no great secret about that. I should think almost everyone in the college knows, apart from one or two of the younger fellows.'

'Tell me about it.'

It appeared that only two crucial ordinances had been decreed for election to the Mastership of Lonsdale College: first, that any nominate must be a layman; second, that such a person must be elected by the eight senior fellows of the college, with a minimum of six votes needed in favour, and with the election declared invalid if even a single vote was cast against. It had been common knowledge five years ago, in spite of the so-called 'secret' nature of the ballot, that when Dr Browne-Smith had been proposed and seconded, one solitary vote had thwarted his election hopes; equally common knowledge was the fact that when Mr Wester-by's name, in turn, had been put forward, one single slip of paper was firmly printed with a 'No'. The third choice – the compromise candidate – had also been one of the college's senior fellows, and it had been a relief for everyone when the present Master had been voted into office, *nem. con.*

'Head of House!' said Morse slowly. 'Great honour, isn't it?' (He was suddenly conscious that he had repeated *verbatim* the question he had asked of Andrews.)

'Some people would give a lot for it, yes.'

'Would *you?*'

The Vice-Master smiled. 'No! You can leave me out of the running, Inspector. You see, I'm in holy orders, and so, as I said, I'm just not eligible.'

'I see,' said Morse. 'Now just getting back to Dr Browne-Smith for a minute. I'd be grateful, sir, if you could tell me something about his, well, his personal life.'

'Such as?' The Vice-Master's eyes were upon him, and Morse found himself wondering how much, or how little, he could ever expect to know of the complex web of relationships within this tight community of Lonsdale.

'What about his health, for example?'

Again the shrewd look, as if the question had been fully expected. 'He was a very sick man, Inspector. But you knew that yesterday, didn't you? By the way, Andrews said you looked just a little surprised when he told you.'

'How long had *you* known?' countered Morse.

'Three weeks, I suppose. The Master called Andrews and me up to his room one evening after Hall. Strictly confidential, he said, and all that – but we had to know, of course, because of Browne-Smith's teaching commitments.'

'When did the Master think . . .?'

'Certainly no longer than the end of the Hilary Term.'

'Mm.'

'And you're wondering whether his teaching days might not be over already. Am I right?'

'How much did Andrews tell you?' asked Morse.

'Everything. You didn't mind, I hope?'

Morse felt oddly uncomfortable with the man, and after asking a few more vague questions about Browne-Smith's lifestyle, he got up to go. 'You getting some holiday soon, sir?'

'Once the Master gets back. We usually alternate so that one of us is here for most of the vac. I know that some people haven't much time for all us lazy academic lay-abouts, but there's a lot to do in a college apart from looking after students. But you'd know that, of course.'

Morse nodded, and knew that he could very soon

learn to dislike this unclerically garbed parson intensely.

'We shall co-operate as much as we can,' continued the Vice-Master. 'You know that. But it would be nice to be kept in the picture – just a little, perhaps?'

'Nothing really to tell you, sir – not yet, anyway.'

'You don't even want to tell me why your sergeant took the key to Westerby's room as well?'

'Ah, that! Yes, I ought to have mentioned that, sir. You see, there's just a possibility that the corpse we found up in the canal wasn't Browne-Smith's after all.'

'Really?'

But Morse declined to elaborate further as he made his farewell and strode away across the quad, sensing those highly intelligent eyes upon him as he turned into the Porters' Lodge. From there he progressed, only some hundred yards, into the bar of the Mitre, where he had agreed to meet Lewis. He would be half an hour early, he realized that; but a thirty-minute wait in a pub was no great trial of patience to Morse.

Once inside Browne-Smith's room, Lewis had taken out of its plastic wrapper the dark-blue jacket found on the corpse and measured it carefully against the jackets in the bedroom wardrobe: it was the same length, the same measurement round the chest, of the same sartorial style, with a single slit at the back and slim lapels. There could be little doubt about it: the jacket had belonged to Browne-Smith. After rehanging the suits,

Lewis methodically looked through the rest of the clothes, but learned only that each of the five pairs of shoes was size nine, and that four brand-new pairs of socks were all of navy-blue cotton with two light blue rings round the tops.

Westerby's rooms opposite were silent and empty now, only the faded brown fitted carpet remaining, with oblong patches of pristine colour marking the erstwhile positions of the heavier furniture. Nothing else at all, except a plastic spoon and an empty jar of Nescafé on the draining-board in the kitchen.

Lewis's highly discreet inquiries in the college office produced (amongst other things) the information that Browne-Smith certainly wore a suit very similar to the one he now unwrapped once more; and the college secretary herself (whom even Lewis considered very beautiful) was firmest of all in such sad corroboration.

The young porter was still on duty when Lewis handed back the two keys, and was soon chatting freely enough when Lewis asked about 'Gilbert Removals'. As far as the porter could remember, Mr Gilbert himself had been down to T Staircase about four or five times; but he'd finished now, for Mr Westerby had at last been 'shifted'.

'Funny you should ask about Mr Gilbert, sergeant. He's like your chief – both of 'em got the jaw-ache by the look of things.'

Lewis nodded and prepared to leave. 'Nuisance, teeth are, yes. Nothing much worse than an abscess on one of your front teeth, you know.'

The porter looked strangely at Lewis for a few

seconds, for the words he had just heard were almost exactly (he could swear it) the words he had heard from the afflicted furniture-remover.

He told Lewis so ... and Lewis told Morse, in the Mitre. Yet neither of them realized, at least for the present, that this brief and seemingly insignificant little episode was to have a profound effect upon the later stages of the case.

CHAPTER NINETEEN

Friday, 25th July

Our two detectives have not yet quite finished with the implications of severe dismemberment.

THE CASE WAS working out well enough, thought Lewis, as he drove Morse back through Summertown. The shops were in the same order as they'd been two hours earlier when he had driven past them: the RAC building, Budgens, Straw Hat Bakery, Allied Carpets, Chicken Barbecue ... yes, just the same. It was only a question of seeing them in reverse order now, tracing them backwards, as it were. Just like this case. Morse had traced things backwards fairly well thus far, if somewhat haphazardly ... And he wanted to ask Morse two questions, though he knew better than to interrupt the great man's thoughts in transit.

In Morse's mind, too, far more was surfacing from the murky waters of a local canal than a bloated, mutilated corpse that had been dragged in by a boat-hook as it threatened to drift down again and out of reach. Other things had been surfacing all the way along the towpath, as clue had followed clue. One thing at least was fairly firmly established: the murderer –

whoever that might be – had either been quite extra-ordinarily subtle, or quite inordinately stupid, in going to the lengths of dismembering a body, and then leaving it in its own clothes. If it *was* in its own suit . . . Lewis had done his job; and Lewis was sure that the suit was Browne-Smith's. But what about the body? Oh yes, indeed – but what about the body?

Back in Morse's office, Lewis launched into his questions: 'It's pretty certainly Browne-Smith's body, don't you think, sir?'

'Don't know.'

'But surely—'

'I said I don't *bloody* know!'

So, Lewis, after a decent interval, asked his other question: 'Don't you think it's a bit of a coincidence that you and this Gilbert fellow should have a bad tooth at the same time?'

Morse appeared to find this an infinitely more interesting question, and he made no immediate reply. Then he shook his head decisively. 'No. Coincidences are far more commonplace than any of us are willing to accept. It's this whole business of *chance,* Lewis. We don't go in much for talking about chance and luck, and what a huge part they play in all our lives. But the Greeks did – *and* the Romans; they both used to worship the goddess of luck. And if you must go on about coincidences, you just go home tonight and find the forty-sixth word from the beginning of the forty-sixth psalm, and the forty-sixth word from the end of it – and see what you land up with! Authorized Version, by the way.'

'Say that again, sir?'

'Forget it, Lewis! Now, listen! Let's just get back to this case we're landed with and what we were talking about at lunchtime. If our murderer wants his victim to be identified, he does not – repeat *not* chop his head off. Quite apart from the facial features – features that could be recognized by some myopic moron from thirty yards away – you've got your balding head, your missing mandibles, and whatever – even the angle of your ears; and all of those things are going to lead to a certain identification. Somebody's going to know who he is, whether he's been floating in the Mississippi for a fortnight, or whether he's been up in Thrupp for three months. Agreed? And if our murderer is still anxious for his corpse to be identified, he does not – repeat *not* cut his hands off, either. Because that removes at one fell chop the one thing we know that gives him a unique and unquestionable individuality – his fingerprints!'

'What about the legs, sir?'

'Shut up a minute! And for Christ's sake try to follow what I'm telling you! It's hard enough for *me*!'

'I'm not finding much trouble, sir.'

'All I'm saying is that if the murderer wants the body to be recognized, he doesn't chop off his head and he doesn't chop off his hands – agreed?'

Lewis nodded: he agreed.

'And yet, Lewis, there are two other clues that lead quite clearly to a positive identification of the body; the suit – quite certainly now it seems it was Browne-Smith's suit; and then the letter – almost as certainly that was written to Browne-Smith. All right, it wasn't all *that* obvious; but you'd hardly need to be a Shylock—'

'"Sherlock", sir.'

'You see what I'm getting at, though?'

Lewis pondered the question, and finally answered, 'No.'

Morse, too, was beginning to wonder whether he himself was following the drift of his own logic, but he'd always had the greatest faith in the policy of mouthing the most improbable notions, in the sure certainty that by the law of averages some of them stood a more reasonable chance of being nearer to the truth than others. So he burbled on.

'Just suppose for a minute, Lewis, that the body *isn't* Browne-Smith's, but that somebody wanted it to *look* like his. All right? Now, if the murderer had left us the head, or the hands, or both, then we could have been quite sure that the body *wasn't* Browne-Smith's, couldn't we? As we know, Browne-Smith was suffering from an incurable brain-tumour, and with a skull stuck on the table in front of him even old Max might have been able to tell us there was something not all that healthy round the cerebral cortex – even if the facial features were badly disfigured. It's just the same with the hands – quite apart from fingerprints. Browne-Smith lost most of his right index-finger in the war, and not even your micro-surgeons can stick an artificial digit on your hand without even a delinquent like Dickson spotting it. So, if the hands, or at least the right hand, had been left attached to the body, and *if all the fingers were intact* – then again we'd have been quite sure that the body *wasn't* Browne-Smith's. You follow me? The two things that could have proved that the body wasn't his are both deliberately and callously removed.'

Lewis frowned, just about managing to follow the line of Morse's argument. 'But what about the suit? What about the letter?'

'All I'm saying, Lewis, is that perhaps someone's been trying mighty hard to convince us that it *was* Browne-Smith's body, that's all.'

'Aren't you making it all a bit too complicated?'

'Could be,' conceded Morse.

'I'm just a bit lost, you see, sir. We're usually looking for a murderer, aren't we? We've never had all this trouble with a body before.'

Morse nodded. 'But we're getting to know more about the murderer all the time! He's a very clever chap. He tries to lead us astray about the identity of the body, and he very nearly succeeds.'

'So?'

'So he's almost as clever as we are; and most of the clever people I know are – guess where, Lewis!'

'In the police force?'

Morse allowed himself a weak smile, but continued with his previous earnestness. 'In the University of Oxford! And what's more, I reckon I've got a jolly good idea about exactly *which* member of the University it is!'

'Uh?' Lewis looked across at his chief with surprise – and suspicion.

But Morse was off again. 'Let's just finish off this corpse. We're left with those legs, right? Now we've got some ideas about the head and the hands, but why chop the legs off?'

'Perhaps he lost a toe in a swimming accident off Bermuda or somewhere. Got his foot caught in the propeller of a boat or something.'

Morse was suddenly very still in his chair, for Lewis's flippant answer had lit another sputtering fuse. He reached for the phone, rang through on an internal extension to Superintendent Strange, and (to Lewis's complete surprise) asked for two more frogmen – if possible immediately – to search the bottom of the canal by Aubrey's Bridge.

'Now about those legs,' resumed Morse. 'At what point would you say they were chopped off?'

'Well, sort of here, sir.' Lewis vaguely put his hand on his femur. 'About half-way between—'

'Between pelvis and patella, that's right. Half-way, though, you say? If we don't know how long his thighs were to start with, where exactly is that "half-way" of yours? It may have been meant to *look* half-way—'

'That's what I told you this morning, sir.'

'I know you did, yes! All I'm doing is to stick a bit more clarity into your thinking. You don't mind, I hope?'

'My mind's perfectly clear already, sir. He might have been a shorter man or a taller man, and, because Browne-Smith's about five-eleven, the odds are probably on him being shorter. It's the length of the femur, you see, that largely determines the height.'

'Oh!' said Morse. 'You don't happen to know how tall Westerby is – or was?'

'Five-five, sir – about that. I asked the college secretary – very nice girl.'

'Oh!'

'And I agree with all you've said, sir. Head, hands, legs – you've explained them all. If the murderer wanted us to think the body was Browne-Smith's, perhaps he couldn't have left any of them.'

The tables were turned now, and it was Morse's turn to look dubious. 'You don't think all this is getting a bit too complicated, do you, Lewis?'

'*Far* too complicated. We've got the suit and we've got the letter – both of them Browne-Smith's – and we know that he's gone missing somewhere. That would be quite enough for me, sir. But you seem to think that the man we're after is almost as clever as you are.'

Morse did not reply immediately, and Lewis noticed the look of curious exhilaration in the Chief Inspector's face. What, he wondered, had he suddenly thought of now?

Dickson called in a few minutes later to report that no one by the name of Simon Rowbotham was registered in the membership of the Pike Anglers' Association or in the membership of any other fishing-club in the vicinity of Oxford; and Lewis was disappointed with this news, for it gave a little more weight to the one freakish objection to his own firm view that the corpse they had found must be Browne-Smith's: the objection (as Morse had pointed out to him the previous morning) that '*Simon Rowbotham*' was an exact anagram of '*O.M.A. Browne-Smith*'.

Chapter Twenty

Saturday, 26th July

An extremely brief envoi to the first part of the case.

AT FIVE MINUTES to four the next morning, Morse awoke and looked at his bedside clock. It seemed quite impossible that it should be so early, for he felt completely refreshed. He got out of bed and drew the curtains, standing for several minutes looking down on the utterly silent road, only a hundred yards from Banbury Road roundabout ... the road that led north out to Kidlington, and thence past the Thames Valley Police HQ up to the turn for Thrupp, where the waters would now be lapping and plopping gently against the houseboats as they lay at their overnight moorings.

Morse went into the bathroom, noticed that his jaw was almost normal again, swallowed the last of the penicillin tablets and returned to bed, where he lay on his back, his hands behind his head ... There were still many pieces of flotsam that needed to be salvaged before the wreck of a man's life could wholly be reconstructed ... salvaged from those canal waters which changed their colour from green to grey to yellow to black ... to white ... Morse almost dozed off again, momentarily imagining that he saw the outlines of a cunningly plotted murder, with himself – yes, Morse! – at the centre of a beautifully calculated deception. Of one thing he was now utterly sure: that, quite contrary to Lewis's happy convictions about the identity of the dead man, *the man they had found was quite certainly not Dr Browne-Smith of Lonsdale.*

Thereafter, Morse was impatient for the morning and for traffic noise and for the sight of people catching buses. Ovid, in the arms of his lover, had cried out to the midnight horses to gallop slow across the vault of heaven. But Morse was without a lover; and at a quarter to five he got up, made himself a cup of tea and looked out once again at the quiet street below, where he sensed a few vague flutterings and stirrings from the chrysalis of night.

And Morse sensed rightly. For the next morning, like Browne-Smith before him, he received a long letter; a strange and extremely exciting letter.

THE END OF THE FIRST MILE

The Second Mile

CHAPTER TWENTY-ONE

Monday, 28th July

Morse, having been put on the right track by the wrong
clues, now finds his judgement almost wholly vindicated.

MORSE OPENED THE door of his office a few minutes
after eight to find Lewis reading the *Daily Mirror*.

'You seem very anxious to further our inquiries this
morning, Lewis.'

Lewis folded up the newspaper. 'I'm afraid you've
made a bad mistake, sir.'

'You mean you *are* busy on the case?'

'Not only that, sir. As I say, you've made a bad mistake.'

'Nonsense!'

'I was trying to do the coffee-break crossword and
there was a clue there that just said "Carthorse (anagram)"—'

'"Orchestra",' interrupted Morse.

'I know that, sir. But "Simon Rowbotham" is *not* an
anagram of "O.M.A. Browne-Smith"!'

'Of course it is!' Morse immediately wrote down the
letters, and was checking them off one by one when
suddenly he stopped. 'My God! You're right. There's
an "o" instead of an "e", isn't there?'

'It was only by chance I checked it when I was—'

But Morse wasn't listening. Was he *wrong*, after all his mighty thoughts and bold deductions? Was Lewis *right* – with his simple-minded assertion that the case was becoming quite unnecessarily complicated? He shook his head in some dismay. Perhaps (he clutched at straws), perhaps if he himself had made a mistake over an anagram, so might Browne-Smith have done in concocting a completely bogus name? But he couldn't convince even himself for a second, and the truth was that he felt lost.

At eight-thirty the phone rang, an excited voice announcing itself as Constable Dickson.

'I've just been reading last week's *Oxford Times*, sir.'

'Not on duty, I hope.'

'I'm off duty, sir. I'm at home.'

'Oh.'

'I've found him!'

'Found who?'

'Simon Rowbotham. I was reading the angling page – and his name's there. He came second in a fishing match out at King's Weir last Sunday.'

'Oh.'

'He lives in Botley, so it says.'

'I don't give a sod if he lives in Bootle.'

'Pardon, sir?'

'Thanks for letting me know, anyway.'

'Remember what you said about those doughnuts, sir?'

'No, I forget,' said Morse, and put the receiver down.

'Shall I go out and see him?' asked Lewis quietly.

'What the hell good would that do?' snapped Morse, thereafter lapsing into sullen silence.

Since it was marked 'Strictly Private and Confidential', the Registry had not opened the bulky white envelope, and it was lying there on Morse's blue blotting-pad when later the two men returned from coffee. Inside the envelope was a further sealed envelope (addressed, like the outer cover, to Chief Inspector E. Morse), and a covering letter from the Manager of the High Street branch of Barclays Bank, dated 26th July. It read as follows:

Dear Sir,
We received the sealed envelope enclosed on Monday, 21st July, with instructions that it be posted to you personally on Saturday, 26th July. We trust you agree that we have discharged our obligation.
                        Yours faithfully . . .

Morse handed the note over to Lewis. 'What do you make of that?'

'Seems a lot of palaver to me, sir. Why not just post it straight to you?'

'I dunno,' said Morse. 'Let's hope it's full of fivers.'

'Aren't you going to open it?'

'Interesting,' said Morse, apparently unhearing. 'If this letter reached the bank on Monday, the 21st, it was

155

probably written on Sunday, the 20th – and Max says that's the likeliest day that someone put the corpse in the canal.'

'But it's probably nothing to do with the case.'

'Well, we'll soon know.' Morse slit the envelope and began reading, and apart from a solitary 'My God!' (after the first few lines of the typewritten script) he read in utter silence, as totally engrossed, it seemed, as a dedicated pornophilist in a sex-shop.

When he had finished the long letter, he wore that look of almost sickening self-satisfaction frequently found on the face of any man whose judgement has been called into question, but thereafter proved correct.

Lewis took the letter now, immediately turning to the last page. 'There's no signature, sir.'

'Read it – just read it, Lewis,' said Morse blandly, as he reached for the phone and dialled the number of the bank.

'Manager, please.'

'He's rather tied up at the minute. Could you—'

'Chief Constable of Oxfordshire here, lad. Just tell him to get to the phone, please.' (Lewis had by now read the first page of the letter.)

'Can I help you?' asked the manager.

'I want to know whether Dr Browne-Smith – Dr O. M. A. Browne-Smith – of Lonsdale College is one of your clients.'

'Yes, he is.'

'We received a letter from you today, sir, and it's my

duty to ask you if it was Dr Browne-Smith himself who asked you to forward it to us.'

'Ah, the letter, yes. I hoped the Post Office wouldn't keep you waiting too long.'

'You haven't answered my question, sir.'

'No, I haven't. And I can't, I'm afraid.'

'I think you can, sir, and I think you will – because we're caught up in a case of murder.'

'Murder? You're not – you're not saying Dr Browne-Smith's been murdered, surely?'

'No, I didn't say that.'

'Could you tell me exactly who it is that's been murdered?'

Morse hesitated – for too long. 'No, I can't, not just for the present. Inquiries are still at a very – er – delicate stage, and that's why we've got to expect the co-operation of everyone concerned – people like yourself, sir.'

The manager was also hesitant. 'It's very difficult for me. You see, it involves the whole question of the confidentiality of the bank.'

Morse sounded surprisingly mild and accommodating. 'I understand, sir. Let's leave it, shall we, for the present? But if it becomes an absolutely vital piece of information, we shall naturally have to come and question you.'

'Yes, I see that. But I shall have to take the matter up with the bank's legal advisers, of course.'

'Very sensible, sir. And thank you for your co-operation.'

Lewis, who had been half-reading the letter (with continued amazement) and also half-listening to this strange telephone conversation, now looked up to see Morse smiling serenely and waiting patiently for him to finish.

When he had done so, but before he had the chance to pass any comment, Morse asked him to give Barclays another ring, to tell them he was Chief Inspector Morse, and to find out whether they had a second client on their books: a Mr George Westerby, of Lonsdale.

The answer was quick and unequivocal: yes, they had.

Chapter Twenty-Two

We have an exact transcript of the long letter, which was without salutation or subscription, studied by Chief Inspector Morse and by Sergeant Lewis, in the mid-morning of Monday, 28th July.

'PERHAPS IT IS not too much to expect that you have made the necessary investigations? It would scarcely need an intellect as (potentially) powerful as your own accurately to have traced the sequence of events thus far. After all, you had my suit, did you not? That, most surely, should have led your assistants to my (agreed, rather limited) wardrobe at Lonsdale, where (I assume) the waist-band inches and the inside-leg measurements have already been minutely matched. But let us agree: the body was not mine. I did try, perhaps amateurishly, to make you think it was; yet I had little doubt that you would quickly piece together a reasonably coherent letter, the torn half of which I left in the back pocket of the trousers. You might therefore have had the reasonable suspicion that the corpse was me – but not for long, if I assess you right.

'But whichever way it is (either your thinking of me as one of the dead or as one of the non-dead), I see it my duty to inform you that I am alive, at least for a little while longer. (You will have discovered that, too?)

Whose, then, is the body you found in the waters out at Thrupp? For it is not, most certainly not, my own. I repeat – whose is it? To find the answer to that question must be your next task, and it is a task in which I am prepared (even anxious) to offer some co-operation. As a child, did you ever play the game called "treasure-hunt", wherein a clue would lead from A to B? From, let us say, a little message hidden underneath a stone to a further message pinned behind a maple tree? Well, let us go on a little, shall we? From B to C, as it were.

'I received the letter and immediately acted upon it. All very odd, was it not? I knew the girl mentioned, of course, for she was one of my own pupils; and, what is more, she was a girl acknowledged by all to be the outstanding classic of the year – if not of the decade. This was common knowledge, and it was totally predictable (why bother to ask me?) that her marks in the Greats papers would be higher than any of her contemporaries of either sex. Therefore the request to communicate (and that to some anonymous third party) this particular girl's result only a week or so before the publication of class-lists struck me as rather suspicious. (A poorly constructed sentence, but I have not time to recast it.) My reward, I was told, for divulging the result some days early would be a memorably pleasant one. You would agree, I think? Even an ageing (I always put the "e" in that word) bachelor like myself may be permitted his mildly erotic day-dreams. And, as I believe, I would hardly be committing the ultimate sin in informing the world of what the world already knew. But I am not telling you the whole truth, even now. Let me go back a little.

'I have a colleague living directly opposite me: a Mr G. Westerby. He and I have been fellow dons for far too many years, and it is an open secret that the relations between the two of us have been almost childishly hostile for a great deal of that time. This colleague (I prefer not to mention his name again) is now retiring; and, although I have never actively sought to learn of his immediate plans, I have naturally gleaned a few desultory facts about his purposes: he is now away on one of his customary cut price holidays in the Greek islands; he is, on his return, to take up residence in some pretentiously fashionable flat in the Bloomsbury district; he has recently hired a firm of removal people to pack up the cheap collection of bric-à-brac his philistine tastes have considered valuable enough to accumulate during his overlong stay in the University. (Please forgive my cynical words.)

'Now – please pay careful attention! One day, only a few weeks ago, I saw a man walking up my own staircase; the man did not see me – not at that point, anyway. He looked around him, at first with the diffidence of a stranger, then with the confidence of an intimate; and he took the key he was holding and inserted it into Westerby's oak. For myself, I took little notice. If someone wished to burgle my colleague's valueless belongings, I felt little inclination to interfere. In fact, I was secretly interested – and amused. I learned that this stranger was the head of a London removals firm; that he had come to size up the task and to pack up the goods. A few days later, I saw this same individual again – although this time he wore a bright-red scarf about his face, as if the wind blew uncommonly keenly, or as if the wretched fellow had recently returned from the dentist's chair. It was only a matter of days after this that I received a letter – istam epistolam; the letter you half-received yourself.

'Does all this sound rather mysterious and puzzling? No! Not to you, surely. For you have already guessed what I am about to say. Yes! I recognized the man; and the man brought back poignantly to me the one episode in my life of which I am bitterly – so bitterly! – ashamed. But again, I am getting ahead of myself – or behind. It depends upon which way you look at it.

'With assorted young assistants, this man reappeared three or four times, presumably to supervise the packing-up of crates and boxes in my colleague's rooms. And on each of these subsequent occasions, the man wore the same gaudy scarf around the lower half of his face, as if (as I have said) a wayward tooth was inflicting upon him the acutest agony . . . or else as if he wished to keep his face concealed. Is one not, in such circumstances, quite justified in adding two and two together, and making of them twenty-two? Was he worried, perhaps, that I should recognize his face? Had he known it, however, his clumsy attempts at deception were futile. Why? Simply because I had already recognized the man. And because of this, I experienced little difficulty in linking the two contiguous events together: first, the arrival in Lonsdale of the one man in the world I had hoped and prayed I would never meet again; second, the arrival of the strangest letter I ever received in the whole of my time in the college. In sum, these two events appeared to me to add to more than twenty-two; yet not to more than I could cope with. Let us go on a bit.

'I followed up my invitation. Why not do so? I have never married. I have never, therefore, known the delights (if such they are) of the marriage-bed. Over-rated as I have frequently considered them, the illicit lure of sexual delights will almost always be a potential attraction to an old, unhonoured person like myself. (I don't think we have a hanging participle in the previous sentence.) And lascivious thoughts, albeit occasional ones, are not wholly alien even from such a dryasdustest man as me.

'Where are we then? Ah, yes. I went. I went through the doors that had been clearly labelled for my atten-tion, and I knew where I was going; I knew exactly. It will be of little value to you to have a comprehensive account of subsequent events, although (to be fair to myself) they were not particularly sordid. The whole drama (I must admit it) was played with a carefully rehearsed verisimilitude, with myself acting a role that was equally carefully rehearsed. Yet at one stage (if I may continue the metaphor), I forgot my lines com-pletely. And so, perhaps, would you have done. For a devastatingly lovely woman – a Siren fit to beguile the wily Ulysses himself – was almost, almost able to rob me of my robe of honour; and, perhaps more importantly, to rob me of my one defence – an army revolver which

I had kept since my days in the desert, and which was even now still bulging reassuringly in my jacket-pocket.

'But again things are getting out of sequence, and we must go back. Who was the man I had seen on Staircase T at Lonsdale College? You will have to know. Yes, I am afraid you will have to know.

'I was a young officer in the desert during the battle of El Alamein. I was, I think, a good officer, in the sense that I tried to look after the men in my charge, left little to needless chance, enforced the orders I was given and faced the enemy with the conviction that this conflict – this one, surely – was as fully justified as any in the annals of Christendom. But I knew one thing that no one else could know. I knew that at heart I was a physical coward; and I always feared the thought that, if there were to come a time when I should be called upon to show a personal, an individual – as against a communal, corporate – act of courage, well, I knew that I would fail. And that moment came. And I failed. It came – I need not relate the shameful details – when a man pleaded with me to risk my own life in trying to save the life of a man who was trapped in a fiercely burning tank. But enough of that. It hurts me deeply, even now, to recall my cowardice.

'Let us now switch forward again. It was all phoney: I soon began to realize that. There were those two bottles of everything, for example: two of them – in whatever the client (in this case, me) should happen to indulge. Why two? The one of them about two thirds empty (or is it one third full?); the other completely intact, with the plastic seal fixed round its top. Why go, then, to the new bottle for the first, perfunctory drinks? I didn't know, but I soon began to wonder. And then her accent! Oh dear! Had she been at an audition, any director worth a tuppence of salt would have told her to flush her Gallic vowels down the nearest ladies' lavatory. And then at one point she opened her handbag – a handbag she must have owned for twenty years. A professional whore with an aged handbag? And not only that. She was introduced to me by an unconvincing old hag as "Yvonne"; so why are the faded gilt initials on the inside flap of her handbag clearly printed "W.S."? You see where all this suspicion is leading? But I had my revolver. I was going to be all right. I _was_ all right. (How I hate underlining words in typescript – but often it is necessary.) It was only when this lovely girl (oh dear, she _was_ lovely!) poured my final drink from the _other_ bottle (not the bottle I had drunk from before) that I knew exactly what my situation was. I asked her to open the curtains a little, and whilst she was doing this I poured the (doubtless doctored) contents of my glass inside my trousers, in order that the impression should be given that I had been incapable of controlling myself. (I know you will understand the sense of what, so delicately, I have tried to express.) You must understand that at this point she was quite openly and wantonly naked, and I myself quite justifiably aroused.

'After that? If I may say so, I performed my part professionally. Making vaguely somnolent noises, I now assumed the role of a man (as the Americans have it) in a totally negative response situation. Then the woman left me; and after hearing whispered communications on the other side of the door, I sensed that someone else was in the room. Let us leave it there.

'I am getting tired with this lengthy typing, but it is important that I should go on a little longer.

'You were a fool when you were an undergraduate – wasting, as you did, the precious talent of a clear, clean mind. It was me (or do you prefer "I"?) who marked some of your Greats papers, and even amidst the widespread evidence of your appalling ignorance there were moments of rare perception and sensitivity. But since that time you have made a distinguished reputation for yourself as a man of the Detective (as Dickens has it), and I was anxious that it should be a worthy brain that was to be pitted against my own. Why else should the body be discovered where it was? Who made sure that it should be found at Thrupp – a place almost in your own back-yard? You will, I suspect, have almost certainly discovered by now why I was not able to leave the head and the hands for your inspection? Yes, I think so. You would have been quite certain that it was not my body had I done so, and I wished to sharpen up your brain, for (believe me!) it will need to be as sharp as the sword of Achilles before your work is finished. Here then is a chance for you to show the sort of quality that was apparent in your early days at Oxford. Perhaps this case of yours will afford for you the opportunity to kill an ancient ghost, since I shall quite certainly (albeit posthumously) award you a "first" this time if you can grasp the inevitable (and basically so simple) logic of all these strange events.

'I shall make no further communications to you; and I advise you not to try to track me down, for you will not find me.

'Post Scriptum I have just read this letter through and wish to apologize for the profusion of brackets. (I am not often over-influenced by the work of Bernard Levin.)'

CHAPTER TWENTY-THREE

Monday, 28th July

Investigations proceed with a nominal line drawn down the middle of needful inquiries.

SO MANY CLUES now, and as Morse and Lewis saw things there were four main areas of inquiry:

1. What were the real facts about that far-off day in the desert when Browne-Smith had faced his one real test of character — and (apparently) failed so lamentably?
2. Where exactly did Westerby (a name cropping up repeatedly now) fit into the increasingly complex pattern?
3. Who was the person whom Browne-Smith had met after his anti-climactic sexual encounter with the pseudonymous 'Yvonne'?
4. And (still, to Morse the most vital question of all) whose was the body they had found?

Obviously the strands of these inquiries would interweave at many points; but it seemed sensible to the two detectives that each should make his own investigations for a day or two, with Lewis concentrating his attentions on the first two areas, and Morse on the second two.

Lewis spent most of the morning on the telephone, ringing, amongst other numbers, those of the War Office, the Ministry of Defence, the HQ of the Wiltshire Regiment, and the Territorial Unit at Devizes. It was a long, frustrating business; but by lunch-time he had a great deal of information, much of it useless, but some of it absolutely vital.

First, he discovered more about Browne-Smith: Captain, acting Major, (Royal Wiltshires); served North Africa (1941–42), wounded El Alamein; Italy (1944–45); awarded the MC (1945).

Second, he learned something about Gilbert. There had been three Gilbert brothers, Albert, Alfred, and John. All had fought at El Alamein; the first two, both full corporals, had survived the campaign (although both of them had been wounded); the third, the youngest brother, had died in the same campaign. That was all.

But it couldn't be quite all, Lewis knew that. And it was from the Swindon branch of the British Legion that he learned the address of a man in the Wiltshires who must certainly have known the Gilbert brothers fairly well. Immediately after lunch, Lewis was driving out along the A420.

'Yes, I knew 'em, Sergeant – s'funny, I wur a sergeant, too, you know. Yes, there wur Alf 'n' Bert – like as two peas in a pod, they wur. One of 'em, 'e got a bit o' the ol' shrapnel in the leg, and I 'ad a bit in the 'ead. We wur at base 'ospital for a while together, but I can't quite recolleck . . . Real lads, they wur – the pair of 'em!'

'Did you know the other one?' asked Lewis.

'Johnny! That wur 'is name. I didn't know 'im very well, though.'

'You don't know how he was killed?'

'No, I don't.'

'They were all tank-drivers, weren't they?'

'All of 'em – like me.'

'Was he killed in his tank?'

For the second time the old soldier looked rather vague and puzzled, and Lewis wondered whether the man's memory could be relied upon.

'There wur a bit of an accident as I recolleck. But 'e wurn't with us that morning, Sergeant – not when we all moved up 'long Kidney Ridge.'

'You don't remember what sort of accident?'

'No. It wur back at base, I seem to . . . But you get a lot of accidents in wartime, Sergeant. More'n they tell the folk back 'ome in Blighty.'

He was an engaging old boy; a sixty-nine-year-old widower for whom, it seemed, the war had been the only intermission of importance in a largely anonymous life, for there was no real sadness in him as he recalled those weeks and months of fighting in the desert – only an almost understandable nostalgia. So Lewis wrote down the facts, such as they were, in his painstakingly slow long-hand, and then took his leave.

*

Morse was away from the office when Lewis returned at 4.30 p.m. and of this fact he was strangely glad. All the way back from Swindon he had been wondering what that 'accident' might have been. He suspected that had Morse been there he would have guessed immediately; and it was a pleasant change to be able to tackle the problem at his own, rather slower, pace. He rang the War Office once again, was put through to the Archives section, and soon began to realize that he was on to something important.

'Yes, we might be able to help in some way. You're Thames Valley Police, you say?'

'That's right.'

'Why are you asking for information about this man?'

'It's in connection with a murder, sir.'

'I see. What's your number? Can't be too careful in these things – you'll know all about that.' He spoke with the monotone bark of a machine-gun.

So Lewis gave him his number, was rung back inside thirty seconds, and was given an extraordinary piece of information. Private John Gilbert of the Royal Wiltshires had not been killed in the El Alamein campaign. He had played no part in it. The night before the offensive, he had taken his army rifle, placed the muzzle inside his mouth, and shot himself through the brain. The incident had been hushed up on the highest orders; and that for obvious reasons. A few had known, of course – *had* to know. But 'officially' John Gilbert died on active service in the desert, and that is how his family and his friends had been informed.

'This is all in the strictest confidence, you understand that?'

'Of course, sir.'

'Never good for morale, that sort of thing, eh?'

Morse was having a far less fruitful day. He realized that
with the first of his self-imposed assignments he could
for the present make little headway, since that would
necessitate some far from disagreeable investigations in
Soho – a journey he had planned for the morrow.
Which only left him with the same old tantalizing
problem that had monopolized his mind from the
beginning: the identity of the corpse. From the embarrassment of clues contained in Browne-Smith's letter,
the shortest odds must now be surely on the man whom
Browne-Smith had finally encountered in London. But
who was that man? Had it been *Gilbert,* as the letter so
obviously suggested? Or was the body *Westerby's*? If
Browne-Smith had killed anyone, then Westerby was
surely the most likely of candidates. Or was the body
that of someone who had not yet featured in the
investigations? Some outsider? Someone as yet
unknown who would make a dramatic entry only
towards the finale of Act Five? A sort of *deus ex machina*?
Morse doubted this last possibility – and amidst his
doubts, quite suddenly the astonishing thought flashed
through his mind that there might just be a *fourth*
possibility. And the more Morse pondered the idea, the
more he convinced himself that there was: the possi-

bility that the puffed and sodden salt-white corpse was that of *Dr Browne-Smith*.

On the way home that evening, Lewis decided to risk his wife's wrath, to face the prospect of almost certainly reheated chips – and to call on Simon Rowbotham in Botley.

Simon Rowbotham invited him into the small terraced house in which he lived with his mother. But Lewis declined, learning over the doorstep that Simon had been one of three anglers who had spotted the body, and that it was he, Simon, who had readily volunteered to dial the police in lieu of looking further upon the horror just emerging from the waters. He often fished out along the banks at Thrupp, a good place for specialists such as himself. As it happened, they were just about to form a new angling club there, for which he had volunteered his services as secretary. In fact (just as Lewis had called) he had been checking a proof of the new association's letter-head for the printer. They had managed to persuade a few well-known people to support them; and clearly, for Simon Rowbotham, the world was entering an exciting phase.

Lewis waited until 8.30 p.m. before ringing Morse (who had been strangely absent somewhere since lunch-time). He found him at his flat and promptly reported on his day's work.

When he had finished, Morse could hardly keep the

excitement out of his voice. 'Just go over that bit about John Gilbert again, will you, Lewis?'

So Lewis repeated, as accurately as he could recall it, the news he had gleaned from the War Office archivist; and he felt very happy as he did so, for he knew that the news was pleasing to his master – a master, incidentally, who now had guessed the whole truth about the desert episode.

'You've done a marvellous day's work, old friend. Well done!'

'Did *you* find out anything new, sir?'

'Me? Well, yes and no, really. I've – I've been thinking about the case for most of the day. But nothing startling.'

'Anyway, have a good day in London tomorrow, sir!'

'What? Ah yes – tomorrow. I'll – er – give you a ring if I find out anything exciting.'

'Perhaps you'll do that, sir.'

'What? Ah yes – perhaps I will.'

A rather sad footnote to the events described in this chapter is that if Lewis had been slightly more interested in the formation of a new angling association and if he had asked to see the proof of the proposed letter-heading (but why should he?), he would have found that one of the two honorary vice-presidents listed at the top left-hand corner of the page was a man with a name which was now very familiar to him: Mr G. Westerby (Lonsdale College, Oxford).

CHAPTER TWENTY-FOUR

Tuesday, 29th July

Morse appears to have a powerful effect on two women, one of whom he has never met.

FOR LEWIS, A 10 a.m. visit to Lonsdale was pleasantly productive, since the college secretary (she liked Lewis) had brought him a cup of coffee, and been quite willing to talk openly about Westerby as a person. So Lewis made his notes. Then he found out something about *cars*, since – in spite of Morse's apparent indifference to the problem – it seemed to him of great importance to discover exactly how the corpse had been transported from London to Thrupp; and he learned that Browne-Smith – doubtless on doctor's orders – had sold his Daimler a month or so ago, whilst Westerby still ran a red Metro, occasionally to be seen in the college forecourt.

'Why would Westerby want a car, though?' asked Lewis. 'He lived in college.'

'I don't know. He's a bit secretive – doesn't tell anyone much about what he does.'

'He must go *somewhere*?'

'I suppose so,' she nodded vaguely.

'Nice little car, the Metro. Economical!'

'Roomy in the back, too. You can take the seats out, you know – get no end of stuff in there.'

'So they tell me, yes.'

'You've got a car, Sergeant?'

'I've got an old Mini, but I don't use it much. Usually go to work on the bus and then use a police car.'

The college secretary looked down at her desk. 'Has Inspector Morse got a car?'

Lewis found it an odd question. 'He's got a Lancia. He's had a Lancia ever since I've known him.'

'You've known him long?'

'Long enough.'

'Is he a nice man?'

'Well, I wouldn't exactly call him "nice".'

'Do you like him?'

'I don't think you "like" Morse. He's not that sort of person, really.'

'But you get on well with him?'

'Usually. You see – well, he's the most remarkable man I've ever met, that's all.'

'He must think *you're* a remarkable man – if he works with you all the time, I mean.'

'No! I'm just, well . . .' Lewis didn't quite know how to finish, but he felt more than a little pride in the shadow of the compliment. 'Do you know him, then, miss?'

She shook her pretty head. 'He spoke to me over the phone once, that's all.'

'Oh, he's terrible over the phone – always sounds so, I don't know, so cocky and nasty, somehow.'

'You mean . . . he's not *really* like that?'

'Not really,' said Lewis quietly. Then he noticed that the gentle eyes of the college secretary had suddenly drifted away from himself, and out towards a man she had never known or even seen. Momentarily he felt a twinge of jealousy.

Morse!

Down the dingy red-carpeted stairs, through the dingy red curtains, Morse, at 11 a.m., followed the same path that Browne-Smith had trodden eighteen days before him. He sat at a table in the Flamenco Topless Bar, and transacted his business with a milky white maiden. It didn't take him long; and, after that, Browne-Smith's spunky antagonist behind the bar had proved no match for him, since for some reason she could not conceive of suggesting to *this* man, with the blue-grey eyes and the thinning, grey-black hair, that he could go across the way to the Sauna if he wanted any further sexual gratification. He seemed to her coldly detached; and when he looked at her with eyes intensely still, she found herself answering his questions almost hypnotically. Thus it was that Morse, in a short space of time, had penetrated the door marked 'Private' at the rear of the drinking lounge.

At 1 p.m. he was riding in a taxi to an address he had known anyway – the address already pencilled firmly in his mind when that same morning he had left the

Number One platform at Oxford on the 9.12 train. Perhaps he should have short-circuited the whole process; but on the whole he thought not, even though he had felt not the vaguest stir of virility as one of the girls had sat opposite him, sipping her exotic juice.

So far so good; and comparatively easy. The outlines of the pattern had been confirmed at every stage: Gilbert (one of twins, as Lewis had told him – interesting!) had quite fortuitously found a client in Oxford; and opposite his client's room he'd seen, in Gothic script, a name that for some reason was indelibly printed on his mind; with (doubtless) considerable ingenuity, he had lured this man to London – lured him to the address which Morse had just given to his taxi-driver, the same address that Morse had memorized from the wooden crates in the rooms of Westerby on Staircase T: 29 Cambridge Way, London, WC1. But what had happened after the suspicious and resourceful Browne-Smith had faced his *second* test of personal courage? What exactly had occurred when 'Yvonne' had left . . . and someone else had entered?

Such thoughts occupied Morse's mind as the taxi made its way (by an extremely circuitous route, it seemed to Morse) to Cambridge Way. Yet there were other thoughts, too: he could, of course, claim full expenses for his train fare (first class, although he usually travelled second), tube fare, taxi fare, subsistence . . . Yes, he might *just* make enough on the day to settle down happily in the buffet car on his return and enjoy a couple of Scotches at someone else's expense. But would he be justified in sticking down on his claimsform such a ludicrous-looking item as 'Flamenco Revenge – £6'? On the whole, he thought, probably not.

He alighted, and stood alone in front of Number 29.

CHAPTER TWENTY-FIVE

Tuesday, 29th July

Lewis retraces some of his steps, and makes some startling new discoveries.

LEWIS WAS BACK at Police HQ by 11.30 a.m., sensing that without further directions from on high he had gone as far as he was likely to go. But just for the moment he felt a little resentful about taking too many orders; and by noon he had taken the firm decision to revisit the scene of the crime. He didn't quite know why.

After drinking half a pint of bitter in the Boat Inn, he walked out along the road by the canal and up to Aubrey's Bridge. But there were no fishermen there this morning, and he turned his attention to his left as he walked slowly along, noting once more the authoritative notices posted regularly along the low, neat terrace: 'No mooring opposite these cottages.' The people here were obviously jealous of their acquired territories – doubtless rich enough, too, to own boats of their own and to regard it as some divine right that they should moor such craft immediately opposite their neatly painted porches.

Then something stirred in Lewis's mind ... If all these people were so anxious to preserve their rights and their privacy; if all those sharp eyes there were jealously watching the waterfront for the first signs of any territorial trespass – then, surely, in this quiet cul-de-sac that led to nowhere, where there was hardly room enough to execute a six-point turn in a car ... yes! Surely, someone must have seen something? For the body must quite certainly have been pushed into the canal from the back of a car. How else? And yet Lewis, who had himself earlier questioned the tenants, had learned nothing of any strange car. Understandably, not every cottage had been inhabited at the time; the owners of some had been away – boating, or shopping in Oxford, or waiting in high places in large cities to motor down for a weekend of rural relaxation in their quiet country cottages.

Lewis had now reached the end of his walk, looking down as he did so at the water wherein the hideous body had been found. From this perusal he learned nothing. As he made his way back, however, he saw that the third cottage from the far end was 'For Sale', and he began to wonder whether such a property might not perhaps make a nice little investment for himself and the missus when he retired. Retired ... And suddenly an exciting thought occurred to him. He knocked loudly on the door of the house for sale. No answer. Then he knocked at the house next door, which was opened by a freckle-faced lad of about twelve years of age.

'Is your mum in – or your dad?'

'No.'

'I was just trying to find out something about the house here.' Lewis pointed to the empty property.

'They want twenny thousand forrit – and it's got a leaky roof.'

'Lot of money,' said Lewis.

'Not worth it. It's been on the market a couple of months.'

Lewis nodded, sizing up this embryo property-evaluator. 'You live here?'

The boy nodded.

'Did you know the people next door – before it was for sale?'

'Not "people".'

'No?'

The young lad looked vaguely suspicious, but he blinked and agreed: 'No.'

'Look!' said Lewis. 'I'm a policeman and—'

'I know. I saw you when you was here before.'

'Shouldn't you have been at school?'

'I had the measles, didn't I? I was watching from the bedroom.'

'You didn't see anything sort of suspicious – before that, I mean?'

The boy shook his head.

'You say it wasn't "people" next door?'

'He's not in any trouble, is he?' The freckled face looked up at Lewis anxiously, as if it were a matter of deep concern to him that any trouble might have befallen the previous owner of the house next door.

'Not so far as I know.'

The boy looked down at the threshold and spoke quietly: 'He was good to me. Took me out in his Metro to King's Weir, once. Super fisherman he was – Mr Westerby.'

A Jaguar's horn blared imperiously as Lewis turned left on to the main road down to Kidlington, and he knew his mind was full of other things. He had just discovered a quite extraordinarily significant link between Westerby and the waterfront at Thrupp. And if someone had taken a body from London to Thrupp in a car (as someone must have done), there would have been no suspicions aroused by the familiar sight of a red Metro. No trouble at all. Not if that someone who had brought the body *had lived there himself.* What was more, this was the only car that had cropped up in the case so far, for Dr Browne-Smith had sold his large, black Daimler . . .

Lewis turned into HQ and sat down at Morse's desk, giving his bubbling thoughts the chance to simmer down. The green box-file containing the few documents on the case was lying open before him, and he riffled through the sheets – most of them his own reports. In fact (he told himself) there were only two *real* clues, anyway, whatever anyone might say: the suit, and the torn letter. Yes ... and that torn letter was here, in his hands now – together with Morse's neatly written reconstruction of the whole. He looked down at the torn half once more, and the final 'G' in line 7 and the final 'J' in line 15 suddenly shot out at him from the page. *Could* it be?

He parked the police car half on the pavement outside the Examination Schools and felt like a nervous punter in a betting-shop who can hardly bear to read the latest 1,2,3. The lists were still posted around the entrance hall, and quickly he found the board announcing the final honours list for Geography and read through the names. Whew! It not only could be – it *was*. 'Jennifer Bennet'. There she perched at the top of the list – that wonderful girl beginning with 'J' whom he had found on a board beginning with 'G'. And the college – Lonsdale. Lewis could hardly believe his eyes, or his luck. And there was more to come, for the bottom name of the examining sextet was none other than Westerby's!

It was an excited Lewis who drove back to Kidlington; but, even as he drove, the conflicting nature of his morning's findings was slowly becoming apparent to him. Most of what he had discovered was pointing with an insistent regularity in one direction – in the direction of George Westerby. And with Browne-Smith as the body and Westerby as the murderer, almost everything fitted the facts beautifully. Except . . . except that last bit. Because if the letter had been written to *Westerby*, and not to Browne-Smith . . . oh dear! Lewis was beginning to feel a little lost. He wondered if Morse had spent such a successful morning in London. He doubted it – doubted it genuinely. But how he longed to talk to Morse!

Back in the office, Lewis typed up his findings and although spelling had never been Lewis's strong suit, yet he felt rather pleased with his present reports, particularly with his little vignette of Westerby:

Londoner. Little dapper bumshious fellow — slightly deaf — pretty secretive. Tends to squint a bit, but this may be the usual cigarette at the corner of his mouth.

CHAPTER TWENTY-SIX

Tuesday, 29th July

Unable to get any answer from the house in Cambridge Way, Morse now reflects upon his meeting with the manager of the Flamenco Topless Bar.

LIKE BROWNE-SMITH BEFORE him, Morse walked slowly up the shallow steps of Number 29 and rang the bell. But he, too, heard no sound of ringing on the other side of the great black door. He rang again, noticing as he did so the same board that Browne-Smith must have seen, with its invitation to apply to 'Brooks & Gilbert (Sole Agents)'. Almost imperceptibly he nodded; almost imperceptibly he smiled. But there was still no sign of any movement in the house, and he bent down to look through the highly polished brass letter-box. He could make out the light-olive carpeting on the wide staircase that faced him; but the place seemed ominously silent. He walked across the street and looked up at the four-storied building, admiring the clean-cut architecture, and the progressively fore-shortened oblongs of the window-frames, behind which – as far as he could see – there was not the slightest tell-tale twitching of the curtainings. So he walked away along the street, entered a small park, and sat down on a bench, where he communed for many minutes with the pigeons, and with his thoughts. On the taxi-journey he had sought in his mind to minimize the risks he had already run that morning; and yet, as he now began to realize, those risks had been decidedly dangerous, especially after he had walked through the door marked 'Private' . . .

He'd started off in the quiet monotone of a man whose authority was beyond that of other men: 'It matters to me not a single fart in the cosmos, lad, whether you tell me about it here and now, or in one of the cells of Her Majesty's nearest nick.'

'I don't know who the bloody hell you think you are, talking to me like that. Let me tell you—'

'Before you tell me anything, just call in one of your tarts out there, preferably the one with biggest tits, and tell her to bring me a large Scotch, preferably Bell's. On the house, I suggest – because I'm here to *help* you, lad.'

'I was going to tell you that I've got friends here who'd gladly kick the guts out of the likes of you.'

' "Friends", you say?'

'Yeah – friends!'

'If you mean what you say, lad, I don't honestly think they're going to thank you very much if you bring *them* into this little business – and get 'em involved with *me*.'

'They're one helluva sight tougher than you, mate!'

'Oh no! You've got it all wrong, lad. And one little thing. You can curse and swear as much as you like with me, but you must never call me "mate" again! Is that understood? I've told you who I am, and I shan't be telling you again.'

The manager swallowed hard. 'I suppose you're going to tell me you've got a van full of squaddies outside. Is that it?'

Morse allowed a vague smile to form at the corners of his mouth. 'No, that's not it. I'm here completely on my own – and what's more no one else knows I'm here at all. Well, let's be honest, *almost* no one. And if we get along, you and me, I shan't even tell anyone that I've been here, either. No need really, is there?'

The manager was biting down hard on the nail of his left index finger, and Morse pressed home his obvious advantage.

'Let me give you a bit of advice. You're not a crook – you're not in the same league as most of the murderous morons I deal with every day. And, even if you were, I wouldn't need a posse of police to go around protecting *me*. You know why, lad?' Morse broke off for a few seconds, before focusing his eyes with almost manic ferocity upon the youngish man seated opposite him. Then he shook his head almost sorrowfully. 'No, you don't know why, do you? So let me tell you. It's because the archangels look after me, lad – always have done. And most especially when I'm pursuing my present calling as the protector of Law and eternal Justice!' Morse managed to give each of these mighty personages a capital letter; and pompous as he sounded, he also sounded very frightening.

Certainly, this was the impact upon the manager, for

he appeared now to have little faith that he would be likely to emerge victorious from any conflict with the archangelic trio. He walked to the door, and sounded suddenly resigned as he asked 'Racquel' to fetch two double Scotches; whilst, for a rather frightened Morse, the prospect of finding himself dead or dying in a Soho side-street was gradually receding.

The manager's story was brief.

The club was registered in the name of Soho Enterprises Limited, although he had never himself met anyone (or so he thought) directly from this syndicate. Business was transacted through a soberly dressed intermediary – a Mr Schwenck – who periodically visited the bar to look around, and who collected takings and paid all salaries. About three weeks or so ago (he couldn't remember exactly), Mr Schwenck had announced that a certain Mr William would very soon be calling; that the said Mr William would make his requests known, and that no questions were to be asked. In fact, the bearded Mr William had requested very little, spurning equally the offers of hospitality from the bar and from the bra-less hostesses. He had taken away a projector and two reels of pornographic film, and announced that he would be back the following morning. And he had been, bringing with him a small blue card (given to the manager) and a cassette of some piano music (given to the girl behind the bar). Thereafter he had stood quietly at the bar, reading a paperback and drinking half a glass of lime-juice. Another man (so the manager had been informed) would probably be coming in that morning; and at some point this new-comer would be directed to the office where he was to be given the blue card, plus an address. That was all.

The young man appeared not overtly dishonest (albeit distinctly uncomfortable) as he told his little tale; and Morse found himself believing him.

'How much in it for you?' he asked.

'Nothing. I'm only—'

'Couple of hundred?'

'I told you—'

'Five hundred?'

'What? Just for—?'

'Forget it, lad! What was on the card?'

'Nothing really. It was just one of those cards that – that let you into places.'

'Which place?'

'I – I don't remember.'

'You didn't write it down?'

'No. I remembered it.'

'You've got a good memory?'

'Good enough.'

'But you just said you *can't* remember.'

'I can't. It was a good while ago now.'

'When exactly was it?'

'I can't—'

'Friday? Friday 11th July?'

'Could have been.'

'Did you get your projector and stuff back all right?'

''Course I did.'

'The next day?'

'Yes – er – I think it was the next day.'

For the first time Morse felt convinced that the man was lying. But why (Morse asked himself) should the man have lied to him on *that* particular point?

'About that address. Was it a number in Cambridge Way by any chance?'

Morse noted the dart of recognition in the manager's eyes, and was about to repeat his question when the telephone rang. The manager pounced on the receiver, clamping it closely to his right ear.

'Yes' (Morse could hear nothing of the caller's voice) 'yes' (a quick, involuntary look across at Morse) 'yes' (unease, quite certainly, in the manager's eyes) 'all right' (sudden relief in the manager's face?).

Morse's hand flashed across the table and snatched the receiver, but he heard only the dull, quiet purr of the dialling tone.

'Only the wife, Inspector. She wants me to take five pounds of potatoes home. Run out, she says. You know how these women are.'

Something had happened, Morse knew that. The young manager had got a shot of confidence from somewhere, and Morse began to wonder whether his patrons, Michael, Raphael and Gabriel, might not, after all, be called upon to fight his cause. He heard the door open quietly behind him – but not to admit the roundly bosomed Racquel with a further double Scotch. In the doorway stood a diminutive Chinaman of about thirty years of age, his brown arms under the white, short-sleeved shirt as sleek and sinewy as the limbs of a Derby favourite in the Epsom paddock. It seemed to Morse a little humiliating to be cowed into instant submission by such a hominid; but Morse was. He rose to his feet, averted his gaze from the twin slits of horizontal hostility in the Chinaman's face, and thanked the manager civilly for his co-operation, rueing the fact that he was himself now far too decrepit even to enlist in the kung-fu classes advertised weekly in the *Oxford Times*. But the Chinaman guided him gently back to his chair; and it was more than half an hour (a period, however, of unmolested confinement) before Morse was allowed to leave the Topless Bar, whence he emerged into the upper world just after 1 p.m., deeply and gratefully inhaling the foul fumes of the cars that circled Piccadilly Circus, and crossing carefully to its west side, where he had a wait of only two minutes outside the Café Royal before a taxi pulled up in front of him.

'Where to, guv?'

Morse told him, infinitely preferring 'guv' to 'mate'.

CHAPTER TWENTY-SEVEN

Tuesday, 29th July, p.m.

In which Morse views a luxury block of flats in central London, catching an enigmatic glimpse of one of its tenants and looking longer upon our second corpse.

MORSE HAD BEEN sitting for over half an hour, pondering these and other things, when the extraordinary thought crossed his mind that he was in the middle of a park in the middle of opening hours with a pub only fifty yards away on the corner of the square. Yet somehow he sensed that events were gathering pace, and he walked past the Duke of Cambridge, went up the steps of Number 29, and rang the bell once more. This time he was in luck, for after a couple of minutes the great black door was opened.

'Yis, guv?'

He was a mournful-looking man in his mid-sixties, sweating slightly, wearing a beige-coloured working overall, carrying a caretaker's long-handled floor-mop, and fiddling with the controls of a stringed, National Health hearing-aid.

Morse explained who he was and, upon producing his identification, was reluctantly admitted across the threshold. The man (announcing himself as Hoskins – pronounced 'oskins) informed Morse that he had been the porter in the flats for just over a year now: 8.45 a.m. to 4.30 p.m., Tuesdays to Fridays, his job consisting mainly of keeping an eye on the properties and doing a bit of general cleaning during working hours. 'Nice little job, guv.'

'Still some flats for sale, I see?'

'No – not nah. Both of 'em sold. Should'a' taken the notice darn, really – still, it's good for business, I s'pose.'

'*Both* of them sold?'

'Yis, guv. One of 'em's a gent from Oxford – bought it a coupla months back, 'e did.'

'And the other one?'

'Few days ago. Some foreign gent, I think it is.'

'The one from Oxford – that's Mr Westerby, isn't it?'

'You know 'im, then?'

'Is he in?'

'No. I 'aven't seen 'im since 'e came to look rarnd, like.' The man hesitated. 'Nuffin wrong, is there?'

'Everything's wrong, Mr Hoskins, I'm afraid. You'd better show me round his flat, if you will.'

Rather laboriously the man led the way up the stairs to the first floor, produced a key from his overall pocket, and opened the door across from the landing with the apprehension of a man who expects to cast his eye upon a carpet swimming with carnage. But the pale-grey carpeting in the small (and otherwise completely unfurnished) ante-room provided evidence only of a recent, immaculate hoovering.

'Main room's through there, guv.'

Inside this second room, half a dozen pieces of heavy, mahogany furniture stood at their temporary sites around the walls, whilst the floor space was more than half covered by oblong wooden crates, several piled on top of others – crates each labelled neatly with the name and new address of a G. O. Westerby, Esq., MA; crates which Morse had recognized immediately, especially the one, already opened, which had contained the head of Gerardus Mercator (now standing on the mantelpiece).

'Mr Westerby already been here?'

'Not seen 'im guv. But o'course, 'e might'a' come later – after I was off. Looks like it, don't it?'

Morse nodded, looking aimlessly around the room, and then trying the two fitted wardrobes, both of which were unlocked, empty, dusty. And Morse frowned, knowing that somewhere something was wrong. He pointed back to the ante-room. 'Did you hoover the carpet in there?'

The man's face (Morse could have sworn it) had paled a few degrees. 'No – I just, as I said, look after the general cleaning, like – stairs and that sort o' thing.'

But Morse sensed that the man was lying, and found no difficulty in guessing why: a caretaker in a block of flats like this ... half a dozen wealthy and undomesti-cated men ... a few nice little backhanders now and again just to dust and to clean ... Yes, Morse could imagine the picture all right; and it might well be that a caretaker in such a block of flats would know rather more about one or two things than he was prepared to admit. Yet Morse was singularly unsuccessful in eliciting even the slightest piece of information, and he changed the course of his questioning.

'Did *you* show Mr Westerby round here?'

'No, chap from the agents, it was – young fellow.'

'Always the same young fellow, is it?'

'Pardon, sir?'

'You say they've just sold the other flat?'

'Ah I see. No, I wasn't 'ere then.'

'It's not Mr Gilbert himself, is it – this young fellow you mention?'

'I wouldn't know – I never met 'im personally, like.'

'I see.' Again Morse sensed that the man was holding something back, and again he aimed blindly in the dark. 'You know when Mr Westerby called again ... when was it, about a week, ten days ago?'

'I told you, sir. I only saw 'im once – the day 'e looked rand the place.'

'I see.' But Morse saw nothing, apart from the fact that far from hitting any bull's-eye he'd probably missed the target altogether. Without any clear purpose he proceeded to look into the small kitchen, and then into the bathroom; but the only thing that mildly registered in his mind was that the parquet flooring in each was sparklingly clean, and he felt quite convinced now that Hoskins (almost certainly in contravention of his contract) was working a very profitable little fiddle for himself with his mop and his cleaning-fluid.

So it was that slowly and disconsolately Morse followed what he now saw as the marginally devious little caretaker down the broad staircase towards the front door. And at that point, had it not been for one fortuitous occurrence, perhaps the simple yet quite astounding truth of the present case might never have beached upon the shores of light. For Morse had heard a lift descending, and now he saw a dark-skinned, grey-suited man emerge from the side of the entrance-hall.

'Afternoon, sir,' said Hoskins, touching some imaginary lock on his balding pate.

The affluent-looking Arab was walking in the opposite direction from the front door, and as he watched him Morse whispered to his companion: 'Where's *he* going?'

'There's a back entrance 'ere, guv...'

But Morse hardly heard, for the Arab himself had looked over his shoulder, and was in turn looking back towards Morse with a puzzled, vaguely worried frown.

'Who's he?' asked Morse very quietly.

''E lives on the—'

But again Morse was not listening, for his thoughts were travelling via the unsuspected lift towards the higher storeys. 'He finishes work early, doesn't he?'

''E can afford to, guv.'

'Yes. Like you can, sometimes, Hoskins! Take me up to the flat that's just been sold!'

The small but extraordinarily efficient lift brought them swiftly up to the top storey, where Hoskins nervously fingered a bouquet of silvery keys, finally finding the correct one, and pushing open the door for the policeman to enter.

Things were at last falling into place in Morse's mind, and as they stood by the opened door his aim was more deliberate.

'Did they give you the afternoon off, Hoskins?'

'What afternoon, guv?' the man protested. But not for long.

It had been on the Friday, he confessed. He'd had a phone call, and been given a couple of fivers – huh! – just for staying away from the place.

Morse was nodding to himself as he entered the rooms. Yes . . . the Gilbert twins: one of them a housing agent; the other a removals man. Sell some property – and also recommend a highly reputable and efficient removals firm; buy some property – and also recommend the same paragon of pantechniconic skills. Very convenient, and very profitable. Over the years the two brothers must have worked a neatly dovetailed little business . . .

Now, again, Morse looked around him at a potentially luxurious flat in central London: the small entrance hall, the living room, the bedroom, the kitchen, the bathroom – all newly decorated. No carpets yet, though; no curtains, either. But there was not a flick of cigarette ash, not even a forgotten tin-tack, on the light-oak boards, as spotless as those of an army barrack floor before the CO's inspection.

'You've been cleaning in here, too?' asked Morse.

The walls were professionally painted in lilac emulsion, the doors and fitted cupboards in brilliant-white gloss. And Morse, suddenly thinking back to his own bachelor flat with the heavy old walnut suite his mother had left him, began to envisage some lighter, brighter, modernistic furniture for himself as he opened one of the fitted wardrobes in the bedroom with its inbuilt racks and airy, deep recesses. And not just one of them!

But the second one was locked.

'You got the key for this, Hoskins?'

'No, sir. I only keep the keys for the doors. If people wants to lock things up . . .'

'Let's look in the kitchen!'

Beside the sink, Morse found a medium-sized screwdriver, the only object of any kind abandoned (it seemed) by the previous owner.

'Think this'll open it, Hoskins?'

'I – I don't want to get you in any trouble, sir – or me. I shouldn't really 'ave . . . I just don't think it's right to mess up the place and damage things, sir.'

(The 'sir's were coming thick and fast.)

It was time, Morse thought, for some reassurance. 'Look, Hoskins, this is my responsibility. I'm doing my duty as a police officer – you're doing your duty as a good citizen. You understand that?'

The miserable man appeared a modicum mollified and nodded silently. And indeed it was he, after a brief and ineffectual effort from Morse, who proved the more successful; for he managed to insert the screwdriver far enough into the gap between the side of the cupboard door and the surrounding architrave to gain sufficient leverage. Then, with a joint prizing, the lock finally snapped, the wood splintered, and the door swung slowly open. Inside, slumped on the floor of the deep recess, was the body of a man, the head turned

COLIN DEXTER

towards the wall; and almost exactly half-way between
the shoulder-blades was a round hole in the dead man's
sports-jacket, from which was oozing still a steady drip
of bright-red blood, feeding a darker pool upon the
floor. Almost squeamishly, Morse inserted his left hand
under the lifeless, lolling head . . . and turned it towards
him.

'My God!'

For a few moments the two men stood looking down
on the face that stared back up at them with open,
bulging eyes.

'Do you know who it is?' croaked Morse.

'I never seen him before, sir. I swear I 'aven't.' The
man was shaking all over, and Morse noticed the ashen-
grey pallor in his cheeks and the beads of sweat upon
his forehead.

'Take it easy, old boy!' said Morse in a kindly,
understanding voice. 'Just tell me where the nearest
telephone is – then you'd better get off home for a
while. We can always—'

Morse was about to lay a comforting hand upon the
man's shoulder; but he was already too late, for now he
found another body slumped about his feet.

Five minutes later, after dialling 999 from the telephone in the living-room, and after sending the old
boy off home (having elicited a full name and home
address from those gibbering lips), Morse stood once
again looking down at the corpse in the cupboard
recess. A tiny triangle of white card was showing above
the top pocket of the jacket, and Morse bent down to

extract it. There were a dozen or so similar cards there, but he took only one and read it – his face betraying only the grimmest confirmation. He'd known anyway, because he'd recognized the face immediately. It was the face of the man whom Morse had last (and first) seen in the rooms of George Westerby, Geography don at Lonsdale College, Oxford: the face of A. Gilbert, Esq., late proprietor of the firm Removals Anywhere.

CHAPTER TWENTY-EIGHT

Tuesday, 29th July

Morse meets a remarkable woman, and learns of another
woman who might be more remarkable still.

ON THE LEFT sat a very black gentleman in a very smart
pin-striped suit, studying the pink pages of the *Financial
Times*; on the right sat a long-haired young brunette,
wearing enormous earrings, and reading *Ulysses*; in the
middle sat Morse, impatiently fingering a small white
oblong card; and all the while the tube-train clattered
along the stations on the northbound Piccadilly line.

To Morse it seemed an inordinately long journey,
and one during which he found it almost impossible to
concentrate his mind. Perhaps it had been improper
for him (as the plain-clothes sergeant had diffidently
hinted) to have fled the scene of the recent crime so
precipitately; quite certainly it had bordered upon the
criminally negligent (as the plain-clothes sergeant had
more forcefully asserted) that he had allowed the one
and only other witness to have left the premises in
Cambridge Way – whatever the state of shock that had
paralysed the man's frame. But at least Morse had
explained where he was going – had even given the

address and the telephone number. And he could always do his best to explain, to apologize . . . later.

Arsenal. (Nearly there.)

The brunette's eyes flickered over Morse's face, but flashed back immediately to Bloom, as though the latter were a subject of considerably greater interest.

Finsbury Park. (Next stop.)

Suddenly Morse stiffened bolt upright in his seat, and this time it was the gentleman from the city whose bloodshot eyes turned suspiciously towards his travelling companion, as though he half expected to find a man in the initial throes of an epileptic fit.

That screwdriver . . . and that small, round hole in the middle of those sagging shoulder-blades . . . and he, Morse, a man who had lectured so often on proper procedure in cases of homicide, *he* had just left his own fine set of fingerprints around the bulbous handle of – the murder-weapon! Oh dear! Yes, there might well come, and fairly soon, the time for more than an apology, more than a little explanation.

For the moment, however, Morse was totally convinced that he was right (as indeed for once he was) in recognizing the signs of a tide in the affairs of men that must be taken at the flood; and when he emerged from the underground into the litter-strewn streets of Manor House, he suspected that the gods were smiling happily upon him, for almost immediately he spotted Berrywood Court, a tall tenement block only some hundred yards away down Seven Sisters Road.

*

Mrs Emily Gilbert, an unlovely woman in her late fifties (her teeth darkly stained) capitulated quickly to Morse's urgent questioning. She'd known it was all silly; and she'd told her husband it might be dangerous as well. But it was just a joke, he'd said. Some joke! She'd met another woman there in Cambridge Way – an attractive Scandinavian-looking woman who (so Mrs G. had thought) had been hired from one of the better-class clubs in Soho. They'd both been briefed by Albert (her husband) and – well, that was it really. This man had come to the place, and she (Mrs G.) had left the pair of them together in a first-floor flat (yes, Mr Westerby's flat). Then, after an hour or so, Albert had come up to tell her (she was waiting in an empty top-floor flat) that he was very pleased with the way things had gone, that she (Mrs G.) was a good old girl, and that the odd little episode could now be happily forgotten.

She had a strangely intense and rather pleasing voice, and Morse found himself gradually reassessing her. 'This other woman,' he asked, 'what was her name?'

'I was told to call her "Yvonne".'

'She didn't tell you where she lived? Where she worked?'

'No. But she was "class" – you know what I mean? She was sort of tasteful – beautifully made-up, lovely figure.'

'You don't know where she lives?'

'No. Albert'll probably be able to tell you, though.'

'Do you know where *he* is, Mrs Gilbert?'

She shook her head. 'In his sort of business you're off all the time. I know he's got a few jobs on in the Midlands – and one in Scotland – but he's always on the move. He just turns up here when he gets back.'

At this point, Morse felt a curious compassion for Emily Gilbert, for she seemed to him a brave sort of woman – yet one who would need to be even braver very soon. He knew, too, that time was running out; knew he had to find out more before he broke the cruel news.

'Just tell me anything you can, please, about this other woman – this "Yvonne". Anything you can remember.'

'I've told you – I don't—'

'Didn't you talk together?'

'Well, yes – but—'

'You don't have any idea where I can find her?'

'I think she lives south of the Thames somewhere.'

'No name of the road? No number of the house? Come on! Think, woman!'

But Morse had pushed things too far, for Mrs Gilbert now broke down and wept, and Morse was at a loss as to what to do, or what to say. So he did nothing; and such masterly inactivity proved to be the prudent course, for very soon she had wiped her wide and pleasing eyes and apologized sweetly for what she called her 'silliness'.

'Have you any children?' asked Morse.

She shook her head sadly.

It was hardly the most propitious moment, but Morse now rose from the sofa and placed his right hand firmly on her shoulder. 'Please be brave, Mrs Gilbert! I've got to tell you, I'm afraid, that your husband is dead.'

With a dramatic, convulsive jerk, her right hand snapped up to meet Morse's, and he felt the sinewy vigour of her fingers as they sought to clutch the comfort of his own. Then Morse told her, in a very quiet, gentle voice, as much (and as little) as he knew.

When he had finished, Mrs Gilbert asked him no questions, but got up from her chair, walked over to the window, lit a cigarette, and stared out over the long, bleak reservoir that lay below, where a swan glided effortlessly across the still waters. Then, finally, she turned towards him, and for the first time Morse realized that she must have been an adequately attractive woman ... some few little summers ago. Her eyes, still glistening with tears, sought his.

'I lied to you, Inspector, and I shouldn't have done that. I *know* that other woman, you see. My husband occasionally gets – got involved in his brother's – well, let's say his brother's side of things, and he met her in one of the clubs a few weeks ago. I – I found out about it. You see – he wanted to leave me and go and – and go and live with her. But she—'

Mrs Gilbert broke off, and Morse nodded his understanding.

'But she didn't want him.'

'No, she didn't.'

'Did you tell him you'd found out?'

Mrs Gilbert smiled a wan sort of smile and she turned back to the window, her eyes drifting over and beyond the reservoir to where a DC10 droned in towards Heathrow. 'No! I wanted to keep him. Funny, isn't it? But he was the only thing I had.'

'It blew over?'

'Not really very much time for that, was there?'

Morse sat and looked once more at this very ordinary woman he had come to visit, and his mind drifted back to Molly Bloom in *Ulysses*, and he knew that Mrs Gilbert, too, was a woman who had offered, once, a presence and a bosom and a rose.

'Please tell me about this other woman.'

'I don't know her real name – they call her "Yvonne" at the clubs. But I know her initials – W.S. – and I know where she lives – 23A Colebourne Road, just south of Richmond Road. It's only about five minutes walk from the tube-station . . .'

'You went to *see* her?'

'You don't know much about women, do you?'

'No, perhaps not,' agreed Morse. But he was impatient now. He felt like a man with an enormously distended bladder who has been kept talking on the phone for half an hour, and he walked across to the door. 'Will you be all right, Mrs Gilbert?'

'Don't worry about me, Inspector. I'll give the GP a ring when you've gone, and he'll give me a few tablets. They should take care of me for a little while, shouldn't they?'

'Yes, I'm sure they will. I know how you must be feeling—'

'Of course you don't! You've not the faintest idea. It's not today – it's not tonight. It's *tomorrow*. Can't you see that? You tell me Albert's dead, and in an odd sort of way it doesn't register. It's a shock, isn't it? And I'd be more than happy to live through one shock after another, but . . .'

The tears were running freely again, and suddenly she moved towards him and buried her head on his shoulder. And Morse stood there by the door, awkward and inept; and (in his own strange way) almost loving the woman who was weeping out her heart against him.

It was several minutes before he was able to disengage himself and finally to stand upon the threshold of the opened door.

'Please look after yourself, Mrs Gilbert.'

'I will. Don't worry about that.'

'If there's anything I can do to help . . .'

She almost smiled. 'Be gentle with the girl, Inspector. You see, I know you're anxious to get away from here and see her, and I just want you to know that she's the loveliest girl – woman – I've ever met in all my life – that's all.'

Tears were spurting again now, and Morse leaned forward and kissed her lightly on the forehead, in the sure knowledge that this woman had somewhere touched his feelings deeply. And as he walked slowly away up the road towards Manor House tube-station he doubted whether Albert Gilbert had ever really known the woman he had asked to marry him.

For all his conviction that the tide was running fully in his favour, the open doors of the Manor Hotel proved irresistible, and Morse wondered as he drained his pints and watched the pimps and prostitutes walk by whether, in a life so full of strange coincidence, he might at last be facing the wildest and most wonderful coincidence of them all: 'W.S'! Browne-Smith had mentioned those initials ... and Emily Gilbert had just repeated them ... and those were the selfsame glorious initials of a girl whom once he'd known, and loved too well.

Twenty minutes after Morse had left the seventh floor of Berrywood Court, a key was inserted into the outer door of the Gilberts' flat, and a man walked in and flung his jacket carelessly down upon the sofa.

Two minutes later, Albert Gilbert, of Removals Anywhere, was talking (somewhat incoherently) over the phone to his GP, explaining how, for no apparent reason, his wife had fainted quite away on his return, and desperately demanding some instructions, since even now she showed no signs of sense or sanity returning.

CHAPTER TWENTY-NINE

Tuesday, 29th July

All men, even those of a pessimistic nature, fall victim at
certain points in their lives to the most extravagant of
hopes.

As Mrs Gilbert had told him, Colebourne Road was
no more than five minutes' walk from East Putney tube
station. But Morse appeared in no hurry, and when he
reached the street-sign he stopped awhile and stood
beneath it, deep in thought. Surely he couldn't be so
utterly and stupidly sentimental as to harbour even the
faintest hope that he was just about to see once more
the woman whom he'd worshipped all those years ago.
No, he told himself, he couldn't. And yet a wild,
improbable hope lived on; and as if to nourish the
hope, he entered the Richmond Arms on the corner of
the street and ordered a double Scotch. As he drank,
his thoughts went back to the time when he'd visited
his old mother in the Midlands, and gone off to an
evening Methodist service to see if a girl, a very precious
girl, was still in her place in the choir-stalls, still raising
her eyes to his at the end of each verse of every hymn
and smiling at him sweetly and seraphically. But she

To Brian Bedwell

THE WAY THROUGH
THE WOODS

CHAPTER FORTY

The Final Discovery

THE HEAD OF Gerardus Mercator (as indeed the whole of Westerby's estate) was bequeathed to the Fellows of Lonsdale, and that fine head is still to be seen in an arched recess on the east side of High Table.

And what of that other fine head? It was finally found in the early March of the following year by two twelve-year-old boys playing on a Gravesend rubbish-tip. How the head ever reached such a distant and unlikely site remains a minor mystery; but it posed no other problems. The notes of the pathologist who first examined the skull recorded signs of a massive haemorrhage in the chambers of the upper brain, doubtless caused by the bullet still embedded there. Later forensic tests were to show that this bullet had been fired from a .38 Webley pistol – the make of pistol issued to officers of the Royal Wiltshire Regiment serving in the desert in 1942.

'I'm awfully sorry about that! I sometimes get a bit cross, I'm afraid.'

'I did notice, yes.'

'You've forgiven me?'

'Of course! You're a bit of a genius, aren't you? Your sergeant thinks so, anyway. And some geniuses are a bit – well, sort of unusual, so they tell me.'

'I wish I'd spoken to you niccly.'

She smiled once again – a little sadly: 'I'm glad I've seen you.' Then, brightly: 'You enjoying yourself?'

'I am now.'

For a few seconds their eyes met, and Morse was reminded of some of the great lost days and a face that shone beyond all other faces.

'Would you like some coffee, Inspector?'

'Er, no. No thanks.'

A tall, gangling, bespectacled man in his mid-thirties had joined them.

'Ah, Anthony! Let me introduce you to Chief Inspector Morse!'

Morse shook the man's limp hand, and looked upon him briefly with distaste.

'Anthony's one of the Research Fellows here, and – and we're going to be married next term, aren't we, darling?'

Morse mumbled his congratulations, and after a few minutes announced that he must go. It was still only ten o'clock, and he could spend half an hour with himself in the Mitre. Red wine always made him a little sentimental – and more than a little thirsty.

hadn't been there – hadn't been there for thirty years, perhaps – and he'd sat by a pillar alone that night. Morse walked to the bar ('Same again, please – Bell's'), and the name of Wendy Spencer tripped trochaically across his brain … It couldn't be the same woman, though. It *wasn't* the same woman. And yet, ye gods – if gods ye be – please make it her!

Morse's heart was beating at an alarming rate and his throat felt very dry as he rang the bell of Number 23. There was a light downstairs, a light upstairs; and the odds were very strongly on her being in.

'Yes?' The door was opened by a youngish, dark-complexioned woman.

'I'm a police inspector, Miss—'

'Mrs – Mrs Price.'

'Ah yes – well, I'm looking for someone I think lives here. I'm not quite sure of her name but—'

'I can't help you much then, can I?'

'I think she's sometimes called "Yvonne".'

'There's no one here by that name.'

The door had already closed an inch or two, but now there was another voice. 'Anything *I* can do to help?'

A taller woman was standing behind Mrs Price, a woman in a white bathrobe, a woman with freshly showered and almost shining skin, a woman awkwardly re-making the tumbled beauty of her hair.

'He says he's a police inspector – says he's looking for someone called "Yvonne",' explained an aggressive Mrs Price.

'Do you know her surname, Inspector?'

Morse looked at the white-clad woman who now had moved towards the centre of the doorway, and a crushing wave of disappointment broke over him. 'Not yet, I'm afraid. But I know she lives here – or she was staying – shtaying here until very recently.'

'Well you must have got it wrong—' began Mrs Price.

But the woman in white was interrupting her: 'Leave this to me, Angela – it's all right. I think I may be able to help you, Inspector. Won't you come in?'

Morse climbed the narrow stairs, noting the slim ankles of the woman who preceded him.

'Would you like a drink?' she asked, as they sat opposite each other in the small but beautifully furnished living-room.

'Er – no. Perhaps not.'

'You've had enough already, you mean?'

'Does it show?'

She nodded – a faint smile upon lips that were thin and completely devoid of make-up. 'It's the "s"s that are always difficult, isn't it? When you've had too much drink, I mean – or when you begin wearing false teeth.'

Morse looked at her own, most beautifully healthy teeth. 'How would you know about that?'

'I sometimes drink too much.'

Morse let it go, for things were going very nicely – the conversation moving already on to a plane of easy familiarity. But it wasn't to last.

'What do you want, Inspector?' A hard, no-nonsense tone had come into her voice.

So Morse told her; and she listened in silence,

occasionally crossing one naked leg over the other and then covering her knees with a sharp little tug at the robe, like some puritanical parson's wife at a vicarage tea-party. And almost from the start Morse felt the virtual certainty that 'Yvonne' had now been found – found sitting here in front of him, her head slightly to one side, sweeping up her blonde hair with her left hand and re-inserting a few of the multitudinous pins with her right.

When Morse had finished the first part of his tale, she reached for her handbag. 'Do you smoke, Inspector?'

Morse patted his jacket pocket, and suspected that he must have left his own recently purchased packet in the pub.

'Here, have one of these.' Her bag was open now, the flap towards him; and seeing the faded gilt initials Morse knew that his silly hope was finally extinguished.

'You're very kind,' he heard himself say.

Had she seen something vulnerable in this strange inspector of police? In his mien? In his eyes? On his lips? Perhaps, indeed, she had, for her voice had been more gentle, and she now stood up and lit his cigarette, unconscious (or uncaring) that her robe was partly open at the top as she leaned towards him. Then she sat back in her chair again, and told him her own side of the story, still occasionally recrossing her lovely legs, but now no longer too concerned about concealing them.

She'd known Bert Gilbert for only a few weeks. He'd come into the sauna one morning – very much in control of himself – and asked her if she'd be willing to

entertain a very special client of his; yes, at the address Morse had mentioned; and, yes, with a sequel much as he'd described it. After that Gilbert had obviously taken a liking to her, spent a fair amount of money on her, and wanted to keep seeing her. *Had* kept seeing her. But he'd got jealous and morose, and was soon telling her that he wanted her to pack up her job and go to live with him. For her part, the whole thing had been the old familiar story of an ageing man behaving like an infatuated schoolboy – and she'd told him so.

That was all.

'What's your name?' asked Morse.

Her eyes were looking down at the thickly piled carpet: 'Winifred – Winifred Stewart. Not much of a name, is it? Some people are christened with horrid names.'

'Mm.'

She looked up. 'What's your name?'

'They call me Morse: Inspector Morse.'

'But that's your *surname*.'

'Yes.'

'You don't want to tell me your Christian name?'

'No.'

'Like that, is it?' (She was smiling.)

Morse nodded.

'What about that drink? You've sobered up a bit, you know.'

But (quite amazingly) Morse had hardly heard her. 'Do you – do you go with lots of men?'

'Not lots, no. I'm a very expensive item.'

'You earn a lot of money?'

'More than you do.' Her voice had grown harsh again, and Morse felt sad and dejected.

'Do you get much pleasure from – er—'

'From having sex with clients? Not much, no. Occasionally though – if you want me to be honest.'

'I'm not sure I do,' said Morse.

She stood up and poured herself a glass of dry Vermouth, without renewing her offer to the Chief Inspector. 'You don't know much about life, do you?'

'Not much, no.' He seemed to her to look so lost and tired now, and she guessed he must have had a busy day. But had she known it, his mind was working at a furious rate. There was *something* (he knew it!) that he'd been missing all the way along; something he doubted he would learn from this disturbingly attractive woman; something that she probably couldn't tell him, anyway, even when she came (as he knew she would) to the second part of the tale she had to tell.

'When did you last see Gilbert?' he asked.

'I'm not sure—'

'You say you saw him quite a few times after you entertained his special client?'

It was puzzling to Morse how the tone of her voice could vary so vastly (and so suddenly) between the gentle and jarring. It was the latter again now.

'You mean did I go to bed with him?'

Morse nodded. And for the first time she was aware of the cold, almost merciless eyes that stared upon her, and she felt the sensation of a psychological and almost physical stripping as she answered him, her top lip quivering.

COLIN DEXTER

'Yes!'

'Was that after you'd met your *second* special client?'

Her startled eyes looked into his, and then down to the Wilton again. 'Yes,' she whispered.

'Please tell me all about that,' said Morse quietly.

For a few moments she said nothing; then she picked up her glass and quickly drained it.

'Before I do – would you like to come to bed with me?'

'No.'

'Are you sure?' She stood up and loosened her belt, allowing the sides of her bathrobe to fall apart before drawing them together again and retying the belt tightly around her waist.

'Quite sure,' lied Morse.

So Winifred Stewart (it was now past eight o'clock) told Morse about her second special client, a Mr Westerby, who also hailed from Oxford. And Morse listened very carefully, nodding at intervals and seemingly satisfied. But he *wasn't* satisfied. It was all interesting – of course it was; but it merely corroborated what he'd already known, or guessed.

'What about that drink?' he asked.

Mrs Angela Price looked knowingly at her husband when she finally heard the quiet voices on the doorstep. It was a quarter to midnight, and BBC 1 had already finished its transmission.

*

216

Lewis had finally gone to bed about ten minutes before Morse found a taxi on the Richmond Road. He'd hoped that Morse would have been back before now, and had tried repeatedly to get in touch with him, both at HQ and at his home. For he had received a remarkable piece of news that same afternoon from the young porter at Lonsdale, who had received a card by second post; a card from Greece; a card from Mr Westerby.

At 2 a.m., Winifred Stewart was still lying awake. The night was sultry and she wore no nightdress as she lay upon her bed, covered only by a lightweight sheet. She thought of Morse, and she felt inexpressibly glad that she had met him; longed, too, with one half of her mind, that he would come to visit her again. And yet she knew, quite certainly, that if he did her soul would be completely bared and she would tell him all she knew. Two thirds of the tragic tale had now been told; and if ever he began to guess the final truth . . . Yet, with the other half of her mind she didn't want him back – ever – for she was now a very frightened woman.

At 3 a.m. she went to the bathroom to take some Disprin tablets.

At 4 a.m. she was still awake, and suddenly she felt the night had grown so very cold.

CHAPTER THIRTY

Wednesday, 30th July

In which 'The Religion of the Second Mile' is fully explained, and Morse is peremptorily summoned to his superior.

AS HE SAT back comfortably in a first-class compartment of the 10 a.m. '125' from Paddington, Morse felt the residual glow of a great elation. For now (as he knew) the veil of the temple had been rent in twain.

The previous night he had missed the last train to Oxford and only just managed to find, on the highest floor of a cheap hotel, a cramped and claustrophobic room in which the water-pipes had groaned and gurgled through the early hours. But it was in this selfsame mean and miserable room that Morse, as he lay on his back in the darkness with both hands behind his head, had finally seen the amazing light of truth. Half occupied with the lovely woman he had left so recently, half with the older problems that beset him still, his mind had steadfastly refused to rest. He sensed that he was *almost* there, and the facts of the case raced round and round his brain like an ever-accelerating whirligig. The old facts . . . and the new facts.

Not that he had learned much that was surprisingly new from Mrs Emily Gilbert. Nor, for that matter, from Miss Winifred Stewart – except for the confirmation that she had, indeed, agreed to entertain a second special guest from Oxford whose name was Mr Westerby. There had been a few other things, though. She'd told him, for example, that Emily had been simultaneously wooed by each of the Gilbert brothers; that, of the two, Alfred was considerably the more interesting and cultured – particularly because of his love of music; but that it was Albert who had won the prize with his livelier, albeit coarser, ways. The brothers were still very much alike (she'd told him) – extraordinarily so in appearance – but if they'd been holidaying together in Salzburg Alfred would have gone to a Mozart concert and Albert to *The Sound of Music* . . . Yes, that was something new; but it hardly seemed to Morse of much importance. Far more important was what she *hadn't* told him, for he had sensed the deep unease within her when she'd told him of her time with Westerby: not the unease of a woman telling obvious untruths; the unease, rather, of a woman telling something less than all she knew . . .

It was at that very point in his whirling thoughts that Morse had jerked himself up in his bed, switched on the bedside lamp, and reached for the only object of comfort that the sombre room could offer him: the Gideon Bible that rested there beside the lamp. In two minutes his fumbling and excited fingers had found what he was seeking. There it was – St Matthew, Chapter

Five, Verse Forty-One: 'And whosoever shall compel thee to go a mile, go with him twain.' He remembered vividly from his youth a sermon on that very text – from a wild, Welsh minister: 'The Religion of the Second Mile'. And it was with the forty-watt bulb shedding its feeble light over the Gideon Bible that Morse smiled to himself in unspeakable joy, like one who has travelled on a longer journey still – that third and final mile . . .

At last he knew the truth.

'In two minutes we shall be arriving at Oxford station,' came the voice over the microphone. 'Passengers for Banbury, Birmingham, Charlbury . . .' Morse looked at his watch: 10.41 a.m. No need for any great rush now – no need for any rush at all.

He walked from the station up to the bus-stop in Cornmarket; and at 11.30 was back at Police HQ in Kidlington, where a relieved-looking Lewis awaited him.

'Good time, sir?'

'Marvellous!' said Morse, seating himself in the black leather chair and beaming benignly.

'We expected you back yesterday.'

'"We"? Who's that supposed to mean?'

'The super was after your blood last night, sir – *and* this morning.'

'Ah, I see.'

'I said you'd ring him as soon as you got in.'

Morse dialled Strange's number immediately. Engaged.

'How about you, Lewis? You have a good time?'

'I don't know, sir. There's *this*.'

He handed over the postcard he had picked up the previous evening from Lonsdale, and Morse looked down at a glossy photograph of ancient stones. He turned the card over, and read that such crumbling masonry was nothing less than the remains of the royal palace of Philip II of Macedon (382–336 BC). Then he saw the large Hellas stamp, featuring sea shells set against a blue-green background; then the message, neatly penned and very brief: 'Wonderful weather. Any mail to Cambridge Way. Staying on a further week. Regards to the Master – and to your good selves. G.W.'

'Lovely place, Greece, Lewis.'

'I wouldn't know, I'm afraid.'

'Perhaps Westerby doesn't know either,' said Morse slowly.

'Pardon, sir?'

'You'd better keep it, of course – but he's not in Greece. It's a forgery – you can see that, surely!'

'But—'

'Look, Lewis! Look at that franking.'

Lewis looked closely but saw little more than a blackened circle, with whatever lettering there may have been so smudged that it was quite illegible. He could, though, just about decipher one or two of the letters: there was an 'O' (certainly) and an 'N' (possibly) near the beginning of one word, and the next

word probably ended in an 'E'. But he could make nothing of it, and looked up to find that Morse was smiling still.

'I shouldn't take too much notice of it, Lewis. It's not too difficult to get hold of a Greek postage-stamp, is it? And then if you get a date-stamp and push it vaguely one way instead of banging it straight down you'll get the same sort of blur as that. You see, someone just brought the card into the Lodge and left it handily upon a pile of mail. It's all a fake! And, if you like, I'll tell you where the date-stamp comes from: it comes from *Lonsdale College*.'

The phone rang before Lewis could make any answer, and a harsh voice barked across the line: 'That you, Morse? Get over here – and get over here quick!'

'I think you're in the dog-house,' said Lewis quietly.

But Morse appeared completely unconcerned as he rose to his feet and put his jacket on.

'I'll tell you something else about that card, Lewis. We know a man, don't we, who's been writing a book about our Mister Philip Two of Macedon – remember?'

Yes, Lewis did remember. Just as Morse had done, he'd seen the typescript on the desk in Browne-Smith's room, as well as the pile of postcards that had lain beside it. And, as Morse walked across to the door, he felt annoyed and disappointed with himself. There was one thing Morse hadn't mentioned, though.

'Is the handwriting a fake as well, sir?'

'I haven't the faintest idea,' replied Morse. 'Why don't you go and find out, if you can? No rush, though.

THE RIDDLE OF THE THIRD MILE

I think the super and I may well be in for rather a
longish session.'

'Siddown, Morse!' growled Strange, his long gaunt face
set grimly and angrily. 'I heard last night – and again
this morning – from the Metropolitan Commissioner.'
His eyes fixed Morse's as he continued. 'It seems that a
member of *my* force – *you*, Morse! – was witness to a
major crime in London yesterday; that you left the
scene of this crime without adequate explanation and
in defiance of normal police procedures; that you
allowed the only other witness of this crime to go off
home – God! – a home incidentally which doesn't exist;
that you then went off to see a woman up in North
London to tell her that her husband had just been
murdered; and if all that's not enough,' the blood was
rising in his face, 'you couldn't even get the name of
the bloody corpse right!'

Morse nodded agreement, but said nothing.

'You realize, don't you, that this is an extremely
serious matter?' Strange's voice was quieter now. 'It
won't be in my hands, either.'

'No, I understand that. And you're right, of course –
it's a very serious matter. The only thing is, sir, I don't
think that even you quite understand how desperately
serious it is.'

Strange had known Morse for many years and had
marvelled many times at the exploits of this extraordinary and exasperating man. And there was something

223

about the way in which Morse had just spoken that signalled a warning. It would be wise for him to listen, he knew that.

So he listened.

It was more than two hours later when Strange's middle-aged secretary saw the door open and the two men emerge. Earlier she had been informed that, short of a nuclear explosion, her boss was not to be disturbed; and she did know a little (how not?) of the reason for Morse's summons from on high. Yet now she saw that it was Strange's face which looked, of the two, the more drained and set; and she bent her head a little closer to the clattering keys, as if her presence there might cause embarrassment. The two men had said nothing more to each other, she was sure of that – except that Strange had murmured a muted 'Thank you' as Morse had walked across the room. Then, after Morse was gone, and just before her boss had closed his office door, she thought she heard him speak once more: 'My God!'

THE END OF THE SECOND MILE

The Third Mile

CHAPTER THIRTY-ONE

Friday, 1st August

Like some latter-day Pilgrim, one of the protagonists in this macabre case is determined to rid himself of his burden.

TWO DAYS AFTER the events described in the previous chapter, a man looked about him with extreme circumspection before inserting one of his keys into the door at the rear entrance of the luxury flats in Cambridge Way. The coast was clear. Apart from the uniformed police constable standing outside the front entrance, he guessed (and guessed correctly) that at last he was alone. He moved silently up the carpeted staircase and let himself into the room that faced the first landing; there was just one thing he had to do. Once inside the flat he fixed his rather ancient hearing-aid into his right ear (exactly as he'd done three days before), flicked over the lock on the Yale (a precaution he'd earlier omitted to take), and took from his pocket a newly purchased screwdriver – a larger, shinier, more effective instrument than the one which had bored its way through Gilbert's spine. He'd known the truth, of course, on that previous visit; known it immediately

he'd entered the main sitting-room. For, although the crates seemed all (quite properly) still unopened, from the mantelpiece Mercator's head had stared at him accusingly . . .

After performing his grisly task – it took him only a few minutes – he retraced his steps to the rear entrance and let himself out into the bright afternoon sunlight, where he promptly hailed a taxi. He saw the driver's eyes flick to the mirror as his hearing-aid began to oscillate; so he turned off the volume and took it out. It had served its purpose well today, and he put it away and sought to relax as the taxi threaded its way through the heavy traffic. But his mind could give him little rest . . . If only on that terrifying day . . . But no! Awaiting Gilbert had been an almost certain early retribution. Money! That was all that Gilbert had demanded – then more money. An odd compulsion (as it appeared to the man in the taxi); certainly when compared with the motivations that dominated his own life – the harbouring of inveterate hatreds, and the almost manic ambition, sometimes so carefully concealed, for some degree of worldly fame.

'Here we are, sir: Paddington.'

Why Paddington? Why not Euston, or Victoria, or Liverpool Street? Why *any* railway station? Perhaps it was the anonymity of such a place – a place at which he could deposit the burden of his sin that lay so heavily in the supermarket carrier-bag he tightly clutched as he walked through the swing doors of the Station Hotel and turned right to the gentlemen's toilet. No one else was there, and he closed the door behind him in the

furthest of the cubicles that faced the open pissoir. Here, he lifted the plastic ring of the lavatory seat, climbed on to the circular fixture and lifted the covering of the porcelain cistern. But the water-filled cavity was far too narrow – and suddenly he was jerked into a frozen stillness, for he heard the door-catch click in a nearby cubicle. Something had to be done quickly. He felt inside the carrier-bag and took out a flat package wrapped round with a copy of *The Times* – a package which, judging from its shape, might have held two sandwiches, and which now plopped into the water and sank immediately to the bottom of the cistern.

Still carrying the bulk of his burden, he walked out of the hotel into the main-line station, where he drifted aimlessly about until he saw the planks and scaffolding at the furthest end of Platform One. He made his way slowly along this platform, intermittently turning his eyes upwards to take in Brunel's magnificent wrought-iron roof that arched above him. He had already seen the skip – half-full of building rubble and general rubbish ... Apart from a solitary orange-coated workman a few yards up the line, he was alone. Suddenly turning, he dropped his bag into the skip and sauntered back towards the unmanned ticket-barrier. He would have enjoyed a pot of searing hot tea and a buttered scone in the cool lounge of the Station Hotel, but he dared not trust himself. He was shaking visibly and the sweat was cold upon his forehead. It was time to return to base, to lie down awhile, to tell himself that the task he'd so much dreaded was now accomplished – if not accomplished well.

Crossing over Praed Street, he walked down to the bottom of Spring Street and entered a small hotel just off to the left. No one was on duty at the reception-desk, and he lifted the hinged board, took his key (Number 16) off its wall-hook, and climbed the stairs. Although he had now been in the same hotel for many days, he still felt some hesitation about which way up the key went in; and again, now, he fiddled and scraped a bit before opening the door and admitting himself to the small but neatly furnished room. He took off his jacket, placed it at the bottom of the single bed, wiped his forehead with a clean white handkerchief from the antique wardrobe – and experienced a vast relief at finding himself safely back in this temporary home. The Gideon Bible, in its plum-coloured boards, still lay on the table beside the pillow; the window, as he had left it, was still half-open, providing easy access (he was glad of it!) to the fire-escape that zigzagged down the narrow side of the hotel to the mean-looking courtyard below. Turning round, he saw that the door to the wash-room was open, too, and he promised himself (but in a little while) a cool and guilt-effacing shower.

For the moment he lay down on top of the coverlet, with that curious amalgam of elation that springs from defiance of danger and knowledge of accomplishment. As a boy, he'd known it when climbing Snowdon with a Scout troop: for all the other boys, the route alongside one precipitous face had seemed a commonplace occurrence – yet for himself a source of great and secret pride ... It was strange that he should only have experienced that marvellous elation again so very late

in life, and then so often in such a short period of time
... He closed his eyes, and almost moved his mind
towards some neutral gear, untroubled, disengaged ...

But only a minute later his body was jarred into
panic-stricken dread. Someone was standing over him;
someone who said 'Good afternoon' – and nothing
more.

'You! *You!*'

His eyeballs bulged in fear and incredulous surprise,
and if either of these emotions could be said to have
been in the ascendant, perhaps it was that of surprise.
But even as he cowered upon the coverlet, the packing
twine was cutting deep into his neck; and soon his
frantic spluttering and croaking grew quieter and
quieter – until it was completely stilled. So died George
Westerby, late Scholar and Senior Fellow of Lonsdale
College in the University of Oxford.

CHAPTER THIRTY-TWO

Saturday, 2nd August

It is a characteristic of the British people that they complain about their railways. In this case, however, there appears little justification for such complaint.

IT WAS 9.50 A.M. the following morning when the winsome receptionist looked up from her desk and took the room-key.

'Nice morning again, Mr Smith?'

He nodded and smiled – that distinctively lop-sided smile of his. Since he'd been there, she'd almost always been on duty in the mornings; often, too, in the evenings, when she'd taken his order for an early-morning pot of tea – and also for *The Times*.

'I've got to leave this morning; so if you'll make out my bill, please?'

He sat down in one of the armchairs just opposite the reception desk, and breathed in very deeply. He'd spent another deeply troubled night, fitfully falling into semi-slumber, then waking up to find his blue pyjamas soaked in chilling sweat. Throughout these hours his head had thumped away as though some alien fiend were hammering inside his skull; and it was only after

early tea that finally he'd slept a little while. He woke just after 9 a.m., his head still aching, yet now with a dulled and tolerable pain. For a few minutes he had lain there almost happily, upon the creased and tumbled pillow. But soon the same old host of thoughts was streaming through the portals of his brain, his eyeballs rolling round beneath the shuttered lids. And one thought fought a leading way through all the crowd – and one decision was made.

'Mr Smith? Mr *Smith*?'

He heard her, and rose to pay the bill. Sometimes (as well he knew) his brain could play him false; but this particular contingency he had anticipated, and he paid his dues with ready cash, in notes of high denomination.

He left the Station Hotel (as Westerby had done before him) and walked to the ticket-office. Then, for many minutes, he stood in front of the high departures-board. But he could read nothing. His eyes no sooner focused on the times of trains for Oxford than the letters (white) upon their background (black) had leap-frogged astigmatically across his retina, leaving him in dizzied indecision.

He stepped to the nearest ticket-barrier.

'Can you tell me my best bet for Oxford, please?'

'Platform 9. Half-past ten. But you'll have to—'

'Thank you.'

The train was already in the platform and he pulled himself up into an empty first-class compartment, putting his ticket carefully into his wallet and leaning back against the head-rest . . .

Half an hour later he jerked forward as the train halted with something less than silken braking-power, and he looked out of the window: Reading. Still the solitary occupant of the compartment, he leant back again and closed his wearied eyes. Not long ... and he'd be there!

Thirty-five minutes later he was jerked to a second awakening.

'Tickets, please!'

He was gratified that he could find his ticket so easily, but his head was throbbing wildly.

'This your ticket, sir?'

'Yes. Why?'

'I'm afraid you've missed your connection. We've just gone past Didcot. You're on your way to Swindon.'

'What? I don't understand—'

'You should have changed at Didcot for the Oxford train. You must have nodded off.'

'But I've got to get to Oxford. I've – I've just *got* to get there.'

'Nothing we can do, sir. You'll have to get the next train back from Swindon—'

'But it's urgent!'

'As I say, you'll just have to wait till we get to Swindon.' The collector punched the ticket and handed it back. 'We won't worry about any excess fare, sir. Genuine mistake, I'm sure.'

The next few minutes registered themselves in his mind as an aeon of frenzied agony. Sitting forward in his seat, he bit deep into the nails of his little fingers,

fighting with all his powers to keep control of a brain that stood unsurely on a precipice.

Then the train stopped – more gently this time.

He was glad to find his legs steady as he got to his feet, and he felt much calmer now. He put the sweat-soaked handkerchief away inside his trouser pocket, took his case from the luggage-rack, opened the left-hand door of the carriage – and stepped down into nothing. He fell on to the sharp stones of a slight embankment on the south side of the line, and lay there hurt and wholly puzzled. Yet, strangely, he felt profoundly comfortable there: it seemed so easy now to sleep. The sun was blazing down from the clear-blue sky, and his head – at last! – was free from pain.

'You all right, sir?'

The ticket collector was crouching beside him, and he heard some faintly sounding voices from afar.

'I'm sorry . . . I'm sorry . . .'

'Let me just help you up, sir. You'll be all right.'

'No! Please don't bother. I'm just sorry, that's all . . .'

He closed his eyes. But the sun was blazing still beneath his eyelids, glowing like some fiery orange, whirring and – ever larger – spinning down towards him.

But still there was no pain.

'I'll go and get some help, sir. Shan't be a minute.'

The ticket collector vaulted nimbly up the shallow embankment, but already it was too late.

'Before you do that, please do one thing for me. I want to get a message to a Chief Inspector Morse – at

the Thames Valley Police Headquarters. Please tell him I was – I was on my way to see him. Please tell him that *I* did it – do you understand me? Please tell him ... that ...'

But the man beside the track was speaking to himself; and even the curious heads that poked through nearby carriage-windows could make no sense of all the mumbled words.

Suddenly the sun exploded in a yellow flash and a jagged, agonizing pain careered across his skull. With a supreme effort of will he opened his eyes once more; but all was dark now, and the sweat was pouring down his face and seeping inside his gaping mouth. He *had* a handkerchief, he knew: it was in his trouser pocket. But he wanted a clean one. Yes, he had plenty of clean ones. Why, he'd only bought a box of Irish-linen ones so very recently ... from the shop in the Turn ... only a hundred yards away from Lonsdale College ...

Another man now knelt beside the body – a young neurosurgeon who was travelling up to Swindon General Hospital. But he could do nothing; and after a little while he looked up at the ticket collector – then slowly shook his head.

CHAPTER THIRTY-THREE

Saturday, 2nd August

Whose was the body found in the Thrupp canal? It becomes increasingly clear now that there are very few contenders remaining.

IN RECENT YEARS Lewis had seldom spent two nights away from Oxford, and he didn't care much for London. But it had been a busy and a fruitful time.

Late the previous Wednesday afternoon, Morse had insisted that it was to be he, Lewis, who should drive up the next morning. There was much to do (Morse had said): many loose ends to tie up; statements to be taken; and, not least, some needful explanations to be made. So Lewis had taken his instructions, had performed them more than adequately, and now (indulging his one real weakness in life) was driving far too fast along the M40 back to Oxford. It was mid-morning.

His London colleagues had been a friendly bunch, most of them speaking in a careless, aitchless Cockney – yet all of them shrewd and competent men. They could forgive Morse readily, of course, but none of them seemed to understand his actions very well. And Lewis, himself being only semi-enlightened, was unable

to throw much further light. But certain things were now clear. The man found murdered in the top-storey flat in Cambridge Way was Alfred Gilbert, Esq., estate agent, and late bachelor of some parish or other in central London. The murder weapon (so plain for all to see!) had been the screwdriver so conveniently found at the scene of the crime, upon whose handle were some smudgy prints that might or (as Lewis hoped) might not be soon identifiable. For the present there were few other clues. Of 'Mr Hoskins' the police could find no trace, nor expected to do so, since the residents of Cambridge Way had always had a woman as their part-time concierge. But the police had been mildly mollified when Lewis had been able to produce Morse's description of the man – from his age to his height, from chest-measurement to weight, from the colour of eyes to the size of his shoes.

After that, Lewis had done exactly as Morse had instructed. There had been three visits, three interviews, and three statements (slowly transcribed). First, the statement from the manager of the Flamenco Topless Bar; second, that from Miss Winifred Stewart, hostess at the Sauna Select; third, that from Mrs Emily Gilbert at her home in Berrywood Court. All three, in their various ways, had seemed to Lewis to be nervously defensive, and more than once he had found himself seriously doubting whether any of the trio was over-anxious to come completely clean. But Morse had blandly told him that any further investigations were not only futile but also quite unnecessary; and so he

had ignored some obvious evasions, and merely written down what each had been prepared to tell him.

Then, without much difficulty, he'd been able to discover at least something about the Gilbert brothers. Albert and the late Alfred had been public partners in a property-cum-removals firm, and private partners in a company christened Soho Enterprises – the latter owning, in addition to the topless bar, two dubious bookshops and a small (and strictly members-only) pornographic cinema. The London police knew a good deal about these activities anyway and inquiries were still proceeding, but already it seemed perfectly clear that even sex was suffering from the general recession. Of which fact Lewis himself was glad, for he found the Soho area crude and sordid; and had the tempter looked along those streets, he could have entertained only the most desperate hope of pushing that broad and solid back through any of the doorways there. Finally, Lewis had been instructed to discover, if it were at all possible, the whereabouts of Albert Gilbert, Esq., although Morse had held out little prospect on that score – and Morse (as usual) had been right.

At the Headington roundabout Lewis was debating whether to call in for a few minutes and tell the missus he was safely home. But he didn't. He knew the chief would be waiting.

During the previous two days Morse had hardly over-exerted himself, fully recognizing his own incompetence

in such matters as mounting a man-hunt or supervising the search (yes – yet another one!) of the waters out at Thrupp. But he *had* done two things, in each case retracing the ground that Lewis had trodden before him. First, he had visited the Blood Transfusion Centre at the Churchill Hospital, where he asked to look through the current records; where after only a couple of minutes he nodded briefly; where he then asked to see the records for the previous five years, in this second instance spending rather longer before nodding again, pushing the drawers of the filing-cabinet to, thanking the clerk, and departing. Second, he'd driven down to the Examination Schools, where he spent more than an hour with the Curator, finally thanking him, too, and leaving with the contented look of a man who has found what he sought. Now, again, as he sat at his desk that Saturday morning, he looked contented – and with even better reason, for the call had come through at 9.30. He'd *known* there must be something in the waters of the Thrupp canal . . .

The sight of Lewis gladdened him even more. 'Get some egg and chips while you were away?'

Lewis grinned. 'Once or twice.'

'Well, let's hear from you. By the way, I hope you've noticed: hardly any swelling at all now, is there?'

Twenty minutes later the phone rang.

'Morse here. Can I help you?'

Lewis observed that the Chief Inspector's pale, ill-

shaven face was tautening as he listened. Listened only; till finally he said, 'I'll be there as soon as I can,' and with a look of unwonted agitation slowly put the receiver down.

'What was all that about, sir?'

'That was London on the line – Westerby's just been found – he's been murdered – they found him this morning – in a bedroom near Paddington – strangled with packing-twine.'

It was Lewis's turn now to reflect with puzzlement on this troublous news. From what Morse had told him earlier, the case was almost over – with just a few arrests to come. So what on earth did *this* mean? But already Morse was on his feet and looking in his wallet.

'Look, Lewis! You just get those reports of yours sorted out and typed up – then get off home and see the missus. Nothing more for you today.'

'You sure there's nothing I can do?'

'Not got a couple of fivers to spare, have you?'

After Morse had left, Lewis rang his wife to say that he'd be in for a latish lunch. Then, beginning to get his documents in order, he reached for *Chambers Dictionary*; Morse was a fanatic about spelling.

The phone rang ten minutes later: it was the police surgeon.

'Not there? Where the 'ell's he got to, then?'

'One or two complications in the case, I'm afraid.'

'Well, just tell the old bugger, will you, that the leg he's found would make the height about 5 foot 10 inches – 5 foot 11 inches. All right? Doesn't help all

COLIN DEXTER

that much, perhaps, but it might cut out a few of the
little 'uns.'

'*What* leg?' Lewis felt utterly confused.

'Didn't he tell you? Huh! Secretive sod, isn't he?
He's had half a dozen divers out this last couple of days
... Still, he was right, I suppose. Lucky, though! Just
tell him anyway – if he comes back.'

'Perhaps he knew all the time,' said Lewis quietly.

The phone was going all the time now. A woman's
voice was put through from the operator: but, no, she
would speak to no one but Morse. Then Strange
(himself, this time), who slammed down the receiver
after learning that Morse had gone to London. Then
another woman's voice – one Lewis thought he almost
recognized: but she, too, refused to deal with any
underling. Finally, a call came through from Dickson,
on reception; a call that caused Lewis to jolt in
amazement.

'You *sure*?'

'Yep. Swindon police, it was. Said he was dead when
the ambulance got there.'

'But they're sure it's *him*?'

'That's what they said, Sarge – sure as eggs is eggs.'
Lewis put down the phone. It would be impossible to
contact Morse in transit: he never drove anything other
than his privately owned Lancia. Would Morse be
surprised? He'd certainly *looked* surprised about an hour
ago on learning of the death of Westerby. So what
about this? What about Dickson's latest information?
That the body just recovered from a shallow embankment on the Didcot–Swindon railway-line was certainly

that of Oliver Browne-Smith, late fellow of Lonsdale College, Oxford.

About the time that Lewis received his last call that morning, Morse was turning left at Hanger Lane on to the North Circular. He'd still (he knew) a further half-hour's driving in front of him, and with a fairly clear road he drove in a manner that verged occasionally upon the dangerous. But already he was too late. It had been a quarter of an hour earlier that the ambulance had taken away the broken body that lay directly beneath a seventh-storey window in Berrywood Court, just along the Seven Sisters Road.

Later the same afternoon, a business executive, immaculately dressed in a pin-striped suit, walked into the furthest cubicle of the gentlemen's toilet at the Station Hotel, Paddington. When he pulled the chain, the cistern seemed to be working perfectly, as though the presence of a pair of human hands as yet was causing little problem to the flushing mechanism.

CHAPTER THIRTY-FOUR

Monday, 4th August

In which Morse and Lewis retrace their journey as far as the terminus of the first milestone.

IT WAS WITH growing impatience that Lewis waited from 8.15 a.m. onwards. Morse had arrived back in Oxford late the previous evening and had called in to see him, readily accepting Mrs Lewis's offer to cook him something, and thereafter settling down to watch television with the joyous dedication of a child. He had refused to answer Lewis's questions, affirming only that the sun would almost certainly rise on the morrow, and that he would be in the office – early.

At 9 a.m. there was still no sign of him, and for the umpteenth time Lewis found himself thinking about the astonishing fact that, of the four dubiously associated and oddly assorted men who had played their parts in the case, not *one* of them could now lay the slightest claim to be mistaken for the corpse that still lay in Max's deep-refrigeration unit: Browne-Smith had died of a brain haemorrhage beside a railway-track; Westerby had been strangled to death in a cheap hotel near Paddington; Alfred Gilbert had been found mur-

dered in a room a couple of floors above Westerby's flat in Cambridge Way; and Albert Gilbert had thrown himself from a seventh-storey window in Berrywood Court. So the same old question still remained unanswered, and the simple truth was that they were running out of bodies.

But there *were* one or two items that Lewis had discovered for himself, and at 9.30 a.m. he browsed through his neatly typed reports once more. He'd learned, for example – from the manager of the topless bar – that Browne-Smith seemed to have been unaccountably slow in identifying himself by the agreed words: 'It's exactly twelve o'clock, I see.' Then (after applying a good deal of pressure) he'd learned from the same source that the ciné equipment had definitely not been returned to the bar the next day; in fact, it had been nearer a week before any of the bar-clients could indulge their voyeuristic fantasies again. There was a third fact, too: that neither the manager nor any of his hostesses had previously set eyes upon the man with the brownish beard who had sat beside the bar that fateful Friday when Browne-Smith had been tempted down from Oxford . . .

Morse finally arrived just before 9.45 a.m., his lower lip caked with blood.

'Sorry to be late. Just had her out. No trouble. Hardly felt a thing. "Decayed beyond redemption" – that's what the little fellow said.' He sat down expansively in his chair. 'Well, where do you want me to start?'

'At the beginning, perhaps?'

COLIN DEXTER

'No. Let's start before then, and get a bit of the background clear. While you were off gallivanting in London, Lewis, I called in to see your pal at the Examination Schools, and I asked him just one thing: I asked him what he thought were the potential areas for any crooked dealings in this whole business of the final lists. And he made some interesting suggestions. First, of course, there's the possibility of someone getting results ahead of the proper time. Now this isn't perhaps one of the major sins; but, as you told me yourself, all that waiting can become a matter of great anxiety: sometimes perhaps *enough* anxiety to make one or two people willing to pay – pay in *some* way – for learning results early. That's only the start of it, though. You see if there's some undergraduate who's *nearly* up to the first-class honours bracket, he's put forward for a viva-voce examination, but he's never told which particular part of his work he's going to be re-examined in. Now, if he *did* know, he'd be able to swot up on that side of things and get ready to catch all the hand-grenades they lobbed at him. Agreed? But let's go on a stage further. Our budding "first" would be an even shorter-odds favourite if he knew the *name* of the man who was going to viva him: he could soon find out this fellow's hobby-horses, read his books, and generally tune himself in to the right wavelength. Which leads on to the final consideration. If he did know exactly who it was who was going to settle his future, there'd always be the potential for a bit of *bribery* – the offer of money in return for that glowing recommendation for a "first". You see, Lewis? The whole process is full of loop-holes!

I'm not saying anyone wriggles through 'em: I'm just telling you they're *there*. And, depending on what the rewards are, there might be a few susceptible dons who could feel tempted to go along with one or two suggestions, don't you think?'

Lewis nodded. 'Perhaps a few might, I suppose.'

'No "perhaps", Lewis – just a few *did*!'

Again Lewis nodded – rather sadly – and Morse continued.

'Then we found a corpse with a great big question-mark on the label round its neck.'

'It hadn't got a neck, sir.'

'That's true.'

'And there isn't a question-mark any longer?'

'Patience, Lewis!'

'But we had the letter to go on.'

'Even that, though. If we hadn't had a line on things to start with, the whole thing would have been a load of gobbledygook. Would *you* have made much of it without—'

'I wouldn't have made anything of it, anyway.'

'Don't underestimate yourself, Lewis – let me do it for you!'

'What about that blood-donor business?'

'Ah! Now if you've been a donor for a good many years you get a lot of little tiny marks – '

'As a matter of fact I got my gold badge last year – for fifty times, that is – in case you didn't know.'

'Oh!'

'So I don't really need you to tell me much about *that*.'

'But you *do*. Do you know when you have to pack up giving blood? What age, I mean?'

'No.'

'Well, you bloody should! Don't you read any of the literature? It's *sixty-five*.'

Lewis let the information sink in. 'You mean that Browne-Smith wouldn't have been on the current records . . .'

'Nor Westerby. They were both over sixty-five.'

'Ye-es. I should have looked in the old records.'

'It's all right. I've already checked. Browne-Smith *was* a donor until a couple of years ago. Westerby never: he'd had jaundice and that put him out of court, as I'm sure you'll know!'

'But the body *wasn't* Browne-Smith's.'

'No?' Morse smiled and wiped the blood gently from his mouth. 'Whose was it then?'

But Lewis shook his head. 'I'm just here to listen, sir.'

'All right. Let's start at the beginning. George Westerby is just finishing his stint at Lonsdale. He's looking for a place in London, and he finds one, and buys it. The estate agent tells him that all the removals from Oxford can easily be arranged, and that suits Westerby fine. He's got two places: his rooms in Lonsdale, and his little weekend cottage out at Thrupp. So Removals Anywhere come on to the scene – and the supremely important moment in the case arrives: Bert Gilbert notices the name opposite Westerby's rooms on T Staircase – the name of Dr O. M. A. Browne-Smith – the name of a man he'd always ranked among the

legion of the damned – the man who'd been responsible for his younger brother's death.

'Now, very soon after this point – I'm sure of it! – we get a switch of brothers. Bert reports his extraordinary finding to his brother, and it's Alfred – by general consent the abler of the two – who now takes over. He finds out as much as he can about Browne-Smith, and devises a plan that makes it ridiculously easy for Browne-Smith to go along with things. He writes a letter on Westerby's typewriter – he's in Westerby's rooms whenever he likes now, remember – inviting Browne-Smith to do him a very small favour, and one that would entail no real compromise to Browne-Smith's academic integrity. This offer, as we know, was taken up, and off Browne-Smith goes to London. But we also know – because he told us – that Browne-Smith played his own cards with equal cunning. And in the end Gilbert's plan misfired – whatever that plan had been originally.

'Gilbert came into the room to find that Browne-Smith wasn't unconscious, as he'd expected. So they talked together straightaway; and it wasn't long before Gilbert discovered that the military records of young brother John were hardly a striking example of dedication to duty. In fact, far from being killed in action, he'd shot himself the night before El Alamein – and one of the few people who knew all this was Browne-Smith, John Gilbert's platoon officer. So when the whole story was out at last, there couldn't have been much wind left in the Gilberts' sails, because it was quite clear to them that Browne-Smith hadn't the

COLIN DEXTER

slightest responsibility, direct or indirect, for their brother's death! Now, at that point everything could have been over, Lewis. And if it had been, certainly four of the five people who've died in this case would still be alive. But . . .'

Yes, Lewis understood all this. It seemed simpler, though, now that Morse had put it into words. 'But then,' he said quietly, 'Browne-Smith saw the chance to duplicate—'

' "Replicate" – that's the word I'd use, Lewis.'

'—to replicate the process with Westerby.'

'That's it. That's the end of the first mile, and we're soon going to start on the second.'

'Off we go then, sir!'

'Do you fancy a cup of coffee?'

Lewis got to his feet. 'Any sugar?'

'Just a little, perhaps. You know it's a funny thing. There were no end of tins of coffee in Alfred Gilbert's flat, and not a single drop of alcohol!'

'Not everybody drinks, sir.'

''Course they do! He was just an oddball – that's for certain. And I'll tell you something else. When I was a lad I heard of a Methodist minister who was a bit embarrassed about being seen reading the Bible all the time – you know, on trains and buses. So he had a special cover made – a sort of cowboy cover with a gun-slinger on his horse; and he had this stuck round his Bible when he was reading Ezekiel or something. Well, I found a book in Gilbert's flat that was exactly the opposite. It had a cover on it called *Know Your Köchel Numbers*—'

'Pardon, sir?'

'"Köchel". He was the chap who put all Mozart's works into some sort of chronological order and gave 'em all numbers.'

'Oh.'

'I had a look in this book – and do you know what I found? It was a load of the lewdest pornography I've ever seen. I – er – I brought it with me, if you want to borrow it?'

'No, sir. You read it yourself. I—'

'I *have* read it.' The numbed lips were smiling almost guiltily: 'Read it twice, actually.'

'Did you find anything else in the flat?'

'Found a beard – a brownish beard. Sort of theatrical thing, stuck with Elastoplast.'

'That all?'

'Found a scarf, Lewis. Not quite so long as mine, but a nice scarf. Still, that was hardly a surprise, was it?'

'Just a little sugar, you say?'

'Well, perhaps a bit more than that.'

Lewis stood at the door. 'I wonder whether Gilbert had *his* tooth out.'

'Didn't need to, Lewis. He had false teeth – top and bottom.'

CHAPTER THIRTY-FIVE

Monday, 4th August

Gently we journey along the second mile, which appears to Morse to be adequately posted.

DURING THE FEW minutes that Lewis was away, Morse was acutely conscious of the truth of the proposition that the wider the circle of knowledge the greater the circumference of ignorance. He was (he thought) like some tree-feller in the midst of the deepest forest who has effected a clearing large enough for his immediate purposes; but one, too, who sees around him the widening ring of undiscovered darkness wherein the wickedness of other men would never wholly be revealed. On his recent visit to London he had felled a few more trees; and doubtless he and Lewis (before the case was closed) would fell a few more still. But the men who might have directed his steps through the trackless forest were now all dead, leaving him with an odd collection of ugly, jagged stumps; ugly, jagged, awkward clues that could only tell a stark, truncated version of the truth. But that was all he had and – almost – it was enough, perhaps.

'Tell me more about the Gilberts,' said Lewis, handing across a paper cup of tepid coffee.

'Well, you know as much about their background as I do. Just remember one thing, though. We learned they were identical twins, so closely alike that even their friends got them muddled up occasionally. But when you get to your sixties, Lewis, you're bound to differ a bit: general signs of ageing, spots on the chin, gaps in the teeth, hair-style, scars, whether you're fatter or thinner, the way you dress – almost everything is going to mark some ever-widening difference as the years go by. Now, I never saw Bert Gilbert alive – and I didn't go and look at him when he was dead. You see, it was *Alfred* Gilbert I met in Westerby's rooms that day – with a scarf wrapped round the bottom half of his face and a phoney tale about an abscessed tooth.'

'He was frightened Browne-Smith would recognize him.'

'Not just that, though. As it happened, Browne-Smith had already recognized his brother – although Alfred Gilbert wasn't to know *that*. Like all visitors, Bert had already reported to the Porters' Lodge a couple of times, and Alfred was anxious that *no one* should know that he and his brother had switched roles. He carefully selected a young assistant who'd only just joined the firm and who wouldn't know and wouldn't care which brother did what anyway—'

'But why all the bother, sir? Seems so unnecessary.'

'Ah! But you're missing the point. The plan they'd concocted demanded far more shrewdness – and, yes, far more *knowledge* – than poor Bert could ever have

coped with. Just think! It involved a close knowledge of Browne-Smith's position and duties in the College – and in the University. It involved an equally close knowledge of how final examinations work, and all the complicated procedures of results and so on. It's not *easy* to find all that stuff out. Not unless—'

'Unless *what*, sir?'

'When I went to London I found out quite a lot about Alfred Gilbert. He *wasn't* a bachelor. In fact, he was divorced about ten years ago, and his ex-wife—'

'I suppose you went to see her.'

'No. She's living in Salisbury – but I rang her up. They had one child, a son. Know what they christened him, Lewis?'

'John?'

Morse nodded. 'After the younger brother. He was a bright lad, it seems, won a place at Oxford to read Music, and got a very good "second". In fact,' Morse continued with great deliberation, 'he had viva for a "first".'

Lewis sat back in his chair. All the pieces seemed to be falling neatly into place – or almost all of them.

'Back to the main sequence of events, though. Browne-Smith went to London on Friday the 11th of July, and that doesn't leave much time before most of the class-lists are due to be posted up. So if he decides – as he does – that he's going to repeat the broad outlines of the plan, he's got to get a move on. The Gilbert brothers had to be in on it, too, of course, and no doubt Browne-Smith agrees to pay them hand-somely. There's no time for any chancy postal delay, so

Browne-Smith drafts a careful letter to Westerby, and that letter, too, was probably written on Westerby's typewriter the next day, Saturday the 12th, when Alfred Gilbert went up to Oxford again, and when Westerby was out clearing up his odds and ends at Thrupp. The letter – "By Hand" it must have been – was left on Westerby's desk, I should think—'

'How do you know all this?'

'I don't really. But what I know for sure is that Westerby turned up at an address in London at 2 p.m. on Tuesday the 15th.'

'Not Cambridge Way, though, surely? That was his *own* address.'

'No – but Alfred Gilbert wasn't short of a few vacant properties, was he? And in fact it wasn't all that far from Westerby's flat, a little place—'

'Yes, all right, sir. Go on!'

'Now we come to the most fateful moment in the case. Westerby was given the same treatment as Browne-Smith: same pattern all through, same woman, same bottles of booze, with a few drops of chloral hydrate or something slipped in. But Westerby's not so canny as Browne-Smith was, and very soon he's lying there dead to the world on a creaking bed. *But what exactly happened then?* That's the key to the case, Lewis. Messrs. W and S are waiting outside—'

'*Who*, sir?'

'They're in your statement, Lewis – the men who made the arrangements at the topless bar. Haven't you heard of W. S. Gilbert?'

'Yes, but—'

'You know what "W. S." stands for, don't you? William Schwenck!'

'Oh.'

'You know, there's *something* to be said in the Gilberts' favour: at least they had a warped sense of humour. You remember the name Soho Enterprises is registered under?'

Lewis remembered: Sullivan! He shook his head and then nodded. He knew he wasn't being very bright.

'Anyway,' continued Morse, 'Browne-Smith and Westerby are left alone. And when Westerby gradually comes round – with a splitting headache, I should think – he finds his age-long antagonist sitting on the bed beside him. And they talk – and no doubt soon they have a blazing row ... and please remember that Browne-Smith's got his old army revolver with him! And yet ... and yet, Lewis ...'

'He doesn't use it,' added Lewis in a very quiet voice.

'No. Instead they stay there talking together for a long, long time; and finally they bring one of the Gilbert brothers in – and at that point the road is twisting again to take us forward on the third and final mile.'

Morse finished his coffee, and held out the plastic cup. 'I enjoyed that, Lewis. Little more sugar this time, perhaps?'

The phone rang whilst Lewis was gone. It was Max.

'Spending most of your time in Soho, I hear, Morse.'

'I'll let you into a secret, Max. My sexual appetite grows stronger year by year. What about yours?'

'About that leg. Lewis tell you about it?'

'He did.'

'Remember that piece you put in the paper? You got the colour of your socks wrong.'

'What do you expect? I hadn't got a leg to *go* on, had I?'

'They were purple!'

'Nice colour – purple.'

'With green suede shoes?'

'You don't dress all that well yourself sometimes.'

'You said they were blue!'

'Just sticking the blinker out in the middle of a blizzard.'

'What? *What?*'

'I've not had your report yet.'

'Will it help?'

'Probably.'

'You know who it is?'

'Yes.'

'Want to tell me?'

So Morse told him; and for once the humpbacked man was lost for words.

CHAPTER THIRTY-SIX

Monday, 4th August

We near the end, with two miles and four furlongs of the long and winding road now completed.

'WE FOUND THE body,' resumed Morse, 'on Wednesday the 23rd, and the odds are that it had been in the water about three days. So the man must have been murdered either the previous Saturday or Sunday.'

'He could have been murdered a few days before that, surely?'

'No chance. He was watching the telly on the Friday night!'

Lewis let it go. If Morse was determined to mystify him, so be it. He'd not interfere again unless he could help it. But one plea he did make. 'Why don't you simply tell me what you think happened – even if you're not quite sure about it here and there?'

'All right. A *third* man goes to London on Saturday the 19th, taking up an offer which nobody in this case seems able to refuse. This time, though, all the initial palaver is probably dispensed with, and there's no intermediary stop at the topless bar. This third man is murdered – by Browne-Smith. And if *both* the Gilberts

were there, we've got four men on the scene with a body on their hands – a body they've got to get rid of. Of the four men, Westerby is wetting his pants with panic; and after a few tentative arrangements are made with him, he goes off – not, as we know, back to Oxford, but to a cheap hotel near Paddington. The other three – I think that Bert had probably kept out of the way while Westerby was still there – now confer about what can and what must be done. The body can't just be dumped anyhow and anywhere – for reasons that'll soon be clear, Lewis. It's going to be necessary, it's agreed, to sever the head, and to sever the hands. That gruesome task is performed, in London, by one of the Gilberts – I should think by Bert, the cruder of the pair – who promises Browne-Smith that the comparatively uncumbrous items he's just detached can be disposed of safely and without difficulty. Then two of the three, Browne-Smith and Bert Gilbert, drive off to Oxford in Westerby's Metro – and with Westerby's prior consent. It's probably the only car immediately available anyway; but it's got one incalculable asset, as you know, Lewis.

'Once in Oxford – this is late Sunday evening now – Browne-Smith lets himself into Lonsdale via the back door in The High and goes into his rooms and takes one item only – a suit. I'm pretty sure, by the way, that it must have been on a second trip to his rooms, later – after Westerby decided he'd little option but to cancel his Greek holiday – that he took the Lonsdale College stamp and one of his Macedonian postcards. Anyway, the two men drive out to Thrupp – the only likely stretch of water either of 'em can think of – where they

stop, without any suspicion being roused, in Westerby's car, outside Westerby's cottage, to which Bert Gilbert has the key. Once inside with the body, Gilbert is willing (what he was paid for all this we shall never know!) to perform the final grisly task – of taking off the dead man's clothes and re-dressing him in Browne-Smith's suit. Then, long after the Boat Inn is closed, the two men carry the body the hundred yards or so along to the one point where no boats are moored or can be moored: the bend in the canal by Aubrey's Bridge. The job's done. It must have been in the early hours when the two of them get back to London, where the faithless Bert returns to his faithful Emily, and Browne-Smith to his room in the Station Hotel at Paddington. All right so far?'

'Are you making some of it up, sir?'

'Of course I bloody am! But it fits the clues, doesn't it? And what the hell *else* can I do? They're all *dead*, these johnnies. I'm just using what we *know* to fill in what we *don't* know. You don't object, do you? I'm just *trying*, Lewis, to match up the facts with the psychology of the four men involved. What do *you* think happened?'

Morse always got cross (as Lewis knew) when he wasn't sure of himself, especially when 'psychology' was involved – a subject Morse affected to despise; and Lewis regretted his interruption. But one thing worried him sorely: 'Do you really think Browne-Smith would have had the belly for all that business?'

'He wasn't a congenital murderer, if that's what you

mean. But the one real mystery in this case is that one man – Browne-Smith – actually did so many inexplicable things. And there's more to come! What we've got to do, Lewis, is not to explain behaviour but to consider *facts*. And there's a very sad but also a very simple *factual* explanation of all this, as you know. I rang up a fellow in the Medical Library to learn something about brain-tumours, and he was telling me about the completely irrational behaviour that can sometimes result ... Yes ... I wonder just what Olive Mainwearing of Manchester actually *did* ...'

'Pardon, sir?'

'You see, Lewis, we're not worried about his belly – we're worried about his *mind*. Because he acted with such a weird combination of envy, cunning, remorse, and just plain *ambivalence*, that I can't begin to fathom his motives.' Morse shook his head. 'I'll tell you one thing, Lewis. I'm just beginning to realize what a fine thing it is to have a mind like mine that's mainly motivated by thoughts of booze and sex – infinitely healthier! But let's go on. Just one more point about the body. Murderers aren't usually quite as subtle as people think; and you were absolutely right, as you know, when you mentioned that pleasure-cruiser off the Bahamas or somewhere. In Max's first report he said the legs were sheared off far more neatly than the other bits – and it's now clear that a boat-propeller hit the body and lopped the legs off. Well done!'

Lewis remained silent, deciding not to raise the subject of the corpse's socks.

'Back to Browne-Smith. His actions that next week are even stranger in some ways. *Abyssus humanae conscientiae!*'

Again, even more praiseworthily, Lewis remained silent.

'On the Monday his conscience was crucifying him, and he writes me – *me* – a long letter. I just don't know why we had the devious delivery through the bank ... unless he thought he'd be giving himself a few days' grace in which he could cancel his confession. Because that's what it was. But it was something else, too. If you read the letter carefully, it contains a much more subtle message: in spite of vilifying Westerby throughout, it completely and deliberately exonerates him! And make no mistake; it was certainly Browne-Smith himself who wrote that letter. I *knew* him, and no one else could have caught that dry, exact, pernickity style. It's almost as though with one half of his fevered brain he *wanted* us – wanted *me*, one of his old pupils – to find out the whole truth; and yet at the same time the other half of his brain was trying to stop us all the time with those messages and cards ... I dunno, Lewis.'

'I think the psychologists have a word for that sort of thing,' ventured Lewis.

'Well we won't bother about that, will we!'

The phone rang in the ensuing silence.

'That's good ... Well done!' said Morse.

'Can you describe them a bit?' asked Morse.

'Yes, I thought so,' said Morse.

'No. Not the nicest job in the world, I agree. It'll be all right if I send my sergeant?' asked Morse.

'Fine. Tomorrow, then. And I'm grateful to you for ringing. It'll put a sort of finishing touch to things,' said Morse.

'Who was that, sir?'

'Do you know, there've been some thousands of occasions in my life when I've looked forward to a third pint of beer, but I can't ever recollect looking forward to a third cup of coffee before!'

He held out the plastic cup, and once more Lewis walked away.

CHAPTER THIRTY-SEVEN

Monday, 4th August

*Morse almost completes his narrative of the main events
— with a little help from his imaginative faculties.*

ONLY RECENTLY HAD Morse encountered the use of
the word 'faction' in the sense of a combination of fact
and fiction. Yet such a combination was all he could
claim in any convincing reconstruction of the final
events of the present case. While Lewis was away,
therefore, he reminded himself of the few awkward
facts remaining that had to be fitted somehow into the
puzzle: the fact that he had been forcibly (significantly?) detained for an extra half-hour after his
interrogation of the manager of the topless bar; that
the door of Number 29, Cambridge Way had (for what
reason?) been finally opened to him; that the head of
Gerardus Mercator had been prominently (accusingly?) displayed on the mantelpiece of Westerby's
living-room; that an affluent Arab, doubtless a resident
in the property, had looked round at him with such
puzzlement (and suspicion?); and that somehow (via
Browne-Smith?) Bert Gilbert had discovered Westerby's
address in London, and (via the fire-escape?) managed

to enter Westerby's room. Thus it was that when Lewis returned Morse was ready with his eschatology.

'The manager of the Flamenco, Lewis, has a wife, called "Racquel". When I got there, he tipped her the wink that something was seriously askew, and she made an urgent phonecall to "Mr Sullivan" – alias Alfred Gilbert – who in turn told her that whatever happened they'd got to keep me in the place for a while. Why? Clearly because there was something that had to be done quickly, something that *could* be done quickly, before I turned up in Cambridge Way. The Gilberts, you see, were already collecting their pickings from Browne-Smith, but not as yet from Westerby. And so to remind Westerby that *he* was still up to his neck in hot water, too, they'd decided on a most appropriate niche for a corpse's head – that space in one of Westerby's crates where another head had originally nestled. It was imperative, therefore, that one of the Gilberts – Alfred, as it turned out – should go and clear away the damning evidence waiting in Westerby's flat. But late that same morning Westerby himself decided that it was reasonably safe now for him to return to his flat, and the first thing he saw there was the head of Mercator on the mantelpiece, and he suspected the grim truth immediately. Which is more than I did, Lewis! When Alfred Gilbert let himself in, Westerby was probably just opening the fateful crate; and somehow Westerby killed him—'

'Sir! That's not good enough. *How* did he do it? And why should he *need* to do it? They were both accomplices, surely?'

Morse nodded. 'Yes, they were. But just think a
minute, Lewis, and try to picture things. Alfred Gilbert
is in a frenetic rush to reach Cambridge Way. He
doesn't know *why* the police have got on to Cambridge
Way, but he does know what they'll find if they visit
Westerby's flat. They'll find what he himself and his
brother have left there, almost certainly with the intention of some future blackmail. And, as I say, that
evidence has got to be removed with the utmost
urgency. So he lets himself into the flat, never expecting to find Westerby there, and never, I suspect, actually
seeing him anyway. Westerby's got his hearing-aid
plugged in, although, as your own notes say, Lewis, he's
only slightly deaf; and when he hears the scrape of the
key in the lock, he beats a panic-stricken retreat into
the bathroom, where he watches the intruder through
the hinged gap of the partially open door.

'Now Westerby himself hasn't the faintest idea that
the police are on their way, has he? What he *suspects* –
what he's been strongly suspecting even before opening
the crate – is that it's been Gilbert – who else? – who's
misled him so wickedly. Instead of Gilbert getting rid
of the murdered man's head, that same head is resting
even now in one of his own crates! He's just found it! I
think he sees in a flash how crude, how indescribably
callous, his so-called accomplice has been. He sees
something else, too, Lewis. He sees Gilbert walking
straight over to the crate, and at that point he *knows*
who it is who's been plotting to implicate him further –
doubtless for even more money – in this tragic and
increasingly hopeless mess. He feels in his soul a savage

compulsion to rid himself of that fiend who's kneeling over the crate, and he creeps back into the room and with all the force he can muster he stabs his screwdriver between those shoulder-blades.

'Then? Well, I can only guess that Westerby must have dragged him into the bathroom straightaway: because while there were no blood-stains on the carpet, the bathroom floor had only just been cleaned. Yes, I saw that, Lewis!

'Next, using the bunch of keys he found in Gilbert's pocket, Westerby took the body up in the lift to the top-floor flat – a flat he knew was still vacant – a flat he'd probably looked over himself when he was deciding on his future home. He locked away the body in a cupboard there, then went down again, cleaned up his own flat in his apron, and heard – at last! – someone ringing the main doorbell – me! – and *answered* it. *Why*, Lewis? Surely that's utter folly for him! Unless – unless he'd previously arranged to *meet* someone in Cambridge Way. And the only man he'd have been anxious to meet at that point is the one man he's been avoiding like the plague for the last five years of his life – Browne-Smith! But instead – he finds *me*! And he now gives the performance of his life – impersonating a concierge called "Hoskins". You knew, Lewis, he was a Londoner? Yes. It's in your admirable notes on the man. I ought to have seen through the deception earlier, though; certainly I ought to have read the signs more intelligently when one of the tenants turned round and stared so curiously at me. But it *wasn't* just me: he was staring at *two* strangers!

'During that same lunch-time there were other things afoot. Alfred Gilbert had left a message for his brother, and now it was Bert Gilbert who got round to Cambridge Way as quickly as he could. There – I'm almost sure of it! – he met Browne-Smith; and Browne-Smith told Bert Gilbert that he'd seen *me* go in, admitted by Westerby. At that moment, Bert must have seen the emergency signals flashing at full beam. He had no key – Alfred had taken the bunch – either to the front door or the back; so the two of them agreed to split up, with Browne-Smith watching the front and Bert Gilbert the back. What happened then? Gilbert saw Westerby leave! So he went round to tell Browne-Smith; and both of them were very puzzled, and very frightened. *I* was still in there, and so was Alfred Gilbert! Probably it was at that point that Bert Gilbert got to know from Browne-Smith where Westerby was staying, because it's clear that later on he *did* know. For the moment, however, they observed from a discreet distance – only to find that I didn't come *out* before the police went *in*. So they knew something had gone terribly wrong. Later, of course, they both learned of the murder of Alfred Gilbert, and they both drew their own conclusion – the *same* conclusion.

'In the days that followed Gilbert must have watched and waited, because he knew that it would now be imperative for Westerby to return to the flat to find out, one way or the other, whether the police had discovered those objects hidden in a relidded crate – objects, Lewis, which must have been a cause of recurrent nightmares to him. When Westerby finally risked

his expedition, Gilbert made no attempt to abort the mission, because it was just as valuable for himself as for Westerby. He followed his quarry back from the flat to Paddington – for all I know he might even have followed him into the gents where the London lads found the corpse's hands. By the way, Lewis, you'd better tell the missus you've got another trip tomorrow.

'But then Gilbert stopped tailing Westerby, and went along to that nearby hotel, where he found an easy access to Westerby's room – either by the fire-escape or by the seldom-tenanted reception desk. But let's leave those details to our metropolitan colleagues, shall we? They're going to find one or two people who saw something, surely? It's not our job. After Westerby got back to his room? Well, I dunno. But I'd like to bet that Westerby almost jumped out of his wilting wits when he found himself confronted by the man he thought he'd killed! You see, I doubt if at any stage Westerby was aware that there *were* two Gilberts – even less that they were still extraordinarily alike in physical appearance. Whatever the truth of that may be, Westerby was strangled in his room, and the long and tragic sequence of events has almost run its Aeschylean course.

'Not quite though. Browne-Smith had now decided that things had gone far too far, and I vaguely suspect that he was on his way to see *me* last Saturday. At least, we've got the evidence of the ticket-collector that Browne-Smith had some very urgent business here in Oxford. Pity . . . but perhaps it was for the best, Lewis. Then, the same Saturday, Bert Gilbert went home and found – as the police found – a note from his wife,

Emily, saying that she couldn't stand any more of it, and that she'd left him. And Bert Gilbert – without any doubt the bravest of the three brothers – now faced both the fear of discovery and the knowledge of failure. So he opened his seventh-floor window – and he jumped . . . Poor sod! Perhaps you think it's a bit out of character, Lewis, for Bert Gilbert to do something as cowardly as that? But it was in the family, if you remember . . .'

During this account, Morse had forgotten his coffee, and he now looked down with distaste at the dark brown skin that had formed on its surface.

'Are the pubs open yet?' he asked.

'As always, sir, I think you know the answers to your own questions better than I do.'

'Well, they will be, I should think, by the time we get to Thrupp. Yes, we're going to have a quiet little drink together, my old friend, at the end of yet another case.'

'But you haven't told me yet—'

'You're quite right. There's one big central jigsaw-piece that's missing, isn't there?'

CHAPTER THIRTY-EIGHT

Monday, 4th August

The Third Milestone

IN NORMAL CIRCUMSTANCES, thought Lewis, Morse would have looked a good deal happier as he mumbled 'Cheers' before burying his nose in the froth; but there was a sombre expression in the chief's face as he spoke quietly across a small table in the lounge-bar of the Boat Inn.

'If this case ever comes to court, Lewis, there'll be several crucial witnesses – but the most important of all of them will be the man who tries to tell the judge about the power of hatred that can spring from thwarted ambition; and there were two men in Lonsdale College who had exemplified that terrible hatred for many years.

'The particular reason for their hatred was an unusual one, perhaps – but also an extremely simple one. Each of them had failed to be elected to the Mastership of Lonsdale, the position they'd both craved. Now, as we found out, the College rules require a minimum of six of the eight votes available to be cast in favour of any candidate, and not a single vote against. So a man

would be elected with six votes in his favour and two abstentions – but not with one abstention, *and one against.* Which, in Browne-Smith's case, is exactly what happened! Again, in Westerby's case, it's exactly what happened! So you hardly need to be a roaring genius to come up with the explanation that Westerby had probably voted against Browne-Smith, and Browne-Smith against Westerby. Hence the mutual, simmering hatred of those two senior fellows.

'But let me tell you a very strange thing, Lewis. In fact, you *do* need to be a genius to understand it! Not so much now, of course – but certainly at any earlier point in the case. Let's recap. The first man who went to London was confronted with a ghost from his past – the ghost of cowardice in war. But it was *the wrong ghost* that the Gilbert brothers conjured up that day, because Browne-Smith had nothing whatsoever to do with the death of their younger brother. Then a second man went to London, and you know what I'm going to say, don't you, Lewis? He, too, was confronted with *the wrong ghost* from his own past. Westerby had *not* voted against Browne-Smith – he'd abstained. And, in turn, Westerby learned that Browne-Smith had *not* cast the solitary vote against his own election: he, too, had abstained. Yet *someone* had voted against each of them; and as they spoke together that night in London the blindingly obvious fact must have occurred to them – that it could well have been *the same man* in each case! And if it was, then they knew beyond any reasonable doubt exactly who that man must be!

'So we find a third man going to London to face his

own particular ghost – this time *the right ghost*. And soon a man is found in the canal here: a man minus a very distinguished-looking head that was framed with a luxuriant crop of grey hair; a man minus the hands – particularly minus the little finger of his left hand on which he wore the large, onyx dress-ring that he never took off, and which his murderers couldn't remove from his fleshy finger; a man minus one of those flamboyant suits of his that were famed throughout the University; a man, Lewis, who had voted against two of his colleagues in the last election for the Mastership; a man – *the* man – who by his own machinations had finally been adopted as a compromise, third-choice candidate, and duly elected *nem. con.*; the man whose own ambition was even greater than that of his other colleagues, and his practical cunning infinitely more so; the same man who at the beginning of the case invited me to try to find out what had happened to Browne-Smith – not because he was worried, but because it was his *duty* – as Head of House! Yes, Lewis! The man we found in the water here was the *Master of Lonsdale.*'

273

CHAPTER THIRTY-NINE

A Premature Epilogue

AT THE END of the Michaelmas term that followed the events recorded in these chapters, it was no great surprise for Morse (or indeed for anyone) to hear that the man whom Dr Browne-Smith had once described as 'quite a good young man' had been elected to the Mastership of Lonsdale. More of a surprise for Morse was subsequently to receive an invitation to a buffet supper in Lonsdale to celebrate Andrews' election. And, without enthusiasm, he went.

Little was said that night about the tragic past, and Morse mingled amiably enough with the college members and their guests. The food was excellent, the wine plentiful; and Morse was just on his way out, feeling that after all it hadn't been so bad, when an extraordinarily attractive woman came up to him – a woman with vivacious eyes and blonde hair piled up on her head.

'You're Chief Inspector Morse, I think.'

He nodded, and she smiled.

'You don't know me, but we spoke on the phone once – only once! I, well, I just thought I'd like to say "hello", that's all. I'm the college secretary here.' Her left hand went up to her hair to re-align a straying strand – a hand that wore no ring.

THE AUTHOR WISHES TO RECORD HIS GRATITUDE
TO THE AUTHORITIES OF BOTH WYTHAM WOODS AND
BLENHEIM PARK FOR THE INFORMATION AND HELP
THEY SO READILY GAVE HIM.
ALSO TO DETECTIVE INSPECTOR JOHN
HAYWARD, OF THE THAMES VALLEY
POLICE, AND TO SIMON JENKINS,
EDITOR OF *THE TIMES*

ACKNOWLEDGEMENTS

The author and publishers wish to thank the following who have kindly given permission for use of copyright materials:

Extract from *A Portrait of Jane Austen* by David Cecil, published by Constable Publishers;

Extract from *The Rehearsal* by Jean Anouilh, published by Methuen London;

The Observer, for a quote by Aneurin Bevan © *The Observer*;

Faber & Faber Ltd for the extract from 'La Figlia Che Piange' in *Collected Poems 1909–1962* by T. S. Eliot;

Oxford University Press for the extract from 'AUSTIN, Alfred (1835–1913)' from the *Oxford Companion to English Literature* edited by Margaret Drabble (5th edition 1985);

Don Manley for the extract from the *Chambers Crossword Manual* (Chambers 1992);

Extract from *Marriage and Morals* by Bertrand Russell, published by Unwin Hyman;

Kate Champkin for the extract from *The Sleeping Life of Aspern Williams* by Peter Champkin;

Extract from *Further Fables of Our Time*, published by Hamish Hamilton, 1956, in the UK and Commonwealth and Simon and Schuster in the US. Copyright © 1956 James Thurber. Copyright © 1984 Helen Thurber;

Weather and rain have undone it again,
And now you would never know
There was once a road through the woods
Before they planted the trees.
It is underneath the coppice and heath
And the thin anemones.
Only the keeper sees
That, where the ring-dove broods,
And the badgers roll at ease,
There was once a road through the woods.

From *The Way Through the Woods*
by Rudyard Kipling

River Thames or Isis

Woodland Boundary

GREAT WOOD

Common Piece

The Keeper's Lodge

Lords Common

Cow Park

Woodland Boundary

Lords Copse

Chalet

Rough Common

Beacon Hill

The Five Sisters

Burket's Plantation

THE SINGING WAY

My Lady's Seat

The Broad Oak

Reji's Seat

RADBROOK COMMON

THE SINGING

Bowling Alley Plantation

Duck Pond

Woodland Boundary

Healings Copse

Cowleaze Copse

Froghole Cottage

To Oxford →

Bean Wood

Oaken Holt

WYTHAM WOODS
or THE WOODS OF HAZEL

1 Mile
(approx)

3/4

1/2

1/4

0
Scale

N

Woodland
Boundary

Forest rides &
footpaths

Wytham

White Hart Inn

All Saints
Church

Wytham Abbey

Oxford Western Bypass

Woodland Boundary

Marley
Lodge

MARLEY
WOOD

Singing
Pond

HARP

PASTICKS

WAY

Boundary

THE
FOLLIES

Marley
Wood
Plantation

Botley
Lodge

CAR
PARK

Higgen's
Copse

PROLEGOMENON

Though your sins be as scarlet, they shall be whiter, yea whiter, than snow

(*Isaiah*, ch. 1, v. 18)

Whereof one cannot speak, thereof one must be silent
(Wittgenstein, *Philosophical Investigations*)

'I MUST speak to you.'

'Speak on, my child.'

'I've not often come to your church.'

'It is not my church – it is God's church. We are all children of God.'

'I've come to confess a big sin.'

'It is proper that all sins should be confessed.'

'Can all sins be forgiven?'

'When we, sinful mortals as we are, can find it in our hearts to forgive each other, think only of our infinitely merciful Father, who understands our every weakness – who knows us all far better than we know ourselves.'

'I don't believe in God.'

'And you consider that as of any great importance?'

'I don't understand you.'

'Would it not be of far greater importance if God did not believe in *you*?'

'You're speaking like a Jesuit.'

1

'Forgive me.'

'It's not you – it's *me* who wants forgiveness.'

'Do you recall Pilgrim, when at last he confessed his sins to God? How the weight of the great burden was straightway lifted from his shoulders – like the pain that eases with the lancing of an abscess?'

'You sound as if you've said that all before.'

'Those self-same words I have said to others, yes.'

'Others?'

'I cannot talk of them. Whatever it is that men and women may confess to me, they confess – through me – to God.'

'You're not really needed at all, then – is that what you are saying?'

'I am a servant of God. Sometimes it is granted me to help those who are truly sorry for their sins.'

'What about those who aren't?'

'I pray that God will touch their hearts.'

'Will God forgive them – whatever they've done? You believe that, Father?'

'I do.'

'The scenes of the concentration camps . . .'

'What scenes have you in mind, my child?'

'The "sins", Father.'

'Forgive me, once again. My ears are failing now – yet not my heart! My own father was tortured to death in a Japanese camp, in 1943. I was then thirteen years old. I know full well the difficulties of forgiveness. I have told this to very few.'

'Have you forgiven your father's torturers?'

2

'God has forgiven them, if they ever sought His forgiveness.'

'Perhaps it's more forgivable to commit atrocities in times of war.'

'There is no scale of better or of worse, whether in times of peace or in times of war. The laws of God are those that He has created. They are steadfast and firm as the fixed stars in the heavens – unchangeable for all eternity. Should a man hurl himself down headlong from the heights of the Temple, he will break himself upon the law of God; but never will he break the universal law that God has once ordained.'

'You *are* a Jesuit.'

'I am a man, too. And all men have sinned and fallen short of the glory of God.'

'Father . . .'

'Speak on, my child.'

'Perhaps you will report what I confess . . .'

'Such a thing a priest could never do.'

'But what if I *wanted* you to report it?'

'My holy office is to absolve, in the name of our Lord and Saviour, Jesus Christ, the sins of all who show a true repentance. It is not my office to pursue the workings of the Temporal Power.'

'You haven't answered my question.'

'I am aware of that.'

'What if I *wanted* you to report me to the police?'

'I would be unsure of my duty. I would seek the advice of my bishop.'

'You've never been asked such a thing before?'

'Never.'

'What if I repeat my sin?'

'Unlock your thoughts. Unlock those sinful thoughts to me.'

'I can't do that.'

'Would you tell me everything if I could guess the reasons for your refusal?'

'You could never do that.'

'Perhaps I have already done so.'

'You know who I am, then?'

'Oh yes, my child. I think I knew you long ago.'

CHAPTER ONE

A perpetual holiday is a good working definition of Hell
(George Bernard Shaw)

MORSE never took his fair share of holidays, so he told himself. So he was telling Chief Superintendent Strange that morning in early June.

'Remember you've also got to take into consideration the time you regularly spend in pubs, Morse!'

'A few hours here and there, perhaps, I agree. It wouldn't be all that difficult to work out how much—'

'"Quantify", that's the word you're looking for.'

'I'd never look for ugly words like "quantify".'

'A useful word, Morse. It means – well, it means to say how much . . .'

'That's just what I said, isn't it?'

'I don't know why I argue with you!'

Nor did Morse.

For many years now, holidays for Chief Inspector Morse of Thames Valley CID had been periods of continuous and virtually intolerable stress. And what they must normally be like for men with the extra handicaps of wives and children, even Morse for all his extravagant imagination could scarcely conceive. But for this year, for the year of our Lord nineteen hundred and ninety-two, he was resolutely determined that

5

things would be different: he would have a holiday away from Oxford. Not abroad, though. He had no wanderlust for Xanadu or Isfahan; indeed he very seldom travelled abroad at all – although it should be recorded that several of his colleagues attributed such insularity more than anything to Morse's faint-hearted fear of aeroplanes. Yet as it happened it had been one of those same colleagues who had first set things in motion.

'Lime, mate! Lime's marvellous!'

Lime?

Only several months later had the word finally registered in Morse's mind, when he had read the advertisement in *The Observer.*

THE BAY HOTEL
Lyme Regis

Surely one of the finest settings of any hotel in the West Country! We are the only hotel on the Marine Parade and we enjoy panoramic views from Portland Bill to the east, to the historic Cobb Harbour to the west. The hotel provides a high standard of comfort and cuisine, and a friendly relaxed atmosphere. There are level walks to the shops and harbour, and traffic-free access to the beach, which is immediately in front of the hotel.

For full details please write to The Bay Hotel, Lyme Regis, Dorset; or just telephone (0297) 442059.

'It gets tricky,' resumed Strange, 'when a senior man takes more than a fortnight's furlough – you realize that, of course.'

'I'm not taking more than what's due to me.'

'Where are you thinking of?'

'Lyme Regis.'

'Ah. Glorious Devon.'

'Dorset, sir.'

'Next door, surely?'

'*Persuasion* – it's where some of the scenes in *Persuasion* are set.'

'Ah.' Strange looked suitably blank.

'And *The French Lieutenant's Woman*.'

'Ah. I'm with you. Saw that at the pictures with the wife . . . Or was it on the box?'

'Well, there we are then,' said Morse lamely.

For a while there was a silence. Then Strange shook his head.

'You couldn't stick being away that long! Building sand-castles? For *over a fortnight?*'

'Coleridge country too, sir. I'll probably drive around a bit – have a look at Ottery St Mary . . . some of the old haunts.'

A low chuckle emanated from somewhere deep in Strange's belly. 'He's been dead for ages, man – more Max's cup o' tea than yours.'

Morse smiled wanly. 'But you wouldn't mind me seeing his *birth*-place?'

'It's gone. The rectory's gone. Bulldozed years ago.'

'Really?'

Strange puckered his lips, and nodded his head. 'You think I'm an ignorant sod, don't you, Morse? But let me tell you something. There was none of this child-centred nonsense when I was at school. In those days we all had to learn things off by heart – things like yer actual Ancient Bloody Mariner.'

'My days too, sir.' It irked Morse that Strange, only a year his senior, would always treat him like a representative of some much younger generation.

But Strange was in full flow.

'You don't forget it, Morse. It sticks.' He peered briefly but earnestly around the lumber room of some olden memories; then found what he was seeking, and with high seriousness intoned a stanza learned long since:

> 'All in a hot and copper sky
> The bloody sun at noon
> Right up above the mast did stand
> No bigger than the bloody moon!'

'Very good, sir,' said Morse, uncertain whether the monstrous misquotation were deliberate or not, for he found the chief superintendent watching him shrewdly.

'No. You won't last the distance. You'll be back in Oxford within the week. You'll see!'

'So what? There's plenty for me to do here.'

'Oh?'

'For a start there's a drain-pipe outside the flat that's leaking—'

Strange's eyebrows shot up. 'And you're telling me *you're* going to fix *that?*'

'I'll get it fixed,' said Morse ambiguously. 'I've already got a bit of extra piping but the, er, diameter of the cross-section is . . . rather too narrow.'

'It's too bloody *small*, you mean? Is *that* what you're trying to say?'

Morse nodded, a little sheepishly.

The score was one-all.

CHAPTER TWO

Mrs Austen was well enough in 1804 to go with her
husband and Jane for a holiday to Lyme Regis. Here we
hear Jane's voice speaking once again in cheerful tones.
She gives the news about lodgings and servants, about
new acquaintances and walks on the Cobb, about some
enjoyable sea bathing, about a ball at the local Assembly
Rooms

(David Cecil, *A Portrait of Jane Austen*)

'IF I MAY SAY SO, sir, you really are rather lucky.'

The proprietor of the only hotel on the Marine
Parade pushed the register across and Morse quickly
completed the Date – Name – Address – Car Registration – Nationality columns. As he did so, it was out of
long habit rather than any interest or curiosity that his
eye took in just a few details about the half-dozen or so
persons, single and married, who had signed in just
before him.

There had been a lad amongst Morse's fellow pupils
in the sixth form who had possessed a virtually photographic memory – a memory which Morse had much
admired. Not that his own memory was at all bad; short
term, in fact, it was still functioning splendidly. And
that is why, in one of those pre-signed lines, there was
just that single little detail which very soon would

be drifting back towards the shores of Morse's con-
sciousness . . .

'To be honest, sir, you're *very* lucky. The good lady
who had to cancel – one of our regular clients – had
booked the room as soon as she knew when we were
opening for the season, and she especially wanted – she
always wanted – a room overlooking the bay, with bath
and WC *en suite* facilities, of course.'

Morse nodded his acknowledgement of the anonymous woman's admirable taste. 'How long had she
booked for?'

'Three nights: Friday, Saturday, Sunday.'

Morse nodded again. 'I'll stay the same three nights
– if that's all right,' he decided, wondering what was
preventing the poor old biddy from once more enjoying her private view of the waves and the exclusive use
of a water-closet. Bladder, like as not.

'Enjoy your stay with us!' The proprietor handed
Morse three keys on a ring: one to Room 27; one (as
he learned) for the hotel's garage, situated two minutes' walk away from the sea front; and one for the
front entrance, should he arrive back after midnight.
'If you'd just like to get your luggage out, I'll see it's
taken up to your room while you put the car away. The
police allow our guests to park temporarily of course,
but . . .'

Morse looked down at the street-map given to him,
and turned to go. 'Thanks very much. And let's hope
the old girl manages to get down here a bit later in the
season,' he added, considering it proper to grant her a
limited commiseration.

'Afraid she won't do that.'

'No?'

'She's dead.'

'Oh dear!'

'Very sad.'

'Still, perhaps she had a pretty good innings?'

'I wouldn't call forty-one a very good innings. Would you?'

'No.'

'Hodgkin's disease. You know what that's like.'

'Yes,' lied the chief inspector, as he backed towards the exit in chastened mood. 'I'll just get the luggage out. We don't want any trouble with the police. Funny lot, sometimes!'

'They may be in your part of the world, but they're very fair to us here.'

'I didn't mean—'

'Will you be taking dinner with us, sir?'

'Yes. Yes, please. I think I'd enjoy that.'

A few minutes after Morse had driven the maroon Jaguar slowly along the Lower Road, a woman (who certainly looked no older than the one who had earlier that year written in to book Room 27) turned into the Bay Hotel, stood for a minute or so by the reception desk, then pressed the Please-Ring-For-Service bell.

She had just returned from a walk along the upper level of Marine Parade, on the west side, and out to the Cobb – that great granite barrier that circles a protective arm around the harbour and assuages the incessant pounding of the sea. It was not a happy walk. That late afternoon a breeze had sprung up from the south, the sky had clouded over, and several people now promenading along the front in the intermittent drizzle were struggling into lightweight plastic macs.

'No calls for me?' she asked, when the proprietor reappeared.

'No, Mrs Hardinge. There's been nothing else.'

'OK.' But she said it in such a way as if it weren't OK, and the proprietor found himself wondering if the call he'd taken in mid-afternoon had been of greater significance than he'd thought. Possibly not, though, for suddenly she seemed to relax, and she smiled at him – most attractively.

The grid that guarded the drinks behind reception was no longer in place and already two couples were seated in the bar enjoying their dry sherrics; and with them one elderly spinster fussing over a dachshund, one of those 'small dogs accepted at the management's discretion: £2.50 *per diem*, excluding food'.

'I think I'll have a large malt.'

'Soda?'

'Just ordinary water, please.'

'Say when.'

'"When"!'

'On your room-bill, Mrs Hardinge?'

'Please! Room fourteen.'

She sat on the green leather wall-seat just beside the main entrance. The whisky tasted good and she told herself that however powerful the arguments for total abstinence might be, few could challenge the fact that

13

after alcohol the world almost invariably appeared a kinder, friendlier place.

The Times lay on the coffee table beside her, and she picked it up and scanned the headlines briefly before turning to the back page, folding the paper horizontally, then vertically, and then studying one across.

It was a fairly easy puzzle; and some twenty minutes later her not inconsiderable cruciverbalist skills had coped with all but a couple of clues – one of them a tantalizingly half-familiar quotation from Samuel Taylor Coleridge – over which she was still frowning when the lady of the establishment interrupted her with the evening's menu, and asked if she were taking dinner.

For a few minutes after ordering Seafood Soup with Fresh Garden Herbs, followed by Guinea Fowl in Leek and Mushroom Sauce, she sat with eyes downcast and smoked a king-sized Dunhill cigarette. Then, as if on sudden impulse, she went into the glass-panelled telephone booth that stood beside the entrance and rang a number, her lips soon working in a sort of silent charade, like the mouth of some frenetic goldfish, as she fed a succession of 20p's into the coin-slot. But no one could hear what she was saying.

CHAPTER THREE

Have you noticed that life, real honest-to-goodness life,
with murders and catastrophes and fabulous inheritances,
happens almost exclusively in the newspapers?

(Jean Anouilh, *The Rehearsal*)

MORSE found his instructions fairly easy to follow. Driving from the small car park at the eastern end of Marine Parade, then turning right, then left just before the traffic lights, he had immediately spotted the large shed-like building on his left in the narrow one-way Coombe Street: 'Private Garage for Residents of The Bay Hotel'. Herein, as Morse saw after propping open the two high wooden gates, were eighteen parking spaces, marked out in diagonal white lines, nine on each side of a central KEEP CLEAR corridor. By reason of incipient spondylosis, he was not nowadays particularly skilled at reversing into such things as slanting parking bays; and since the garage was already almost full, it took him rather longer than it should have done to back the Jaguar into a happily angled position, with the sides of his car equidistant from a J-reg Mercedes and a Y-reg Vauxhall. It was out of habit as before that he scanned the number plates of the cars there; but when about a quarter of an hour earlier he'd glanced through the hotel register, at least *something* had clicked in his mind.

15

Now though? Nothing. Nothing at all.

There was no real need for Morse immediately to
explore the facilities of Room 27, and the drinks-bar
faced him as he turned into the hotel. So he ordered a
pint of Best Bitter, and sat down in the wall-seat, just by
the entrance, and almost exactly on the same square
footage of green leather that had been vacated ten
minutes earlier by one of the two scheduled occupants
of Room 14.

He should have been feeling reasonably satisfied
with life, surely? But he wasn't. Not really. At that
particular moment he longed for both the things he
had that very morning solemnly avowed to eschew for
the remaining days of his leave: cigarettes and newspapers. Cigarettes he had given up so often in the past
that he found such a feat comparatively simple; never
previously however had he decided that it would be of
some genuine benefit to his peace of mind to be wholly
free for a week or so from the regular diet of disasters
served up by the quality dailies. Perhaps that was a silly
idea too, though . . .

His right hand was feeling instinctively for the
reassuring square packet in his jacket pocket, when the
maîtresse d'hotel appeared, wished him a warm welcome, and gave him the menu. It may have been a
matter of something slightly more than coincidence
that Morse had no hesitation in choosing the Seafood
Soup and the Guinea Fowl. Perhaps not, though – and
the point is of little importance.

'Something to drink with your meal, sir?' She was a
pleasantly convivial woman, in her late forties, and

16

Morse glanced appreciatively at the décolletage of her black dress as she bent forward with the wine list.

'What do you recommend?'

'Half a bottle of Médoc? Splendid vintage! You won't do much better than that.'

'A bottle might be better,' suggested Morse.

'A bottle it shall be, sir!' – the agreement signed with mutual smiles.

'Could you open it now – and leave it on the table?'

'We always do it that way here.'

'I, er, I didn't know.'

'It likes to breathe a little, doesn't it?'

'Like all of us,' muttered Morse; but to himself, for she was gone.

He realized that he was feeling hungry. He didn't often feel hungry: usually he took most of his calories in liquid form; usually, when invited to a College gaudy, he could manage only a couple of the courses ordained; usually he would willingly exchange an entrée or a dessert for an extra ration of alcohol. But this evening he was feeling hungry, quite definitely; and just after finishing his second pint of beer (still no cigarette!) he was glad to be informed that his meal was ready. Already, several times, he had looked through the glass doors to his left, through to the dining room, where many now sat eating at their tables, white tablecloths overlaid with coverings of deep maroon, beneath the subdued lighting of crystal chandeliers. It looked inviting. Romantic, almost.

As he stood by the dining-room door for a moment,

the maîtresse was quickly at his side, expressing the hope that he wouldn't mind, for this evening, sharing a table? They had quite a few non-residents in for dinner . . .

Morse bade the good lady lose no sleep over such a trivial matter, and followed her to one of the farthest tables, where an empty place was laid opposite a woman, herself seated half-facing the wall, reading a copy of *The Times*, an emptied bowl of Seafood Soup in front of her. She lowered the newspaper, smiled in a genteel sort of way, as though it had taken her some effort to stretch her painted lips into a perfunctory salutation, before reverting her attention to something clearly more interesting than her table companion.

The room was almost completely full, and it was soon obvious to Morse that he was going to be the very last to get served. The sweet-trolley was being pushed round, and he heard the elderly couple to his right ordering some caramelized peaches with nuts and cream; but – strangely for him! – he felt no surge of impatience. In any case, the soup was very soon with him, and the wine had been there already; and all around him was goodwill and enjoyment, with a low, steady buzz of conversation, and occasionally some muted laughter. But the newspaper opposite him, for the present, remained firmly in place.

It was over the main course – his only slightly after hers – that Morse ventured his first, not exactly original, gambit:

'Been here long?'

She shook her head.

'Nor me. Only just arrived, in fact.'

'And me.' (She *could* speak!)

'I'm only here for a few days . . .'

'Me, too. I'm leaving on Sunday.'

It was the longest passage of speech Morse was likely to get, he knew, for the eyes had drifted down again to the Guinea Fowl. Stayed on the Guinea Fowl.

Bugger you! thought Morse. Yet his interest, in spite of himself, was beginning to be engaged. Her lower teeth – a little too long maybe? – were set closely together and slightly stained with nicotine; yet her gums were fresh and pink, her full mouth undoubtedly attractive. But he noticed something else as well: her mottled, tortoise-shell eyes, though camouflaged around with artificial shadow, seemed somehow darkened by a sadder, more durable shadow; and he could see an intricate little criss-cross of red lines at the outer side of either eye. She might have a slight cold, of course.

Or she might earlier have been weeping a little . . .

When the sweet-trolley came, Morse was glad that he was only halfway down the Médoc, for some cheese would go nicely with it ('Cheddar . . . Gouda . . . Stilton . . .' the waitress recited); and he ordered Stilton, just as the woman opposite had done.

Gambit Number Two appeared in order.

'We seem to have similar tastes,' he ventured.

'Identical, it seems.'

'Except for the wine.'

'Mm?'

'Would you, er, like a glass of wine? Rather good! It'll go nicely with the Stilton.'

This time she merely shook her head, disdaining to add any verbal gloss.

Bugger you! thought Morse, as she picked up *The Times* once more, unfolded the whole broadsheet in front of her, and hid herself away completely – together with her troubles.

The fingers holding the paper, Morse noticed, were quite slim and sinuous, like those of an executant violinist, with the unpainted nails immaculately manicured, the half-moons arching whitely over the well-tended cuticles. On the third finger of her left hand was a narrow-banded gold wedding ring, and above it an engagement ring with four large diamonds, set in an unusual twist, which might have sparkled in any room more brightly lit than this.

On the left of the opened double-page spread (as Morse viewed things) her right hand held the newspaper just above the crossword, and he noticed that only two clues remained to be solved. A few years earlier his eyes would have had little trouble; but now, in spite of a sequence of squints, he could still not quite read the elusive wording of the first clue, which looked like a quotation. Better luck with the other half of the paper though, held rather nearer to him – especially with the article, *the quite extraordinary article*, that suddenly caught and held and dominated his attention. At the foot of the page was the headline: 'Police pass sinister verses to Times' man', and Morse had almost made out the whole of the first paragraph –

THE LITERARY correspondent of *The Times*, Mr Howard Phillipson, has been called upon by the Oxfordshire police to help solve a complex riddle-me-ree, the answer to which is believed to pinpoint the spot where a young woman's body

– when the waitress returned to the table.

'Coffee, madame?'

'Please.'

'In the bar – or in the lounge?'

'In the bar, I think.'

'You, sir?'

'No. No, thank you.'

Before leaving, the waitress poured the last of the Médoc into Morse's glass; and on the other side of the table the newspaper was folded away. To all intents and purposes the meal was over. Curiously, however, neither seemed over-anxious to leave immediately, and for several moments they sat silently together, the last pair but one in the dining room: he, longing for a cigarette and eager to read what looked like a most interesting article; wondering, too, whether he should make one last foray into enemy territory – since, on reflection, she really did look rather attractive.

'Would you mind if I smoked?' he ventured, half-reaching for the tempting packet.

'It doesn't matter to me.' She rose abruptly, gathering up handbag and newspaper. 'But I don't think the management will be quite so accommodating.' She spoke without hostility – even worse, without interest, it seemed – as she pointed briefly to a notice beside the door:

> IN THE INTEREST OF PUBLIC HEALTH, WE
> RESPECTFULLY REQUEST YOU TO REFRAIN FROM
> SMOKING IN THE DINING AREA. THANK YOU FOR
> YOUR CO-OPERATION.

Bugger you! thought Morse.

He'd not been very sensible though, he realized that. All he'd had to do was ask to borrow the newspaper for a couple of minutes. He could *still* ask her, of course. But he wasn't going to – oh no! She could stick her bloody paper down the loo for all he cared. It didn't matter. Almost every newsagent in Lyme Regis would have a few unsold copies of yesterday's newspapers, all ready to be packaged off mid-morning to the wholesale distributors. He'd seen such things a thousand times.

She'd go to the bar, she'd said. All right, *he* would go to the lounge ... where very soon he was sitting back in a deep armchair enjoying another pint of bitter and a large malt. And just to finish off the evening, he told himself, he'd have a cigarette, just one – well, two at the very outside.

It was growing dark now – but the evening air was very mild; and as he sat by the semi-opened window he listened again to the grating roar of the pebbles dragged down by the receding tide, and his mind went to a line from 'Dover Beach':

But now I only hear its melancholy, long withdrawing roar.

Much-underrated poet, Matthew Arnold, he'd always thought.

In the bar, Mrs Hardinge was drinking her coffee, sipping a Cointreau – and, if truth be told, thinking for just a little while of the keen blue eyes of the man who had been sitting opposite her at dinner.

CHAPTER FOUR

The morning is wiser than the evening.

(Russian proverb)

MORSE rose at 6.45 the following morning, switched on his room-kettle, and made himself a cup of coffee from one of the several sachets and small milk-tubs provided. He opened the curtains and stood watching the calm sea, and a fishing boat just leaving the Cobb. Blast! He'd meant to bring his binoculars.

The gulls floated and wheeled across the esplanade, occasionally hanging motionless, as if suspended from the sky, before turning away like fighter-aircraft peeling from their formation and swooping from his vision.

The sun had already risen, a great ball of orange over the cliffs to the east, over Charmouth – where they said someone had discovered a dinosaur or a pterodactyl, or something, that had lived in some distant prehistoric age, some figure with about twelve noughts after it. Or was it twenty?

Deciding that he really ought to learn more about the world of natural history, Morse drained his coffee and without shaving walked down to the deserted ground floor, out of the hotel, and left along Marine Parade – where his search began.

The newsagent on the corner felt pretty sure that he

hadn't got a previous day's *Times*. *Sun*, yes; *Mirror*, yes; *Express*, yes . . . but, no – no *Times*. Sorry, mate. Turning left, Morse struggled up the steep incline of Broad Street. Still out of breath, he enquired in the newsagent's shop halfway up on the left. *Telegraph, Guardian, Independent* – any good? No? Sorry, sir. Morse got another 'sir' in the newsagent's just opposite – but no *Times*. He carried on to the top of the hill, turned left at a rather seedy-looking cinema, then left again into Cobb Road, and down to the western end of Marine Parade – where a fourth newsagent was likewise unable to assist, with the chief inspector reduced in rank to 'mate' once more.

Never mind! Libraries kept back numbers of all the major dailies; and if he were desperate – which he most certainly *wasn't* – he could always go down on his knees and beg Mrs Misery-guts to let him take a peek at her newspaper. If she'd still got it . . . Forget it, Morse! What's it matter, anyway?

What's *she* matter?

Strolling briskly now along the front, Morse breathed deeply on the early-morning air – cigarettes were going to be *out* that day. Completely out. He had, he realized, just walked a sort of rectangle; well, a 'trapezium' really – that was the word: a quadrilateral with two parallel sides. And doubtless he would have told himself it wouldn't be a bad idea to brush up on his geometry had he not caught sight of a figure in front of him, about two hundred yards distant. For there, beneath the white canopy of the buff-coloured Bay Hotel, with its yellow two-star AA sign, stood Mrs

25

Hardinge, Mrs Crabcrumpet herself, dressed in a full-length black leather coat, and searching in a white shoulder-bag. For a purse, probably? But before she could find it she raised her right hand in greeting as a taxi drew up along the lower road, its driver manoeuvering 180 degrees in the turning area, then getting out and opening the near-side rear door for the elegant, luggageless woman who had just walked down the ramp. Morse, who had stopped ostensibly to survey the ranks of fruit machines in the Novelty Emporium, looked down at his wrist-watch: 7.50 a.m.

The ground floor was still deserted, and as yet no delicious smell of fried bacon betrayed the opening of the hostelry's daily routine. Morse passed by the giant potted-palm, passed by the statue of a maiden perpetually pouring a slow trickle from her water-jug into the pool at her feet, and was starting up the stairs when his eye fell on the reception desk to his right: a jar of artificial flowers; a tray of mineral water; a yellow RNLI collecting box; and below a stack of brochures and leaflets – the hotel register. He glanced around him. No one.

He looked swiftly along the linear information once again:

3.7.92 – Mr and Mrs ¢ A Hardinge – 16 Cathedral Mews, Salisbury – H 35 LWL – British – Rm 14

It had been the Oxfordshire letter-registration, LWL, which had caught his eye that previous evening. Now it was something else: that ¢. It was her all right though, for he'd seen the room number on her key-ring at dinner. And frowning slightly as he mounted the stairs, he found himself wondering how many married women were unable to write out the accepted formula for their wedded state without getting the wrong initial. Perhaps she was only recently married? Perhaps she was one of those liberated ladies who had suddenly decided that if only *one* initial were required it was going to be hers? Perhaps ... perhaps they weren't 'Mr and Mrs' at all, and she had been momentarily confused about what names they were going under *this* time?

The latter, he thought – a little sadly.

Breakfast (8.45 a.m.–9.30 a.m.) was for Morse a solitary affair, yet he was finding it, as ever, the biggest single joy of any holiday. After some Kellogg's Corn Flakes and a mixed grill, he strolled along the edge of the sea once more, feeling pleasantly replete and (he supposed) about as content as he was ever likely to be. The weather forecast was good, and he decided that he would drive out west to Ottery St Mary and then, if the mood took him, north up to Nether Stowey, and the Quantocks.

As he reached the second-floor landing after his return to the hotel, Room 14 was almost directly in front of him; and with the door slightly ajar, as one blue-uniformed room-maid came out with a hoover, he could see another maid inside the room replenishing the sachets of coffee and tea and the little tubs of milk. He took his chance. Knocking (not too hesitantly), he put his head round the door.

'Mrs Hardinge in?'

'No, sur.' She looked no more than eighteen, and Morse felt emboldened.

'It's just that she promised to keep yesterday's newspaper for me – we had dinner here together last night. *The Times*, it was.'

The maid gave Morse a dubious look as he cast a swift glance over the room. The bed nearer the window had been slept in – the pillow deeply indented, a flimsy black negligée thrown carelessly over the duvet. But had *Mr* Hardinge slept in the other? The bed could have been made up already, of course ... but where was his case and his clothes and his other impedimenta?

'I'm afraid there's no newspaper as I can see 'ere, sur. In any case, I wouldn't—'

'Please, please! I fully understand. I mean, if it's not in the waste-paper basket . . .'

'No, it's not.'

'There'd be another basket, though? In the bathroom? It's just that she *did* say . . .'

The young girl peered cautiously round the bathroom door, but shook her head.

Morse smiled affably. 'It's all right. She must have left it somewhere else for me. Probably in *my* room. Huh! Sorry to have bothered you.'

Back in Room 27, he found his own bed made up, the floor hoovered, and his coffee cup washed and placed upside-down on its matching saucer. He stood for several minutes looking out at the sea again, telling himself he must re-read *The Odyssey*; and soon, almost unconsciously, finding himself smoking one of his forbidden cigarettes and wondering why the brown leather suitcase he had just seen lying closed on the set of drawers in Room 14 bore, in an attractive Gothic script, the gilt letters 'C S O'. The only thing he knew with such initials was Community Service Order – but that seemed wholly unlikely. Must be *her* initials, surely. But whatever the C stood for – Carole? Catherine? Claire? Celia? Constance? – it was going to be obvious even to an under-achiever in the new seven-year-old reading tests that the O didn't stand for 'Hardinge'. It may reasonably have been the lady's surname before she got married. But the case was a new one – a very new one . . .

So what, Morse! So bloody *what*!

He sat down and wrote a note.

Dear Mrs H, I shall be most grateful if you can save yesterday's Times for me. Not the Business/Sport section; just the main newspaper – in fact I only really want to look at the bit on p. 1 (and probably a continuation on an inside page) about the 'Sinister Verses' article. Your reward, which you <u>must</u> accept, will be a drink on me at the bar before dinner, when I promise to adhere religiously to every one of the management's ordinances.

Room 27

Leaving this innocent, if rather pompous, communication with the proprietor, Morse walked along to the private garage, pondering the reason why the female half of Room 14 had not made use of car H 35 LWL instead of ordering a taxi. Pondering only briefly though, since he thought he now knew why Mrs C.

Something (Hardinge?) had been acting so strangely. Well, no – not 'strangely', not if you looked at it from *her* point of view. Forget it, Morse! Get your road atlas out and trace the easiest route to Ottery St Mary.

Soon the Jaguar was on its way, with the sun growing warmer by the minute, and hardly a cloud in the bluest of skies. By the time he reached Honiton, Morse had almost forgotten the rather odd fact that when he had looked just now around the other cars in the hotel's garage, there had been no sign whatsoever of any vehicle with the registration H 35 LWL.

CHAPTER FIVE

Extract from a diary dated 26 June 1992 (one week
before Morse had found himself in Lyme Regis)

Words! Someone – a Yank I think – said you can stroke
people with words. I say – sod words! Especially sod the
sight of words. They're too powerful. 'Naked's powerful.
'Breasts' are powerful. Larkin said he thought the most
splendid verb in the language was 'unbutton'. But when
the words are a joke? Oh God, help me! Please God,
help me! Yesterday Tom wrote me a letter from his new
house in Maidstone. Here's part of what he wrote

> I've got a pair of great tits in the garden here. Now
> don't you go and think that when I look down from
> my study window with the binoes you bought me
> there's this bronzed and topless and vasty bosomed
> signora sunning herself on a Lilo. No! Just a
> wonderfully entertaining little pair of great tits
> who've taken up residence – a bit late aren't they? –
> in the nesting-box we fixed under the beech tree.
> Remember that line we learned at school?
> Titvre tu patulae recubans sub tegmine fagi . . .

Those are Tom's words. Wouldn't you think that any
normally civilized soul would be delighted with the
thought of those little blue black white yellow birds (my

31

speciality!!) slipping their slim little selves into a nesting-box? Wouldn't you think that only a depraved and perverted mind would dwell instead upon that picture of a woman on a sunbed? Wouldn't you think that any sensitive soul would rejoice in that glorious Virgilian hexameter instead of seeing another 'tit' in the opening word? Christ, it was only a pun wasn't it! The Greek term is 'paronomasia'. I'd forgotten that but I just looked it up in my book of literary terms. And still the words follow me. Looking through the p's I found 'pornography' again. Words! Bloody hell. God help me!

> 'Common subjects of such exotic pornography are
> sadism, masochism, fetishism, transvestism,
> voyeurism (or scoptolagnia), narcissism, pederasty,
> and necrophilia. Less common subjects are
> coprophilia, kleptolagnia, and zoophilia.'

Should it be a fraction of comfort that my tastes don't yet run to these last three 'less common' perversions — if that's the right word. What does the middle one mean anyway? It's not in Chambers.

(Later) Dinner in SCR <u>very</u> good — 'Barbue Housman'. I phoned C afterwards and I almost dare to believe she's really looking forward to next weekend. I just wish I could go to sleep and wake up on the 3rd. But I seem to spend half my time wishing my life away. I have drunk too much. Oh God, let me sleep well!

CHAPTER SIX

... and hence through life
Chasing chance-started friendships
(Samuel Taylor Coleridge,
'To the Revd George Coleridge')

IN MID-AFTERNOON Morse looked back on his Coleridge pilgrimage with considerable disappointment.

Half a dozen miles west of Honiton he had turned left off the A30 for the little market town of Ottery St Mary. Parking had proved a virtually insuperable problem; and when he finally got to the Information Office he learned only that 'Coleridge was born here in 1772 at the Rectory (gone), the tenth child of The Revd J. Coleridge, vicar 1760–81, and master of the Grammar School (gone). The rapidly growing family soon occupied the old School House (gone) ...'. St Mary's was still there though, and he walked around the large church consulting some printed notes on 'Points of Interest', fixed to a piece of wood shaped like a hand-mirror. He began to feel, as he read, that it was high time he re-familiarized himself with 'corbels' and 'mouldings' and 'ogees'; but it was something of a surprise that the author of the notes appeared never to have heard of Coleridge. Indeed it was only by accident that as he was leaving the church he spotted a memorial plaque on the churchyard wall, with a low-relief bust of the poet beneath the outspread wings of an albatross.

An hour and a half later, after a fast drive up the M5, Morse was equally disappointed with the village of Nether Stowey. 'The small thatched cottage, damp and uncomfortable' wherein Coleridge had lived in 1796 was now enlarged, tiled, and (doubtless) centrally heated, too. More to the point, it was closed to the public – on Saturdays; and today was Saturday. Inside the church the leaflet available for visitors ('Please take – quite free!') was a singularly uninformative document, and Morse felt no inclination to heed the vicar's exhortation to join the church fellowship – 'emphasis ever on joyous informality'. He put 50p in a slot in the wall and joylessly began the drive back to Lyme Regis.

Perhaps Strange had been right all along. Perhaps he, Morse, was the sort of person who could never really enjoy a holiday. Even the pint of beer he'd drunk in a rather dreary pub in Nether Stowey had failed to satisfy, and he didn't really know what he wanted. Or rather he did: he wanted a cigarette for a start; and he wanted something to engage his brain, like a cryptic crossword or a crime – or the previous day's issue of *The Times*. But there was something else too, though he was hardly prepared to admit it even to himself: he would have wished Mrs Hardinge (or Mrs Whatever) to be beside him in the passenger seat.

A voice in his brain told him that he was being quite extraordinarily foolish. But he didn't listen.

*

At 3.45 p.m. he parked the Jaguar in the hotel garage: only three other cars there now – none of the three with the Oxon registration.

At the Corner Shop on Marine Parade, he succumbed to two temptations, and resisted a third. He bought twenty Dunhill International, and a copy of *The Times*; but the magazine with the seductively posed, semi-clad siren on its glossy cover remained on the top shelf – if only because he would be too embarrassed and ashamed to face the hard-eyed man behind the counter.

Back in the hotel, he took a leisurely bath and then went down to the residents' lounge, where he unfolded the cover from the full-sized billiard table, and for half an hour or so pretended he was Steve Davis. After all, didn't *The Oxford Companion to Music* devote one entire page to 'Mozart on the Billiard Table'? Morse, however, was unable to pot virtually anything, irrespective of angle or distance; and just as carefully as he had unfolded the cover he now replaced it, and returned to his room, deciding (if life should allow) to brush up on his cuemanship as well as on that glossary of architec tural terms. This was exactly why holidays were so valuable, he told himself: they allowed you to stand back a bit, and see where you were going rusty.

It was whilst lying fully clothed on his single bed, staring soberly at the ceiling, that there was a knock on the door and he got up to open it. It was the proprietor himself, carrying a Sainsbury's supermarket carrier bag.

'Mrs Hardinge wanted you to have this, Mr Morse. I tried to find you earlier, but you were out – and she insisted I gave it to you personally.'

What was all this to Morse's ears? Music! Music! Heavenly music!

Inside the carrier bag was the coveted copy of *The Times*, together with a 'Bay Hotel' envelope, inside which, on a 'Bay Hotel' sheet of note-paper, was a brief letter:

For 27 from 14. I've seen a paperback called The Bitch by one of the Collins sisters. I've not read it but I think it must be all about me, don't you? If I'm not at dinner I'll probably be in soon after and if you're still around you can buy me a brandy. After all these newspapers do cost honest money you know!

For Morse this innocent missive was balm and manna to the soul. It was as if he'd been trying to engage the attention of a lovely girl at a dinner party who was apparently ignoring him, and who now suddenly leaned forward and held her lips against his cheek in a more than purely perfunctory kiss.

Strangely, however, before reading the article, Morse picked up the bedside phone and dialled police HQ at Kidlington.

CHAPTER SEVEN

I read the newspaper avidly. It is my one form of continuous fiction

(Aneurin Bevan, quoted in *The Observer*, 3 April 1960)

POLICE PASS SINISTER VERSES TO TIMES' MAN

THE LITERARY correspondent of *The Times*, Mr Howard Phillipson, has been called upon by the Oxfordshire police to help solve a complex riddle-me-ree, the answer to which is believed to pinpoint the spot where a young woman's body may be buried.

The riddle, in the form of a five-stanza poem, was sent anonymously by a person who (as the police believe) knows the secret of a crime which for twelve months has remained on the unsolved-case shelves in the Thames Valley Police HQ at Kidlington, Oxfordshire.

'The poem is a fascinating one,' said Mr Phillipson, 'and I intend to spend the weekend trying to get to grips with it. After a brief preliminary look I almost think that the riddle has a strong enough internal logic to be solvable within its own context, but we must wait and see.'

According to Detective Chief Inspector Harold Johnson of Thames Valley CID the poem would fairly certainly appear to have reference to the disappearance of a Swedish student whose rucksack was found in a layby on the northbound carriageway of the A44, a mile or so south of Woodstock, in July 1991. Documents found in the side-panels of the rucksack had identified its owner as Karin Eriksson, a student from Uppsala, who had probably hitchhiked her way from London to Oxford, spent a day or so in the University City – and then? Who knows?

'The case was always a baffling one,' admitted DCI Johnson. 'No body was ever found, no suspicious circumstances uncovered. It is not unknown for students to be robbed of their possessions, or lose them. And of course some of them run away. But we've always thought of this as a case of potential murder.'

At the time of her disappearance, Miss Eriksson's mother informed the police that Karin had phoned her from London a week or so previously, sounding 'brisk and optimistic', albeit rather short of cash. And the Principal of the secretarial college where Karin was a student described her as 'an attractive, able, and athletic young lady'. Since the discovery of the rucksack, no trace whatever has been found, although senior police officers were last night suggesting that this new development might throw fresh light on one or two possible clues discovered during the earlier investigation.

The poem in full reads as follows:

Find me, find the Swedish daughter –
    Thaw my frosted tegument!
Dry the azured skylit water,
    Sky my everlasting tent.

Who spied, who spied that awful spot?
    O find me! find the woodman's daughter!
Ask the stream: 'Why tell'st me not
    The truth thou know'st – the tragic slaughter?'

38

Ask the tiger, ask the sun
    Whither riding, what my plight?
Till the given day be run,
    Till the burning of the night.

Thyme, I saw Thyme flow'ring here
    A creature white trapped in a gin,
Panting like a hunted deer
    Licking still the bloodied skin.

With clues surveyed so wondrous laden,
    Hunt the ground beneath thy feet!
Find me, find me now, thy maiden,
    I will kiss thee when we meet.

A. Austin
(1853–87)

The lines were typed on a fairly old-fashioned machine, and police are hopeful that forensic tests may throw up further clues. The only immediately observable idiosyncracies of the typewriter used are the worn top segment of the lower-case 'e', and the slight curtailment of the cross-bar in the lower-case 't'.

'To be truthful,' admitted Chief Inspector Johnson, 'not many of my colleagues here are all that hot on poetry, and that's why we thought *The Times* might help. It would be a sort of poetic justice if it could.' Final word with Mr Phillipson: 'It might all be a cruel hoax, and the link with the earlier case does appear rather tenuous, perhaps. But the police certainly seem to think they are on to something. So do I!'

Morse read the article at his own pace; then again, rather more quickly. After which, for several minutes, he sat where he was, his eyes still, his expression quite emotionless – before turning to the back page and reading the clue he hadn't quite been able to see the evening before:

'Work without hope draws nectar in a—' (Coleridge) (5).

Huh! If the poem was a 'riddle', so was the answer! A quotation from Coleridge, too! Half smiling, he sat back in his chair and marvelled once more at the frequency of that extraordinarily common phenomenon called 'coincidence'.

Had he but known it, however, a far greater coincidence had already occurred the previous evening when (purely by chance, surely?) he had been ushered into the dining room to share a table with the delectable occupant of Room 14. But as yet he couldn't know such a thing; and taking from his pocket his silver Parker pen, he wrote 'I' and 'V' in the empty squares which she had left in S-E-E – before reaching for the telephone again.

'No, sir – Superintendent Strange is still not answering. Can anyone else help?'

'Yes, perhaps so,' said Morse. 'Put me through to Traffic Control, will you?'

CHAPTER EIGHT

Extract from a diary dated 2 July 1992 (one day before
Morse had found himself in Lyme Regis)

I must write a chapter on 'Gradualism' in my definitive
opus on pornography, for it is the <u>gradual</u> nature of the
erotic process that is all important, as even that old
fascist Plato had the nous to see. Yet this is a factor
increasingly forgotten by the writers and the film-
directors and the video-makers. If they ever knew it.
'Process' is what it should be all about. The process
typified in the lifting of a full-length skirt to a point just
above the ankle, or the first unfastening of a button on
a blouse! Do I make things clear? Without the skirt,
what man will glory in the ankle? Without the blouse,
what man will find himself aroused by the mere button?
Nudity itself is nothing: it is the intent of nudity which
guarantees the glorious engagement. Never did nudity in
itself mean very much to me, even when I was a young
boy. Never did I have any interest in all those Italian
paintings of naked women. Likewise it seems to me that
few of our licentious and promiscuous youth take
overmuch notice of the women who flaunt their bodies
daily in the tabloid press. Such young men are more
interested in back-page soccer stories. Is there a moral
here?

I've just read through all that shit I've just written

and it makes me sound almost sane. Almost as if I'd laugh outright at any quack who suggested that I ought to go along and see somebody. But in truth there's not much to laugh about considering the wreck I've now become – I've always been perhaps. These others are bloody lucky. Christ, how lucky they are! They have their erotic fancies and imaginings and get their fixes from their filthy mags and porno flicks and casual sex. But me? Ha! I study those articles in the quality press about the effects of pornography on the sex-crime statistics. That's what the civilized sex maniacs do. Does then pornography have the effect that is claimed? I doubt it. Yet I wish it did. Yes! Then almost everyone would be committing some dreadful sex-offence each day. I know – of course I do! – that such a state of affairs wouldn't be all that bloody marvellous for the goody-goody girls who've been guarding their virginity. But at least I would be normal! I would be normal.

Come on Time! Hurry along there! It is tomorrow that I see her and I can hardly wait to watch the hours go by. Why do I wait? Because although I have never really loved my wife (or my children all that much) I would sacrifice almost everything in my life if by so doing I could spare her the despairing humiliation of learning about my own shame.

(Later) I picked up The Guardian in the SCR and read about a Jap who murdered a young model and feasted off her flesh for a fortnight. They didn't keep him in jail very long because he was manifestly crackers. But when they transferred him to a loony asylum he kicked up such a fuss that they didn't keep him there long either. Why? Because the authorities became convinced that he was normal. After they'd let him go he said to a newspaper reporter: 'My time in the mental ward was like Hell. Everyone else in there was real crazy, but the doctors saw that I wasn't like the rest of them. They saw I was normal. So they let me go.' I wasn't too upset about what this weirdo said. What really upset me was what the reporter said. He said the most distressing aspect of this strange and solitary cannibal was the fact that he really believed himself to be normal! Don't you see what I'm saying?

CHAPTER NINE

And I wonder how they should have been together!
(T. S. Eliot, *La Figlia Che Piange*)

HE MADE his way from the dining room to the bar.
The meal had been a lonely affair; but Morse was never
too worried about periods of loneliness, and felt himself
unable to appreciate the distinction that some folk
made between solitude and loneliness. In any case, he'd
enjoyed the meal. Venison, no less! He now ordered a
pint of Best Bitter and sat down, his back to the sea,
with the current issue of *The Times*. He looked at his
wrist-watch, wrote the time (8.21) in the small rectangle
of space beside the crossword, and began.

At 8.35, as he struggled a little over the last two clues,
he heard her voice:

'Not finished it yet?'

Morse felt a sudden rush of happiness.

'Mind if I join you?' She sat down beside him, to his
right, on the wall-seat. 'I've ordered some coffee. Are
you having any?'

'Er, no. Coffee's never figured all that prominently
in my life.'

'Water neither, by the look of things.'

Morse turned towards her and saw she was smiling at
him. 'Water's all right,' he admitted ' – in moderation.'

'Not original!'

'No. Mark Twain.'

A young bow-tied waiter had brought the coffee, and she poured an almost full cup before adding a little very thick cream; and Morse looked down at those slim fingers as she circled the spoon in a slow-motion, almost sensual stir.

'You got the paper?'

Morse nodded his gratitude. 'Yes.'

'Let me tell you something – I'm not even going to ask why you wanted it so badly.'

'Why not?'

'Well, for one thing, you told me in your note.'

'And for another?'

She hesitated now, and turned to look at him. 'Why don't you offer me a cigarette?'

Morse's new-found happiness scaled yet another peak.

'What's your name?' she asked.

'Morse. They, er, call me Morse.'

'Odd name! What's your surname?'

'That *is* my surname.'

'As well? Your name's Morse Morse? Like that man in *Catch 22*, isn't it? Major Major Major.'

'Didn't he have *four* Majors?'

'You read a lot?'

'Enough.'

'Did you know the Coleridge quotation? I could see you looking at the crossword last night.'

'Hadn't you got the paper twixt thee and me?'

'I've got X-ray eyes.'

Morse looked at her eyes, and for a few seconds looked deeply *into* her eyes – and saw a hazel-green concoloration there, with no sign now of any bloodshot webbing. 'I just happened to know the quote, yes.'

'Which was?'

'The answer was "sieve".'

'And the line goes?'

'Two lines actually, to make any sense of things:

> "Work without Hope draws nectar in a sieve,
> And Hope without an object cannot live."'

'You *do* read a lot.'

'What's your name?'

'Louisa.'

'And what do you do, Louisa?'

'I work for a model agency. No, that's wrong. I am a model agency.'

'Where are you from?'

'From a little village just south of Salisbury, along the Chalke Valley.'

Morse nodded vaguely. 'I've driven through that part once or twice. Combe Bissett? Near there, is it?'

'Quite near, yes. But what about you? What do *you* do?'

'I'm a sort of glorified clerk, really. I work in an office – nine-to-five man.'

'Whereabouts is that?'

'Oxford.'

'Lovely city!'

'You know Oxford?'

'Why don't you buy me a large brandy?' she asked softly in his ear.

Morse put the drinks on his room-bill and returned with one large brandy and one large malt Scotch. Several other couples were enjoying their liqueurs in that happily appointed bar and Morse looked out from the window at the constantly whitening waves before placing the drinks side by side on the table.

'Cheers!'

'Cheers!'

'You're a liar,' she said.

The three words hit Morse like an uppercut, and he had no time to regain his balance before she continued, mercilessly:

'You're a copper. You're a chief inspector. And judging from the amount of alcohol you get through you're probably never in your office much after opening time.'

'Is it *that* obvious – I'm a copper, I mean?'

'Oh no! Not obvious at all. I just saw your name and address in the register and my husband – well, he happens to have heard of you. He says you're supposed to be a bit of a whizz-kid in the crime world. That's all.'

'Do I know your husband?'

'I very much doubt it.'

'He's not here—'

'What are *you* doing in Lyme?'

'Me? I dunno. Perhaps I'm looking for some lovely, lonely lady who wouldn't call me a liar even if she thought I was.'

'You deny it? You deny you're a copper?'

Morse shook his head. 'No. It's just that when you're on holiday, well, sometimes you want to get away from the work you do – and sometimes you tell a few lies, I suppose. Everyone tells a few lies occasionally.'

'They do?'

'Oh yes.'

'Everyone?'

Morse nodded. 'Including you.' He turned towards her again, but found himself unable to construe the confusing messages he read there in her eyes.

'Go on,' she said quietly.

'I think you're a divorced woman having an affair with a married man who lives in Oxford. I think the pair of you occasionally get the opportunity of a weekend together. I think that when you do, you need an accommodation address and that you use your own address, which is not in the Chalke Valley but in the Cathedral Close at Salisbury. I think you came here by coach on Friday afternoon and that your partner, who was probably at some conference or other in the area, was scheduled to get here at the same time as you. But he didn't show up. And since you'd already booked your double room you registered and took your stuff up to your room, including a suitcase with the initials "C S O" on it. You suspected something had gone sadly wrong, but as yet you daren't use the phone to find out. You had no option but to wait. I think a call did come through eventually, explaining the situation; and you were deeply disappointed and upset – upset enough to shed a tear or two. This morning you hired a taxi to take you to meet this fellow who had let you down, and I think you've spent the day together somewhere. You're back here now because you'd booked the weekend break anyway, and your partner probably gave you a cheque to cover the bill. You'll be leaving in the morning, hoping for better luck next time.'

Morse had finished – and there was a long silence between them, during which he drained his whisky, she her brandy.

'Another?' asked Morse.

'Yes. But I'll get them. The cheque he gave me was more than generous.' The voice was matter-of-fact, harder now, and Morse knew that the wonderful magic had faded. When she returned with the drinks, she changed her place and sat primly opposite him.

'Would you believe me if I said the suitcase I brought with me belongs to my mother, whose name is Cassandra Samantha Osborne?'

'No,' said Morse. For a few seconds he thought he saw a sign of a gentle amusement in her eyes, but it was soon gone.

'What about this – this "married man who lives in Oxford"?'

'Oh, I know all about him.'

'You *what*?' Involuntarily her voice had risen to a falsetto squeak, and two or three heads had turned in her direction.

'I rang up the Thames Valley Police. If you put any car number through the computer there—'

'—you get the name and address of the owner in about ten seconds.'

'About *two* seconds,' amended Morse.

'And you did *that?*'

'I did that.'

'God! You're a regular shit, aren't you?' Her eyes blazed with anger now.

'S'funny, though,' said Morse, ignoring the hurt. 'I know *his* name – but I still don't know *yours.*'

'Louisa, I told you.'

'No. I think not. Once you'd got to play the part of Mrs Something Hardinge, you liked the idea of "Louisa". Why not? You may not know all that much about Coleridge. But about Hardy? That's different. You remembered that when Hardy was a youth he fell in love with a girl who was a bit above him in class and wealth and privilege, and so he tried to forget her. In fact he spent all the rest of his life trying to forget her.'

She was looking down at the table as Morse went gently on: 'Hardy never really spoke to her. But when he was an old man he used to go and stand over her unmarked grave in Stinsford churchyard.'

It was Morse's turn now to look down at the table.

'Would you like some more coffee, madame?' The waiter smiled politely and sounded a pleasant young chap. But 'madame' shook her head, stood up, and prepared to leave.

'Claire – Claire Osborne – that's my name.'

'Well, thanks again – for the paper, Claire.'

'That's all right.' Her voice was trembling slightly and her eyes were suddenly moist with tears.

'Shall I see you for breakfast?' asked Morse.

'No. I'm leaving early.'

'Like this morning.'

'Like this morning.'

'I see,' said Morse.

'Perhaps you see too much.'

'Perhaps I don't see enough.'

'Goodnight – Morse.'

'Goodnight. Goodnight, Claire.'

When an hour and several drinks later Morse finally decided to retire, he found it difficult to concentrate on anything else except taking one slightly swaying stair at a time. On the second floor, Room 14 faced him at the landing; and if only a line of light had shown itself at the foot of that door, he told himself that he might have knocked gently and faced the prospect of the wrath to come.

But there was no light.

Claire Osborne herself lay awake into the small hours, the duvet kicked aside, her hands behind her head, seeking to settle her restless eyes; seeking to fix them on some putative point about six inches in front of her nose. Half her thoughts were still with the conceited, civilized, ruthless, gentle, boozy, sensitive man with whom she had spent the earlier hours of that evening;

the other half were with Alan Hardinge, Dr Alan
Hardinge, fellow of Lonsdale College, Oxford, whose
young daughter, Sarah, had been killed by an articu-
lated lorry as she had cycled down Cumnor Hill on her
way to school the previous morning.

CHAPTER TEN

Mrs Kidgerbury was the oldest inhabitant of Kentish
Town, I believe, who went out charing, but was too
feeble to execute her conceptions of that art
(Charles Dickens, *David Copperfield*)

WITH A sort of expectorant 'phoo', followed by a
cushioned 'phlop', Chief Superintendent Strange sat
his large self down opposite Chief Inspector Harold
Johnson. It was certainly not that he enjoyed walking
up the stairs, for he had no pronounced adaptability
for such exertions; it was just that he had promised his
very slim and very solicitous wife that he would try to
get in a bit of exercise at the office wherever possible.
The trouble lay in the fact that he was usually too feeble
in both body and spirit to translate such resolve into
execution. But not on the morning of Tuesday, 30 June
1992, four days before Morse had booked into the Bay
Hotel . . .

The Chief Constable had returned from a fortnight's
furlough the previous day, and his first job had been to
look through the correspondence which his very competent secretary had been unable, or unauthorized, to
answer. The letter containing the 'Swedish Maiden'

verses had been in the in-tray (or so she thought) for about a week. It had come (she thought she remembered) in a cheap brown envelope addressed (she *did* almost remember this) to 'Chief Constable Smith (?)'; but the cover had been thrown away – sorry! – and the stanzas themselves had lingered there, wasting as it were their sweetness on the desert air – until Monday the 29th.

The Chief Constable himself had felt unwilling to apportion blame: five stanzas by a minor poet named Austin were not exactly the pretext for declaring a state of national emergency, were they? Yet the 'Swedish' of the first line combined with the 'maiden' of the penultimate line had inevitably rung the bell, and so he had in turn rung Strange, who in turn had reminded the CC that it was DCI Johnson who had been – was – in charge of the earlier investigations.

A photocopy of the poem was waiting on his desk that day when Johnson returned from lunch.

It had been the following morning, however, when things had really started to happen. This time, certainly, it *was* a cheap brown envelope, addressed to 'Chief Constable Smith (?), Kidlington Police, Kidlington' (nothing else on the cover), with a Woodstock postmark, and a smudged date that could have been '27 June', that was received in the post room at HQ, and duly placed with the CC's other mail. The letter was extremely brief:

> Why are you doing nothing about my letter?
> Karin Eriksson

The note-paper clearly came from the same wad as that used for the first letter: 'Recycled Paper – OXFAM ● Oxford ● Britain' printed along the bottom. There was every sign too that the note was written on the same typewriter, since the four middle characters of 'letter' betrayed the same imperfections as those observable in the Swedish Maiden verses.

This time the CC summoned Strange immediately to his office.

'Prints?' suggested Strange, looking up from the envelope and note-paper which lay on the table before him.

'Waste o' bloody time! The envelope? The postman who collected it – the sorter – the postman who delivered it – the post room people here – the girl who brought it round – my secretary . . .'

'*You*, sir?'

'And me, yes.'

'What about the letter itself?'

'You can try if you like.'

'I'll get Johnson on to it—'

'I don't want Johnson. He's no bloody good with this sort of case. I want Morse on it.'

'He's on holiday.'

'First I've heard of it!'

'You've been on holiday, sir.'

'It'll have to be Johnson then. But for Christ's sake tell him to get off his arse and actually *do* something!'

For a while Strange sat thinking silently. Then he said, 'I've got a bit of an idea. Do you remember that correspondence they had in *The Times* a year or so back?'

'The Irish business – yes.'

'I was just thinking – thinking aloud, sir – that if you were to ring *The Times*—'

'Me? What's wrong with *you* ringing 'em?'

Strange said nothing.

'Look! I don't care what we do so long as we do *something* – quick!'

Strange struggled out of his seat.

'How does Morse get on with Johnson?' asked the CC.

'He doesn't.'

'Where is Morse going, by the way?'

'Lyme Regis – you know, where some of the scenes in *Persuasion* are set.'

'Ah.' The CC looked suitably blank as the Chief Superintendent lumbered towards the door.

'There we are then,' said Strange. 'That's what I reckon we ought to do. What do you say? Cause a bit of a stir, wouldn't it? Cause a bit of interest?'

Johnson nodded. 'I like it. Will *you* ring *The Times*, sir?'

'What's wrong with *you* ringing 'em?'

'Do you happen to know—?'

'You – can – obtain – Directory – Enquiries,' intoned Strange caustically, 'by dialling one-nine-two.'

Johnson kept his lips tightly together as Strange continued: 'And while I'm here you might as well remind me about the case. All right?'

So Johnson reminded him of the case, drawing together the threads of the story with considerably more skill than Strange had thought him capable of.

CHAPTER ELEVEN

Nec scit qua sit iter
(He knows not which is the way to take)
(Ovid, *Metamorphoses II*)

KARIN ERIKSSON had been a 'missing person' enquiry a year ago when her rucksack had been found; she was a 'missing person' enquiry now. She was not the subject of a murder enquiry for the simple reason that it was most unusual – and extremely tricky – to mount a murder enquiry without any suspicion of foul play, with no knowledge of any motive, and above all without a *body*.

So, what *was* known about Miss Eriksson?

Her mother had run a small guest-house in Uppsala, but soon after the disappearance of her daughter had moved back to her roots – to the outskirts of Stockholm. Karin, the middle of three daughters, had just completed a secretarial course, and had passed her final examination, if not with distinction at least with a reasonable hope of landing a decent job. She was, as all agreed, of the classic Nordic type, with long blonde hair and a bosom which was liable to monopolize most men's attention when first they met her. In the summer of 1990 she had made her way to the Holy Land without much money, but also without much trouble it appeared, until reaching her destination, where she may or may not have been the victim of attempted rape by an Israeli soldier. In 1991 she had determined to embark on another trip overseas; been determined too, by all accounts, to keep well clear of the military, wherever she went, and had attended a three-month martial arts course in Uppsala, there showing an aptitude and perseverance which had not always been apparent in her secretarial studies. In any case, she was a tallish (5 foot 8½ inches), large-boned, athletic young lady, who could take fairly good care of herself, thank you very much.

The records showed that Karin had flown to Heathrow on Wednesday, 3 July 1991, with almost £200 in one of her pockets, a multi-framed assemblage of hiking-gear, and with the address of a superintendent in a YWCA hostel near King's Cross. A few days in London had apparently dissipated a large proportion of her English currency; and fairly early in the morning of Sunday, 7 July, she had taken the tube (perhaps) to Paddington, from where (perhaps) she had made her way up to the A40, M40 – towards Oxford. The statement made by the YWCA superintendent firmly suggested that from what Karin had told her she would probably be heading – in the long run – for a distant relative living in mid-Wales.

In all probability K. would have been seen on one of the feeder roads to the A40 at about 10 a.m. or so that day. She would have been a distinctive figure: longish straw-coloured hair, wearing a pair of faded-blue jeans, raggedly split at the knees à la mode. But particularly noticeable – this from several witnesses – would have been the yellow and blue Swedish flag, some 9 inches by 6 inches, stitched across the main back pocket of her rucksack; and around her neck (always) a silk, tasselled scarf in the same national colours – sunshine and sky.

Two witnesses had come forward with fairly positive sightings of a woman, answering Karin's description, trying to hitch a lift between the Headington and the Banbury Road roundabouts in Oxford. And one further witness, a youth waiting for a bus at the top of the Banbury Road in Oxford, thought he remembered seeing her walking fairly purposefully down towards Oxford that day. The time? About noon – certainly! – since he was just off for a drink at the Eagle and Child in St Giles'. But more credence at the time was given to a final witness, a solicitor driving to see his invalid mother in Yarnton, who thought he could well have seen her walking along Sunderland Avenue, the horn-beam-lined road linking the Banbury Road and the Woodstock Road roundabouts.

At this point Johnson looked down at his records, took out an amateurishly drawn diagram, and handed it across to Strange.

'That's what would have faced her, sir – if we can believe she even got as far as the Woodstock Road roundabout.'

With little enthusiasm, Strange looked down at the diagram and Johnson continued his story.

Karin could have gone straight over, of course – straight along the A40, a road where it would be very much easier for a hitchhiker to get a lift than along the motorways and dual-carriageways she'd already negotiated successfully. In addition, the A40 would lead pretty directly towards the address of her third cousin, or whatever, near Llandovery. But it had not seemed to the detectives who considered the matter that she had taken the 'Witney' option – or the 'Wolvercote' – or the 'City Centre' one; but had taken the road that led to Woodstock . . .

CHAPTER TWELVE

Sigh out a lamentable tale of things,
Done long ago, and ill done
(John Ford, *The Lover's Melancholy*)

AT ABOUT 7.15 (Johnson continued) on the sunny
Tuesday morning of 9 July 1991, George Daley, of 2
Blenheim Villas, Begbroke, Oxon, had taken his eight-
year-old King Charles spaniel for an early-morning walk
along the slip-road beside the Royal Sun, a roadside
ale-house on the northern stretch of the A44, a mile or
so on the Oxford side of Woodstock. At the bottom of
a hawthorn hedge, almost totally concealed by rank
cow-parsley, Daley had spotted – as he claimed – a
splash of bright colour; and as he ventured down, and
near, he had all but trodden on a camera before seeing
the scarlet rucksack.

Of course at this stage there had been no evidence
of foul play – still wasn't – and it was the camera that
had claimed most of Daley's attention. He'd promised
a camera to his son Philip, a lad just coming up for his
sixteenth birthday; and the camera he'd found, a heavy,
aristocratic-looking thing, was a bit too much of a
temptation. Both the rucksack and the camera he'd
taken home, where cursorily that morning, in more

detail later that evening, he and his wife Margaret had considered things.

'Finders keepers', they'd been brought up to accept. And well, yes, the rucksack clearly – and specifically – belonged to someone else; but the camera had no name on it, had it? For all they knew, it had no connection at all with the rucksack. So they'd taken out the film, which seemed to be fully used up anyway, and thrown it on the fire. Not a crime, was it? Sometimes even the police – Daley had suggested – weren't all that sure what should be entered in the crime figures. If a bike got stolen, it was a crime all right. But if the owner could be persuaded that the bike hadn't really been stolen at all – just inadvertently 'lost', say – then it didn't count as a crime at all, now did it?

'Was he an ex-copper, this fellow Daley?' asked Strange, nodding his appreciation of the point.

Johnson grinned, but shook his head and continued.

The wife, Margaret Daley, felt a bit guilty about hanging on to the rucksack, and according to Daley persuaded him to drop it in at Kidlington the next day, Wednesday – originally asserting that he'd found it that same morning. But he hadn't really got his story together, and it was soon pretty clear that the man wasn't a very good liar; and it wasn't long before he changed his story.

The rucksack itself? Apart from the pocket-buttons rusting a bit, it seemed reasonably new, containing, presumably, all the young woman's travelling possessions, including a passport which identified its owner as one Karin Eriksson, from an address in Uppsala, Sweden. Nothing, it appeared, had been tampered with overmuch by the Daleys, but the contents had proved of only limited interest: the usual female toiletries, including toothpaste, Tampax, lipstick, eye-shadow, blusher, comb, nail-file, tweezers, and white tissues; an almost full packet of Marlboro cigarettes with a cheap 'throwaway' lighter; a letter, in Swedish, from a boyfriend, dated two months earlier, proclaiming (as was later translated) a love that was fully prepared to wait until eternity but which would also appreciate a further rendezvous a little earlier; a slim money-wallet, containing no credit cards or travellers' cheques – just five ten-pound notes (newish but not consecutively numbered); a book of second-class English postage-stamps; a greyish plastic mac, meticulously folded; a creased postcard depicting Velasquez's 'Rokeby Venus' on one side, and the address of the Welsh relative on the other; two clean (cleanish) pairs of pants; one faded-blue dress; three creased blouses, black, white, and darkish red . . .

'Get on with it,' mumbled Strange.

Well, Interpol were contacted, and of course the Swedish police. A distraught mother, by phone from Uppsala, had told them that it was very unusual for Karin not to keep her family informed of where she was and what she was up to – as she had done from London the previous week.

A poster ('Have you seen this young woman?') displaying a blown-up copy of the passport photograph had been printed, and seen by some of the citizens of Oxford and its immediate environs in buses, youth clubs, information offices, employment agencies, those sorts of places.

'And that's when these people came forward, these witnesses?' interrupted Strange.

'That's it, sir.'

'And the fellow you took notice of was the one who thought he saw her in Sunderland Avenue.'

'He was a very good witness. Very good.'

'Mm! I don't know. A lovely leggy blonde – well-tanned, well-exposed, eh, Johnson? Standing there on the grass verge facing the traffic ... Bit odd, isn't it? You'd've thought the fellow would've remembered her for *certain* – that's all I'm saying. Some of us still have the occasional erotic day-dream, y'know.'

'That's what Morse said.'

'Did he now!'

'He said even if most of us were only going as far as Woodstock we'd have taken her on to Stratford, if that's what she wanted.'

'*He'd* have taken her to Aberdeen,' growled Strange.

The next thing (Johnson continued his story) had been the discovery, in the long grass about twenty yards from where the rucksack had been found – probably fallen out of one of the pockets – of a slim little volume titled *A Birdwatchers' Guide*. Inside was a sheet of white paper, folded vertically and seemingly acting as a bookmark, on which the names of ten birds had been written in neat capitals, with a pencilled tick against seven of them:

HOBBY ✓
RED KITE
LESSER SPOTTED WOODPECKER
BREADED TIT ✓
CORN BUNTING ✓
TREE PIPIT ✓
REDSTART ✓
NIGHTINGALE ✓
GRASSHOPPER WARBLER ✓
NUTHATCH

The lettering matched the style and slope of the few scraps of writing found in the other documents, and the easy conclusion was that Karin Eriksson had been a keen ornithologist, probably buying the book after arriving in London and trying to add to her list of sightings some of the rarer species which could be seen during English summers. The names of the birds were written in English and there was only the one misspelling: the 'breaded tit' – an interesting variety of the 'bearded plaice' spotted fairly frequently in English restaurants. (It had been the pedantic Morse who had made this latter point.)

Even more interesting, though, had been the second enclosure within the pages: a thin yellow leaflet, folded this time across the middle, announcing a pop concert in the grounds of Blenheim Palace on Monday, 8 July – the day before the rucksack was found: 8 p.m.–11.30 p.m., admission (ticket only) £4.50.

That was it. Nothing else really. Statements taken –

enquiries made – searches organized in the grounds of Blenheim Palace – but . . .

'How much did Morse come into all this?' asked a frowning Strange.

Johnson might have known he'd ask it, and he knew he might as well come clean.

CHAPTER THIRTEEN

He that reads and grows no wiser seldom suspects his
own deficiency, but complains of hard words and obscure
sentences, and asks why books are written which cannot
be understood

(Samuel Johnson, *The Idler*)

THE TRUTH was that Morse had *not* figured on the
scene at all during the first few days of the case – for it
was not a case of homicide; and (as was to be hoped)
still wasn't. Yet the follow-up investigations had been
worrying, especially of course the steadily growing and
cumulative evidence that Karin Eriksson had been a
responsible young woman who had never previously
drifted into the drink-drugs-sex-scene.

Only after the case had grown a little cold had Morse
spent a couple of hours one afternoon with Johnson, in
that late July, now a year ago – before being side-
tracked into a squalid domestic murder out on the
Cowley Road.

'I reckon he thought it all a bit – a bit of a joke, sir,
quite honestly.'

'Joke? *Joke?* This is no bloody joke, Johnson! Like
as not, we shall be opening a couple of extra lines
on the switchboard once these bloody newspapers get
hold of it. It'll be like an air disaster! And if the

public come up with some brighter ideas than the police . . .'

Johnson gently reminded him: 'But it's *your* idea, sir – this business of sending the letters to *The Times*.'

'What did you mean – about Morse?' asked Strange, ignoring the criticism.

'What I meant, sir, is that he, well, he only skipped over the details with me, and he sort of said the first things that came into his head, really. I don't think he had time to think about things much.'

'He'd have *ideas* though, wouldn't he, Morse? Always did have. Even if he'd been on a case a couple of minutes. Usually the wrong ideas of course, but . . .'

'All I'm saying is that he didn't seem to take the case at all seriously. He was sort of *silly* about things, really—'

Strange's voice sounded suddenly thunderous: 'Look here, Johnson! Morse may be an idiot, you're right. But he's never been a fool. Let's get *that* straight!'

For Johnson, the differentiation between what he had hitherto regarded as virtual synonyms – 'idiot' and 'fool' – was clearly beyond his etymological capacities; and he frowned a guarded puzzlement as his superior officer continued:

'Some people are occasionally right for the wrong reasons. But Morse? He's more often than not wrong for the right reasons. The *right* reasons . . . you understand me? So even if he sometimes drinks too much . . .'

Johnson looked down at the file in front of him: he knew, alas, exactly what Strange was saying. 'Would you rather Morse took over the case, sir?'

'Yes, I think I would,' said Strange. 'So would the CC, if you must know,' he added cruelly.

'So when does he get back from leave . . .?'

Strange sighed deeply. 'Not soon enough. Let's see what happens with this newspaper angle.'

'He's pretty sure to see it – if they print it.'

'What? Morse? Nonsense! I've never seen him reading anything. He just spends half an hour on the crossword, that's all.'

'Ten minutes – last time I watched him,' said Johnson honestly, if somewhat grudgingly.

'Wasted his life, Morse has,' confided Strange, after a pause.

'Should've got married, you mean?'

Strange began to extricate himself from his chair. 'I wouldn't go as far as that. Ridiculous institution – marriage! Don't you think so?'

Johnson, himself having married only six months previously, forebore any direct response, as Strange finally brought his vertebrae to the vertical, from which vantage point he looked down on the papers that Johnson had been consulting.

'Isn't that Morse's writing?' he queried presbyopically.

Yes, it was Morse's handwriting; and doubtless Johnson would have preferred Strange not to have seen it. But at least it would prove his point. So he picked out the sheet, and handed it over.

'Mm.' Chief Superintendent Strange held the piece of paper at arm's length, surveying its import. Unlike Morse, he was an extremely rapid reader; and after only ten seconds or so he handed it back to Johnson: 'See what you mean!'

Johnson, in turn, looked down again at the sheet Morse had left him – the one he'd found on his desk that morning a year ago now, when Morse had been transferred to what had appeared more urgent enquiries:

I never got to grips with the case as you know but I'd have liked answers to the following half-dozen qq:
(a) Had Daley or his missus owned a camera themselves?
(b) What was the weather like on Tuesday 9th July?
(c) 'It's striped: what about ze panties?' (5)
(d) What's the habitat of 'Dendrocopus Minor'?
(e) What beer do they serve at the Royal Sun (or at the White Hart!)?
(f) What's the dog's name?

Strange now lumbered to the door. 'Don't ignore all this bloody nonsense, Johnson. That's what I'm telling you. Don't take *too* much notice of it; but don't *ignore* it, understand?'

For the second time within a short while the etymological distinction between a couple of unequivocal synonyms had completely escaped Inspector Johnson's reasonably bright but comparatively limited brain.

'As you say, sir.'

'And, er, and one other thing ... the wife's just bought a new dog – little King Charles, lovely thing! Two hundred pounds it cost. Pisses everywhere, of course – and worse! But he's, you know, he's always glad to see you. More than the wife sometimes, eh? It's just that we've only had the bloody thing a fortnight, and we still haven't christened it.'

'The dog's name was "Mycroft". Good name – be a good name for *your* dog, sir.'

'Imaginative, yes! I'll, er, mention it to the missus, Johnson. Just one little problem, though . . .'

Johnson raised his rather bushy eyebrows.

'Yes. She's a *she*, Johnson!'

'Oh.'

'Anything else Morse said?' pursued Strange.

'Well, yes. He, er, thought – he said he had a gut-feeling—'

'Huh!'

'—that we'd been searching for a body in the wrong *place.*'

'In Blenheim, you mean?'

Johnson nodded. 'He thought we ought to have been looking in Wytham Woods.'

'Yes. I remember him saying that.'

'Only after we'd drawn a blank in Blenheim, though.'

'Better wise after the event than never.'

Augh, shut up! Johnson was becoming a little weary of all the innuendos: 'If you recall, sir, it wasn't just Morse who was in favour of a wider operation. But we hadn't got the personnel available for a search of Wytham Woods. You said so. I came to ask you myself.'

Strange was stung into retaliation. 'Look, Johnson! You find *me* a body and I'll find *you* all the bloody personnel you need, all right?'

It was the chicken-and-egg business all over again, and Johnson would have said so – but Strange was already guiding his bulk downstairs, via the hand-rail on the HQ wall.

CHAPTER FOURTEEN

Only the keeper sees
That, where the ring-dove broods,
And the badgers roll at ease,
There was once a road through the woods
(Rudyard Kipling, *The Way Through the Woods*)

IT WAS to be Morse's last breakfast at the Bay Hotel, that morning of Monday, 6 July 1992, six days after the long meeting just recorded between Strange and Johnson at Kidlington HQ in Oxfordshire. He would have wished to stay a further couple of days – but there were no vacancies; and, as the proprietor reminded him, he'd already had more than his share of luck.

As he waited for his mixed grill he re-read the article, again high-profile page-one news – the article promised the previous Friday by Howard Phillipson, literary editor of *The Times*:

A PRELIMINARY ANALYSIS

INTEREST in the 'Swedish Maiden' verses printed in these columns last week (Friday, July 3) has been sweeping this newspaper's offices, but I am myself now somewhat more diffident than I originally was about solving the fascinating riddle-me-ree presented by the five stanzas. I had earlier assumed that there might well be sufficient 'internal logic' in the information received by the Thames Valley Police to come to some firm conclusions. I am no longer so strongly of this opinion.

Only with considerable hesitation therefore do I offer my own amateurish analysis of the riddle, in the fairly certain knowledge that very soon the cryptologists and cabbalists, criminologists and cranks, will be making their own considerably more subtle interpretations of these tantalizing lines.

For what it is worth, however, I suggest that the parameters of the problem may be set, albeit rather vaguely. In modern mathematics (as I understand the situation) pupils are asked, before tackling any problem: 'What roughly do you think the answer might be? What sort of answer might you logically expect?' If, say, the problem involves the speed of a supersonic jet flying the Atlantic, the answer is perhaps unlikely to be 10 m.p.h., and any pupil coming up with such an improbable answer is advised to look back through his calculations and find out where he might have dropped a couple of noughts. If we are set to discover the time taken by those famous taps to fill the family tub, the answer is still rather more likely to be ten minutes than ten hours. Permit me then to make a few general comments on what would appear to be the sort of solution we might expect. (The verses are reprinted on page 2.)

Clearly the poem is cast in a 'sylvan' setting: we have 'woodman'; 'stream'; 'riding' (sic!); 'Thyme flow'ring'; 'trapped'; 'hunted deer'; etc. There will be no prizes, I realize, for such an analysis, but the neglect of the obvious is always the beginning of unwisdom.

The setting of some wood or forest therefore must be our donné, and my suggestion to the Thames Valley CID would be to concentrate their doubtless limited resources of manpower within two of the local areas which seem to hold the greatest promise: the forested area around Blenheim Palace, and the Wytham Woods – the latter becoming increasingly famous for its fox and badger research.

Let us now turn to the more specific import of the stanzas. The speaker of the poem, the 'persona', is clearly no longer a living being. Yet her dramatic message is quite unequivocal: she has been murdered; she has been drowned (or perhaps just dumped) in one of the lakes or streams situated in the wood(s); if such waters are searched and dredged her corpse will be found; finally the police may have been (somewhat?) remiss in not pursuing their enquiries with rather greater perseverance.

What can be gathered from the nature of the verses themselves? Their composer is certainly no Herrick or Housman, yet in terms of technical prosody the writer is more than competent. Vocabulary ('tegument', 'azured', etc.) is more redolent of the Senior Common Room than the Saloon Bar; and the versification, punctuation, and diction, all point to a literate and well read man – or woman!

Can anything more specific be said about the writer? For some while, as I read and re-read the verses, I toyed with the idea of their author being a relative of the dead girl. The reason for my thinking was the continued emphasis, throughout the poem, of the 'find me' motif; and I was reminded of the Homeric heroes of the *Iliad* where death in battle was a fully expected and wholly honourable end – but where the most terrible fate of all was to die unrecognized, unburied, *unfound*, in some unknown and far-off land. Is the poem then above all a desperate cry for the Christian burial of the body? This would be most understandable. We have seen in recent years so many tragic instances (in the Middle

East, for example) where the simple return of a dead body has paved the way for some peace initiative.

But I no longer believe this to be the case. My firm conviction now is that the verses have been sent to the police by a person for whom the period – now a year – between the murder of Karin Eriksson and the present time has become an intolerable Hell. A person who is very near to breaking point. A person who wishes the crime at last to be uncovered, and who is now prepared to pay the penalty. In short, the murderer!

Dare I go any further? I learned two further (hitherto unpublished) facts from Detective Chief Inspector Johnson. First, that the letter-writer was able to spell, correctly, the not very easy or obvious 'Eriksson'; second, that the writer was aware of the previous Chief Constable's surname, but not that of the current incumbent. On the old adage then that one might just as well be hanged for a sheep as a lamb, I reckon the murderer to be male; to be between thirty and thirty-five years old; to have a degree in English literature; to have lived until about six or nine months ago in Oxfordshire; to have revisited the scene of his crime during the last month, say, whilst staying at one of the more upmarket hostelries in Woodstock, Oxon.

I rest my case, m'lud!

'Hi!' she said. 'Mind if I join you?'

'Please do,' said Morse, carefully mounting the last segment of his fried egg on the last square of his fried bread.

'You ever read about cholesterol?' Her voice was very cultured, the two 't's of her simple question affectedly exaggerated.

Morse swallowed his latest mouthful and looked at the slim, expensively dressed woman who now sat opposite him, ordering black coffee and a croissant – nothing more.

'They say we've all got to die of something.' He tried to make it sound reasonably cheerful.

'Ridiculous attitude!' The lips, expertly outlined in some pale-crimson shade, looked severe, yet the grey eyes in the delicate, oval face might almost have been mocking him.

'I suppose it is,' he said.

'You're overweight anyway, aren't you?'

'I suppose so,' he repeated lamely.

'You'll have high blood pressure in your mid-fifties – unless you're there now? Then you'll probably have a stroke in your early sixties; and like as not die of a heart attack before you're seventy.' She had already drained her coffee cup, and held up an elegant, imperious hand to the waitress. 'What's your job?'

Morse sighed, and considered the last piece of toast in the rack. 'I'm a policeman, and I come from Oxford, and I'm on holiday here until about ten o'clock this morning. I'm single and maybe I'm not much of a catch, but if I'd known I was going—'

'—going to meet a beautiful girl like me! Surely you can be more original than that?' The eyes were mocking him again.

Morse took the toast and started buttering it. 'No, I can't. I can't do much better than that.'

'Perhaps you underrate yourself.'

'What about you? What do you do?'

'Why don't *you* tell *me*. You're a policeman, you say?'

For half a minute or so Morse looked at her, cocking his head slightly to the right. Then he gave his judgement: 'You're a beautician, possibly a dietitian too, which you probably spell with a "t" and not a "c"; you're in your late twenties, and you went to school at Cheltenham Ladies'; you're married but you sometimes leave off your wedding ring – like now; you're fond of pets but you tend to think children are something of an exaggerated pastime. And if you come for a walk with me along the prom, I'll try to fill in a few more of the details as we go along.'

'That's much better.'

'Well? How did I do?'

She smiled and shook her head. 'Is your name Sherlock Holmes?'

'Morse.'

'Am I *that* transparent?'

'No. I, er, saw you come in with your husband last night – when you went straight to bed and he—'

'He stayed at the bar!'

'We had one or two drinks together, and I asked him who the beautiful woman was—'

'And he said, "That's not a beautiful woman: that's my wife!"?'

'Something like that.'

'And he talked about me?'

'He talked nicely about you.'

'He was drunk.'

'He's sleeping it off?' Morse pointed to the ceiling.

She nodded her dark curls. 'So he won't mind much if you take me on that walk, will he, Mr Morse? When you've finished your toast, of course. And wouldn't *you* spell dietitian with a "t"?'

CHAPTER FIFTEEN

At the very smallest wheel of our reasoning it is possible
for a handful of questions to break the bank of our
answers

(Antonio Machado, *Juan de Mairena*)

ON THE same morning that Morse was packing his
single suitcase ('On the day of their departure guests
are respectfully requested to vacate their rooms by
10.30 a.m.') Sergeant Lewis knocked on Johnson's
door, soon seating himself opposite the chief inspector,
and beside Sergeant Wilkins.

'Good of you to spare a few minutes.'

'If I can help in any way . . .' said Lewis warily.

'You know Morse better than most.'

'Nobody knows him all *that* well.'

'You've got a reasonable idea how his mind works
though.'

'He's got a strange sort of mind—'

'Not many'd disagree with you.'

'He's good at some things.'

'Such as?'

'He's not bad at catching murderers for a start.'

'And you do realize the odds are we're trying to
catch another murderer now, don't you, Sergeant?'

'If it *is* murder.'

'Did Morse think it was murder?'

'As I remember, sir, he was only on it with you for a day or so.'

'Less than that.' (Wilkins had made his first contribution.)

'You're following this – this newspaper business, I presume, Lewis?'

'Everybody reads *The Times* before the *Sun* now.'

'What do you make of this?' Johnson handed a photocopy of Morse's 'half-dozen qq.' across the desk.

Lewis looked down at the list and smiled. 'Bit of a joke – some of this, isn't it?'

'Take my advice, Lewis, and don't try telling that to the Super!'

'I don't know the answer to any of 'em,' admitted Lewis, 'except (e) – well, part of (e). It's a "Morrell's" pub, the Royal Sun. I've brought quite a few pints there, I reckon.'

'What, for Morse, you mean?'

'Who else?'

'But has he ever bought *you* any, Lewis? That's the real question, eh, Wilkins?'

The two men sniggered. And suddenly Lewis hated them both.

'What about the White Hart?' continued Johnson.

'Lot of "White Harts" about.'

'Yes, we know that!' Johnson gestured to Wilkins, the latter now reading from his notes: 'Headington, Marston, Wolvercote, Wytham, Minster Lovell, Eynsham . . .'

'I expect Morse could probably add to the list,' ventured Johnson.

Lewis, determining henceforth to be as minimally helpful as possible, made only a brief comment: 'She'd've got past the first two.'

Johnson nodded. 'What about Eynsham and Minster Lovell? Just off the A40, both of them – if she ever travelled along the A40, that is.'

Lewis said nothing.

'What about the other two: Wolvercote and Wytham? Which would you put your money on?'

'Wytham, I suppose.'

'Why's that?'

'The woods there – easy enough to hide a body.'

'Did you know that Morse asked the Chief Super about a search of Wytham Woods last year?'

Lewis did, yes. 'Only after the search in Blenheim didn't come up with anything.'

'Do you know how big Wytham Woods *is*, man?'

Lewis had a good idea, yes. But he merely shrugged his shoulders.

'Why would Morse be interested in the dog?'

'Don't know. He told me once he'd never had any pets when he was a lad.'

'Perhaps he should get one now. Lots of bachelors have dogs.'

'You must suggest it to him, sir,' replied Lewis, with a note of confidence in his voice, and a strange exhilaration flooding his limbs, for he suddenly realized that it was Johnson who was on the defensive here, not himself. They were trying to pick his (Lewis's) brains because they were envious of his relationship with Morse!

'What about the camera?' continued Johnson.

'You can ask the Daleys, can't you? If they're still there.'

'Odd question though, wouldn't you say?'

'I just don't know, sir. I think Morse told me he had a "Brownie" given him once, but he said he never really understood how to work it.'

Sitting back in an almost relaxed manner now, Lewis looked down at the questions again. 'Should be easy to check on (b) – about the weather . . .'

Again Johnson waved a hand, and Wilkins consulted his notes: 'According to Radio Oxford . . . the ninth of July . . . "Dry, sunny, seventy-two to seventy-four degrees Fahrenheit; outlook settled; possibility of some over-night mist".'

'Nice, warm day, then,' said Lewis blandly.

'What about (c)?'

'Crossword clue, sir. He's pretty hot on crosswords.'

'What's the answer?'

'No good asking me. Sometimes I can't even do the *Mirror* coffee-break one.'

'"Ze-bra" – that's the answer.'

'Really? Well that's another one crossed off.'

'What about this "Dendrocopus Minor"?' There was a note of exasperation in Johnson's voice now.

'Pass,' said Lewis with a gentle smile.

'For Christ's sake, man, we're on a potential *murder* enquiry – not a bloody *pub*-quiz! Don't you realize that? As a matter of fact it's the Lesser something bloody Woodpecker!'

'We learn something new every day.'

'Yes, we do, Sergeant. And I'll tell you something else, if you like. Its habitat is woodlands or parklands and there are a few pairs nesting in Wytham!'

Lewis's new-found confidence was starting to ebb away as Johnson glared at him aggressively. 'You don't seem all that anxious to help us, Sergeant, do you? So let me just tell you why I asked you along here. As you probably know, we're starting searching Blenheim all over again today, and we're going to search and search until we're blue in the bloody face, OK? But if we still don't find anything we're going to hand over to Morse – and to *you*, Sergeant. I just thought you might like to know what we're *all* up against, see?'

Lewis was conscious of a sinking sense of humiliation. 'I – I didn't know that, sir.'

'Why should you? They don't tell even you everything, do they?'

'Why might they be taking you off?' asked Lewis slowly.

'They – "they" – are taking me off because they don't think I'm any fucking good,' said Johnson bitterly as he rose to his feet. 'That's why!'

CHAPTER SIXTEEN

Between 1871 and 1908 he published twenty volumes
of verse, of little merit
('Alfred Austin', *The Oxford Companion to English Literature*,
edited by Margaret Drabble)

MORSE was spending the last three days of his West
Country holiday at the King's Arms in Dorchester
(Dorchester, Dorset). Here he encountered neither
models nor beauticians; but at last he began to feel a
little reluctant about returning to Oxford. On the
Wednesday he had explored Hardy's Dorchester on
foot (!) a.m., and spent the whole p.m. in the Dorset
County Museum. Nostalgic, all of it. And when finally
he returned to 'the chief hotel in Casterbridge' he sat
drinking his beer in the bar before dinner with the
look of a man who was almost at ease with life.

On the Thursday morning he drove out through the
countryside that provided much of the setting for *Tess
of the d'Urbervilles*, along the A352 to the east of Dorchester, following the Vale of the Great Dairies, past Max
Gate and Talbothays towards Wool. As he was driving
through Moreton, he wondered whether there was any
follow-up to the Phillipson analysis (there had been no
mention in the Tuesday or Wednesday editions), and
he stopped and bought the last copy of *The Times* from

the village newsagent's. The answer was yes – yes, there was; and he sat for a while in the sunshine beside the wall of the cemetery containing the grave of Lawrence of Arabia, reading the long letter which (as with succeeding letters) now found its place naturally in the newspaper's correspondence columns:

From Professor (Emeritus) René Gray

Sir, my mind, doubtless like the minds of many of your regular readers, has been much exercised these past few days following the publication (July 3) of the letter received by the Thames Valley Police. I beg the courtesy of your columns to make one or two observations.

This is not a poem by Alfred Austin, though the words 'A. Austin' appear beneath it. The name 'Austin' does not seem to refer to a make of motor car: 'A'-registration Austins date from 1983–84, and there is no resemblance between this date and those given in brackets. The dates given are not Austin the poet's dates. He was born in 1835, and died in 1913. There is a remote possibility that the last two digits of his birth-date have been transposed for some reason, but the death-date is plainly wrong. Dying in 1913, he was 78 years old at the time of his death. By a strange coincidence the transposition of these digits gives us the '87' which is written here. I conclude that the dates are not all they seem, and most likely constitute the key to the cypher.

The figures do not appear to give geographical co-ordinates. They do not match the format of Ordnance Survey co-ordinates, and they are not co-ordinates of latitude and longitude, since Great Britain lies between the 50th and 60th lines of latitude and between the longitudes 2°E and 10°W. We are left with six digits which somehow must give the clue to the interpretation of the words of the message.

I have not been able to work out the cypher. I have tried the first word, followed by the eighth, followed by the fifth after that (giving either 'Find ... my ... the skylit', or 'Find ... frosted ... skylit ... me'). I have re-transposed the sequences of digits, to no better effect. I have tried lines, first words of lines, last words of lines. I have taken the digits in pairs, i.e. as 18, 53 (or 35) and 87 with the same result. I have alternated the beginnings of the lines with the ends of the lines, and vice versa.

I have simplified the expression '1853–87' by interpreting the hyphen as a minus sign. The answer, '1766', does not produce any happier result. The only sensible word produced is yielded by taking letters in that sequence in the first line, thus giving 'F-i-s-h', but the message does not continue. (A red herring, possibly!)

There are a large number of other combinations and permutations, but no method other than trial and error for seeing whether any make any sense.

The overriding advantage of the mechanical method of deciphering is that the poem itself does not have to make sense; a random sequence of words would fulfil exactly the same purpose of concealing the message. Hence odd words such as 'tiger' need not fall into the category of important words at all: in its place, 'chairman' or 'post-box' would do equally well; these words meet the requirements of the metre, but would not be included in the deciphered message. Likewise, the upper case 'T' in the middle of line 13 is not significant. The fact that the poem does make some kind of sense in places thus merely adds to the bafflement.

If this line of thinking is correct, it does not matter

what the poem says, or what it means. What is needed is the services of a skilled cryptographer.	Yours faithfully, RENÉ GRAY, 137 Victoria Park Road, Leicester

Morse read the letter once only, and decided to wait until his return to the King's Arms (where he had the two earlier cuttings) in order to have a more careful look at the good professor's analysis and suggested methodology. He sounded an engaging sort of fellow, Gray – especially with that bit about the 'chairman' and the 'post-box'.

Back in Dorchester that afternoon, Morse went into the public library and looked up 'Austin' in *The Oxford Companion to English Literature.* He'd heard of Austin the poet – of course he had; but he'd never known anything much about him, and he was certainly unaware that any poem, or even line, produced by the former poet laureate had merited immortality.

From the library Morse walked on to the post office, where he bought a black and white postcard of Dorchester High Street, and stood for an inordinate length of time in the queue there. He didn't know the price of the stamp for a postcard, and didn't wish to waste a first-class stamp if, as he suspected, the official tariff for postcards was a few pence lower. It was, he realized, quite ridiculous to wait so long for such a little saving.

But wait Morse did.

*

Lewis received the card the following morning, the message written in Morse's small, neat, and scholarly hand:

> Mostly I've not been quite
> so miserable since last year's
> holiday, but things are
> looking up here in D.
> Warmest regards to you
> (and to Mrs Lewis) – but
> not to any of our other
> colleagues. Have you been
> following the Swedish lass?
> I reckon I know what the
> poem means.
> Definitely home Sat.
>
> M

This card, with its curmudgeonly message, was delivered to police HQ in Kidlington – since Morse had not quite been able to remember Lewis's Headington address. And by the time it was in Lewis's hands, almost everyone in the building had read it. It might, naturally, have made Lewis a little cross – such contravention of the laws of privacy.

But it didn't. It made him glad.

CHAPTER SEVENTEEN

Extract from a diary dated Friday, 10 July 1992

Please God let me wake from this dream! Please God may she not be dead! Those words – the ones I so recently wrote – for them may I be forgiven! Those terrible words! – when I disavowed my love for my own flesh and blood, for my own children, for my daughter. But how could I be forgiven? The fates decree otherwise and ever have so decreed. The words may be blotted out but they will remain. The paper may be burned in the furnace but the words will persist for evermore. Oh blackness! Oh night of the soul! Throw open the wide door of Hell, Infernal Spirits, for it is I who approach – all hope of virtue, all hope of life abandoned! I have reached the Inferno and there now read that grim pronouncement of despair above its portal.

I am sunk deep in misery and anguish of mind and spirit. At my desk I sit here weeping bitter tears. I shout Forgive me! Forgive me! And then I shout again Forgive me! Everyone forgive me! Had I still belief in God I would seek to pray. But I cannot. And even now – even in the abyss of my despair – I have not told the truth! Let it be known that tomorrow I shall once more be happy – some of tomorrow's hours will bring me happiness again. She is coming. She is coming here. She herself has arranged and organized. She it is who has wished to come! For my sake is this? Is this for my need – my grief's sake? Yet such considerations are of minor consequence. She is coming, tomorrow she is <u>coming</u>. More precious to me is that woman even than the mother who suffers all that pain ...

(Later.) I am so low I wish I were dead. My selfishness my <u>self</u>-pity is so great that I can have no pity for the others – the others who grieve so greatly. I have just re-read one of Hardy's poems. I used to know it by heart. No longer though and now my left forefinger traces the lines as slowly I copy it out:

> I seem but dead man held on end
> To sink down soon ... O you could not know
>   That such swift fleeing
>   No soul foreseeing –
> Not even I – would undo me so.

I never really managed to speak to you my daughter. I never told you my darling daughter because I did not know – and now you can never know why and can never understand.

I have reached a decision. This journal shall be discontinued. Always when I look back on what I have written I see nothing of any worth – only self-indulgence – theatricality – over-emotionalism. Just one plea I make. It was never forced or insincere or hypocritical. No, never!
    But no more.

CHAPTER EIGHTEEN

A 'strange coincidence' to use a phrase
By which such things are settled now-a-days
(Lord Byron, *Don Juan*)

CLAIRE OSBORNE turned right from the A40 down into Banbury Road, knowing that she would have to drive only three or four hundred yards along it, since she had received a detailed map through the post. She was a little surprised – a lot surprised – when she spotted, on her right, the Cotswold House, a considerably more striking and attractive building than the 'suburban, modern, detached' blurb of *The Good Hotel Guide* had led her to expect. She experienced an unexpected feeling of delight as she parked her Metro MG (what a disaster not taking that to Lyme!) on the rusty-red asphalt in front of the double-fronted guest-house, built of honey-coloured Cotswold stone in the leafy environs of North Oxford.

Flower-baskets in green, red, purple, and white hung all around her as she rang the bell at the front door, on which a white notice announced 'No Vacancies'. But Claire had earlier found a vacancy, and booked it: a vacancy for two.

The door was opened by a tall, slim man, with a shock of prematurely grey hair, black eyebrows, a slightly diffident smile, and a soft Irish brogue.

'Hello.'

'Hello. My name's Mrs Hardinge, and I think you'll find—'

'Already found, Mrs Hardinge. And I'm Jim O'Kane. Now do come in, won't you? And welcome to the Cotswold House.' With which splendid greeting he picked up her case and led her inside, where Claire felt immediately and overwhelmingly impressed.

Briefly O'Kane consulted the bookings register, then selected a key from somewhere, and led the way up a semi-circular staircase.

'No trouble finding us, I trust?'

'No. Your little map was very helpful.'

'Good journey?'

'No problems.'

O'Kane walked across the landing, inserted a key in Room 1, opened the door, ushered his guest inside, followed her with the suitcase, and then, with a courteous, old-world gesture, handed her a single key – almost as if he were presenting a bouquet of flowers to a beautiful girl.

'The key fits your room here *and* the front door, Mrs Hardinge.'

'Fine.'

'And if I could just remind you' – his voice growing somewhat apologetic – 'this is a non-smoking guest-house . . . I *did* mention it when you rang.'

'Yes.' But she was frowning. 'That means – everywhere? Including the bedrooms?'

'Especially the bedrooms,' replied O'Kane, simply if reluctantly.

Claire looked down at the single key. 'My husband's been held up in London—'

'No problem! Well, only *one* problem perhaps. We're always a bit pushed for parking – if there are *two* cars . . .?'

'He'll have his car, yes. But don't worry about that. There seems to be plenty of room in the side-streets.'

O'Kane appeared grateful for her understanding, and asked if she were familiar with Oxford, with the North Oxford area. And Claire said, yes, she was; her husband knew the area well, so there was no trouble there.

Wishing Mrs Hardinge well, Mr O'Kane departed – leaving Claire to look with admiration around the delightfully designed and decorated accommodation. *En suite*, too.

O'Kane was not a judgemental man, and in any case the morality of his guests was of rather less importance to him than their comfort. But already the signs were there: quite apart from the circumstantial evidence of any couple arriving in separate cars, over the years O'Kane had observed that almost every wedded woman arriving first would show an interest in the in-house amenities and the like. Yet Mrs Hardinge(?) had enquired about none of these ... he would have guessed too (if asked) that she might well pay the bill from her own cheque-book when the couple left – about 50 per cent of such ladies usually did so. In the early days of his business career, such things had worried O'Kane a little. But not so much now. Did it matter? Did it really matter? Any unwed couple could get a *mortgage* these days – let alone a couple of nights' accommodation in a B & B. She was a pleasantly spoken, attractive woman; and as O'Kane walked down the stairs he hoped she'd have a happy time with that Significant Other who would doubtless be arriving soon, ostensibly spending the weekend away from his wife at some Oxford conference.

Oxford was full of conferences . . .

Claire looked around her. The co-ordinated colour scheme of décor and furnishing was a sheer delight – white, champagne, cerise, mahogany – and reproductions of late-Victorian pictures graced the walls. Beside the help-yourself tea and coffee facilities stood a small fridge, in which she saw an ample supply of milk; and two wine glasses – and two champagne glasses. For a while she sat on the floral-printed bedspread; then went over to the window and looked out, over the window-box of busy Lizzies, geraniums, and petunias, down on to the Banbury Road. For several minutes she stood there, not knowing whether she was happy or not – trying to stop the clock, to live in the present, to grasp the moment . . . and to hold it.

Then – her heart was suddenly pounding against her ribs. A man was walking along the pavement towards the roundabout. He wore a pink, short-sleeved shirt, and his forearms were bronzed – as if perhaps he might recently have spent a few days beside the sea. In his left hand he carried a bag bearing the name of the local wineshop, Oddbins; in his right hand he carried a bag with the same legend. He appeared deep in thought as he made his way, fairly slowly, across her vision and proceeded up towards the roundabout.

What an amazing coincidence! – the man might have thought had she pushed open the diamond-leaded window and shouted 'Hi! Remember me? Lyme Regis? Last weekend?' But that would have been to misunderstand matters, for in truth there was no coincidence at all. Claire Osborne had seen to that.

There was a soft knock on her door, and O'Kane asked if she – if either of them – would like a newspaper in the morning: it was part of the service. Claire smiled. She liked the man. She ordered *The Sunday Times*. Then, for a little while after he was gone, she wondered why she felt so sad.

It was not until just before 9 p.m. that Dr Alan Hardinge arrived – explaining; excusing, but as vulnerable, as loving as ever. And – bless him! – he had brought a bottle of Brut Imperial, *and* a bottle of Skye Talisker malt. And almost, *almost* (as she later told herself) had Claire Osborne enjoyed the couple of hours they'd spent together that night between the immaculately laundered sheets of Room 1 in the Cotswold House in North Oxford.

Morse had arrived home at 2.30 p.m. that same day. No one, as far as he knew, was aware that he had returned (except Lewis?); yet Strange had telephoned at 4 p.m. Would Morse be happy to take on the case? Well, whether he would be happy or not, Morse was *going* to take on the case.

'What case?' Morse had asked, disingenuously.

At 5 p.m. he had walked down to Summertown and bought eight pint-cans of newly devised 'draught' bitter, which promised him the taste of a hand-pulled, cask-conditioned drop of ale; and two bottles of his favourite Querry claret. For Morse – considerably out of condition still – the weight felt a bit too hefty; and outside the Radio Oxford building he halted awhile and looked behind him in the hope of seeing the oblong outline of a red double-decker coming up from the city centre. But there was no bus in sight, so he walked on. As he passed the Cotswold House he saw amongst other things the familiar white sign 'No Vacancies' on the door. He was not surprised. He had heard very well of the place. He wouldn't mind staying there himself.

Especially for the breakfasts.

CHAPTER NINETEEN

> I like to have a thing suggested rather than told in full.
> When every detail is given, the mind rests satisfied, and
> the imagination loses the desire to use its own wings
> (Thomas Aldrich, *Leaves from a Notebook*)

STRANGE had been really quite pleased with all the
publicity. Seldom had there been such national interest
in a purely notional murder; and the extraordinary if
possibly unwarranted ingenuity which the public had
already begun to exercise on the originally printed
verses was most gratifying – if not as yet of much
concrete value. There had been two further offerings
in the Letters to the Editor page in the Saturday, 11
July's issue of *The Times*:

From Gillian Richard

Sir, Professor Gray (July 9) seems to me too lightly to dismiss one factor in the Swedish Maiden case. She is certainly, in my view, alive still, but seemingly torn between the wish to live – and the wish to die. She has probably never won any poetry competition in her life, and I greatly doubt whether she is to be found as a result of her description of the natural world. But she is *out* there, in the natural world – possibly living rough; certainly not indoors. I would myself hazard a guess, dismissed by Professor Gray, that she is in a

---

car somewhere, and here the poem's attribution (A. Austin 1853–87) can give us the vital clue. What about an A-registration Austin? It would be a 1983 model, yes; and might we not have the registration number, too? I suggest A 185 – then three letters. If we suppose 3=C, 8=H, and 7=G (the third, eighth, and seventh letters of the alphabet), we have A 185 CGH. Perhaps then our young lady is languishing in an ageing Metro? And if so, sir, we must ask one question: who is the owner of that car? Find her!

Yours etc.,
GILLIAN RICHARD,
26 Hayward Road,
Oxford.

From Miss Polly Rayner

Sir, I understand from your report on the disappearance a year ago of a Swedish student that her rucksack was found near the village of Begbroke in Oxfordshire. It may be that I am excessively addicted to your own crossword puzzles but surely we can be justified in spotting a couple of 'clues' here? The '-broke' of the village name is derived from the Anglo-Saxon word 'brok', meaning 'running water' or 'stream'. And since 'beg' is a synonym of 'ask', what else are we to make of the first three words in line 7: 'Ask the stream'? Indeed, this clue is almost immediately confirmed two lines later in the injunction 'ask the sun'. 'The Sun' is how the good citizens of Begbroke refer to their local hostelry, and it is in and around that hostelry where in my view the police should re-concentrate their enquiries.

Yours faithfully,
POLLY RAYNER,
President,
Woodstock Local History Society,
Woodstock,
Oxon.

That was more like it! Strange had earlier that day put the suggested car registration through the HQ's traffic computer. No luck! Yet this was just the sort of zany, imaginative idea that might well unlock the mystery, and stimulate a few more such ideas into the bargain. When he had rung Morse that same Saturday afternoon (he too had read the postcard!) he had not been at all surprised by Morse's apparent – surely only 'apparent'? – lack of interest in taking over the case immediately. Yes, Morse still had a few days' leave remaining – only to the Friday, mind! But, really, this case was absolutely up the old boy's street! Tailor-made for Morse, this case of the Swedish Maiden . . .

Strange decided to leave things alone for a while though – well, until the next day. He had more than enough on his plate for the minute. The previous evening had been a bad one, with the City and County police at full stretch with the (virtual) riots on the Broadmoor Lea estate: car-thefts, joy-riding, ram-raids, stone-throwing . . . With Saturday and Sunday evenings still to come! He felt saddened as he contemplated the incipient breakdown in law and order, contempt for authority – police, church, parents, school . . . Augh! Yet in one awkward, unexplored little corner of his mind, he knew he could *almost* understand something of it all – just a fraction. For as a youth, and a fairly privileged youth at that, he remembered harbouring a secret desire to chuck a full-sized brick through the window of one particularly well-appointed property . . .

But yes – quite definitely, yes! – he would feel so very much happier if Morse could take over the responsibility of the case; take it away from his own, Strange's, shoulders.

Thus it was that Strange had rung Morse that Saturday afternoon.

'*What* case?' Morse had asked.

'You know bloody well—'

'I'm still on furlough, sir. I'm trying to catch up with the housework.'

'Have you been drinking, Morse?'

'Just starting, sir.'

'Mind if I come and join you?'

'Not this afternoon, sir. I've got a wonderful – odd, actually! – got a wonderful Swedish girl in the flat with me just at the moment.'

'Oh!'

'Look,' said Morse slowly, 'if there *is* a breakthrough in the case. If there *does* seem some reason—'

'You been reading the correspondence?'

'I'd sooner miss *The Archers*!'

'Do you think it's all a hoax?'

Strange heard Morse's deep intake of breath: 'No! No, I don't. It's just that we're going to get an awful lot of false leads and false confessions – you know that. We always do. Trouble is, it makes us look such idiots, doesn't it – if we take everything *too* seriously.'

Yes, Strange accepted that what Morse had just said was exactly his own view. 'Morse. Let me give you a ring tomorrow, all right? We've got those bloody yoiks out on Broadmoor Lea to sort out . . .'

'Yes, I've been reading about it while I was away.'

'Enjoy your holiday, in Lyme?'

'Not much.'

'Well, I'd better leave you to your . . . your "wonderful Swedish girl", wasn't it?'

'I wish you would.'

After Morse had put down his phone, he switched his CD player on again to the Immolation Scene from the finale of Wagner's *Götterdämmerung*; and soon the pure and limpid voice of the Swedish soprano, Birgit Nilsson, resounded again through the chief inspector's flat.

CHAPTER TWENTY

When I complained of having dined at a splendid table without hearing one sentence worthy to be remembered, he [Dr Johnson] said, 'There is seldom any such conversation'

(James Boswell, *The Life of Samuel Johnson*)

IN THE small hours of Sunday, 12 July, Claire Osborne still lay awake, wondering yet again about what exactly it was she wanted from life. It had been all right – it usually was 'all right'. Alan was reasonably competent, physically – and so loving. She liked him well enough, but she could never be in love with him. She had given him as much of herself as she could; but where, she asked herself, was the memorability of it all? Where the abiding joy in yet another of their brief, illicit, slightly disturbing encounters?

'To hell with this sex lark, Claire!' her best friend in Salisbury had said. 'Get a man who's interesting, that's what I say. Like Johnson! Now, he was interesting!'

'*Doctor* Johnson? He was a great fat slob, always dribbling his soup down his waistcoat, and he was smelly, and never changed his underpants!'

'Never?'

'You know what I mean.'

'But everybody wanted to hear him *talk*, didn't they? That's what I'm saying.'

'Yeah. I know what you mean.'

'Yeah!'

And the two women had laughed together – if with little conviction.

Alan Hardinge had earlier said little about the terrible accident: a few stonily spoken details about the funeral; about the little service they were going to hold at the school; about the unexpected helpfulness of the police and the authorities and support groups and neighbours and relatives. But Claire had not questioned him about any aspect of his own grief. She would, she knew, be trespassing upon a territory that was not, and never could be, hers . . .

It was 3.30 a.m. before she fell into a fitful slumber.

At the breakfast table the following morning she explained briefly that her husband had been called away and that there would be just her: coffee and toast, please – nothing more. A dozen or so newspapers, room-numbered in the top-right corner, lay in a stag-gered pile on a table just inside the breakfast room – *The Sunday Times* not amongst them.

Jim O'Kane seldom paid too much attention to the front page of the 'Sundays'; but ten minutes before Claire had put in an appearance, he'd spotted the photograph. Surely he'd seen that young girl before! He took *The Sunday Times* through to the kitchen where, under the various grills, his wife was watching the progress of bacon, eggs, tomatoes, mushrooms, and sausages. He pointed to the black and white photograph on the front page:

'Recognize her?'

Anne O'Kane stared at the photograph for a few seconds, quizzically turning her head one way, then the other, seeking to assess any potential likeness to anyone she'd ever met. 'Should I?'

'I think *I* do! You remember that young blonde girl who called – about a year ago – when we had a vacancy – one Sunday – and then she called again – later – when we hadn't?'

'Yes, I do remember,' Anne said slowly. 'I *think* I do.' She had been quickly reading the article beneath the photograph, and she now looked up at her husband as she turned over half a dozen rashers of bacon. 'You don't mean . . .?'

But Jim O'Kane *did* mean.

Claire was on her last piece of toast when she found her hostess standing beside her with the newspaper. 'We pinched this for a minute – hope you didn't mind.'

'Course not.'

'It's just that' – Anne pointed to the reproduction – 'well, it looks a bit like a young girl who called here once. A young girl who disappeared about a year ago.'

'Long time, a year is.'

'Yes. But Jim – my husband – he doesn't often forget faces; and I think,' she added quietly, 'I think he's right.'

Claire glanced down at the photograph and the article, betraying (she trusted) not a hint of her excitement. 'You'd better tell them – the police, hadn't you?'

'I suppose we should. It's just that Jim met one of the men from CID recently at a charity do, and this fellow said one of the biggest problems with murders is all the bogus confessions and hoax calls you always get.'

'But if you *do* recognize her—'

'Not one hundred per cent. Not really. What I do remember is that this girl I'm thinking of called and asked if we'd got a room and then when she knew what it would cost she just sort of ... Well, I think she couldn't afford it. Then she called back later, this same girl ...'

'And you were full?'

Anne O'Kane nodded sadly, and Claire finished a last mouthful of toast. 'Not always easy to know what to do for the best.'

'No.'

'But if your husband knows this CID man he could always just, you know, mention it unofficially, couldn't he?'

'Ye-es. Wouldn't do any harm. You're right. And he only lives just up the road. In one of the bachelor flats.'

'What's his name? Lord Peter Wimsey?'

'Morse. Chief Inspector Morse.'

Claire looked down at her empty plate, and folded her white linen table napkin.

'More toast?' asked Anne O'Kane.

Claire shook her head, her flawlessly painted lips showing neither interest nor surprise.

CHAPTER TWENTY-ONE

It is only the first bottle that is expensive

(French proverb)

CLAIRE OSBORNE had discovered what she wanted that same morning. However, it was not until the following morning, 13 July (Sunday spent with Alan Hardinge), that she acted upon her piece of research. It had been terribly easy – just a quick look through the two-inch-thick phone-book for Oxford and District which lay beside the pay-phone: several Morses, but only one 'Morse, E.' – and the phone number, to boot! Leys Close, she learned from the Oxford street-map posted on the wall just inside the foyer, looked hardly more than two hundred yards away. She could have asked the O'Kanes, of course . . . but it was a little more exciting not to.

It was another fine sunny morning; and having packed her suitcase and stowed it in the boot of the Metro, and with permission to leave the car ('Shouldn't be all that long,' she'd explained), she walked slowly up towards the roundabout, soon coming to the sign 'Residents Only: No Public Right of Way', then turning left through a courtyard, before arriving at a row of two-storey, yellow-bricked, newish properties, their woodwork painted a uniform white. The number she sought was the first number she saw.

COLIN DEXTER

After knocking gently, she noticed, through the window to her left, the white shelving of a kitchen unit and a large plastic bottle of Persil on the draining board. She noticed, too, that the window directly above her was widely open, and she knew that he must be there even before she saw the vague silhouette behind the frosted glass.

What the hell are you doing here? – is that what she'd expected him to say? But he said nothing as he opened the door, bent down to pick up a red-topped bottle of semi-skimmed Co-op milk, stood to one side, inclined his head slightly to the right, and ushered her inside with an old-world gesture of hospitality. She found herself in a large lounge with two settees facing each other, the one to her left in a light honey-coloured leather, to which Morse pointed, and in which she now sat – a wonderfully soft and comfortable thing! Music was playing – something with a sort of heavyweight sadness about it which she thought she almost recognized. Late nineteenth century? Wagner? Mahler? Very haunting and beautiful. But Morse had pressed a panel in the sophisticated bank of equipment on the shelves just behind the other settee, a smaller one in black leather, in which he seated himself and looked across at her, his blue eyes showing a hint of amusement but nothing of surprise.

'No need to turn it off for me, you know.'

'Of course not. I turned it off for *me*. I can never do two things at the same time.'

Looking at the almost empty glass of red wine which stood on the low coffee table beside him, Claire found herself doubting the strictly literal truth of the statement.

'Wagner, was it?'

Morse's eyes lit up with some interest. 'It does show some Wagnerian harmonic and melodic traits, I agree.'

What a load of crap, the pompous oaf! Blast him. Why didn't he just *tell* her? She pointed to the bottle of Quercy: 'I thought you couldn't cope with two things at once?'

'Ah! But drinking's like breathing, really. You don't have to think about it, do you? And it's good for you – did you know that? There's this new report out saying a regular drop of booze is exceedingly good for the heart.'

'Not quite so good for the liver, though.'

'No.' He smiled at her now, leaning back in the settee, his arms stretched out along the top, wearing the same short-sleeved pink shirt she'd seen him in the previous Saturday. He probably needed a woman around the house.

'I thought you were supposed to wait till the sun had passed the yard-arm, or something like that.'

'That's an odd coincidence!' Morse pointed to *The Times* on the coffee table. 'It was in the crossword this morning: "yard-arm".'

'What is a yard-arm, exactly?'

Morse shook his head. 'I'm not interested in boats or that sort of thing. I prefer the Shakespeare quote – remember? That line about "the prick of noon"?'

'"The bawdy hand of the dial is now upon the prick of noon"?'

109

'How on earth did you know that?'

'I once played the Nurse in *Romeo and Juliet.*'

'Not the sort of thing for a schoolgirl—'

'University, actually.'

'Oh. I was never on the boards much myself. Just the once really. I had a line "I do arrest thee, Antonio". For some reason it made the audience laugh. Never understood why . . .'

Still clutching her copies of the previous day's *Sunday Times* and the current issue of *The Times*, Claire looked slowly around at the book-lined walls, at the stacks of records everywhere, at the pictures (one or two of them fractionally askew). She especially admired the water-colour just above Morse's head of the Oxford skyline in a bluey-purple wash. She was beginning to enjoy the conversational skirmishing, she admitted that; but there was still something *irritating* about the man. For the first time she looked hard, directly across at him.

'You're acting *now*, aren't you?'

'Pardon?'

'You're pretending you're not surprised to see me.'

'No, I'm not. I saw you sitting outside the Cotswold House yesterday; smoking a cigarette. I was walking down to Cutteslowe for a newspaper.'

'Mind if I smoke now?'

'Please do. I've, er, stopped myself.'

'Since when?'

'Since this morning.'

'Would you like one?'

'Yes, please.'

Claire inhaled deeply, crossed her legs as she sat

down again, and pulled her Jaeger skirt an inch or so below her knees.

'Why didn't you say hello?' she asked.

'I was on the opposite side of the road.'

'Not very pally, was it?'

'Why didn't you say hello to me?'

'I didn't see you.'

'I think you did, though.' His voice was suddenly gentle and she had the feeling that he knew far more about her than he should. 'I think you saw me late Saturday afternoon as well – just after you'd arrived.'

'You *saw* me? You saw me when you walked by with your booze?'

Morse nodded.

Blast him! Blast him! 'I suppose you think you know why I've come here now.'

Morse nodded again. 'It's not because I'm psychic, though. It's just that Jim, Mr O'Kane, he rang me yesterday . . .'

'About this?' She held up the newspapers.

'About the girl possibly calling there, yes. Very interesting, and very valuable, perhaps – I don't know. They're going to make a statement. Not to me though, I'm on holiday. Remember?'

'So it's a bit of a wasted journey. I was going to tell you—'

'Not a wasted journey – don't say that!'

'I – I kept thinking about the girl – all day yesterday . . . well, quite a few times yesterday . . . You know, her calling there and perhaps not having the money and then—'

'How much does a single room cost there now?'

'I'm not sure. And you're acting again! You know perfectly well I booked a *double*, don't you? A double for two nights. You asked O'Kane – you nosey bloody parker!'

For several seconds Morse seemed to look across the room at her with a steady intensity. 'You've got beautifully elegant legs,' he said simply; but she sensed that her answer may have caused him a minor hurt. And suddenly, irrationally, she wanted him to come across the room to her, and take her hand. But he didn't.

'Coffee?' he asked briskly. 'I've only got instant, I'm afraid.'

'Some people prefer instant.'

'Do you?'

'No.'

'I don't suppose I can, er, pour you a glass of wine?'

'What on earth makes you suppose that?'

'Quite good,' she commented, a minute or so later.

'Not bad, is it? You need a lot of it though. No good in small quantities.'

She smiled attractively. 'I see you've finished the crossword.'

'Yes. It's always easy on a Monday, did you know that? They work on the assumption that everybody's a bit bleary-brained on a Monday morning.'

'A lot of people take *The Times* just for the crossword.'

'Yep.'

'And the Letters, of course.'

Morse watched her carefully. 'And the Letters,' he repeated slowly.

Claire unfolded her own copy of *The Times*, 13 July, and read aloud from a front-page article:

CLUES TO MISSING STUDENT

BOTH *The Times* offices and the Thames Valley Police are each still receiving about a dozen letters a day (as well as many phone calls) in response to the request for information concerning the disappearance a year ago of Karin Eriksson, the Swedish student who is thought to be the subject of the anonymous verses received by the police and printed in these columns (July 3). Chief Superintendent Strange of Thames Valley CID himself believes that the ingenious suggestions received in one of the latest communications (see Letters, page 15) are the most interesting and potentially the most significant hitherto received.

'You must have read that?'

'Yes. The trouble is, just like Mr and Mrs O'Kane said, you can't follow up everything. Not even a tenth of the things that come in. Fortunately a lot of 'em are such crack-pot...' He picked up his own copy and turned to page 15, and sat looking (again) at the 'ingenious suggestions'.

'Clever – clever analysis,' he remarked.

'Obviously a very clever fellow – the one who wrote that.'

'Pardon?' said Morse.

113

'The fellow who wrote that letter.'

Morse read the name aloud: 'Mr Lionel Regis? Don't know him myself.'

'Perhaps nobody does.'

'Pardon?'

'See the address?'

Morse looked down again, and shook his head. 'Don't know Salisbury very well myself.'

'It's *my* address!'

'Really? So – are you saying *you* wrote this?'

'Stop it!' she almost shrieked. '*You* wrote it! You saw my address in the visitors' book at Lyme Regis, and you needed an address for this letter, otherwise your – your "ingenious suggestions" wouldn't be accepted. Am I right?'

Morse said nothing.

'You *did* write it, didn't you? *Please* tell me!'

'Yes.'

'Why? Why go to all this silly palaver?'

'I just – well, I just picked someone from the top of my mind, that's all. And you – you were there, Claire. Right at the top.'

He'd spoken simply, and his eyes lifted from her legs to her face; and all the frustration, all the infuriation, suddenly drained away from her, and the tautness in her shoulders was wonderfully relaxed as she leaned back against the soft contours of the settee.

For a long time neither of them spoke. Then Claire sat forward, emptied her glass, and got to her feet.

'Have you got to go?' asked Morse quietly.

'Fairly soon.'

'I've got another bottle.'

'Only if you promise to be nice to me.'

'If I tell you what lovely legs you've got again?'

'*And* if you put the record on again.'

'CD actually. *Bruckner Eight.*'

'Is that what it was? Not all that far off, was I?'

'Very close, really,' said Morse. Then virtually to himself: for a minute or two, very close indeed.

It was halfway through the accord movement and three-quarters of the way through the second bottle that the front doorbell rang.

'I can't see you for the minute, I'm afraid, sir.'

Strange sniffed, his small eyes suspicious.

'Really? I'm a little bit surprised about that, Morse. In fact I'm surprised you can't see *two* of me!'

CHAPTER TWENTY-TWO

> In a Definition-and-Letter-Mixture puzzle, each clue
> consists of a sentence which contains a definition of the
> answer and a mixture of the letters
>
> (Don Manley, *Chambers Crossword Manual*)

THERE WERE just the two of them in Strange's office
the following morning, Tuesday, 14 July.

It had surprised Strange not a little to hear of Morse's
quite unequivocal refusal to postpone a few days of his
furlough and return immediately to HQ to take official
charge of the case; especially in view of the latest letter
– surely the break they'd all been hoping for. On the
other hand there were more things in life than a blonde
damozel who might or might not have been murdered
a year ago. This bloody 'joy'(huh!)-riding, for a start –
now hitting the national news and the newspaper headlines. It all served, though, to put things into perspective
a bit – like the letter he himself had received in the post
('Strictly Personal') that very morning:

> To Chief Superintendent Strange,
> Kidlington Police HQ
>
> Dear Sir,
> It is naturally proper that our excellent whodunnit writers
> should pretend that the average criminal in the UK can

boast the capacity for quite exceptional ingenuity in the commission of crime. But those of us who (like you) have given our lives to the detection of such crime should at this present juncture be reminding everyone that the vast majority of criminals are not (fortunately!) blessed with the sort of alpha-plus mentality that is commonly assumed. Obviously if any criminal is brought to book as a result of the correspondence etc. being conducted in sections of the national press, we shall all be most grateful. But I am myself most doubtful about such an outcome, and indeed in a wider sense I am very much concerned about the precedent involved. We have all heard of trial by TV, and we now seem to be heading for investigation by correspondence column. This is patently absurd. As I read things, the present business is pretty certainly a hoax in any case, with its perpetrator enjoying himself (or I suppose herself?) most hugely as various correspondents vie with one another in scaling ever steeper and steeper peaks of interpretive ingenuity. If the thing is *not* a hoax, I must urge that all investigation into the matter be communicated *in the first instance* to the appropriate police personnel, and most certainly not to radio, TV, or newspapers, so that the case may be solved through the official channels of criminal investigation.

Yours sincerely,
Peter Armitage
(former Assistant Commissioner, New Scotland Yard)
PS I need hardly add, I feel sure, that this letter is not for publication in any way.

But this must almost certainly have been written before its author had seen the latest communiqué from the most intrepid mountaineer so far: the writer of the quite extraordinary letter which had appeared in the correspondence columns of *The Times* the previous morning.

Strange now turned to Lewis. 'You realize it's the break, don't you?'

Lewis, like every other police officer at HQ, had read the letter; and, yes, he too thought it was the break. How else? But he couldn't understand why Strange had asked him – *him* – along that morning. He was very tired anyway, and should by rights have been a-bed. On both Saturday and Sunday nights, like most officers in the local forces, his time had been spent until almost dawn behind a riot-shield, facing volleys of bricks and insults from gangs of yobbos clapping the skidding-skills of youths in stolen cars – amongst whom (had Lewis known it) was a seventeen-year-old schoolboy who was later to provide the key to the Swedish Maiden mystery.

'Lewis! You're listening, aren't you?'

'Sorry, sir?'

'You do *remember* Morse belly-aching about transferring the search from Blenheim to Wytham?'

'Yes, sir. But he wasn't on the case more than a day or so.'

'I know that,' snapped Strange. 'But he must have had some *reason*, surely?'

'I've never quite been able to follow some of his reasons.'

'Do you know how much some of these bloody searches cost?'

'No, sir.'

Nor perhaps did Strange himself, for he immediately changed tack: 'Do you think Morse was right?'

'I dunno, sir. I mean, I think he's a great man, but he sometimes gets things awfully wrong, doesn't he?'

'And he more often gets things bloody *right*!' said Strange with vehemence.

It was an odd reversal of rôles, and Lewis hastened to put the record straight. 'I think myself, sir, that—'

'I don't give a *sod* what you think, Sergeant! If I want to search Wytham Woods I'll bloody well search 'em till a year next Friday if I – if *I* – think it's worth the candle. All right?'

Lewis nodded wordlessly across the table, watching the rising, florid exasperation in the Super's face.

'I'm not sure where I come into all this—' he began.

'Well, I'll tell you! There's only one thing you can do and I can't, Sergeant, and that's to get the morose old bugger back to work here – smartish. I'm under all sorts of bloody pressure . . .'

'But he's on holiday, sir.'

'I *know* he's on bloody holiday. I saw him yesterday, drinking shampers and listening to Schubert – with some tart or other.'

'Sure it was *champagne*, sir?'

But quietly now, rather movingly, Strange was making his plea: 'Christ knows why, Lewis, but he'll always put himself out a bit for you. Did you realize that?'

He rang from Morse's own (empty) office.

'Me, sir. Lewis.'

119

'I'm on holiday.'

'Super's just had a word with me—'

'Friday – that's what I told him.'

'You've seen the letter about Wytham, sir?'

'Unlike you and your philistine cronies, Lewis, my daily reading includes the royal circulars in *The Times*, the editorials—'

'What do I tell the Super, sir? He wants us – you and me – to take over straightaway.'

'Tell him I'll be in touch – tomorrow.'

'Tell him you'll ring, you mean?'

'No. Tell him I'll be back on duty tomorrow morning. Tell him I'll be in my office any time after seven a.m.'

'He won't be awake then, sir.'

'Don't be too hard on him, Lewis. He's getting old – and I think he's got high blood pressure.'

As he put down the phone, with supreme contentment, Lewis knew that Strange had been right – about Morse and himself; realized that in the case of the Swedish Maiden, the pair of them were in business again – w.e.f. the following morning.

In his office, Strange picked up the cutting from *The Times* and read the letter yet again. Quite extraordinary!

From Mr Lionel Regis	
Sir, Like most of your other correspondents I must assume that the 'Swedish	Maiden' verses were composed by the person responsible for the murder of that unfortunate young lady. It is of course possible they were

sent as a hoax, but such is not my view. In my opinion it is far more probable that the writer is exasperated by the inability of the police to come anywhere near the discovery of a *body*, let alone the arrest of a murderer. The verses, as I read them, are a cry from the murderer – not the victim – a cry for some discovery, some absolution, some relief from sleepless, haunted nights.

But I would not have written to you, sir, merely to air such vague and dubious generalities. I write because I am a setter of crossword puzzles, and when I first studied the verses I had just completed a puzzle in which the answer to every clue was indicated by a definition of the word to be entered, and also by a sequenced *anagram* of the same word. It was with considerable interest therefore – and a good measure of incredulity – that I gradually spotted the fact that the word WYTHAM crops up, in anagrammatized form, in each of the five stanzas. Thus: THAW MY (stanza 1); [stre]AM WHY T[ell'st] (stanza 2); WHAT MY (stanza 3); [s]AW THYM[e] (stanza 4); and [no]W THY MA[iden] (stanza 5).

The occurrence of *five* such instances is surely way beyond the bounds of coincidence. (I have consulted my mathematical friends on this matter.) 'Whytham', I learn (I am not an Oxford man), is the name of some woods situated to the west of Oxford. If the verse tells us anything then, it is surely that the body sought is to be found in Wytham Woods, and it is my humble suggestion that any further searches undertaken should be conducted in that quarter.

Yours,
LIONEL REGIS,
16 Cathedral Mews,
Salisbury.

Like Lewis, Strange remembered exactly what Morse had said on his postcard: 'I reckon *I* know what the poem means!', and he pushed the newspaper aside, and looked out across the car park. 'Lionel Regis, my arse!' he said quietly to himself.

CHAPTER TWENTY-THREE

On another occasion he was considering how best to welcome the postman, for he brought news from a world outside ourselves. I and he agreed to stand behind the front door at the time of his arrival and to ask him certain questions. On that day, however, the postman did not come

(Peter Champkin,
The Sleeping Life of Aspern Williams)

WEDNESDAY, 15 July, was never going to be a particularly memorable day. No fire-faced prophet was to bring news of the Message or the name of the One True God. Just a fairly ordinary transitional sort of day in which events appeared discrete and only semi-sequential; when some of the protagonists in the Swedish Maiden case were moved to their new positions on the chessboard, but before the game was yet begun.

At a slightly frosty meeting held in the Assistant Chief Constable's office at 10.30 a.m., the Swedish Maiden case was reviewed in considerable detail by the ACC himself, Chief Superintendent Strange, and Detective Chief Inspectors Johnson and Morse. General agreement was reached (only one dissident voice) that perhaps there was little now to be gained from any prolongation of the extensive and expensive search-programme on the Blenheim Palace Estate. The decision was reported too, emanating from 'higher authority', that Morse was now i/c and that Johnson would therefore be enabled to take his midsummer furlough as scheduled. Such official verbiage would fool no one, of course – but it was possibly better than nothing at all.

Amongst the items reviewed was yet another letter, printed that morning in *The Times*:

From Mr John C. Chavasse

Sir, The Wood (singular not plural please) at Wytham is a place most familiar to me and I suspect to almost all generatations of young men who have taken their degrees at Oxford University. Well do I remember the summer weekends in the late 40s when together with many of my fellow undergraduates I cycled up through Lower Wolvercote to Wytham.

  In lines 14 and 15 of the (now notorious!) verses, we find 'A creature white' (*sic*) 'Trapped in a gin' (*sic*),

'Panting like a hunted deer' (*sic*). Now if this is *not* a cryptic reference to a gin-and-whatnot in that splendid old hostelry in Wytham, the White Hart – then I'm a Dutchman, sir! But I am convinced (as an English-man) that such a reference can only serve to corrobor-ate the brilliant analysis of the verses made by Mr Lionel Regis (Letters, July 13).

Yours faithfully,
JOHN C. CHAVASSE,
21 Hayward Road,
Bishop Auckland.

Around the table, 'Mr Lionel Regis' looked slightly sheepish; but not for long, and now it was all an open secret anyway. He realized that there would be little he could do for a day or so – except to re-read all the material that had accumulated from the earlier enquiries; to sit tight; to get Lewis cracking on the admin; and perhaps to try to think a bit more clearly about his own oddly irrational conviction that the young student's body *would* be found – and found in Wytham Wood(s). There *was* that little bit of new evidence, too – the call from the O'Kanes. For if their memories served them to any degree aright, then Karin Eriksson had at some point gone *down* the Banbury Road from the round-about; it was the testimony of the man who had been waiting for a bus there that Sunday noon-time which should have been given credence – not that of the man who had driven along Sunderland Avenue.

Such and similar thoughts Morse shared with Sergeant Lewis in the early afternoon. Already arrangements were well in hand for the availability of about twenty further members of various local forces to supplement the thirty due to be switched immediately from Blenheim. One annoying little hold-up, though. The head forester at Wytham, Mr David Michaels, was unfortunately away that day at a National Trust conference in Durham. But he was expected home later that night, his wife said, and would almost certainly be available the following morning.

Things *were* moving, that afternoon. But slowly. And Morse was feeling restless and impatient. He returned home at 4 p.m., and began typing a list of gramophone records . . .

Before leaving him the previous Monday, a quarter

of an hour after Strange's inopportune interruption, Claire Osborne had asked him to send her his eight Desert Island Discs and the versions he possessed of the Mozart *Requiem*. It was high time she started to improve her mind a bit, she'd said; and if Morse would promise to try to help her...? So Morse had promised, and reiterated his promise as he'd kissed her briefly, sweetly, fully on the lips, at her departure.

'You do know my address, I think?' she'd shouted from the gate.

Morse was still not *quite* sure of numbers seven and eight as he sat and slowly typed his list that afternoon.

A quarter of an hour or so before Morse had begun his labour of love, Philip Daley swaggered loutishly out of his class-room in the Cherwell School, just along the Marston Ferry Road in North Oxford. Only two more days to go! Roll on! School would be finishing on the 17th and he couldn't wait to get shot of it. Shot of it for good and all! His dad (his dad's own words) didn't give a fuckin' toss, though his mum (as he knew very well) would have been glad if he could have settled down to schoolwork and stayed on in the sixth form and maybe landed up with a decent job and all that bullshit. But other thoughts were uppermost in his bitterly discontented mind as he walked up the Banbury Road that afternoon. At lunch-time he'd asked one of the girls from his class, the one with the blouseful, whether she'd go with him to the end-of-term disco; and she'd said he must be bloody jokin' and anyway she'd already got a feller, 'adn't she? Soddin' cunt! As he walked up to the shops he crashed his fist against some ancient wooden fencing there: fuck it, fuck it, *fuck* it! Just wait till Friday, though. He'd show the fuckin' lot of 'em.

It was at 7.15 p.m., twelve hours after reaching HQ earlier that day, that Lewis sat down at his home in Headington to his beloved eggs and chips.

Blast him! thought Claire, as she turned first to one side and then the other in her bed that night. She could not understand at all why he was monopolizing her thoughts – but he was. And blast that other copper – that fat slob of a man who'd stood there talking to him on the doorstep for almost a quarter of an hour. She'd have had to leave very soon anyway, she realized that. But it had meant there had been no time to develop that little passage of intimacy between them ... and now, and again, and again, he was passing through her mind. Bloody nuisance, it all was! Only temporary, she trusted – this inability to sleep, this inability to thrust him from her thoughts. She just hoped she'd get a letter from him in the next *post*, that's all. He said he'd write; he'd promised; and she'd been looking out eagerly for the postman.

On that day, however, the postman did not come.

CHAPTER TWENTY-FOUR

The Grantor leaves the guardianship of the Woodlands to the kindly sympathy of the University ... The University will take all reasonable steps to preserve and maintain the woodlands and will use them for the instruction of suitable students and will provide facilities for research

(Extract from the deed under which Wytham Wood was acquired by the University of Oxford on 4 August 1942 as a gift from Col. ffennell)

MANY Oxonians know 'Wytham' as the village on the way to the wood. But Morse knew the spot as the village, situated on the edge of the wood, which housed the White Hart Inn; and he pointed lovingly to the hostelry the next morning as Lewis drove the pair of them to their meeting with the head forester.

'Did you know,' asked Morse (consulting his leaflet) 'that in the parish of Wytham, a large part of it covered with woods, the ground rises from the banks of the Thames – or "Isis" – to a height of 539 feet at Wytham Hill, the central point of the ancient parish?'

'No, sir,' replied Lewis, turning right just after the pub into a stretch of progressively narrowing roadway that was very soon marked by the sign 'Private Property: University of Oxford'.

'You don't sound very interested—'

'Look!' shouted Lewis. 'See *that*?'

'No!' In his youth Morse had almost invariably been the boy in the group who missed out; whilst his school-mates were perpetually spotting birds' eggs, the blue flash of kingfishers, or gingery foxes momentarily motionless at the edge of cornfields, the young Morse had seldom seen anything; the old Morse had seen nothing now.

'What exactly *was* the cause of all the excitement, Lewis?'

'Deer, sir. Roe deer, I think. Two of them, just behind—'

'Are they different from normal deer?'

'I don't reckon you're going to be too much help in this neck of the woods, sir.'

Morse made no comment on such a nicely turned phrase, as Lewis drove half a mile or so further, with an area of fairly dense woodland on his left, until he reached a semi-circular parking lot, also on his left. 'Cars must be left at one of the two car parks shown on the plan', the map said; and in any case a locked barrier across the road effectively blocked further progress to motor vehicles. Lewis pulled the police car in beside an ancient, rusting Ford.

'Good to see some people care, sir,' ventured Lewis, pointing to an RSPB sticker on one side window and a larger 'Save the Whale' plea on the other.

'Probably here for a snog under the sycamores,' Morse replied cheerfully.

A low, stone-built cottage stood thirty yards or so

back on the further side of the track. 'That must be where Mr Michaels lives, sir. Nice view – looking right across there to Eynsham.'

'C'mon,' said Morse.

It was just past the barrier, which they negotiated via a kissing-gate, set in its V-shaped frame, that the two detectives came, on their left, to a large clearing, some 100 yards square, with fir-saplings planted around the fenced perimeter, in which was set a whole complex of sheds and barns, built in horizontally slatted wood, with piles of spruce- and fir-logs stacked nearby, and with several tractors and pieces of tree-felling machinery standing beside or beneath the open-fronted barns.

From the furthest shed a figure walked down the slope to greet them – a man of about fifty or so, blue-eyed, closely bearded, and little short of six foot – introducing himself as David Michaels, the head forester. They shook hands with the man, Morse being careful to keep slightly behind Lewis as a black and white dog, bounding energetically after his master, sought to introduce himself too.

In the forester's hut, Michaels briefly described the lay-out of the woods (plural!), referring repeatedly to the four Ordnance Survey maps on the inner wall, themselves pinned together in a large oblong to give a synoptic view of the whole area under the forester's charge. There was a University Committee, the policemen learnt, administering Wytham Woods, to whom he (Michaels) was personally responsible, with a University Land Agent acting as Executive Officer; and it was to the latter that the police would need to apply formally.

Permits to walk in the woods (this in answer to Lewis) were issued, on request, to any resident teachers or administrators in the University, and of course to any other citizen, Town or Gown, who was able to provide adequate cause, and no criminal impediment, for wishing to visit the area.

Morse himself became more interested when Michaels moved closer to the maps and expanded on the woods' main attractions, his right forefinger tracing its way through what (to Morse) was a wonderfully attractive-sounding catalogue: Duck Pond; The Follies; Bowling Alley; Cowleaze Copse; Froghole Cottage; Hatchett Lane; Mailey Wood; Pasticks; Singing Way; Sparrow Lane . . . almost like the music of the woods and birds themselves.

But as he watched and listened, Morse's heart was sinking slightly lower. The woodlands were vast; and Michaels himself, now in his fifteenth year there, admitted that there were several areas where he had never – probably *would* never – set foot; parts known only to the badgers and the foxes and the deer and the families of woodpeckers. Yet somehow the mention of the woodpeckers appeared to restore Morse's confidence, and he gratefully accepted the forester's offer of a guided tour.

Lewis sat on the floor in the back of the rugged, powerful, ineffably uncomfortable and bouncy Land-rover, with Bobbie, the only dog allowed in the woods. Morse sat in the front with Michaels, who spent the next ninety minutes driving across the tracks and rides and narrow paths which linked the names of his earlier litany.

For a while Morse toyed with the idea of bringing in the military perhaps – a couple of thousand men from local units, under the command of some finicky brigadier sitting in Caesar's tent and ticking off the square yards one by one. Then he put his thought into words:

'You know I'm beginning to think it'd take an army a couple of months to cover all this.'

'Oh, I don't know,' replied Michaels. Surprisingly? 'No?'

Patiently the forester explained how during the summer months there were dozens of devotees who regularly checked the numbers of eggs and weights of fledglings in the hundreds of bird-boxes there; who laid nocturnal wait to observe the doings of the badgers; who clipped tags and bugging devices to fox-cubs; and so many others who throughout the year monitored the ecological pattern that Nature had imposed on Wytham Woods. Then there were the members of the public who were forever wandering around with their birdwatchers' guides and their binoculars, or looking for woodland orchids, or just enjoying the peace and beauty of it all . . .

Morse was nodding automatically through much of the recital, and he fully took the point that Michaels was making; he'd guessed as much anyway, but things were clearer in his mind now.

'You mean there's a good deal of ground we can probably forget . . .'

'That's it. And a good deal you can't.'

'So we need to establish some priorities,' Lewis chirped up from the rear.

'That was the, er, general conclusion that Mr Michaels and myself had just reached, Lewis.'

'Eighteen months ago, all this was, you say?' asked Michaels.

'Twelve, actually.'

'So if . . . if she'd been . . . just *left* there, you know, without trying to hide her or anything . . .?'

'Oh yes, there probably wouldn't be all that much of her still around – you'll know that better than most. But it's more often "found in a shallow grave", isn't it? That's the jargon. Not surprising though that murderers should want to cover up their crimes: they often dig a bit and put twigs and leaves and things over . . . over the top. But you need a spade for that. In the summer you'd need a *sharp* spade – and plenty of time, and a bit of daylight, and a bit of nerve . . . They tell me it takes a couple of sextons about eight hours to dig a decent grave.'

Perhaps it was the crudity and cruelty of the scene just conjured up which cast a gloom upon them now – and they spoke no more of the murder for the rest of the bumpy journey. Just about birds. Morse asked about woodpeckers, and Michaels knew a great deal about woodpeckers: the green, the great-spotted, the lesser-spotted – all had their habitats within the woods and all were of especial interest to birdwatchers.

'You interested in woodpeckers, Inspector?'

Splendid birds,' muttered Morse vaguely.

*

133

Back in the hut, Morse explained the limitation of his likely resources and the obvious need therefore for some selective approach. 'What I'd really like to know is this – please don't feel offended, Mr Michaels. But if *you* wanted to hide a body in these woods, which places would come to mind first?'

So Michaels told them; and Lewis made his notes, feeling a little uneasy about his spelling of some of the names which Morse had earlier found so memorable.

When twenty minutes later the trio walked down towards the police car, they heard a sharp crack of a gun.

'One of the farmers,' explained Michaels. 'Taking a pot at some pigeons, like as not.'

'I didn't see any guns in your office,' commented Lewis.

'Oh, I couldn't keep 'em *there*! Against the law, that is, Sergeant.'

'But I suppose you must have one – in your job, sir?'

'Oh yeah! Couldn't do without. In a steel cabinet in there' – Michaels pointed to the low cottage – 'well and truly locked away, believe me! In fact, I'm off to do a bit of shooting now.'

'Off to preserve and maintain some of the local species, Mr Michaels?'

But the degree of sarcasm behind Morse's question was clearly ill-appreciated by the bearded woodsman, who replied with a decided coolness: 'Sometimes – quite often – it's essential to keep some sort of stability within *any* eco-system, and if you like I'll tell you a few things about the multiplication-factor of one or two of our randier species of deer. If I had my way, Inspector, I'd issue 'em all with free condoms from that white machine in the gents at the White Hart. But they wouldn't take much notice of me, would they?' For a few seconds Michaels' eyes glinted with the repressed anger of a professional man being told his job by some ignorant amateur.

Morse jumped in quickly. 'Sorry! I really am. It's just that as I get older I can't really think of killing things. Few years ago I'd have trodden on a spider without a thought, but these days – I don't know why – I almost feel guilty about swatting a daddy-long-legs.'

'You wouldn't find *me* killing a daddy-long-legs!' said Michaels, his eyes still hard as they stared unblinkingly back at Morse's. Blue versus blue; and for a few seconds Morse wondered what exactly Michaels *would* kill . . . and would be killing now.

CHAPTER TWENTY-FIVE

For wheresoever the carcase is, there will the eagles be gathered together

(*St Matthew*, ch. 24, v. 28)

REGIS'S (Morse's) cracking of the Swedish Maiden verses had sparked off a whole series of letters about the Great Wood at Wytham. But only one of these letters was to be published by *The Times* that week – the latest in a correspondence which was gripping the interest of that daily's readers:

From Stephen Wallhead, RA

Sir, It was with interest that I read what must surely be the final analysis of the Swedish Maiden affir. I had not myself, of course, come within a mile of the extraordinarily subtle interpretation (Letters, July 13) in which Wytham Woods are suggested – surely *more* than suggested – as the likeliest resting-place of that unfortunate girl. My letter can make only one small addendum; but I trust an interesting one, since the injunction 'Find the Woodman's daughter' (1. 6 of the verses) may now possibly be of some vital significance.

An oil-on-canvas painting, *The Woodman's Daughter*, was worked on by John Everett Millais in 1850–1. It depicts the young son of a squire offering a handful of strawberries to the young daughter of a woodman.

Millais (as always) was meticulous about his work, and the whole picture is minutely accurate in its research: for example, we know from the artist Arthur Hughes that the strawberries in the boy's hand were bought at Covent Garden in March 1851!

The background to this picture shows a woodland area with a clear perspective and a distinctive alignment of trees, and in my view it is at least a possibility that even allowing for decades of cutting-down and replantation the original site could be established. But there is the point, sir! From the diary of one of the artist's friends, Mrs Joanna Matthews, RA, we learn as follows: 'Millais is hard at work painting the background of his picture from nature in *Wytham Wood*' (my italics). Could not such a background point the place where the body is to be found? And may we not further infer that our murderer has not only an intimate knowledge of the woods themselves but also of the Pre-Raphaelite painters?

Yours faithfully,
STEPHEN WALLHEAD,
Wymondham Cottage,
Helpston, Lincs.

Early on the morning of Friday, 17 July, this letter had been seen by Strange, Morse, Lewis, and most of the personnel on duty at Thames Valley HQ. But not by everyone.

'Just tell me exactly what the 'ell we're supposed to be looking for!' Constable Jimmy Watt complained to his colleague, Constable Sid Berridge, as the two of them halted for a while, side by side, in the riding between Marley Wood on their right and Pasticks on their left.

Seventeen of them, there were, working reasonably scientifically through this particular stretch. Watt had been seconded only that day, taken (quite willingly) off traffic duties, while Berridge had already spent the earlier part of his week in Blenheim. And, in truth, their present duties were unwelcome to neither of them, for the temperature was already warm that morning, the sky an almost cloudless Cambridge blue.

'We're looking for a condom, Jimmy – preferably one with a handful of fingerprints on it—'

'Wha'? Bloody year ago?'

'—so's Morse'll be able to discover which 'and he pulled it on with.'

'We used to call 'em "french letters" in my day,' said Watt, with a hint of nostalgia in his voice.

'Yeah. Things change, though.'

'Yeah! Some of us missed out a bit, don't you reckon? The way some of these young 'uns . . .'

'Yeah.'

'Who'd you wanna go in *there* with, though?' Watt pointed to his left, to the dense patch of forestation nearby.

Berridge rose to the challenge: 'Brigitte Bardot? Liz Taylor? Joan Collins? Madonna? Me next-door neighbour's wife—'

'In *there*, though?'

Berridge decided to scale down his previous decision: 'Perhaps not . . . Perhaps only the woman next-door.'

*

It had been an hour earlier, at 8.30 a.m., that a member of the Wytham Trust had addressed their party, and explained why Pasticks could be a reasonably safe each-way bet for a site where a body may have lain undisturbed for a longish time. Why? Well, most people would think that the cutting-down of trees and the selling of the wood to wholesale dealers was invariably going to be a profitable undertaking. Not so! The expense of hiring men to saw down trees, to trim the fallen timber, then to transport and treat it, and finally to sell it to furniture dealers, or fencing designers, or the rest – such expense would always be considerable. And the Trust had long since agreed that it could do little better than see the whole business of thinning the woods, etc., as, well, as tit-for-tat: *they* would pay nothing for the cutting-back of the various copses and spinneys; and in turn the wood-cutters and carters would receive the proceeds from the tens of thousands of assorted tree-trunks that were annually removed from Wytham Woods. But occasionally there was a bit of a hiccup in the system – when, for example, a few of the areas of re-forestation were not quite ready for such biennial decimation; when the thinning of a particular area ought, for whatever reason, to be delayed for a couple of years.

Such a situation had in fact arisen the year before in the very latest plantation (1958–62) – a mixed hard-wood affair of Norwegian spruce, oak, beech, red cedar – in the area called Pasticks. And that wouldn't be a bad place to leave a body! The trees there allowed in very little light; and in the middle of it all were three or four old spinneys that had existed even before the Enclosure Acts. Dense places. Double-dense.

For Berridge and Watt the task certainly looked uninviting. From any point some two or three yards within the wood it seemed almost as if a curtain had been drawn in front of them, cutting them off from any further investigation, with the leafless horizontal and perpendicular branches of the trees there forming a sort of blurring criss-cross mesh of brown across their vision.

It was a good many hours later, at 3.55 p.m., that the deeply and progressively more pessimistic pair of constables heard a shout of triumph from somewhere to their left. A body had been found; and very soon each wing of the search-party had enfolded the scene like the wings of a mother-bird protecting her young.

The foxes had already been there – often enough by the look of it – and the badgers, and the birds of the air . . . for the bones of what appeared to be a single human being had been dragged apart there – in some cases seemingly removed – from their familiar configuration. Yet not so far removed as to render the pristine pattern unrecognizable. A femur still lay in its approximately normal relationship to its pelvis; a few ribs still in roughly parallel formation above it; a shoulder bone in a vaguely formal relationship with the vertebrae; and the vertebrae themselves about two or three feet separated from a comparatively small and badly savaged skull; not far from which was a faded, tasselled neckscarf, still boasting its original colours – the twin proud colours of the Swedish national flag.

CHAPTER TWENTY-SIX

Science is spectrum analysis: art is photosynthesis
(Karl Kraus, *Half Truths One and a Half Truths*)

WORD quickly spread and the verdict in all quarters was the same: here he was – only a couple of days into the investigation, only one day into the search, and eureka! Clever bugger, Morse! A bit lucky, perhaps. Could have been another week before they'd found her if they'd started at the other, the western, side of the woods.

'Touch nothing!', 'Keep your distance!' had been the orders of the day; and it had been around an unmolested, untrodden area of four or five square yards of woodland, carpeted with a thick, darkish-brown pile, that a rather irregular cordon had been drawn.

Morse had arrived on the scene within twenty minutes, and now stood there silently, not venturing beyond the waist-high red and white tape, his eyes recording the evidence before him. He saw the dislocated pattern of the bones; the scattered, residual clothes; and especially he saw the tasselled scarf beside the horridly damaged head. It reminded him of something from a DIY manual, in which various arrows point from the outer-lying parts towards a putative centre, giving instruction for the assemblage of the purchase: 'Bring this part into *there*, attach this part to *that*; connect *here*, it will fit, all of it, if only you take your time, read the instructions carefully, and know that you are going wrong if more than gentle force is required for the final assembly.' Occasionally Morse moved his weight slightly on the packed twigs and spindles beneath his feet; but still he said nothing. And the others standing there were silent too, like awkward mourners at a funeral.

Lewis, busily negotiating that afternoon with the University authorities, would not be with him. But neither of them, neither Morse nor Lewis, would be of much use at this stage. It was Max who was going to be the important personage, and Max had already been informed, was already on his way; Max who ten minutes later made his lumbering progress across the crackling bracken, and stood wheezing heavily beside Morse.

Silently, just as Morse had done earlier, the hump-backed surgeon surveyed the sorry sight which lay at the foot of an evergreen of some sort, the lower branches leafless, brittle, dead. If any attempt had been made to conceal the body, it was not now apparent; and disturbingly (as others had already noticed) a few of the major bones, including the whole of the lower left arm, had been carried away somewhere – to some den or earth or sets. From the look of it the clothes were slightly better preserved than the body: several strips of stained white, and substantial remnants of what looked like blue jeans, perhaps; and some yellowish, straw-coloured hair still gruesomely attached to the skull.

But Morse hadn't kept his eyes long on the skull . . .

'This what you've been looking for, Morse?'

'Yes. I think that's her.'

'Her?'

'I'm certain it's a "her",' said Morse with finality.

'Do you know the last words my old mother said? She'd been baking earlier in the day – the day she died. Then she was taken to her bed, but she still wanted to see how the fruit cake was doing. And it was flat. The bloody thing forgot to *rise*, Morse! And she said, "You know, life's full of uncertainties". Then she closed her eyes – and died.'

'It's the girl,' repeated Morse simply.

Max made no further comment, staring guardedly on as Morse nodded to the scenes-of-crime officer and the police photographer, both of whom had been standing waiting for some while. If there was anything of any import there that Morse should have seen, he was not aware of it; but he still felt nervous about the patch of ground, and instructed both to keep as far as possible from the grisly finds.

After a few minutes of photographic flashing, Max stepped rather gingerly into the area, hooked a pair of ancient spectacles around his large ears, looked down at the scattered skeleton, and picked up a bone.

'Femur, Morse. *Femur, femoris*, neuter. The thigh bone.'

'So?'

Max placed the bone down carefully and turned to

Morse. 'Look, old friend, I don't very often ask you for any forensic guidance, but just for once give me a little advice, will you? What the hell am I supposed to do with this bloody lot?'

Morse shook his head. 'I'm not sure.' But suddenly his eyes glowed as if some inner current had been activated. 'I knew she'd be here, Max,' he said slowly. 'Somehow I *knew* it! And I'm going to find out who murdered our Swedish Maiden. And I want you to help me, Max! Help me paint a picture of what went on in this place.'

The almost Messianic fierceness with which Morse had enunciated these words would have affected most people. But not Max.

'You're the artist, dear boy: I'm just a humble scientist.'

'How long will you be?'

'Looking at the bones, you mean?'

'And the clothes . . . and the underclothes.'

'Ah, yes! I remember. You've always had an interest in underclothes.' He consulted his watch. 'Opening time at six? I'll see you in the upstairs bar at the White Hart—'

'No. I've got a meeting back at HQ at half-past six.'

'Really? I thought *you* were in charge of this case, Morse.'

There were the four of them again: the ACC, Strange, Johnson, and Morse; and for the latter, naturally, congratulations were generous. For Johnson, however, there were very mixed feelings: Morse had come up with the girl's body in a couple of days, whilst he had come up with nothing in a twelve-month. That was the simple truth of the matter. It was good for the *case*, of course; but not much good for his own morale or his rating amongst his colleagues, or for his wife . . . or indeed for his newly acquired mother-in-law. But when, an hour later, the meeting broke up, he shook Morse's hand and wished him well, and almost meant it.

After the ACC and Johnson had left, Strange in turn wished Morse continued success, observing that now Morse had come up with a body, all that remained for him was to come up with a murderer, so that he, Strange, would be able to get a nice little report and send it to the DPP. No problems! Then they'd kick the smart-alec defence lawyers up the arse, and stick the bugger who did it in the nick for the rest of his natural. Put a rope round his bloody neck, too, if Strange had *his* way.

'Just as well we didn't hang the Birmingham Six,' said Morse quietly.

CHAPTER TWENTY-SEVEN

It was a maxim with Foxey – our revered father, gentlemen – 'Always suspect everybody'
(Charles Dickens, *The Old Curiosity Shop*)

ON THE following morning, Saturday, 18 July, Morse appeared, as Lewis saw things, somewhat distanced, somewhat reserved. It was customary for the chief to start, if not always to continue, any case with a surfeit of confidence and exuberance, and doubtless that would soon be the way of things again; just not for the moment.

'Not really all *that* much to go on there, sir.' Lewis nodded to the two red box-files on the table.

'I've done my homework too, you know.'

'Where do we start?'

'Difficult. We ought really to wait till we hear from Max before we do too much.'

'All this DNA stuff, you mean?'

'DNA? He doesn't know what it *stands* for!'

'When's the report due?'

'Today some time, he said.'

'What's that mean?'

'Tonight?' Morse shrugged. But he suddenly sat forward in the black leather chair, appeared to sharpen up, took out his silver Parker pen, and began making a few minimal notes as he spoke:

'There are several people we've got to see pretty soon.'

'Who are you thinking of, sir?'

'Of whom am I thinking? Well, number one, there's the fellow who found the rucksack – Daley. We'll go through his statement with a nit-comb. I never did like the sound of him.'

'You never met him, did you?'

'Number two. There's the YWCA woman who spoke with Karin before she left for Oxford. She sounds nice.'

'But you never—'

'I spoke to her on the phone, Lewis, if you must know. She sounds nice – that's all I said. You don't *mind*, do you?'

Lewis smiled to himself. It was good to be back in harness.

'Number three,' resumed Morse. 'We must have a long session with that Wytham fellow – the Lone Ranger, or whatever he's called.'

'Head forester, sir.'

'Exactly.'

'Did you like *him*?'

Morse turned over the palm of his right hand, and considered his inky fingers. 'He virtually told us where she was, didn't he? Told us where *he* would hide a body if he had to . . .'

'Not likely to have told us if he'd put it there *himself* though, surely? Self-incrimination, that!'

Morse said nothing.

'The witnesses who said they saw her, sir – any good going back over them?'

'Doubt it, but ... Anyway, let's put 'em down, number four. And number five, the parents—'

'Just the mother, sir.'

'—in Uppsala—'

'Stockholm, now.'

'Yes. We shall have to see her again.'

'We shall have to *tell* her first, surely.'

'If it is Karin, you mean?'

'You don't really have much doubt, do you, sir?'

'No!'

'I suppose you'll be going there yourself? To Stockholm, I mean.'

Morse looked up, apparently with some surprise. 'Or you, Lewis. Or *you*!'

'Very kind of you, sir.'

'Not kind at all. Just that I'm scared stiff of flying – you know that.' But the voice was a little sad again.

'You all right?' Lewis asked quietly.

'Shall be soon – don't worry! Now, I just wonder whether Mr George Daley's still working on the Blenheim Estate.'

'Saturday, though. More likely to be off today.'

'Yes ... And his son – Philip, was it? – the lad who had a short-term birthday present of a camera, Karin Eriksson's camera. He was still at school last year.'

'Probably still is.'

'No – not precisely so, Lewis. The state schools in Oxfordshire broke up yesterday, the seventeenth.'

149

'How'd you know that?'

'I rang up and found out. That's how.'

'You've been having a fair old time on the phone!' said Lewis happily, as he got to his feet – and went for the car.

As he drove out along the A44 to Begbroke, Lewis's eyes drifted briefly if incuriously to his left as Morse opened an envelope, took out a single handwritten sheet of A4, and read it; not (in fact) for the first, or even the fourth, time:

Dear Chief Inspector,

V m t f y l and for your interesting choice of records.

It would make a good debate in the Oxford Union – 'This house believes that openness in matters of infidelity is preferrable to deception.' But let me tell you what you want to know. I was married in '76, divorced in '82, remarried in '84, separated in '88. One child, a daughter now aged 20. Work that out, clever-clogs! As you know I consort fairly regularly with a married man from Oxford, and at less frequent intervals with others. So there! And now – Christ! – *you* come along and I hate you for it because you're monopolizing my thoughts just when I'd told myself I was beyond all that nonsense.

I write for two reasons. First to say I reckon I've got some idea how that young girl who monopolizes *your* thoughts may have come by a bit of cash. (Same way I did!) Second to say you're an arrogant sod! You write to me as if you think I'm an ignorant little schoolgirl. Well let me tell you you're not the only sensitive little flower in the whole bloody universe. You quote these poets as if you think you're connected on some direct personal line with them all. Well you're wrong. There's hundreds of extensions, just like in the office I used to work. So there!

Please write again.

Dare I send you a little of my love? C.

Morse hadn't noticed the misspelling before; and as he put the letter away he promised himself not to mention it . . . when he wrote back.

'I'm still not quite sure why we're interviewing Mr Daley, sir.'

'He's hiding something, that's why.'

'But you can't say *that*—'

'Look, Lewis, if he's *not* hiding something, there's not much reason for us interviewing him, is there?'

Lewis, not unaccustomedly, was bewildered by such zany logic; and he let it go.

Anyway, Morse was suddenly sounding surprisingly cheerful.

CHAPTER TWENTY-EIGHT

Be it ever so humble there's no place like home for
sending one slowly crackers

(Diogenes Small, *Obiter Dicta*)

GEORGE DALEY, on overtime, was planting out flowers
in the Blenheim Garden Centre when he looked up
and saw the two men, the shorter of them flashing a
warrant card briefly in front of his face. He knew what
it was all about, of course. *The Oxford Mail* had been
taking a keen interest in the resurrected case; and it
would be only a matter of time, Daley had known,
before the police would be round again.

'Mr Daley? Chief Inspector Morse. And this is
Sergeant Lewis.'

Daley nodded, prodded his splayed fingers round a
marigold, and got to his feet. He was a man in his mid-
forties, of slim build, wearing a shabby khaki-green
pork-pie hat. This he pushed back slightly, revealing a
red line on his sweaty forehead.

'It's that thing I found, I suppose?'

'Those things – yes,' said Morse carefully.

'I can only tell you the same as I told 'em at the time.
I made a statement and I signed it. Nothin' else as I can
do.'

Morse took a folded sheet of A4 from his inside

152

pocket, opened it out, and handed it to Daley. 'I'd just like you to read this through and make sure it's – well, you know, see if there's anything else you can add.'

'I've told you. There's nothin' else.' Daley rubbed a hand across an unshaven cheek with the sound of sandpaper on wood.

'I'd just like you to read it through *again*,' said Morse simply. 'That's all.'

'I shall need me specs. They're in the shed—'

'Don't worry now! Better if you give yourself a bit of time. No rush. As I say, all I want you to do is to make sure everything's there just as you said it, nothing's been missed out. It's often the little things, you know, that make all the difference.'

'If there was anythin' else I'd've told the other inspector, wouldn't I?'

Was it Lewis's imagination, or was there a momentary glint of anxiety in the gardener's pale eyes?

'Are you in this evening, Mr Daley?' asked Morse.

'Wha' – Saturday? I usually go over the pub for a jar or two at the weekends but—'

'If I called at your house about – what, seven?'

George Daley stood motionless, his eyes narrowed and unblinking as he watched the two detectives walk away through the archway and into the visitors' car park. Then his eyes fell on the photocopied statement once more. There was just that one thing that worried him, yes. It was that bloody boy of his who'd fucked it all up. More trouble than they were worth, kids. Especially *him*! Becomin' a real troublemaker he was, gettin' in all hours – like last night. Three bloody thirty a.m. With his mates, he'd said – after the end-of-term knees-up. He'd got a key all right, of course, but his mother could never sleep till he was in. Silly bitch!

'Where to, sir?' queried Lewis.
    'I reckon we'll just call round to see Mrs Daley.'
    'What do you make of Mr?'
    'Little bit nervous.'
    'Most people get a bit nervous with the police.'
    'Good cause, some of 'em,' said Morse.

Lewis had earlier telephoned Margaret Daley about her husband's whereabouts, and the woman who opened the door of number 2 Blenheim Villas showed no surprise. She appeared, on first impressions, a decided cut or two above her horticultural spouse: neatly dressed, pleasantly spoken, well groomed – her light-brown hair professionally streaked with strands of blonde and grey.
    Morse apologized for disturbing her, looked around him at the newly decorated, neatly furnished, through-lounge; offered a few 'nice-little-place-you-have-here' type compliments; and explained why they'd called and would be calling again – one of them, certainly – at seven o'clock that evening.
    'It was you, Mrs Daley, wasn't it, who got your husband to hand the rucksack in?'

154

'Yes – but he'd have done it himself anyway. Later on. I know he would.'

The shelves around the living area were lined with china ornaments of all shapes and sizes; and Morse walked over to the shelf above the electric fire, and carefully picked up the figure of a small dog, examining it briefly before replacing it on its former station.

'King Charles?'

Margaret Daley nodded. 'Cavalier King Charles. We had one – till last February. Mycroft. Lovely little dog – lovely face! We all had a good cry when the vet had to put him down. Not a very healthy breed, I'm afraid.'

'People living next to us have one of those,' ventured Lewis. 'Always at the vet. Got a medical history long as your arm.'

'Thank you, Lewis. I'm sure Mrs Daley isn't over-anxious to be reminded of a family bereavement—'

'Oh, it's all right! I quite like talking about him, really. We all – Philip and George – we all loved him. In fact he was about the only thing that'd get Philip out of bed sometimes.'

But Morse's attention appeared to have drifted far from dogs as he gazed through the french windows at the far end of the room, his eyes seemingly focused at some point towards the back of the garden – a garden just over the width of the house and stretching back about fifty feet to a wire fence at the bottom, separating the property from the open fields beyond. As with the patch of garden in the front, likewise here: George Daley, it had to be assumed, reckoned he did quite enough gardening in the course of earning his daily bread at Blenheim, and carried little if anything of his horticultural expertise into the rather neglected stretch of lawn which provided the immediate view from the rear of number 2.

'I don't believe it!' said Morse. 'Isn't that *Asphodelina lutea*?'

Mrs Daley walked over to the window.

'There!' pointed Morse. 'Those yellow things, just across the fence.'

'Buttercups!' said Lewis.

'You've, er, not got a pair of binoculars handy, Mrs Daley?'

'No – I – we haven't, I'm afraid.'

'Mind if we have a look?' asked Morse. 'Always contradicting me, my sergeant is!'

The three of them walked out through the kitchen door, past the (open) out-house door, and on to the back lawn where the daisies and dandelions and broad-leaf plantain had been allowed a generous freedom of movement. Morse himself stepped up to the fence, looking down at the ground around him; then, cursorily, at the yellow flowers he had spotted earlier, and which he now agreed to be nothing rarer than buttercups. Mrs Daley smiled vaguely at Lewis; but Lewis was now listening to Morse's apparently aimless chatter with far greater interest.

'No compost heap?'

'No. George isn't much bothered with the garden here, as you can see. Says he's got enough, you know . . .' She pointed vaguely towards Blenheim, and led the way back in.

'How do you get rid of your rubbish then?'

'Sometimes we go down to the waste disposal with it. Or you can buy those special bags from the council. We *used* to burn it, but a couple of years ago we upset the neighbours – you know, bits all over the washing and—'

'Probably against the bye-laws, too,' added Lewis; and for once Morse appeared to appreciate the addendum.

It was Lewis too, as they were leaving, who spotted the rifle amid the umbrellas, the walking sticks, and the warped squash racket, in a stand just behind the front door.

'Does your husband do a bit of shooting?'

'Oh *that*! George occasionally . . . yes . . .'

Gently, for a second time, Lewis reminded her of the law's demands: 'Ought to be under lock and key, that. Perhaps you'd remind your husband, Mrs Daley.'

Margaret Daley watched them through the front window as they walked away to their car. Just a bit of a stiff-shirt, the sergeant had been, about their legal responsibilities. Whereas the inspector – well, he'd seemed much nicer with his interest in dogs and flowers and the decoration in the lounge – *her* decoration. Yet during the last few minutes she'd begun to suspect her judgement a little, and she had the feeling that it would probably be Morse who would be returning that evening. Not that there was anything to worry about, really. Well, just the one thing, perhaps.

*

157

In spite of that day being Saturday – and the first of the holidays – Mrs Julie Ireson, careers mistress at the Cherwell School, Oxford, had been quite willing to meet Lewis just after lunch; and Lewis was anxious to get the meeting over as soon as possible, for he was desperately tired and had been only too glad to accept Morse's strict directive for a long rest – certainly for the remainder of the day, and perhaps for the next day, Sunday, too – unless there occurred any dramatic development.

She was waiting in the deserted car park when Lewis arrived, and immediately took him up to her first-floor study, its walls and shelves festooned with literature on nursing, secretarial courses, apprenticeship schemes, industrial training, FEs, polys, universities ... For Lewis (whose only career advice had been his father's dictum that he could do worse than to keep his mouth mostly shut and his bowels always open), a school-based advice centre for pupils leaving school was an interesting novelty.

A buff-coloured folder containing the achievements of Philip Daley was on the table ready for him. Non-achievements rather. He was now just seventeen years old, and had officially abandoned any potential advancement into further education w.e.f. 7 July – the previous day. The school was prepared to be not overpessimistic about some minor success in the five GCSE subjects in which, the previous term, he had tried (though apparently not overhard) to satisfy his examiners: English; Technical Drawing; Geography; General Science; and Communication Studies. Over the years, however, the reports from his teachers, even in nonacademic subjects, had exhibited a marked lack of enthusiasm about his attitude and progress. Yet until fairly recently he appeared not to have posed any great problem to the school community: limited, clearly, in intellectual prowess; limited too in most technical and vocational skills; in general about average.

Current educational philosophy (Lewis learned) encouraged a measure of self-evaluation, and amongst other documents in the folder was a sheet on which eighteen months previously, in his own handwriting, Philip had filled in a questionnaire about his six main 'Leisure Interests/Pastimes', in order of preference. The list read thus:

1. Football
2. Pop music
3. Photography
4. Pets
5. Motorbikes
6. TV

'He can spell OK,' commented Lewis.

'Difficult to misspell "pets", Sergeant.'

'Yes. But – well, "photography" . . .

'Probably had to look it up in the dictionary.'

'You didn't like him?' said Lewis slowly.

'No, I'm afraid I didn't. I'm glad he's gone, if you must know.' She was younger than Lewis had expected: perhaps more vulnerable too?

'Any particular reason?'

'Just general, really.'

'Well, thanks very much, Mrs Ireson. If I could take the folder?'

'Any particular reason you want to know about him?'

'No. Just general, really,' echoed Lewis.

He slept from 6.30 that evening through until almost ten the following morning. When he finally awoke, he learned there had been a telephone message the previous evening from Morse: on no account was he to come in to HQ that Sunday; it would be a good idea, though, to make sure his passport was in order.

Well, well!

CHAPTER TWENTY-NINE

Every roof is agreeable to the eye, until it is lifted; then
we find tragedy and moaning women, and hard-eyed
husbands

(Ralph Waldo Emerson, *Experience*)

IT WAS two minutes to seven by the Jaguar's fascia
clock when Morse pulled up in the slip-road outside
number 2 Blenheim Villas. He was fairly confident of
his ground now, especially after reading through the
folder that Lewis had left. Certain, of course, about the
electric fire in the Daleys' main lounge; almost certain
about the conversion of the old coal-house into a utility
room, in which, as they'd walked out to the garden,
he'd glimpsed the arrangement of washing-machine
and tumble-drier on newly laid red tiles; not *quite* so
certain about the treeless back garden though, for
Morse was ridiculously proud about never having been
a boy scout, and his knowledge of camp-fires and cocoa-
barbecues, he had to admit, was almost nil.

For once he felt relieved to be on his own as he
knocked at the front door. The police as a whole were
going through a tough time in public esteem: allegations of corrupt officers, planted evidence, improper
procedures – such allegations had inevitably created
suspicion and some hostility. And – yes, Morse knew it

– he himself was on occasion tempted to overstep the procedural boundaries a little – as shortly he would be doing again. It was a bit like a darts player standing a few inches in front of the oche as he threw for the treble-twenty. And Lewis would not have brooked this; and would have told him so.

In the lounge, in a less than convivial atmosphere, the Daleys sat side by side on the settee; and Morse, from the armchair opposite, got down to business.

'You've managed to go through the statement again, Mr Daley?'

'You don't mind the wife being here?'

'I'd prefer it, really,' said Morse innocently.

'Like I said, there's nothin' as I can add.'

'Fine.' Morse reached across and took the now rather grimy photocopy and looked through it slowly himself before lifting his eyes to George Daley.

'Let me be honest with you, sir. It's this camera business that's worrying me.'

'Wha' abou' i'?' (If the dietitian sometimes had paid overnice attention to her dental consonants, Daley himself almost invariably ignored them.)

Morse moved obliquely into the attack: 'You interested in photography yourself?'

'Me? Not much, no.'

'You, Mrs Daley?'

She shook her head.

'Your son Philip is though?'

'Yeah, well, he's got fairly interested in it recently,

hasn't he, luv?' Daley turned to his wife, who nodded vaguely, her eyes on Morse continuously.

'Bit more than "recently", perhaps?' Morse suggested. 'He put it down on his list of hobbies at school last year – early last year – a few months before you found the camera.'

'Yeah, well, like I said, we was going to get him one anyway, for his birthday. Wasn't we, luv?' Again, apart from a scarce-discernible nod, Margaret Daley appeared reluctant verbally to confirm such an innocent statement.

'But you've never had a camera yourself, you say.'

'Correck!'

'How did you know the film in the camera was finished then?'

'Well, you know, it's the numbers, innit? It tells you, like, when you've got to the finish.'

'When it reads "ten", you mean?'

'Somethin' like that.'

'What if there are twelve exposures on the reel?'

'Dunno.' Daley appeared not to be at all flustered by the slightly more aggressive tone of the question. 'It was probably Philip as said so.' Again he turned to his wife. 'Was his ten or twelve, luv? D'you remember?'

Morse pounced on the answer: 'So he had a camera *before*?'

'Yeah, well, just an el cheapo thing we bought him—'

'From Spain.' (Mrs Daley had broken her duck.)

'Would you know how to get the film *out* of a camera, Mr Daley?'

'Well, not unless, you know—'

'But it says here' – Morse looked down at the statement again – 'it says here that you burnt the film.'

'Yeah, well, that's right, isn't it, luv? We shoulda kept it, I know. Still, as I said – well, we all do things a bit wrong sometimes, don't we? And we said we was sorry about everything, didn't we, luv?'

Morse was beginning to realize that the last three words, with their appropriate variants, were a rhetorical refrain only, and were not intended to elicit any specific response.

'Where did you burn it?' asked Morse quietly.

'Dunno. Don't remember. Just chucked it on the fire, I suppose.' Daley gestured vaguely with his right hand.

'*That's* electric,' said Morse, pointing to the fireplace.

'And we got a grate for a coal-fire next door. All right?' Daley's voice was at last beginning to show signs of some exasperation.

'Did you have a fire that day?'

'How the 'ell am I supposed to remember *that*?'

'Do *you* remember, Mrs Daley?'

She shook her head. 'More than a year ago, isn't it? Could you remember that far back?'

'I've not had a coal-fire in my flat for fifteen years, Mrs Daley. So I could remember, yes.'

'Well, I'm sorry,' she said quietly, 'I can't.'

'Did you know that the temperature in Oxfordshire that day was seventy-four degrees Fahrenheit?' (Morse thought he'd got it vaguely correct.)

'Wha'! At ten o'clock at night?' Clearly Daley was losing his composure, and Morse took full advantage.

'Where do you *keep* your coal? Your coal-house has been converted to a utility-room – your wife showed—'

'If it wasn't here – all right, it wasn't *here*. Musta been in the garden, mustn't it?'

'What do you burn in the garden?'

'What do I burn? What do I *burn*? I burn bloody twigs and leaves and—'

'You haven't got any trees. And even if you had, July's a bit early for leaves.'

'Oh, for Christ's sake! Look—'

'No!' Suddenly Morse's voice was harsh and authoritative. '*You* look, Mr Daley. If you do burn your rubbish out there in the garden, come and show me where!' All pretence was now dropped as Morse continued: 'And if you make up any more lies about *that*, I'll bring a forensic team in and have 'em cart half your lawn away!'

They sat silently, the Daleys, neither looking at the other.

'Was it you who got the film developed, Mr Daley? Or was it your son?' Morse's voice was quiet once more.

'It was Philip,' said Margaret Daley, finally, now assuming control. 'He was friendly with this boy at school whose father was a photographer and had a dark-room an' all that, and they developed 'em there, I think.' Her voice sounded to Morse as if it had suddenly lost its veneer of comparative refinement, and he began to wonder which of the couple was potentially the bigger liar.

'You must tell me what those photographs were.' Morse made an effort to conceal the urgency of his request, but his voice betrayed the fear that all might well be lost.

'He never kept 'em as far as I know—' began Daley.

But his wife interrupted him: 'There were only six or seven out of the twelve that came out. There was some photos of birds – one was a pinkish sort of bird with a black tail—'

'Jay!' said Daley.

'—and there was two of a man, youngish man – probably her boyfriend. But the others, as I say . . . you know, they just didn't . . . come out.'

'I must have them,' said Morse simply, inexorably almost.

'He's chucked 'em out, surely,' observed Daley. 'What the 'ell would he keep 'em for?'

'I must have them,' repeated Morse.

'Christ! Don't you understand? I never even *saw* 'em!'

'Where is your son?'

Husband and wife looked at each other, and husband spoke: 'Gone into Oxford, I should think – Sa'day night . . .'

'Take me to his room, will you?'

'We bloody *won't*!' growled Daley. 'If you wanna look round 'ere, Inspector, you just bring a search-warrant, OK?'

'I don't need one. You've got a rifle behind the front door, Mr Daley, and it's odds-on you've got a box of cartridges somewhere lying around. All I need to do to take your floorboards up if necessary is to quote to you – just *quote*, mind – Statutory Instrument 1991 No. 1531.

Do you understand? The pair of you? That's *my* only legal obligation.'

But Morse had no further need for inaccurate improvisations regarding the recently enacted legislation on explosives. Margaret Daley rose to her feet and made to leave the lounge.

'You won't search Philip's room with *my* permission, Inspector. But if he has kept them photos I reckon I just might know . . .'

Morse heard her on the stairs, his heart knocking against his ribs: Please! Please! Please!

No word passed between the two men seated opposite each other as they heard the creak of floorboards in the upstairs rooms. Nor was much said when Margaret Daley returned some minutes later holding seven coloured prints which she handed to Morse – wordlessly!

'Thank you. No others?'

She shook her head.

After Morse was gone, Margaret Daley went into the kitchen where she turned on the kettle and spooned some instant Nescafé into a mug.

'I suppose you're out boozing,' she said tonelessly, as her husband came in.

'Why the 'ell didn't you tell *me* about them photos?'

'Shut up!' She spat out the two words viciously and turned towards him.

'Where the 'ell did you find 'em, you—'

'Shut up! And listen, will you? If you must know, I've

167

been looking in his room, George Daley, because if we don't soon get to know what's goin' on and do something about it he'll be in bloody jail or something, that's why! See? There were twelve photos, five of the girl—'

'You stupid bitch!'

'Listen!' she shrieked. 'I never gave him *them*! I've hidden 'em; and now I'm gonna get rid of 'em; and I'm not gonna show 'em to you! You don't give a sod about anything these days, anyway!'

Daley walked tight-lipped to the door. 'Stop moaning, you miserable cunt!'

His wife had taken a large pair of kitchen scissors from a drawer. 'Don't you ever talk to me like that again, George Daley!' Her voice was trembling with fury.

A few minutes after hearing the front door slam behind him, she went upstairs to their bedroom and took the five photographs out of her underwear drawer. All of them were of Karin Eriksson, nakedly or semi-nakedly lying in lewdly provocative postures. She could only guess how often her son had ogled these and similar photographs which he kept in a box at the back of his wardrobe, and which she had discovered when spring-cleaning his room the previous April. She took the five photographs to the loo, where standing over the pan she sliced strip after strip from the face, the shoulders, the breasts, the thighs, and the legs of the beautiful Karin Eriksson, intermittently flushing the celluloid slivers down into the Begbroke sewers.

CHAPTER THIRTY

A man's bed is his resting-place, but a woman's is often
her rack

(James Thurber, *Further Fables for Our Time*)

THE AMBULANCE, its blue light flashing, its siren
wailing, finally pulled into the Casualty Bay of the John
Radcliffe 2 Hospital at 9.15 p.m. The grey face of the
man hurriedly carried through the automatic doors on
a stretcher – the forehead clammy with sweat, the
breathing shallow and laboured – had told its immediate story to the red-belted senior nurse, who straightaway rang through to the medical houseman on duty,
before joining one of her colleagues in taking off the
man's clothes and fastening a hospital gown around his
overweight frame. A series of hurried readings – of
electrocardiograph, blood pressure, chest X-ray – soon
confirmed the fairly obvious: a massive coronary throm-
bosis, so very nearly an immediately fatal one.

Two porters pushed the trolley swiftly along the
corridors to the Coronary Care Unit, where they lifted
the heavy man on to a bed; around which curtains were
quickly drawn, and five leads connected to the man's
chest and linked to monitors, which now gave continuous details of heart rhythm, blood pressure, and pulse
rate, on the screen beside the bed. A very pretty, slightly

plump young nurse looked on as the houseman administered a morphine injection.

'Much hope?' she queried quietly a minute or two later, as the two of them stood at the central desk, where the VDU monitors from each of the small ward's six beds were banked.

'You never know, but . . .'

'Quite a well-known man, isn't he?'

'Taught me as a student. Well, I went to his lectures. Blood – that was his speciality, really; and he was a world authority on VD! Police get him in all the time, too – PMs, that sort of thing.'

The nurse looked at the monitor: the readings seemed significantly steadier now, and she found herself earnestly willing the old boy to survive.

'Give him some Frusemide, Nurse – as much as you like. I'm worried about all that fluid on his lungs.'

The houseman watched the monitor for another few minutes, then went over to the bed again, where the nurse had just placed a jug of water and a glass on the bedside locker.

After the houseman had left, Nurse Shelick remained beside the sick man's bed and looked down at him with that passionate intensity she invariably felt for her patients. Although still in her twenties, she was really one of that old-fashioned school who believed that whatever the advantages of hyper-technology, the virtues of simple human *nursing* were almost as indispensable. She laid the palm of her right hand across the wet, cold brow, and for the next few minutes wiped his face gently with a warm, damp flannel – suddenly aware that his eyes had opened and were looking up at her.

'Nurse?'

'I can hear you – yes?'

'Will you ... will you ... get in touch ... with someone for me?'

'Of course! Of course!' She bent her right ear towards the purple lips, but without quite making out what he was saying.

'Pardon?'

'Morse!'

'I'm sorry. Please say it again. I'm not quite sure—'

'Morse!'

'I still ... I'm sorry ... please.'

But the eyes of the man who lay upon the bed had closed again, and there was no answer to her gently repeated queries.

The time was 11.15 p.m.

The head forester's beautiful young wife was also in bed at this time. She too lay supine; and still lay supine, wakeful and waiting, until finally at 11.35 p.m. she heard the front door being opened, then locked, then bolted.

In spite of four pints of Burton ale and two whiskies at the White Hart, David Michaels knew that he was very sober; far *too* sober – for there was something sadly amiss when a man couldn't get drunk, he knew that. After cleaning his teeth, he went into the bedroom, shed his clothes swiftly, and slid under the lightweight

duvet. She always slept naked, and after their marriage
he had followed her example – often finding himself
erotically aroused not so much by the fact or the sight
of her nakedness as by the very thought of it. And now
as he moved in beside her in the darkened room, he
knew that she was suddenly and wonderfully necessary
once more. He turned his body towards her and his
right hand reached gently across her and fondled her
breast. But with her own right hand she grasped his
wrist, and with surprising strength moved it from her.

'No. Not tonight.'

'Is there something wrong?'

'I just don't want you tonight – can't you
understand?'

'I think I understand all right.' Michaels' voice was
dull and he turned to lie on his back.

'Why did you have to tell them?' she asked fiercely.

'Because I know the bloody place better than anyone
else, that's why!'

'But don't you realize—?'

'I had to tell them something. God! Don't you see
that? I didn't *know*, did I?'

She sat up in bed and leaned towards him, her right
hand on the pillow beside his head. 'But they'll think
you did it, David.'

'Don't be so stupid! I wouldn't be giving them
information if it was *me*. Can't you see that? I'm the
very *last* person they're going to suspect. But if I hadn't
agreed to help . . .'

She said nothing more; and he wondered for a while
whether it would be sensible to go down and make a

couple of cups of piping-hot coffee for them, and then perhaps turn on the bedside lamp and look upon his lovely bride. But there was no need. Seemingly Cathy Michaels had accepted the logic of his words, and her mind was more at ease; for she now lay down again and turned towards him, and soon he felt the silky caress of her inner thigh against him.

CHAPTER THIRTY-ONE

> The background reveals the true being of the man or
> thing. If I do not possess the background, I make the
> man transparent, the thing transparent
>
> (Juan Jiménez, *Selected Writings*)

IT WAS rather like trying to see the answer to a tricky
crossword clue, Morse decided, as at 11 o'clock that
same night he sat in his North Oxford lounge, topping
up his earlier libations with a few fingers of Glenfiddich,
and looking yet again at the photographs that Margaret
Daley had given him. The closer he got to the clue –
the closer he got to the photograph – the less in fact he
saw. It was necessary to stand away, to see things in
perspective, to look *synoptically* at the problem.

As he had just considered the photographs, it was
the man himself, pictured in two of them, who had
monopolized his interest: a small- to medium-sized
man, in his late twenties perhaps, with longish fair hair;
a man wearing a white T-shirt and faded-blue denims,
with a sunburnt complexion and the suggestion of a
day's growth of stubble around his jowls. But the detail
was not of sufficient definition or fidelity for him to be
wholly sure, as if the cameraman himself – or almost
certainly the camera*woman* – had scarcely the experience needed to cope with the problems of the bright

sunlight that so obviously pervaded the garden in which the snaps had been taken. But although Morse knew little (well, nothing) about photography, he was beginning to suspect that there might be slightly more competence in the arrangement of the 'subject' in relation to the 'background' than he'd originally supposed.

The man had been photographed at an oblique angle across the garden, with a house clearly shown to the left of the figure: a three-storey, rosy-bricked house, with a french window on the ground floor, slightly ajar, with another window immediately above it, and one above that, all painted white, and with a black drain-pipe reaching down to ground level; and to the figure's right a smallish tree of some sort with large curly leaves, unidentifiable to Morse who knew little (well, nothing) of such things. But there was even more to learn. Clearly the photographer had been kneeling down, or sitting down, to take the shots, for the man's head showed some way above the line of the garden wall, which rose clearly behind the, shrubs and foliage. Even more to learn though! – Morse decided, as he studied the background yet again. The roof-line of the house stretched away in a slightly convex curve (as it appeared) above the man's head, and then was cut off in the middle of the top of the photograph; but not before suggesting that the house could be one of a terrace, perhaps?

It was amazing, Morse told himself, how much he'd managed to miss when first he'd considered the photographs; and with the strange conviction that there would certainly be a final solution to the mystery if only he looked at it long enough, he stared and stared until he thought he could see two houses instead of one, although whether this was an advance in insight or in inebriation, he couldn't be sure. So what, though? So what if it *were* part of a terrace? The number of three-storeyed, red-bricked terraces in the UK was myriad; and just in Oxford alone it must be . . . Morse shook his head and shook his thoughts. No. It was going to be almost impossible to locate the house and the garden; so the only thing left was the young man's face, really.

Or was it . . .?

Suddenly an exciting thought occurred to him. A straight line could be seen as a curve, so he'd been supposing, either because the camera had looked at it in a particular way, or because in a larger view the line began to bend in a sort of rounded perspective. But such explanations were surely far less probable than the utterly obvious fact that was staring him, literally *staring* him, in the face; the fact that the roof-line of the terraced houses which formed the backdrop here might *look* as if it was curving in a convex fashion for one supremely simple and wholly adequate reason: it *was* curving!

Could it be . . .? Could it be . . .? Did Morse, even now, think he *knew* where it was? He felt the old familiar tingle across his shoulders, and the hairs at the nape of his neck were suddenly erect. He rose from his arm-chair and went over to his bookshelves, whence he extracted the thick Penguin *Oxfordshire*, in the 'Build-ings of England' series; and his right hand shook slightly as he traced 'Park Town' in the index – page 320. On which page he read:

> Laid out in 1853–5. This was North Oxford's first development, built on land originally intended for a workhouse. The trust created for its developments promised elegant villas and [Morse's eyes snatched at the next word] terraces. What it became is this: two crescents [the blood tingled again] N and S of an elliptical central garden, with stone frontages in late-classical style, and bricked at the rear [!] with attractive french windows [!] leading on to small walled [!] gardens.

Phew!
Ye gods!
Bloody hell!
If he were so disposed (Morse knew) he could go and identify the house at that very moment! It *must* be in Crescent S – the sunshine would rule out Crescent N; and with that tree with its big, furry, splayed (beautiful!) leaves; and the drain-pipe, and the windows, and the wall, and the grass . . .

As he sat down again in the black leather settee, Morse's face was betraying a high degree of self-gratification – when the phone rang. It was now a quarter to midnight, and the voice was a woman's – husky, slightly timid, north-country.

*

She identified herself as Dr Laura Hobson, one of the new girls in the path labs; one of Max's protegées. She had been working late with Max – on Morse's bones – when just before 9 p.m. she'd found him lying there on the floor of the lab. Heart attack – severe heart attack. He'd been unconscious most of the time since they'd got him to hospital . . . but the sister had rung her (Dr Hobson) and the possibility was that he (Max) had been trying to ask for him (Morse) – if he (Morse) knew what she (Dr Hobson) was trying to say . . .

Oh dear!

'Which ward's he in?'

'Coronary Care Unit—'

'Yes! But *where?*'

'The JR2. But it's no good trying to see him now. Sister says—'

'You want to bloody *bet?*' snapped Morse.

'Please! There's something else, Inspector. He'd been working on the bones all day and—'

'Bugger the bones!'

'But—'

'Look. I'm most grateful to you, Dr, er . . .'

'Hobson.'

'. . . but please forgive me if I hang up. You see,' suddenly Morse's voice was more controlled, more gentle, 'Max and I – well, we . . . let's say we don't either of us have too many friends and . . . I want to see the old sod again if he's going to die.'

But Morse had already put down the phone, and Dr Hobson heard nothing of the last five words. She too felt very sad. She had known Max for only six weeks.

Yet there was something basically kindly about the man; and only a week before she'd had a mildly erotic dream about that ugly, brusque, and arrogant pathologist.

At least for the present, however, the pathologist appeared to have rallied quite remarkably, for he was talking to Nurse Shelick rationally, albeit slowly and quietly, when he learned of his visitor; and threatened to strike the houseman off the medical register unless Morse (for such it was) were admitted forthwith.

But one patient newly admitted to the JR2 had not rallied that night. Marion Bridewell, an eight-year-old little West Indian girl, had been knocked down by a stolen car on the Broadmoor Lea estate at seven o'clock that evening. She had been terribly badly injured.

She died just after midnight.

CHAPTER THIRTY-TWO

And Apollo gave Sarpedon dead to be borne by swift
companions, to Death and Sleep, twin brethren, who
bore him through the air to Lycia, that broad and
pleasant land

(Homer, *Iliad*, xvi)

'How are you, old friend?' asked Morse with spurious
cheerfulness.

'Dying.'

'You once told me that we're all moving towards death
– at the standard rate of twenty-four hours *per diem*.'

'I was always accurate, Morse. Not very imaginative,
agreed; but always accurate.'

'You've still not told me how—'

'Somebody said . . . somebody said, "Nothing matters
very much . . . and in the end nothing really matters at
all".'

'Lord Balfour.'

'You always were a knowledgeable sod.'

'Dr Hobson rang—'

'Ah! The fair Laura. Don't know how men ever keep
their hands off her.'

'Perhaps they don't.'

'I was thinking of her just now . . . Still have any
erotic daydreams yourself, Morse?'

'Most of the time.'

'Be nice – be nice if she was thinking of me . . .'

'You never know.'

Max smiled his awkward, melancholy smile, but his face looked tired and ashen-grey. 'You're right. Life's full of uncertainties. Have I ever told you that before?'

'Many a time.'

'I've always . . . I've always been interested in death, you know. Sort of hobby of mine, really. Even when I was a lad . . .'

'I know. Look, Max, they said they'd only let me in to see you if—'

'No knickers – you know that?'

'Pardon? Pardon, Max?'

'The bones, Morse!'

'What about the bones?'

'Do you believe in God?'

'Huh! Most of the *bishops* don't believe in God.'

'And you used to accuse *me* of never answering questions!'

Morse hesitated. Then he looked down at his old friend and answered him: 'No.'

Paradoxically perhaps, the police surgeon appeared comforted by the sincerity of the firm monosyllable; but his thoughts were now stuttering their way around a discontinuous circuit.

'You *surprised*, Morse?'

'Pardon?'

'You *were*, weren't you? Admit it!'

'Surprised?'

'The bones! Not a *woman's* bones, were they?'

Morse felt his heart pounding insistently somewhere – everywhere – in his body; felt the blood sinking down from his shoulders, past his heart, past his loins. *Not a woman's bones* – is that what Max had just said?

It had taken the hump-backed surgeon some considerable time to say his say; and feeling a tap on his shoulder, Morse turned to find Nurse Shelick standing behind him. 'Please!' her lips mouthed, as she looked anxiously down at the tired and intermittently closing eyes.

But before he left Morse leaned forward and whispered in the dying man's ear: 'I'll bring us a bottle of malt in the morning, Max, and we'll have a wee drop together, my old friend. So keep a hold on things – please keep a hold on things! . . . Just for me!'

It would have been a joy for Morse had he seen the transient gleam in Max's eyes. But the surgeon's face had turned away from him, towards the recently painted, pale-green wall of the CCU. And he seemed to be asleep.

Maximilian Theodore Siegfried de Bryn (his middle names a surprise even to his few friends) surrendered to an almost totally welcome weariness two hours after Chief Inspector Morse had left; and finally loosed his grip on the hooks just after three o'clock that morning. He had bequeathed his mortal remains to the Medical Research Foundation at the JR2. He had earnestly wished it so. And it would be done.

Many had known Max, even if few had understood

his strange ways. And many were to feel a fleeting
sadness at his death. But he had (as we have seen) a
few friends only. And there was only one man who had
wept silently when the call had been received in his
office in Thames Valley Police HQ at Kidlington at 9
a.m. on Sunday, 19 July 1992.

CHAPTER THIRTY-THREE

What is a committee? A group of the unwilling,
picked from the unfit, to do the unnecessary
  (Richard Harkness, *New York Herald Tribune*, 15 June 1960)

SUNDAY is not a good day on which to do business. Or
to expect others to be at work – or even to be out of
bed. But Dr Laura Hobson was out of bed fairly early
that morning, and awaiting Morse at the (deserted)
William Dunn School of Pathology building at 9.30
a.m.

'Hello.'

'Hello.'

'You're Inspector Morse?'

'Chief Inspector Morse.'

'Sorry!'

'And you're Dr Hobson?'

'I am she.'

Morse smiled wanly. 'I applaud your grammar, my
dear.'

'I am not your "dear". You must forgive me for being
so blunt: but I'm no one's "luv" or "dear" or "darling"
or "sweetheart". I've got a name. If I'm at work I prefer
to be called Dr Hobson; and if I let my hair down over
a drink I have a Christian name: Laura. That's my little
speech, Chief Inspector! You're not the only one who's

heard it.' She was smiling sufficiently as she spoke
though, showing small, very white teeth – a woman in
her early thirties, fair-complexioned, with a pair of
disproportionately large spectacles on her pretty nose;
a smallish woman, about 5 foot 4 inches. But it was her
voice which interested Morse: the broad north-country
vowels in "luv" and "blunt"; the pleasing nairm she had
– and perhaps the not unpleasant prospect of meeting
her sometime orver a drink with her hair doon . . .

They sat on a pair of high stools in a room that
reminded Morse of his hated physics lab at school, and
she told him of the simple yet quite extraordinary
findings. The report on which Max had been working,
though incomplete, was incontestable: the bones discovered in Wytham Woods were those of an adult male,
Caucasian, about 5 foot 6 inches in height, slimly built,
brachycephalic, fair-haired . . .

But Morse's mind had already leaped many furlongs
ahead of the field. He'd been sure that the bones had
been those of Karin Eriksson. All right, he'd been
wrong. But now he *knew* whose bones they were – for
the face of the man in the photograph was staring back
at him, unmistakably. He asked only for a photocopy of
Dr Hobson's brief, preliminary report, and rose to go.

The pair of them walked to the locked outer door in
silence, for the death of Max was heavy on her mind
too.

'You knew him well, didn't you?'

Morse nodded.

'I feel so sad,' she said simply.

Morse nodded again. '"The cart is shaken all to pieces, and the rugged road is at its end."'

She watched him, the slightly balding grey-haired man, as he stood for a few seconds beside his Jaguar. He held the photocopied report in his left hand, and raised it a few inches in farewell. She relocked the door, and walked thoughtfully back to the lab.

Morse wondered about driving up to the JR2, but decided against it. There was little time anyway. An urgent meeting of senior police officers had been summoned for 11 a.m. at the HQ building, and in any case there was nothing he could do. He drove along Parks Road, past Keble College, and then turned right into the Banbury Road. He had a few minutes to spare, and he took the second right turn now, and drove on slowly into Park Town, driving clockwise along the North Crescent, and along the South Crescent ... There would be little chance of doing much that day though, and in any case it would be better to postpone things for twenty-four hours or so.

Senior personnel from both the City and the County Forces were meeting at a time of considerable public disquiet – and criticism. Hitherto the impression had been abroad that known ringleaders were joy-riding and shop-ramming almost with impunity; and that the police were doing little to check the teenage tearaways who were terrifying many sections of the community on the Broadmoor Lea estate. There was little justification for such a view, since the police were continually finding themselves hamstrung by the refusal of the local inhabitants to come out and name names and co-operate in seeking to clean up their crime-ridden neighbourhood. But the death of Marion Bridewell had changed all that.

During this Sunday, 19 July, major decisions were taken, and their immediate implementation planned: a string of arrests would be made in a co-ordinated swoop the following morning, with special sittings of magistrates' courts scheduled for the following two evenings; council workmen would be sent in during the next few days to erect bollards and to construct sleeping-policeman humps across selected streets; police presence on the estate during the next week would be doubled; and a liaison committee of police officers, local head-teachers, social workers, and church ministers would be constituted forthwith.

It was a long and sometimes ill-humoured meeting; and Morse himself contributed little of any importance to the deliberations, for in truth his mind was distanced, and only once had his interest been fully engaged. It had been Strange's inveterate cynicism about committees which had occasioned the little contretemps:

'Give us a week or two at this rate,' he growled, 'and we'll have a standing committee, a steering committee, an *ad hoc* committee – every committee you can put a name to. What we should be doing is hitting 'em where it hurts. *Fining* 'em; fining their dads; docking it off their dads' wages. That's what I reckon!'

The Chief Constable had agreed quietly. 'Splendid idea – and the new legislation, I think, is going to be a big help to us. But there's just one snag, isn't there? You see, a good many of these young lads haven't *got* any fathers, Superintendent.'

Strange had looked disconcerted then.

And Morse had smiled his second smile of the day.

CHAPTER THIRTY-FOUR

The newly arrived resident in North Oxford is likely to find that although his next-door neighbour has a first-class degree from some prestigious university this man is not quite so clever as his wife

(*Country Living*, January 1992)

MORSE was on his own when finally, in mid-morning the following day, he drove down to Park Town, this time again slowly circling the two crescents on either side of the elliptical central garden, well stocked with trees and flowering shrubs. There were plenty of parking spaces, and after his second circuit he pulled in the Jaguar along the south side and walked past the fronts of the dozen Italianate properties which comprised the attractive stone-faced terrace. At the eastern end he turned down an alley-way, and then into the lane, about three yards wide, which ran behind the properties. To his right the continuous brick wall which protected the small back gardens was only about five feet in height, and he realized that it would not even be necessary to enter any of the gardens to find the one he was looking for. It was all childishly easy – no Holmesian intellect needed here; indeed a brief Watsonian reconnoitre would have established the spot almost immediately. Thus it was that after only a couple of minutes Morse found himself leaning over the curved coping-stones of the western-most property, and finding the details on his photographs so easily matchable here: the configuration of the black drain-pipes, the horizontal TV aerial, and then, crucially, the tree upon whose lower bough a child's red swing was now affixed. At the left of the garden, as Morse observed it, was a wooden garden seat, its slats disintegrating; and he felt thrillingly certain that it was from this seat, in this very garden, that someone – and most probably Karin Eriksson herself – had taken the two photographs of the fairheaded, bracycephalic, slimly built . . . what else had Dr Hobson said? He couldn't remember. And it didn't matter. Not at all.

He walked to the imposing front door of the end property, designated 'Seckham Villa' by a small plaque on the right-hand wall of the porch; and below it, three bells: second floor Dr S. Levi; first floor Ms Jennifer Coombs; ground floor Dr Alasdair McBryde. An area clearly where D.Phils and Ph.Ds proliferated. He rang the bottom bell.

The door was opened by a tallish, heavily bearded man in his mid-thirties, who studied Morse's authorization cautiously before answering any questions. He was over from Ostrylia (he said) with his wife, to pursue some research project in micro-biology; they had been in the flat since the previous August, and would be returning home in two weeks' time; he'd learned of the property from a friend in Mansfield College who had been keeping an eye open for suitable accommodation the previous summer.

The previous August . . .

Was this to be Morse's lucky day?

'Did you know the people – did you *meet* the people who were here before you?'

'Fried not,' said the Australian.

'Can I – have a quick look inside?'

Rather unenthusiastically, as it seemed, McBryde led the way into the lounge, where Morse looked around the rather splendid, high-ceilinged room, and tried to attune his senses to the vaguest vibrations. Without success. It was only when he looked out through the french window at the sunlit patch of lawn that he felt a frisson of excitement: a dark-haired little girl in a pink dress was swinging idly to and fro beneath the tree, her white ankle-socked feet just reaching the ground.

'Your daughter, sir?'

'Yeah. You got any kids yourself, Inspector?'

Morse shook his head. 'Just one more thing, sir. Have you got your book, you know, your rent-book or whatever handy? It's important I get in touch with the, er, people who were here just before you last year . . .'

McBryde stepped over to an escritoire beside the french window and found his Property Payment book, the legend 'Finders Keepers' on the cover.

'I'm not in arrears,' said McBryde with the suggestion of his first smile.

'So I see. And I'm not a bailiff, sir,' said Morse, handing back the book.

The two men walked back towards the entrance, and McBryde knocked very gently on the door to his right, and put his ear to the panel.

'Darling? Darling?'

But there was no reply.

At the front door Morse asked his last question.

'Finders Keepers – that's the Banbury Road office, is it?'

'Yeah. You off there now?'

'I think I'll drop in straightaway, yes.'

'Is your car parked here?'

Morse pointed to the Jaguar.

'Well, I should leave it here, if I were you. Only five minutes' walk, if that – and you'll never park in North Parade.'

Morse nodded. Good idea. And the Rose and Crown was just along in North Parade.

Before leaving Park Town however, Morse strolled across into the central oval-shaped garden separating the Crescents, where he read the only notice he could find, fixed to the trunk of a cedar tree:

THIS GARDEN, LAID OUT CIRCA 1850, IS MAINTAINED
BY THE RESIDENTS FOR PLEASURE AND PEACE.
PLEASE RESPECT ITS AMENITIES.
NO DOGS, BICYCLES, BALL GAMES, OR TRANSISTORS.

For a few minutes Morse sat on one of the wooden seats, where someone had obviously not respected the amenities, for an oblong plate, doubtless commemorating the name of a former inhabitant, had been recently prised from the back. It was a restful spot though, and Morse now walked slowly round its periphery, his mind half on Max's death, half on the photographs taken in the back garden of the ground-floor flat at Seckham Villa. As he turned at the western edge of the garden, he realized that this same Seckham Villa was immediately across the road from him, with the maroon Jaguar parked just to the left of it. And as once again he admired the attractive frontages there, he suspected perhaps that a heavily bearded face had suddenly pulled itself back behind the rather dingy curtains in the front room of Seckham Villa, where Mrs Something McBryde lay suffering from goodness knows what. Was her husband slightly more inquisitive than he'd appeared to be? Or was it the Jaguar – which often attracted some interested glances?

Thoughtfully Morse walked out of Park Town, then left into the Banbury Road. Finders Keepers was very close. So was North Parade. So was the Rose and Crown.

CHAPTER THIRTY-FIVE

Doing business without advertising is like winking at a girl in the dark. You know what you are doing, but nobody else does
(Stewart Henderson Britt, *New York Herald Tribune*, 30 October 1956)

AFTER two pints of cask-conditioned ale in the Rose and Crown, Morse walked the short distance to Finders Keepers, where he was soon ushered through the outer office, past two young ladies busy with their VDUs, and into the inner sanctum of Mr Martin Buckby, the dark, smartly suited manager of Property Letting Services. It was fairly close to lunch-time, but the manager would be only too glad to help – of course he would.

Yes, his department was responsible for letting a good many of the Park Town properties, most of which had been converted from single homes into two, sometimes three, flats and were more often than not let out to graduates, occasionally to students. Naturally the accommodation varied, but some of the flats, especially those on the ground floor – or first floor, as some of them called it – were roomy, stylish, and well maintained. The letting year usually divided itself into two main periods: October to June, covering the academic year at Oxford University; and then June/July to the end of September, when very frequently various over-seas tenants were interested in short-term leases. Advertisements for the availability of such accommodation were regularly placed in *The Oxford Times*, and occasionally in *Property Weekly*. But only advertised once, for the flats were almost invariably snapped up straight-away. Such adverts gave a brief description of the property available, and the price asked: about £200–£250 a week for a short-term let (at current rates) and slightly less, proportionately, for a long-term let. Business, in the first instance, was usually conducted by phone, often through agents; and someone – either the client himself or a representative of an agency – would go along to view the property ('Very important, Inspector!') before the paperwork was completed, either there in the firm's offices or, increasingly now, directly by fax interchange with countries overseas. A deposit would be lodged, a tenancy agreement signed, reference given – that was how it worked. There was no *guarantee* of bona fides, of course, and basically one had to rely on gut-reaction; but the firm experienced very few problems, really. When the client was due to move in, a representative would go along to open the property, hand over keys, explain the workings of gas, electricity, stop-cocks, central heating, fuses, thermostats, everything, and to give the client a full inventory of the property's effects – this inventory to be checked and returned within seven days so that there could be no subsequent arguments about the complement of fish-knives or feather pillows. The system worked well. The only example of odd behaviour over the previous

year, for example, had been the overnight disappearance of a South American gentleman who had taken
his key with him – and absolutely nothing else. And
since, as with all short-term lets, the whole of the rental
was paid in advance, as well as an extra deposit of £500,
no harm had been done there – apart from the need
to change the lock on the front door and to get a
further clutch of keys cut.

'Did you report that to the police, sir?'

'No. Should I have done?'

Morse shrugged.

He had a good grasp now of the letting procedure;
yet his mind was always happier (he explained) with
specific illustrations than with generalities; and if it
were proper for him to ask, for example, what Dr
McBryde was paying for the ground-floor flat at Seckham Villa . . .?

Buckby found a green folder in the filing cabinet
behind him and quickly looked through it. 'Thirteen
hundred pounds per month.'

'Phew! Bit steep, isn't it?'

'It's the going rate – and it's a lovely flat, isn't it?
One of the best in the whole crescent.' Buckby picked
out a sheet from the folder and read the specification
aloud.

But Morse was paying scant attention to him. After
all, that was the manager's job, wasn't it? To make the
most of what Morse had seen with his own eyes as a
pretty limited bit of Lebensraum, especially for a married couple with one infant – at least one infant.

'Didn't you just say that the maximum for a short-term let was two hundred and fifty pounds a week?'

Buckby grinned. 'Not for *that* place – well, you've seen it. And what makes you think it's a *short*-term let, Inspector?'

The blood was tingling at the back of Morse's neck, and subliminally some of the specifications that Buckby had recited were beginning to register in his brain. He reached over and picked up the sheet.

> Hall, living room, separate dining room, well-fitted kitchen, two bedrooms, studio/study, bathroom, full gas CH, small walled garden

Two bedrooms . . . and a sick wife sleeping in one of them . . . studio . . . and a little girl sitting on a swing . . . God! Morse shook his head in disbelief at his own idiocy.

'I really came to ask you, sir, if you had any record of who was living in that property last July. But I think – I *think* – you're going to tell me that it was Dr Alasdair McBryde; that he hasn't got a wife; that the people upstairs have got a little dark-haired daughter; that the fellow probably hails from Malta—'

'Gibraltar, actually.'

'You've got some spare keys, sir?' asked Morse, almost despairingly.

In front of Seckham Villa the Jaguar sat undisturbed; but inside there were to be no further sightings of Dr

McBryde. Yet the little girl still sat on the swing, gently stroking her dolly's hair, and Morse unlocked the french window and walked over the grass towards her.

'What's your name?'

'My name's Lucy and my dolly's name's Amanda.'

'Do you live here, Lucy?'

'Yes. Mummy and Daddy live up there.' Her bright eyes lifted to the top rear window.

'Pretty dolly,' said Morse.

'Would you like to hold her?'

'I would, yes – but I've got a lot of things to do just for the moment.'

Inside his brain he could hear a voice shouting, 'Help, Lewis!' and he turned back into the house and wondered where on earth to start.

CHAPTER THIRTY-SIX

Nine tenths of the appeal of pornography is due to the indecent feelings concerning sex which moralists inculcate in the young; the other tenth is physiological, and will occur in one way or another whatever the state of the law may be

(Bertrand Russell, *Marriage and Morals*)

LEWIS arrived at Seckham Villa at 2.15 that afternoon, bringing with him the early edition of *The Oxford Mail*, in which many column-inches were devoted to the wave of car crime which was hitting Oxfordshire – hitting the national press, too, with increasing regularity. Everyone and everything in turn was blamed: the police, the parents, the teachers, the church, the recession, unemployment, lack of youth facilities, car manufacturers, the weather, the TV, the brewers, left-wing social workers, and right-wing social workers; original sin received several votes, and even the Devil himself got one. Paradoxically the police seemed to be more in the dock than the perpetrators of the increasingly vicious crimes being committed. But at least the operation that morning had been successful, so Lewis reported: the only trouble was that further police activity in Wytham Woods was drastically curtailed – four men only now, one of them standing guard over the area cordoned off in Pasticks.

The temporarily dispirited Morse received the news with little surprise, and briefly brought Lewis up to date with his own ambivalent achievements of the morning: his discovery of the garden where in all probability Karin Eriksson had spent some period of time before she disappeared; and his gullibility in allowing McBryde – fairly certainly now a key figure in the drama – more than sufficient time to effect a hurried escape.

At the far end of the ground-floor entrance passage, fairly steep stairs, turning 180 degrees, led down to the basement area in Seckham Villa, and it was here that the first discovery was made. The basement comprised a large, modernized kitchen at the front; and behind this, through an archway, a large living area furnished with armchairs, a settee, coffee tables, bookshelves, TV, HiFi equipment – and a double-bed of mahogany, stripped down to a mattress of pale blue; and beside the bed, a jointed series of square, wooden boards, four of them, along which, for the length of about ten feet, ran two steel rails – rails where, it was immediately assumed, a cine-camera had recently and probably frequently been moving to and fro.

Morse himself (with Lewis and one of the DCs) spent most of his time that afternoon in this area, once the fingerprint men, the senior scenes-of-crime officer and the photographer had completed their formal tasks. Clear fingerprints on the (unwashed) non-stick saucepan and cutlery found in the kitchen sink would doubtless match the scores of others found throughout the flat, would doubtless be McBryde's, and (as Morse saw things) would doubtless advance the investigation not one whit. No clothing, apart from two dirty pairs of beige socks found in one of the bedrooms; no toiletries left along the bathroom shelves; no videos; no correspondence; no shredded letters in either of the two waste-paper baskets or in the dustbin outside the back door. All in all it seemed fairly clear that the flat had been slimmed down – recently perhaps? – for the eventuality of a speedy get-away. Yet there were items that had *not* been bundled and stuffed into the back of the white van which (as was quickly ascertained) McBryde had used for travelling; and cupboards in both the ground-floor and the basement contained duvets, sheets, pillow-cases, blankets, towels, and table cloths – clearly items listed on the tenant's inventory; and the kitchen pantry was adequately stocked with tins of beans, fruit, salmon, spaghetti, tuna fish, and the like.

Naturally however it was the trackway beside the basement double bed which attracted the most interest, much lifting of eyebrows, and many lascivious asides amongst those investigators whose powers of detection, at least in this instance, were the equal of the chief inspector's. Indeed, it would have required a man of monumental mutton-headedness not to visualize before him the camera and the microphone moving slowly alongside the mattress to record the assorted feats of fornication enacted on that creaking charpoy. For himself Morse tried not to give his imagination too free a rein. Sometimes up at HQ there were a few pornographic videos around, confiscated from late-night raids or illegal trafficking. Often had he wished to view some of the crude, corrupting, seductive things; yet equally often had he made it known to his fellow officers that he at least was quite uninterested in such matters.

In a corner of the kitchen, bundled neatly as if for some subsequent collection by Friends of the Earth, was a heap of old newspapers, mostly the *Daily Mail*, and various weeklies and periodicals, including *Oxford Today*, *Oxcom*, *TV Times*, two RSPB journals, and the previous Christmas offers from the Spastic Society. Morse had glanced very hurriedly through, half hoping perhaps to find the statutory girlie magazine; but apart from spending a minute or so looking at pictures of the black-headed gulls on the Loch of Kinnordy, he found nothing there to hold his interest.

It was Lewis who found them, folded away inside one of the free local newspapers, *The Star*. There were fourteen A4 sheets, stapled together, obviously photo-copied (and photocopied ill) from some glossier and fuller publication. On each sheet several photographs of the same girl were figured (if that be the correct verb) in various stages of undress; and at the bottom of each sheet there appeared a Christian name, followed by details of height, bust, waist, hips, dress- shoe- and glove-measurements, and colour of hair and eyes. In almost every case the bottom left-hand picture was of the model completely naked, and in three or four cases striking some sexually suggestive pose. The names were of the glitzy showgirl variety: Jayne, Kelly, Lindy-Lu, Mandy . . . and most of them appeared (for age was not given) to be in their twenties. But four of the sheets depicted older women, whose names were possibly designed to reflect their comparative maturity: Elaine, Dorothy, Mary, Louisa ... The only other information given (no addresses here) was a (i), (ii), (iii), of priority 'services', and Lewis, not without some little interest himself (and amusement), sampled a few of the services on offer: sporting-shots, escort duties, lingerie, stockings, leather, swim-wear, summer dresses, bras, nude-modelling, hair-styling, gloves. Not much to trouble the law there, surely. Three of the girls though were far more explicit about their specialisms, with Mandy listing (i) home videos, (ii) pornographic movies, (iii) overnight escort duties; and with Lindy-Lu, pictured up to her thighs in leather boots, proclaiming an accomplished proficiency in spanking.

And then, as Morse and Lewis were considering these things, the big discovery was made. One of the two DCs who had been given the job of searching the main lounge above had found, caught up against the top of one of the drawers in the escritoire, a list of names and addresses: a list of clients, surely! Clients who probably received their pornographic material in plain brown envelopes with the flap licked down so very firmly. And there, fourth from the top, was the name that both Morse and Lewis focused on immediately: George Daley, Blenheim Villas, Begbroke, Oxon.

Morse had been delighted with the find – of course he had! And his praise for the DC had been profuse and (in Lewis's view) perhaps a trifle extravagant. Yet now as he sat on the settee, looking again at the unzippings and the unbuttonings of the models, reading through the list of names once more, he appeared to Lewis to be preoccupied and rather sad.

'Everything all right, sir?'

'What? Oh yes! Fine. We're making wonderful progress. Let's keep at it!'

But Morse himself was contributing little towards any further progress; and after desultorily walking around for ten minutes or so, he sat down yet again and picked up the sheet of addresses. He would have to tell Lewis, he decided – not just yet but ... He looked again at the seventeenth name on the list: for he was never likely to forget the name that Kidlington HQ had given him when, from Lyme Regis, he'd phoned in the car registration H 35 LWL:

Dr Alan Hardinge.

He picked up the pictures of the models and looked again through their names and their vital statistics and their special proficiencies. Especially did he look again at one of the maturer models: the one who called herself 'Louise'; the one who'd had all sorts of fun with her names at the Bay Hotel in Lyme Regis; the woman who was photographed here, quite naked and totally desirable.

Claire Osborne.

'Pity we've no address for – well, it must be a modelling agency of some sort, mustn't it?'

'No problem, Lewis. We can just ring up one of these johnnies on the list.'

'Perhaps *they* don't know.'

'I'll give you the address in ten minutes if you really want it.'

'I don't want it for myself, you know.'

'Of course not!'

Picking up his sheets, Morse decided that his presence in Seckham Villa was no longer required; and bidding Lewis to give things another couple of hours or so he returned to HQ; where he tried her telephone number.

She was in.

'Claire?'

'Morse!' (She'd recognized him!)

'You could have told me you worked for an escort agency!'

'Why?'

Morse couldn't think of an answer.

'You thought I was wicked enough but not quite so wicked as that?'

'I suppose so.'

'Why don't you get yourself in your car and come over tonight? I'd be happy if you did . . .'

Morse sighed deeply. 'You told me you had a daughter—'

'So?'

'Do you still keep in touch with the father?'

'The father? Christ, come off it! I couldn't tell you who the father *was!*'

Like the veil of the Temple, Morse's heart was suddenly rent in twain; and after asking her for the name and address of the modelling agency (which she refused to tell him) he rang off.

Ten minutes later, the phone went on Morse's desk, and it was Claire – though how she'd got his number he didn't know. She spoke for only about thirty seconds, ignoring Morse's interruptions.

'Shut up, you silly bugger! You can't see more than two inches in front of your nose, can you? Don't you realize I'd have swapped all the lecherous sods I've ever had for you – and instead of trying to understand all you ask me – Christ! – is who fathered—'

'Look, Claire—'

'No! *You* bloody look! If you can't take what a woman tells you about herself without picking over the past and asking bloody futile questions about why and who he was and—' But her voice broke down completely now.

'Look, please!'

'No! You just fuck off, Morse, and don't you ring me again because I'll probably be screwing somebody and enjoying it such a lot I won't want to be interrupted—'

'Claire!'

But the line was dead.

For the next hour Morse tried her number every five minutes, counting up to thirty double-purrs each time. But there was no answer.

Lewis had discovered nothing new in Seckham Villa, and he rang through to HQ at 6 p.m., as Morse had wished.

'All right. Well, you get off home early, Lewis. And get some sleep. And good luck tomorrow!'

Lewis was due to catch the 7.30 plane to Stockholm the following morning.

CHAPTER THIRTY-SEVEN

To be buried while alive is, beyond question, the most
terrifying of those extremes which has ever fallen to the
lot of mere mortality

(Edgar Allan Poe, *Tales of Mystery and Imagination*)

THE DEATH of Max was still casting a cloak of gloom
round Morse as he sat in his office the following
morning. During the previous night his thoughts had
been much preoccupied with death, and the mood
persisted now. As a boy, he had been moved by those
words of the dying Socrates, suggesting that if death
were just one long, unbroken, dreamless sleep, then a
greater boon could hardly be bestowed upon mankind.
But what about the body? The soul might be able to
look after itself all right, but what about the physical
body? In Morse's favourite episode from *The Iliad*, the
brethren and kinsfolk of Sarpedon had buried his body,
with mound and pillar, in the rich, wide land of Lycia.
Yes! It was fitting to have a gravestone and a name
inscribed on it. But there were those stories that were
ever frightening – stories about people prematurely
interred who had awoken in infinite and palpitating
terror with the immovable lid of the coffin only a
few inches above them. No! Burning was better than
burying, surely ... Morse was wholly ignorant of the

immediate procedures effected once the curtains closed over the light-wooded coffins at the crematoria . . . like the curtains closing at the end of *Götterdämmerung*, though minus the clapping, of course. All done and finished quickly, and if somebody wanted to sprinkle your mortal dust over the memorial gardens, well, it might be OK for the roses, too. He wouldn't mind a couple of hymns either: 'The day thou gavest', perhaps. Good tune, that. So long as they didn't have any prayers, or any departures from the Authorized Version of Holy Writ . . . Perhaps Max had got it right, neatly side-stepping the choice of interment or incineration: the clever old sod had left his body to the hospital, and the odds were strongly on one or two of his organs giving them plenty to think about. Huh!

Morse smiled to himself, and suddenly looked up to see Strange standing in the doorway.

'Private joke, Morse?'

'Oh, nothing, sir.'

'C'mon! Life's grim enough.'

'I was just thinking of Max's liver—'

'Not a pretty sight!'

'No.'

'You're taking it a bit hard, aren't you? Max, I mean.'

'A bit, perhaps.'

'You seen the latest?'

Strange pushed a copy of *The Times* across the desk, with a brief paragraph on the front page informing its readers that 'the bones discovered in Wytham Woods are quite certainly not those of the Swedish student whose disappearance occasioned the original verses and their subsequent analysis in this newspaper. (See Letters, page 13)'.

'Anything to help us there?' asked Morse dubiously, opening the paper.

'Scraping the barrel, if you ask me,' said Strange.

Morse looked down at page 13:

From Mr Anthony Beaulah

Sir, like the text of some early Greek, love-lyric, the lines on the Swedish student would appear to have been pondered over in such exhaustive fashion that there is perhaps little left to say. And it may be that the search is already over. Yet there is one significant (surely?) aspect of the verses which has hitherto received scant attention. The collocation of 'the tiger' with 'the burning of the night' (lines 9 and 12) has indeed been commented upon, but in no *specific* context. In my view, sir, one should perhaps interpret the tiger (the cat) as staring back at drivers in the darkness. And the brilliantly simple invention which has long steered the benighted driver through the metaphorical forest of the night? Cat's eyes!

I myself live too far away from Oxford to be able to test such a thesis. But might the police not interpret this as a genuine clue, and look for some stretch of road (in or around Wytham?) where cat's eyes have recently been installed?

Yours
ANTHONY BEAULAH,
Felsted School,
Essex.

'Worth getting Lewis on it?' queried Strange, when Morse had finished reading.

'Not this morning, sir. If you remember he's, er, on

his holidays.' Morse looked at his wrist-watch. 'At this minute he's probably looking out of the window down at Jutland.'

'Why didn't *you* go, Morse? With all these Swedish blondes and that . . .'

'I thought it'd be good experience for him.'

'Mm.'

For a while the two were silent. Then Strange picked up his paper and made to leave.

'You made a will yet, Morse?'

'Not much to leave, really.'

'All those records of yours, surely?'

'Bit out of date, I'm afraid. We're all buying CDs now.'

'Perhaps *they'll* be out of date soon.'

Morse nodded. Strange was not in the habit of saying anything quite so perceptive.

CHAPTER THIRTY-EIGHT

Men are made stronger on realization that the helping
hand they need is at the end of their own right arm
(Sidney J. Phillips, speech, July 1953)

ON THE forty-kilometre bus ride from Arlanda airport
southwards towards Stockholm, Lewis enjoyed what for
him was the fairly uncommon view of a foreign country.
After a while the tracts of large pine and fir woods
changed to smaller coppices and open fields; then farm-
houses, red, with barns that were red too, and a few
yellow, wooden, Dutch-roofed manor houses, just before
the outskirts of Stockholm, with its factories and tidy,
newish buildings – and all so very clean and litter-free.
In wooded surroundings within the city itself, three- and
four-storeyed blocks of flats took over; and finally the
end of the journey, at the Central Station terminal.

Lewis had never studied a foreign language at
school, and his travel abroad had hitherto been
restricted to three weeks in Australia, two weeks in Italy,
and one afternoon in a Calais supermarket. The fact
that he had no difficulty therefore in summoning a taxi
was wholly due to the excellent English of the young
driver, who soon brought Lewis into the suburb of
Bromma – more specifically to an eight-storey block of
white flats in Bergsvägen.

The Stockholm CID had offered to send one of its own men to meet him, but Lewis had not taken advantage of this when he'd arranged the details of his visit the previous morning. Seldom was it that he could assert any independent judgement in an investigation; and here was his chance.

The entrance hall was of polished pink granite, with the long list of tenants' names displayed there:

ANDREASSON	8A
ENGSTRÖM	8B
FASTÉN	7A
OLSSON	7B
KRAFT	6A
ERIKSSON	6B

Sixth floor!

Lewis felt excited at the sight of the name; it was almost as if . . . as if he felt he was going to make some significant discovery.

The door, bearing the name-plate ERIKSSON, was opened by a woman in her mid-forties, of medium height, plumply figured, hazel-eyed, and with short, brownish-blonde hair.

'Mrs Eriksson?'

'Irma Eriksson,' she insisted as he shook her hand, and entered the apartment.

The small hallway was lined with cupboards, with what looked like a home-woven mat on one wall and a large mirror on the other. Through the open door to the right Lewis glimpsed a beautifully fitted kitchen, fresh and gleaming, with a copper kettle and old plates on its walls.

'In here, Mr Lewis.' She pointed smilingly to the left and led the way.

Her English was very good, utterly fluent and idiomatic, with only a hint of a foreign accent, just noticeable perhaps in the slight lengthening of the short 'i' vowels ('Meester Lewis').

The place was all so *clean*; and so particularly clean was the parquet flooring that Lewis wondered whether he should offer to take off his shoes, for she herself stood there in her stockinged feet as she gestured him to a seat on a low, brown-striped settee.

As he later tried to describe the furnishings to Morse, he felt more conscious than anything about the huge amount of stuff that had been packed into this living room: two coffee tables of heavy, dark wood; lots of indoor plants; groups of family portraits and photographs all around; dozens of candle holders; a large TV set; pretty cushions everywhere; vases of flowers; a set of Dala horses; two crucifixes; and (as Lewis learned later) a set of Carl Larsson prints above the bricked fireplace. Yet in spite of all the clutter, the whole room was light and airy, the thin curtains pulled completely back from the south-facing window.

Conversation was easy and, for Lewis, interesting. He learned something of the typical middle-class housing in Swedish cities; learned how and why the Erikssons had moved from Uppsala down to Bergsvägen almost a year ago after ... after Karin had, well, whatever had happened. As Lewis went briefly through the statement she had made a year ago, Irma Eriksson was watching him closely (he could see that), nodding here and there, and at one or two points staring down sadly at a small oriental carpet at her feet. But yes, it was all there; and no, there was nothing she could add. From that day to this she had received no further news of her daughter – none. At first, she admitted, she'd hoped and hoped, and couldn't bring herself to believe that Karin was dead. But gradually she had been forced to such a conclusion; and it was better that way, really – to accept the virtual certainty that Karin had been murdered. She was grateful – how not? – for the recent efforts the English police had made – again! – and she had been following the newspaper correspondence of course, receiving cuttings regularly from an English friend.

'Can I get you coffee? And a leetle Swedish Schnapps, yes?'

When she went out to the kitchen, Lewis could scarcely believe that it had been himself who had answered 'yes' to the first, and 'yes' to the second. So often in his police career he'd prayed for Morse to be on hand to help him; but not now. He stood up and walked slowly round the room, staring long at some of the photographs; and especially at one of them: at three young ladies standing arm in arm, dressed in Swedish national costume.

'Ah! I see you've found my beautiful daughters.'

She had moved in silently, and now stood beside him, still in her stockinged feet, some five or six inches shorter than the six-foot sergeant; and he could smell the sweet summer freshness of her, and he felt an unfamiliar tic in a vein at his right temple.

'Katarina, Karin, Kristina.' She pointed to each in turn. 'All of them better looking than their momma, no?'

Lewis made no direct reply as he still held the framed photograph. So much alike the three of them: each with long, straight gold-blonde hair; each with clear-complexioned, high-cheekboned faces.

'That's Karin – in the middle, you say?' Lewis looked at her again, the one who was looking perhaps just a little more serious than her sisters.

Momma nodded; then, unexpectedly, took the photograph from Lewis's hands and replaced it – with no explanation for her slightly brusque behaviour.

'How can I help you any more?' She sat cross-legged opposite Lewis in an armchair, tossed back her small, squat glass of Schnapps, before sipping the hot, strong coffee.

So Lewis asked her a lot of questions, and was soon to be forming a much clearer picture of the daughter about whom her mother spoke so lovingly now.

Karin had been a reasonably clever girl, if occasionally somewhat idle; she had left her secondary school in Uppsala at the age of eighteen, with good prospects before her; attractive, *very* good at swimming and tennis; and with a series of badges and diplomas from school societies and guides' groups for birdwatching, orienteering, rock-climbing, judo, embroidery, and amateur musicals. It was just after she had left school that Irma's husband, Staffan Eriksson, had moved in with a darkly seductive brunette he had met on a business trip to Norway and, well, that was about it really. She uncrossed her legs and looked over at Lewis with a gentle smile.

'Another Schnapps?'

'Why not?' said Mr Lewis.

Katarina (Irma Eriksson resumed), the eldest daughter (should it be 'elder' now, though?), was married and working with the European Commission in Strasbourg as an interpreter; the youngest (younger) daughter, Kristina – still only eighteen – was in her last year of schooling, studying social sciences. She was living at home, there in the flat, and if Mr Lewis would like to see her . . .? If Mr Lewis were *staying* in Stockholm?

The troublesome tic jerked in Lewis's temple once more, as he turned the conversation back to Karin.

What was Karin *like* – as a person? Well, her mother supposed she would call her 'independent' – yes, above all, independent. The summer before she'd gone to England, she'd spent two months on a kibbutz near Tel Aviv; and the year before that she'd joined a group of enthusiastic environmentalists in the Arctic Circle. But she was never (for the first time Irma Eriksson had seemed to struggle with her English vocabulary) she was never an 'easy' young girl. No! That wasn't the word at all! She was never the sort of girl who went to bed, you know . . .?

'Was she – do you think she was a virgin, Mrs Eriksson?'

' "Irma", please!'

'As far as you know . . . Irma?'

'I'm not sure. Apart from the trouble in Israel, if she had sex with anyone it would be with someone she liked. You know how I mean, don't you?'

'She was fond of birdwatching, you said?' Lewis was losing his way. (Or was he?)

'Oh, yes! Never did she go out on any holiday or walk without taking the binoculars.' (The idiom was breaking down – just a bit.)

There was just the one thing left now which Morse had asked him to confirm: the passport and the work-permit procedures for a young lady like Karin.

No problem. For the first time Lewis thought he saw the underlying grief behind the saddened eyes, as she explained that Sweden did not belong to the EC; that all Swedish nationals needed to apply for work-permits in the UK if they proposed to stay for any length of time; that even for au pair work it was wholly prudent so to do. But Karin had not applied for such a permit; she gave herself only three weeks in the UK; and for this, her Swedish passport, valid for a ten-year period, would have been sufficient.

Lewis was suddenly aware that if there *had* been anything mildly flirtatious in the woman's manner, the situation had now changed.

'You kept Karin's passport, didn't you?' she continued quietly.

Lewis nodded, and his slight frown prompted her quick explanation:

'You see, I suppose we hoped she might – if she were

still alive – she might apply for a new passport – if she'd *lost* it. Do you see . . .?'

Lewis nodded again.

'And she hasn't, has she, Mr Lewis? So!' She got up briskly, and put her feet into a pair of black, semi-heeled shoes. 'So!'

'I'm afraid we can't bring you any hopeful news – not really,' said Lewis, himself now rising to his feet.

'It's all right. I knew from the start, really. It's just . . .'

'I know. And thank you. You've been very helpful. Just one more thing – if I could just *borrow* a photo of the three girls . . .?'

As they stood in the hallway, Lewis ventured a genuine compliment:

'You know, I always envy people like you, Mrs – Irma – you know, people who can speak other languages.'

'We start learning English early though. In the fourth grade – ten years of age. Well, I was twelve myself, but my daughters all learn from ten.'

They shook hands, and Lewis walked down to the ground floor, where he stood for several minutes beside a play area surrounded by a low palisade of dark-brown wooden slats – not a potato-crisp packet in sight. It was early afternoon now on a beautiful summer's day, with a cloudless blue sky and a yellow sun – like the colours of the flag on the rucksack found at Begbroke, Oxfordshire.

Standing on her high balcony, Irma Eriksson

watched him go. As soon as he had disappeared into the main thoroughfare, she stepped back into her flat and let herself into the rear bedroom, where the ensuing conversation was held in Swedish:

'Was he intelligent?'

'Not particularly. Very nice though – *very* nice.'

'Did you ask him to bed with you?'

'I might have done if *you* hadn't been here.'

'Do you think he suspected anything?'

'No.'

'But you're glad he's gone?'

Irma Eriksson nodded. 'Shall I get you coffee?'

'Please!'

When her mother had left, the young lady looked at herself in the long wall-mirror in the shaded room, deciding that she was looking tired and dark around the eyes. Yet had Lewis seen her there that afternoon he would have been impressed by her pale and elegant beauty; would have been struck immediately too by a very close likeness to the photograph of the student found in the rucksack at Begbroke, Oxfordshire.

CHAPTER THIRTY-NINE

In a world in which duty and self-discipline have lost
out to hedonism and self-satisfaction, there is nothing
like closing your eyes and going with the flow. At least
in a fantasy, it all ends happily ever after
(Edwina Currie, *The Observer*, 23 February 1992)

ALAN HARDINGE had gained a first in both parts of
the Natural Sciences Tripos at Cambridge; had stayed
on in that university for a Ph.D.; then done two years'
research at Harvard before being elected in 1970 to a
fellowship at the 'other place'. A year later he had
courted a librarian from the Bodleian, had married her
six months later, subsequently siring two offspring, both
girls: the one now in her second year at Durham
reading Psychology; the other dead – killed nineteen
days earlier as she cycled down Cumnor Hill into
Oxford.

He had not been wholly surprised to receive the
phone call from Chief Inspector Morse that morning
of Tuesday, 21 July, and a meeting was arranged for 2
p.m. the same day, in Hardinge's rooms, overlooking
the front quad of Lonsdale College.

'What does your wife know about your interests in
Seckham Villa?'

'Nothing. Absolutely nothing. So *please* can we keep

220

Lynne – my wife – out of this? She's still terribly upset and nervy – God knows what . . .'

Dr Hardinge spoke in disjunct bursts, punctuated by the equivalent of verbal dashes. He was a smallish, neat man, with crinkly grey hair, darkly suited still in high summer, when many of his colleagues were walking along the High in T-shirts and trainers.

'I can't promise that, of course—'

'Don't you see? I'd do anything – anything at all – to see that Lynne's not hurt. I know it sounds weak – it *is* weak – it's what we all say – I know – but it's true.' From his hunched shoulders Hardinge's face craned forward like that of an earnest tortoise.

'Know this man?' Morse handed across one of the photographs taken in the garden of Seckham Villa.

Hardinge took a pair of half-lensed spectacles from their case; but appeared not to need them, glancing for only a second or two at the photograph before handing it back.

'James – or Jamie? – Myton. Yes, I know him – knew him – sort of jack-of-all-trades really.'

'How did you get to know him?'

'Look – it'll be better if I tell you – about myself – I think it will.'

Morse listened with interest, and with no moral reproof, as Hardinge stated his apologia for a lifetime of sexual adventurism.

As a boy a series of older women had regularly intruded themselves into his dreams, and he had readily surrendered himself, *almost* without guilt, into the sexual fantasies he found he could so easily conjure up

for himself – fantasies in which there were no conse-
quences, no disappointments. In his twenties he would
willingly have preferred – *did* prefer – to watch the
pornographic films and videos that were then so readily
available. Then he'd met Lynne – dear, honest, trusting
Lynne – who would be utterly flabbergasted and so hurt
and ashamed if she even began to suspect a fraction of
the truth. After his marriage, though, his fantasies
persisted; grew even. He was experiencing a yearning
for ever greater variety in his sexual gratification, and
this had gradually resulted in a string of rather sordid
associations: with private film clubs; imported videos
and magazines; live sex-shows; 'hostess' parties – for all
of which he'd become a regular and eager client. The
anticipation of such occasions! The extraordinarily
arousing words that became the open sesame to such
erotic entertainments: 'Is everybody known?'

'And that's what happened regularly at Seckham
Villa?'

'Fairly regularly – seldom more than five or six of us
– usually people we'd met once or twice before.'

Morse watched the middle-aged, dapper deceiver,
leaning forward all the time, with his aquiline cast of
feature, his pale complexion, his slightly pernickety
enunciation. He felt he should have despised the man
a little; but he couldn't do that. If Hardinge were a
bit of a pervert, he was an extraordinarily honest
one; and with his faded, watery eyes he looked rather
tired and rather lost; weak, and not pretending to be
strong.

'You're not a "medical" doctor, sir?' asked Morse when the carnal confessions were complete.

'No. I just wrote a Ph.D. thesis – you know how these things are.'

'On?'

'Promise not to laugh?'

'Try me.'

' "The comparative body-weight of the great tit within the variable habitats of its North European distribution".'

Morse didn't laugh. Birds! So many people in the case seemed interested in birds . . .

'*Original* research, was that?'

'No other kind, as far as I know.'

'And you were *examined* in this?'

'You don't get a doctorate otherwise.'

'But the person who examined you – well, he couldn't know as much as *you*, could he? By definition, surely?'

'*She*, actually. It's the – well, they say it is – the *way* you go about it – your research; the way you observe, record things, categorize them, and then draw some kind of conclusion. Bit like your job, Inspector.'

'All I was thinking, sir, is that it might not have been difficult for you to fabricate a few of the facts . . .'

Hardinge frowned, his head moving forward on his shoulders once more. 'I am *not*, Inspector, fabricating anything about Seckham Villa – if that's what you're getting at.'

'And you first met Claire Osborne there.'

'She told you that was her name?'

'"Louisa Hardinge", too.'

Hardinge smiled sadly. 'Her one and only tribute to me! But she loves changing her name – all the time – she doesn't really know who she is ... or what she wants, Inspector. She's a sort of chameleon, I suppose. But you'll probably know that, won't you? I understand you've met her.'

'What *is* her name?'

'Her birth-certificate name? I don't really know.'

Morse shook his head. Was there *anyone* telling him the truth in this case?

'She never went to Seckham Villa herself – as far as I know,' resumed Hardinge. 'I met her through an agency. McBryde – you've spoken to him? – through McBryde. They give you photographs – interests – you know what I mean.'

'Measurements?'

'Measurements.'

'And you fell for her?'

Hardinge nodded. 'Not difficult to do that, is it?'

'You still in love with her?'

'Yes.'

'She with you?'

'No.'

'You'll have to give me the address of the agency.'

'I suppose so.'

'How do you manage to get all the stuff without your wife knowing?'

'Plain envelopes – parcels – here – to my rooms. I get lots of academic material delivered here – no problem.'

'No problem,' repeated Morse quietly, with some distaste in his voice at last, as the authority on the great tits wrote down a brief address.

Hardinge watched from his window as the chief inspector walked along to the Porters' Lodge beside the well-watered, weedless lawn of the front quad. He'd seemed an understanding man, and Hardinge supposed he should be grateful for that. If he'd been a little brighter, perhaps, he would have asked one or two more perceptive questions about Myton, though. Certainly Hardinge knew amongst other things the TV company the lecherous cameraman claimed to have worked for. Yet oddly enough the chief inspector had seemed considerably more interested in Claire Osborne than in the most odious man it had ever been his, Hardinge's, misfortune to encounter.

CHAPTER FORTY

> Then the little Hiawatha
> Learned of every bird its language,
> Learned their names and all their secrets
> (Henry Wadsworth Longfellow, *The Song of Hiawatha*)

THAT afternoon PC Pollard was completely 'pissed off' with life as he later reported his state of mind to his Kidlington colleagues. He'd spoken to no one for more than two hours, since the two fellows from the path lab had been along to examine the cordoned off area, to dig several spits out of the brownly carpeted earth where the bones had lain, and to cart them off in transparent polythene bags. Not that they'd said much to him when they had been there just after lunch-time: the sort of men (Pollard had little doubt) with degrees in science and bio-chemistry and all that jazz. He appreciated the need for such people, of course, although he thought the force was getting a bit too full of these smart-alecs from the universities. He appreciated too that it was important to keep people away from the scene of the crime – if it *was* a crime. Exactly who these people were though, he wasn't sure. It was a helluva way from the car park for a couple to carry a groundsheet for a bit of clandestine sex; and they wouldn't go *there*, surely? He'd seen a few birdwatchers as he'd been driven along; but again, not *there*. Too dark and the birds couldn't *fly* in there anyway; it'd be like aeroplanes flying through barrage-balloon cables.

The afternoon was wearing tediously on, and for the umpteenth time Pollard consulted his wrist-watch: 4.25 p.m. A police car was promised up along the Singing Way at 5 p.m.; with further instructions, and hopefully with a relief – unless they'd decided to scrub the whole thing now the ground had been worked over, now the first excitement was over.

4.45 p.m.

4.55 p.m.

Pollard folded away his copy of the *Sun* and picked up the flask they'd given him. He put on his black and white checkered cap, and walked slowly through the woodland riding, wholly unaware that a tiny white-fronted tree-creeper was spiralling up a beech tree to his left; that a little further on a lesser-spotted woodpecker was suddenly sitting very still on a short oak branch as the crunching steps moved alongside.

Another pair of eyes too was watching the back of the shirt-sleeved constable as he walked further and further away; the eyes of a man who made no movement until the woodland around was completely still again, with only the occasional cries of the birds – the thin 'tseet-tseet' of the tree-creeper, and after a while the high 'qui-qui' of the woodpecker – to be heard in that late, still, summer afternoon. For unlike Constable Pollard this man knew much about the woods and about the birds.

The man made his way into the area behind the

cordoned square, and, leaning forward, his eyes constantly fixed to the ground, began to tread slowly, as systematically as the terrain would allow, for about twenty yards or so before turning and retracing his steps along a line four or five feet further into the forest; repeating this process again and again until he had covered an area of roughly fifteen yards square. Once or twice he picked up some object from the densely matted floor, only to throw it aside immediately. Such a pattern of activity he repeated on the left-hand side of the cordoned area – into which he ventured at no point – working his way patiently along, ever watchful, ever alert, and occasionally freezing completely like a statue-waltzer once the music has abruptly stopped. In this fashion he worked for over an hour, like an ox that pulls the ploughshare to the edge of the field, then turns round on itself and plods a parallel furrow, right to left . . . left to right. Boustrophedon.

It was just after 6 p.m. when he found it. *Almost* he had missed it – just the top of the black handle showing. His eyes gleamed with the elation of the hunter pouncing on his quarry; but even as he pocketed his find his body froze once more. A rustle . . . nearby. Very near. Then, just as suddenly, he felt his shoulder muscles relax. Wonderfully so. The fox stood only three yards in front of him, ears pricked, staring him brazenly in the eye – before turning and padding off into the undergrowth, as if deciding that this intruder, at least, was unlikely to molest its time-honoured solitary territory.

*

The police car was very late ('Traffic!' the driver said) and the four of them – the three at the vehicular access points to the woods, and Pollard himself – couldn't alas be relieved until 7 p.m. Priority was still with the joy-riding kids, and no one seemed to know *who* was in charge of things there anyway: Sergeant Lewis had buggered off for a skiing holiday in Sweden – Christ! – and Chief Inspector bloody Morse was temporarily 'unavailable', probably in a pub. Pity the walkie-talkie wouldn't function a bit better, probably all those bloody trees, eh?

The tree-creeper was gone, and the lesser-spotted woodpecker was gone, as Pollard plodded reluctantly back to his post.

And something else was gone too.

CHAPTER FORTY-ONE

Little by little the agents have taken over the world.
They don't do anything, they don't make anything –
they just stand there and take their cut

(Jean Giraudoux, *The Madwoman of Chaillot*)

WHETHER the agency was very busy, or whether the
phone was out of order, or whether someone just didn't
want to speak to him, Morse couldn't know. But it was
4.30 p.m. before he finally got through, and 5 p.m.
before, crawling with the other traffic, he finally pulled
into the small concreted parking area of the Elite
Booking Services in Abingdon Road. The establishment
(as it seemed to Morse) should ideally have been a
glitzy, marble-and-glass affair, with a seductive and
probably topless brunette contemplating her long scarlet fingernails at reception. But things were not so.

The front room of the slightly seedy semi-detached
property was so cluttered with file-cases and cardboard
boxes that room could be found for only two upright
chairs – for the two women proprietors: one, very large,
and certainly ill-advised to be wearing a pair of wide,
crimson culottes; the other rather small and flat-
chested, black-stockinged and minimally skirted. Both
were smoking menthol cigarettes; and judging from the
high-piled ashtrays around the room, both were contin-

uously smoking menthol cigarettes. Instinctively Morse felt that the latter (if either) would be the boss. But it was the large woman (in her late twenties?) who spoke first:

'This is Selina – my assistant. I'm Michelle – Michelle Thompson. How can I help you?'

The smile, on the rounded dimpled cheeks, seemed warm enough – attractive even – and Morse, reluctantly taking Selina's seat, asked his questions and received his answers.

The agency was the receptor, the collator, and the distributor of 'information', from all quarters of the country, which might be of interest and use to assorted businesses, ranging from TV companies to film producers, clothes designers to fashion organizers, magazine editors to well, all right, purveyors of rather less salubrious products. In its Terms and Conditions contracts, the agency dissociated itself officially, legally, completely, from any liability arising from the *misuse* of its services. When a particular client hired a particular model, such a booking was made with the strict proviso that any abuse of contractual obligation was a matter to be settled between model and client – never model and agency. But such trouble was rare – very rare. McBryde had been a client for about two years: a very *good* client, if full and prompt payment were the criterion – 80 per cent of the negotiated fee to the model; 20 per cent to the agency.

Each spring a Model Year Book was produced; there were always new models, of course, and always new clients – with new, differing interests. But one of the

Terms and Conditions ('Terribly important, Inspector!') was that any information originally divulged *to* the agency concerning individual models, and any information subsequently learned *by* the agency about the activities of either clients or models, would always remain a matter of the strictest confidentiality. Must still remain so now, unless, well ... But at least the inspector could understand that once trust was gone ...

'And that's why you never contacted the police?'

'Exactly,' asserted Ms Thompson.

The link with the YWCA in London was very simple. The woman the police had earlier interviewed, Mrs Audrey Morris, was her sister. On the Friday before Karin had hitch-hiked to Oxford, Audrey had phoned to say that they had a young Swedish student with them who was down to her last few pennies; that the YWCA had given her a ten-pound note from the charity fund; that Audrey had written out the name, address, and telephone number of the Elite agency, and assured Michelle that the young lady was shapely, *very* photogenic, and probably sufficiently worldly-wise to know that a suitable session with a photographer might well work wonders for an impoverished pocket.

'You work on Sundays?'

'Sunday's a good day for sin, Inspector. And we had a client willing and waiting – if she came.'

'And she came?'

'She rang us from a call-box in Wentworth Road in North Oxford and Selina here went up in the Mini to fetch her—'

Morse could contain himself no longer. 'Bloody hell! Do you realize how much time and trouble you could have saved us? No wonder we've got so much unsolved crime when—'

'What *crime* exactly are we talking about, Inspector?'

Morse let it go, and asked her to continue.

But that was about it – little more to say. Selina had brought her there, to Abingdon Road: attractive, bronzed, blonde, full-figured, skimpily dressed; with a rucksack – yes, a red rucksack, and with very little else. The client from Seckham Villa had been on the look-out for such and similar offerings. A phone call. A verbal agreement: £100 for a one-hour session – £80 to the girl, £20 to the agency.

'How did she get up to Park Town?'

'Dunno. She said she'd walk up to the centre – only five minutes – and get a bite to eat. Didn't seem to want much help. Independent sort of girl.'

So that was that. At least for the present.

Before he left Morse asked to look through the current Model Year Book, a thick black-covered brochure from which, fairly certainly – or from a previous edition of which – the selected photocopies found at Seckham Villa had been taken. The photographs were all in black and white, but in this edition Morse could find neither Claire nor Louisa amongst the elegant ladies in their semi-buttoned blouses and suspendered stockings. No Karin either among the Ks: just Katie, and Kelly, and Kimberly, and Kylie . . .

'If I can take this?'

'Of course.'

'And I may have to bother you again, I'm afraid – with my sergeant.'

As Morse was leaving the phone rang and Selina made forward as if to take the call. But the senior partner picked up the receiver first, placed her hand over the mouthpiece, and bade her visitor farewell. Thus it was Selina the Silent who accompanied the chief inspector to the door, and who, a little to Morse's surprise, walked out with him to the Jaguar.

'There's something I want you to know,' she said suddenly. 'It's not important, I know, but . . .'

Unlike the Cockney ancestry of her partner's speech, the vowels here were curiously curly: the vowels of Oxfordshire and Gloucestershire.

'I picked her up, you see. She was a lovely girl.'

'Yes?'

'Don't you see? I *wanted* her, Inspector. I asked her if she would see me – afterwards. I've got plenty of money, and she'd got . . . she'd got nothing.' A tear, soon to roll slowly down the thin cheek, had formed in the right eye of Selina, the sleeping, weeping partner of the Agency.

Morse said nothing, trusting that for once his instincts were right.

'She said "no",' continued the woman simply. 'That's what I want you to know really: she wouldn't have done . . . *some* things. She just *wouldn't*. She wasn't for sale – not in the way most of them are.'

Morse laid a hand on a bony shoulder, and smiled at

her understandingly, hoping that he'd assimilated whatever it was she'd wanted to tell him. He thought he
had.

As he drove away, Morse could see the mightily
dimensioned Michelle still busily engaged with the
needs of another client. She was certainly the dominant
partner in the business; but he wondered who might be
the dominant partner in the bed.

He was not back in Kidlington HQ until a quarter to
seven, where he learned that some directive was needed
– pretty soon! – about the personnel in Wytham Woods.
Was the police team there to be disbanded? On the
whole Morse thought it was becoming a waste of time
to maintain any further watch. But logic sometimes
held less sway in Morse's mind than feeling and
impulse, and so he decided that perhaps he *would*
continue with it after all.

He drove out of the HQ car park and turned on the
radio; but he'd just missed it – blast! – and he heard
the signing-off signature-tune of *The Archers* as he
headed towards Oxford, wondering how much else he
might have missed that day.

Turning right at the Banbury Road roundabout he
continued down to Wolvercote and called in at the
Trout, where for more than an hour he sat on the
paved terrace between the sandstone walls of the inn
and the low parapet overlooking the river: drinking,
and thinking – thinking about the strangely tantalizing

new facts he was learning about the death of the
Swedish Maiden.

Lewis rang at 10.15 p.m. He was back. He'd had a
reasonably successful time, he thought. Did Morse want
to see him straightaway?

'Not unless you've got some extraordinary revelation
to report.'

'I wouldn't go quite so far as that.'

'Leave it till the morning, then,' decided Morse.

Not that any decision Morse made that night was to
be of very much relevance, since the routines of virtually every department at police HQ were to be
suspended over the next three or four days. Trouble
had broken out again at Broadmoor Lea, where half
the inhabitants were complaining bitterly of under-
policing and the other half protesting violently about
police over-reaction; council workmen there were
being intimidated; copy-cat criminality was being
reported from neighbouring Bucks and Berks; another
high-level two-day conference had been called for
Thursday and Friday; the Home Secretary had stepped
in to demand a full report; and the investigation of a
possible crime committed perhaps a year earlier in
either Blenheim Park or Wytham Woods or where-
bloody-ever (as the ACC had put the case the following
morning) was not going to be the number-one priority
in a community where the enforcement of Law and
Order was now in real jeopardy.

CHAPTER FORTY-TWO

To some small extent these Greek philosophers made use of observation, but only spasmodically until the time of Aristotle. Their legacy lies elsewhere: in their astonishing powers of deductive and inductive reasoning

(W. K. C. Guthrie, *The Greek Philosophers*)

LEWIS'S report from Sweden had been far more interesting, far more potentially suggestive, than Morse could have hoped. The flesh was being put on the bones, as it were – though no longer those particular bones which had been discovered in Pasticks. The thoughts of others too appeared to be shifting away from any guess-work concerning the likeliest spot in which to dig for the Swedish Maiden, and towards the possible identity of the murderer who had dug the hole in the first place – his (surely a 'he'?) interests, his traits, his psychological identikit, as it were. Especially the thoughts behind the latest letter to *The Times*, which Morse read with considerable interest on the morning of Friday, 24 July.

From the Reverend David M. Sturdy

Sir, like so many of your regular readers I have been deeply impressed by the ingenuity expended by your correspondents on the now notorious Swedish Maiden verses. All of us had hoped that such ingenuity would eventually reap its reward – especially the wholly brilliant analysis (July 13) resulting in the 'Wytham hypothesis'. It was therefore with much disappointment that we read (Tuesday, July 21) the findings of the police pathologist in Oxford.

I cannot myself hope to match the deductive logic of former correspondents. But is it not profitable to take a leaf out of Aristotle's book, and to look now for some *inductive* hypothesis? Instead of asking what the original author intended as clues, we should perhaps be asking an entirely different question, viz., what do the verses tell us about the person who wrote them, especially if such a person were trying to conceal almost as much as he was willing to reveal.

Two things may strike the reader immediately. First, the archaisms so prevalent in the verses ('tell'st', 'know'st', 'Wither', 'thy', 'thee', etc.) which strongly suggest that the author is wholly steeped in the language of Holy Writ. Second, the regular resort to hymnological vocabulary: 'The day thou gavest, Lord, is ended' (l. 11); 'As pants the hart for cooling streams' (l. 15); 'When I survey the wondrous cross' (l. 17) – all of which seem to corroborate the view that the author is a man *regularly* conditioned by such linguistic influences.

May I be allowed therefore to put two and two together and make, not a murderer, but a minister of God's church? May I go even further? And suggest a minister in the Church of Rome, where the confessional is a commonplace, and where in rare circumstances a priest may be faced with a grievous dilemma – the circumstances, say, when a sinner confesses to an appalling crime, and when the priest may be tempted to compromise the sacred principle of confidentiality and to warn society about a self-confessed psychopath, especially so if the psychopath himself has expressed a wish for such a course of action to be pursued.

Might it not be worthwhile then for the Thames Valley CID to conduct some discreet enquiries among the RC clergy within, say, a ten-mile radius of Carfax?

Yours truly,
DAVID M. STURDY
St Andrew's Vicarage,
Norwich.

This letter was also read by Inspector Harold Johnson on holiday with his wife on the Lleyn Peninsula in North Wales. The small village store was not in the habit of stocking *The Times*, but he had picked up a copy on a shopping trip to Pwllheli that morning, and felt puzzled by the reference to 'the findings of the police pathologist in Oxford'. Not just puzzled, either; a whole lot *pleased*, if he were honest with himself. It wasn't very specific, but it must surely mean that the girl still hadn't been found. They'd found some *other* poor sod. Huh! That must have shot bloody Morse in the foot. Shot him up the arse if Strange had his finger on the trigger. He was reading the letter again quickly as his wife was arranging the supermarket carrier bags in the boot of the Maestro.

'What are you smiling at, darling?' she asked.

On Broadmoor Lea, the erection of bollards and concrete blocks, the construction of humps across the streets, and the simpler expedient of digging several holes to the depth of several feet – these activities had put a virtual stop to any possibility of further joy-riding.

All a bit makeshift, but all quite effective. There was revulsion too at the young girl's death. And more public co-operation. The police were winning. Or so it appeared. Marion Bridewell had been knocked down by a car (a shiny new BMW stolen from High Wycombe) with four youths inside. The car itself had been abandoned on the neighbouring Blackbird Leys estate, but a good many of the local inhabitants knew who one or two of them were; and some few bystanders, and some few indeed who had earlier applauded the teenagers' skills, were now semi-willing to testify to names and incidents. Earlier that week fourteen youths and two men in their early twenties had been arrested on the estate, and charged with a variety of motoring offences; six of them were still sitting in the cells. There would very soon be four more of them – the BMW four; and looking at things from the point of view of both the City and the County Constabularies, it was fairly certain that normal police duties could be resumed almost immediately.

The following day, Saturday 25 July, Philip Daley had caught the bus into Oxford at 11 a.m., and his mother had watched him disappear up to the main road before venturing quietly, fearfully, into his bedroom with the hoover. The red-covered pocket diary she'd given him for Christmas had remained unused in his drawer until earlier that month, when the entries had started. The first had been on Saturday the 4th, the writing cramped and ill-fitted into the narrow daily space:

Another tonight. Wow!!! What a squeeler
what a bute. I never been so exited before.

And then the last, a fortnight later:

Finish Finis End! We never meant it
none of us. The screems sounded just like
the tires but we never meant it.

Margaret Daley looked down again at the date,
Saturday, 18 July. Her heart was sinking again within
her, and in her misery she wished that she were dead.

241

CHAPTER FORTY-THREE

It is not the criminal things which are hardest to confess,
but those things of which we are ashamed

(Rousseau, *Confessions*)

MRS MARGARET DALEY pulled her white Mini into
the tarmacadamed area ('For Church Purposes Only')
just above St Michael and All Angels at the northern
end of the Woodstock Road in Oxford – a white,
pebble-dashed edifice, with a steeply angled roof sur-
mounted, at the apex of the gable, by a small stone
cross. Although she was not a regular worshipper –
once a month or so, with the occasional Easter or
Whitsun or Christmas service – Margaret's face was not
unfamiliar there, and on the morning of Sunday, 26
July, she exchanged a few semi-smiling greetings; a few
only, however, for the congregation was thin for the
first Holy Mass at 8 a.m.

The car was George's really, but so often he used the
Blenheim Estate van for getting around that it was
almost always possible for her to have the prior call;
and especially so on Sunday mornings. There had been
very few cars on the road as she had driven down the
dual-carriageway to the Pear Tree roundabout – her
mind deeply and agonizingly preoccupied.

It had begun two years earlier, when George had

bought the video; a bit surprising in any case, because he was no great TV addict, preferring a pint in the Sun most evenings to a diet of soaps. But he *had* bought a video machine; and soon he'd bought a few videotapes to go with it – the highlights of great sporting occasions, mostly: England's 1966 victory in the World Cup; Botham's miracles against the Australians; that sort of thing. The machine had been a rather complex affair, and from the outset there had been a taboo on anyone else manipulating it without his lordship's permission and supervision. It was *his* toy. Such possessiveness had irked young Philip a little, but the situation had been satisfactorily resolved when the lad had been presented with a small portable TV of his own on his fifteenth birthday. But in spite of his growing collection of tapes, her husband seldom actually watched them. Or so she'd thought. Gradually, however, she'd begun to realize that he *did* watch them – when she was away from the house; and particularly so on the regular occasions she was out, twice a week: aerobics on Tuesdays; WI on Thursdays. It had been one Tuesday night when she had been feeling unwell and flushed that she had left the class early and returned home to find her husband jumping up from his seat on the floor beside the TV screen, hurriedly flicking the 'Stop' switch on the video, turning over to the ITV channel, and taking out the tape. The next day, when he was at work, she had managed, for the first time, to get the wretched thing working – and had witnessed a few minutes of wholly explicit and (to her) monstrously disgusting pornography. She had said nothing though; had still said nothing.

But other things were fitting into place. About once every three weeks a brown, plain A4 envelope would be found among George's limited mail, containing, as she'd guessed, some sort of magazine of about thirty or forty pages. Often the post would arrive before George left for work; but she had taken the next opportunity of a later delivery partially to steam open the flap on such a communication, and to discover more than sufficient to confirm her suspicions. But again she'd said nothing; had still said nothing; and would still say nothing. For although it was half of her trouble, it was the half of her trouble that she could the better bear . . .

Perhaps things were slightly easier as she followed the Order of Mass that early Sunday morning, glancing the whiles around her at the familiar stations of the cross as she sat in a pew at the rear of the church. She knew next to no Latin herself – only what she had learned as a young girl from the RC services in the Douay Martyrs' Secondary School in Solihull. But especially had she then loved the sound of some of the long words they'd all sung: words like 'immolatum' from the *Ave Verum Corpus* – a serious-minded word, she'd always thought, sort of grand and sad and musical with all those 'm's in it. Although she'd never really known what it meant, she felt disappointed that they'd got rid of most of the Latin and gone for a thin kind of Englishness in the services; felt this disappointment again now as the Celebrant dismissed them:

'The Mass is ended. Go in peace.'

'Thanks be to God,' she'd replied, and waited in her

place – until only one other solitary soul lingered there, still kneeling, head bowed, in one of the side pews.

After a few mild exhortations in the porchway to his departing flock, Father Richards re-entered the church; and as he did so Margaret Daley rose and spoke to him, requesting a confessional hearing at one of the appropriate times: Saturdays, 11–12 a.m.; 5.30–6.15 p.m. Perhaps it was the earnestness of her manner, perhaps the moist film of her incipient tears, perhaps her voice – unhappy, hesitant, and trembling . . . But whichever, it mattered not. Father Richards took her gently by the arm and spoke quietly into her ear.

'If it will help, my child, come now! Let Christ, through His cross and through His resurrection, set you free from all your sins!'

It was not in the normal confessional box at all; but in a small study in the Manse behind the church that Father Richards heard as much as Margaret Daley felt willing to tell him. But even then she lied – lied when she said she had gone into her son's bedroom to collect his dirty washing, lied about her deepest and most secret fears.

Twice, surreptitiously, Father Richards had looked down at his wrist-watch as he listened. But he refrained from interrupting her until she had told him enough, until he thought he understood enough. The burden of her sin was heavy; yet even heavier (he sensed it) was her guilt at prying into the affairs of others; her

COLIN DEXTER

anguished conviction that it was precisely *because* of her prying, *because* of her snooping, that there had been such terrible secrets to discover. Had she *not* done so ... *the secrets themselves might not have existed.* This was her punishment. Oh God! What could she do?

For a while Father Richards offered no words of consolation; it was important, he knew, for the waters to be drained from the poisoned cistern. But soon – soon he would speak to her. And so it was that he sat and waited and listened until she was dry-eyed again; until her guilt and humiliation and self-pity were for the moment spent. She may have told him a lot or a little, she wasn't sure; but she had told him enough, and now it was time for him to speak.

'You must talk to your son, my child, and you must feel able to forgive him; and you must pray to God for guidance and strength. And this I promise – that I too will pray to God for you.' Momentarily there was a twinkle in the old priest's eyes. 'You know, with the two of us praying for the same thing, He might just listen a little bit harder.'

'Thank you, Father,' she whispered.

The priest placed his hand gently on hers, and closed his eyes as he recited the absolution: 'May God Almighty have mercy on you, forgive your sins, and lead you in the paths of righteousness.'

An 'Amen' was called for, but Margaret Daley had been unable to enunciate a single word, and now walked out of the Manse, and fiddled in her handbag for the car keys. The Mini was the only car remaining on the parking area, but another person was standing there, probably waiting for a lift, it seemed; the person who had been kneeling in the church after everyone else had gone; a person who now turned round and looked into Margaret's face – then looked past her face, unrecognizing, and turned away. The look had lasted but a second, yet in that second Margaret Daley's scalp had thrilled with sudden fear.

CHAPTER FORTY-FOUR

Impressions there may be which are fitted with links and which may catch hold on each other and render some sort of coalescence possible

(John Livingstone Lowes, *The Road to Xanadu*)

ON THE morning of Monday, 27 July, Morse and Lewis were back in business at Kidlington HQ: Lewis (at Morse's insistence) once more going through his Swedish trip in meticulous detail – especially through the furnishings and the photographs on view in Irma Eriksson's living room; and Morse (as always) seeking to convince himself that there was probably some vital clue he'd already missed; or, if not *missed* exactly, some clue whose true significance had hitherto eluded him. Since early that morning he had, as it were, been shaking the atoms laterally in the frying pan, hoping that a few hooks and eyes might link together and forge some new chain of thought; a new *train* of thought ... train *spotting* ... *bird*-spotting ... birds ... yes, birds (like dogs!) had figured all over the place so far, especially the lesser-spotted woodpecker – 'spotted' (that word again!) – yet still the link refused to make itself. He considered once again Karin's list of hope-fully-soon-to-be-identified British birds, and realized that as yet he had made no contact with the woman

248

who lived down near Llandovery ... the home of the
red kites ... Llandovery, out into Wales along the A40
... A40, the third of the possibilities ... the third of
the roads that led off from the Woodstock Road roundabout. Inspector Johnson had done his pedestrian best
with the road out to Blenheim Park; and he himself,
Morse, had done his (equally pedestrian?) best with the
road posted down to Wolvercote and Wytham. But what
if *both* of them had been wrong? Morse had re-read the
statement made by Mrs Dorothy Evans (not an aunt, it
appeared, but some second or third cousin, twice or
thrice removed) in which she'd affirmed quite simply
that Karin Eriksson had never visited her, never even
telephoned her at that time; in fact had not seen 'little
Karin' since that now largish girl was ten years old. No!
The solution to the murder lay there in Oxford, in the
environs of Oxford, Morse was convinced of that.

At 10.30 a.m. he decided that he had to speak to
David Michaels once more; the man who had pointed
the way – almost literally so – to the body found in
Pasticks; the man who knew the woodland ridings out
at Wytham better than almost any man alive.

From the very roundabout where Karin Eriksson might
well have made her fatal decision, Lewis drove down
through the twisting road of Lower Wolvercote, past
the Trout Inn, and then up the hill towards Wytham
village.

'What exactly *is* a handbrake-turn?' Morse had asked
suddenly.

'Don't you know – really?'

'Well, of course, I've got a vague idea . . .'

'Just a minute, sir. Wait till we're round this next bend and I'll show you.'

'No! I didn't—'

'Only a joke, sir.'

Lewis laughed at his chief's discomfiture, and even Morse managed to produce a weak smile.

The police car drove up to the T-junction at Wytham village, turned left, then immediately right, past the dovecote in the car park of the White Hart, then right again into the lane that led up into Wytham Woods. On a gate-post to the right was fixed a bold notice, black lettering on an orange background:

> WYTHAM AMATEUR
> OPERATIC SOCIETY
> *presents*
> THE MIKADO
> BY
> GILBERT & SULLIVAN
> Thursday July 30th, Friday
> July 31st, & Saturday August 1st
> TICKETS £3.50
> (Senior Citizens & Children £2.50)

'The wife's very fond of Gilbert and Sullivan. Far better than all your Wagner stuff, that,' ventured Lewis.

'If you say so, Lewis.'

'Full o' tunes – you know what I mean?'

'We don't go in for "tunes" in Wagner – we go in for "continuous melody".'

'If you say so, sir.'

They drove up to the semi-circular clearing at the edge of the Great Wood.

'We did it at school. I wasn't in it myself, but I remember, you know, everybody dressing up in all that oriental clobber.'

'*The Mikado,* you mean? Oh, yes. Well done!'

Morse seemed for a while almost half asleep, as Lewis stopped the car and looked across at the stone cottage where Michaels lived.

'We're in luck, sir.' Lewis wound down his window and pointed to the forester, a rifle under his right arm, its barrel tilted earthwards at 45 degrees, the black and white Bobbie happily sniffling the route ahead of him.

'Start the car up again, Lewis,' said Morse very quietly.

'Pardon?'

'Back to the village!' hissed Morse.

As the car momentarily drew alongside, it was Morse's turn to wind his window down.

'Morning, Mr Michaels. Lovely morning!'

But before the forester could reply, the car had drawn away; and in his rear-view mirror Lewis could see Michaels standing and staring after them, a look of considerable puzzlement on his face.

*

They were almost the first customers in the White Hart, and Morse ordered a pint of Best Bitter for himself.

'Which would you prefer, sir? We've got—'

'Whatever the locals drink.'

'Straight glass or handle?'

'Straight. Optical illusion, I know, but it always looks as if it holds more.'

'Both hold exactly—'

But Morse had turned to Lewis: 'You'd better not have too much. You're driving, remember.'

'Orange juice – that'll be fine, sir.'

'And, er . . .' Morse fiddled in his trouser pockets. 'I don't seem to have any coins on me. I'm sure the landlord doesn't want to change a twenty this early in the day.'

'Plenty of change—' began the landlord, but Morse had turned to the wall with his pint and was studying a medieval map of the old parishes around Wytham . . .

At the time Morse was lifting his first pint, Alasdair McBryde was standing beside reception at the Prince William Hotel in Spring Street, just opposite Paddington railway station. After leaving Oxford – with what a frenetic burst of mental and physical energy! – he had driven the swiftly, chaotically loaded van via the M40 up to London, where he'd parked it in a lock-up garage off the Seven Sisters Road before taking the tube, and a suitcase, to Paddington – to the Prince William. It gave him considerable confidence that he could, if necessary, be standing in front of the departure board of the mainline BR station within one minute of stepping outside this hotel – or if need be by *jumping* outside it, for the sole window of his *en suite* bedroom was no more than six feet above the pavement.

The hotel proprietor was a small, perpetually semi-shaven Italian who spent half his working hours at reception studying the racing columns of the *Sporting Life.* He looked up as McBryde took out his wallet.

'You stay another day, Mr Mac?'

'Mc' had been the only part he could read of the semi-legible scrawl with which his guest had signed the register. And there was no typed name on any cheque to help; no cheque at all – just the two crisp twenty-pound notes he received each day for the following night's B & B, with the repeated injunction (as now) from Mr Mac: 'Give the change to the breakfast girl!' Not a big tip though, for the daily rate was £39.50.

Soon Luigi Bertolese was again reading through the runners in the 2 p.m. at Sandown Park, and looking especially at a horse there named 'Full English', with some moderate form behind him. He looked down too at one of the twenties, and wondered if the Almighty had whispered a tip in his ear.

'So you see, old friend? You *see?*' Morse beamed hugely as he finished his second pint. 'It was all due to *you.* Again!'

Lewis *could* see: for once was able to see perfectly clearly. And this for him was the joy of working with the strange man called Morse; a man who was somehow

able to extricate himself from the strait-jacketing circumstances of any crime and to look at that crime from
some exterior vantage point. It wasn't fair really! Yet
Lewis was very proud to know that he, with all his
limitations, could sometimes (as now) be the catalytic
factor in the curious chemistry of Morse's mind.

'You having any lunch, sir?'

Morse had been talking for half an hour or so,
quietly, earnestly, excitedly. It was now 12.15 p.m.

'No. Today I'll take my calories in liquid form.'

'Well, I think I'll get myself—'

'Here!' Morse took the precious twenty-pound note
from his wallet. 'Don't go mad with it! Get yourself a
cheese sandwich or something – and another pint for
me.' He pushed his glass across the slightly rickety
table. 'And get a beer-mat or something and stick it
under one of these legs.'

For a few seconds as he stood at the bar Lewis looked
back at his chief. Several other customers were now
seated around, and one youth looked almost embarrass-
ingly blissful as he gazed into the bespectacled eyes of
the rather plain young woman sitting beside him. He
looked, Lewis decided, almost as happy as Chief Inspector Morse.

CHAPTER FORTY-FIVE

His addiction to drinking caused me to censure
Aspern Williams for a while, until I saw as true
that wheels must have oil unless they run on nylon
bearings. He could stay still and not want oil, or
move – if he could overcome the resistance
(Peter Champkin, *The Waking Life of Aspern Williams*)

IN HER laboratory, Dr Laura Hobson had now begun
to write her report, after resuming her analysis of the
Wytham bones. Not really 'resuming' though, for the
bones had hardly left her over the weekend. Quite early
on she'd spotted the slight groove on the lower-left rib:
it might have been the sharp incision of a rodent's
tooth, of course; but it looked so distinctive, that thinly
V-shaped mark. It was almost as if someone had deliberately made a notch in the rib – with a knife or similar
instrument. It might be important? But no, that was the
wrong way of looking at things. It *might* be important –
no question mark; and Laura was oddly anxious to
score a few Brownie-points on her first real enquiry. In
any case she'd very much like to ingratiate herself a
little with the strange policeman who had monopolized
her thoughts these last few days. It was odd how you
couldn't shake someone out of your mind, however
hard you tried. And for Laura that weekend Morse

should, she felt, have been reported to the Monopolies' Commission . . .

Once more she studied the scene-of-crime photographs, and she could identify quite easily the bone that was engaging her interest now. It had obviously lain *in situ* – not disseminated as so many of the others; and she felt fairly certain that the incision which her patient investigation had revealed was unlikely to have been caused by the tooth of some wild creature, tearing away a morsel from the still-fleshed bones. *Could* the notch have been caused by a knife, she wondered: after all, she was working, was she not, upon a *murder*? So if it wasn't the foxes or the badgers or the birds . . . Again she adjusted the focus of the powerful microscope upon the top of the rib-bone, but she knew there could never be any *definite* forensic findings here. The very most she would suggest in her report was that the marked incision made slantwise across the top of the bottom-left rib-bone might possibly have been caused by some incisor tooth, or more probably some sharp implement – a knife, say. And if it *were* a knife that had been driven through the lower chest, it could well be, probably *was*, the cause of death. The body would have bled a good deal, with the blood saturating the clothing (if any?) and then seeping into the soil beneath the body; and not even the intervening months of winter, not even the last of the leaves and the accumulating débris from the growth all round, would ever completely obliterate such traces. That angle, though, was being pursued in the University Agricultural Research Station (coincidentally situated out at Wytham) and doubtless she would be hearing something soon. So what, though? Even if there were clear signs of blood to be found there, at the very most *she* would have a blood group, and *Morse* would be able to assume that the body had been murdered *in situ*. Big deal.

Morse! She'd heard he was a bit of a stickler for spelling and punctuation, and she wanted to make as good an impression as she could. Halfway down the first page of her report she was doubtful about one word, and spying a *Chambers Dictionary* on Max's shelves she quickly looked up the spelling of 'noticeable'.

It was the *Pocket Oxford Dictionary* that was being consulted (over 'proceeding') by another report-writer that afternoon, in the Thames Valley Police HQ. Orthographic irregularities were not an uncommon phenomenon in Lewis's writing; but he was improving all the time, and (like his chief) was feeling very happy with life as he transcribed the full notes he had taken on his Swedish investigation.

At 4 p.m., Mrs Irma Eriksson knocked lightly on the door of her daughter's bedroom, and brought in a tray carrying a boiled egg and two rounds of buttered toast. The flu had been virulent, but the patient was feeling a good deal better now, and very much more relaxed.

As was her mother.

*

At 6.45 p.m. the first – well, the first serious – rehearsal was under way for *The Mikado*. It was quite extraordinary, really, how much local talent there always was; even more extraordinary was how willingly, eagerly almost, this local talent was prepared to devote so much of its time to amateur theatricals, and to submit (in this instance) to the quite ridiculous demands of a producer who thought he knew – and in fact *did* know – most of the secrets of pulling in audiences, of ensuring laudatory reviews in the local press, of guiding the more talented vocalists into the more demanding rôles, and above all of soothing the petty squabbles and jealousies which almost inevitably arise in such a venture.

Three hours, his wife had said – about that; and David Michaels had been waiting outside the village hall since 9.30 p.m. It wasn't all that far from home – back down the lane, past the pub, then right again up the road into the woods – little more than a mile, in fact; but it was now beginning to get really dark, and he was never going to take any chances with his lovely wife. His talented wife, too. She'd only been a member of the chorus-line in the Village Review the previous Christmas; but it had been agreed by all that a bigger part would be wholly warranted in the next production. So she'd been auditioned; and here she was as one of the three little Japanese girls from school. Nice part. Easy to learn.

She finally emerged at 10.10 p.m. and a slightly impatient Michaels drove her immediately along to the White Hart.

'Same as usual?' he asked, as she hitched herself up on to a bar stool.

'Please.'

So Michaels ordered a pint of Best Bitter for himself; and for his wife that mixture of orange juice and lemonade known as 'St Clements' – a mixture designed to keep the world's bell-ringers in a state of perpetual sobriety.

An hour later, as he drove the Land-rover back up to the cottage, Michaels felt beside the gear-lever for his wife's hand, and squeezed it firmly. But she had been very silent thus far; and remained so now, as she tucked the libretto under her arm and got out, locking the passenger door behind her.

'It's going to be all right, is it?' he asked.

'Is *what* going to be all right?'

'What do you think I mean? The Mickadoo!'

'Hope so. You'll enjoy *me*, anyway.'

Michaels locked his own side of the Land-rover. 'I want to enjoy you now!'

She took his hand as they walked to the front porch.

'Not tonight, David. I'm so very tired – please understand.'

Morse too was going home at this time. He was somewhat over-beered, he realized that; yet at least he'd everything to celebrate that day. Or so he told himself as he walked along, his steps just occasionally slightly unbalanced, like those of a diffident funambulist.

*

Dr Alan Hardinge decided that Monday evening to stay in college, where earlier he'd given a well-rehearsed lecture on 'Man and his Natural Environment'. His largely American audience had been generously appreciative, and he (like others that evening) had drunk too much – drunk too much wine, had too many liqueurs. When at 11.30 p.m. he had rung his wife to suggest it would be wiser for him to stay in his rooms overnight, she had raised not the slightest objection.

Neither Michaels, nor Morse, nor Hardinge, was destined to experience the long unbroken sleep that Socrates had spoken of, for each of the three, though for different reasons, had much upon his mind.

CHAPTER FORTY-SIX

A fool sees not the same tree that a wise man sees
(William Blake, *The Marriage of Heaven and Hell*)

WEDNESDAY, the 29th July, was promising to be a busy day; and so it proved.

Inspector Johnson had returned from his holiday the day before, and was now au fait with most of the latest developments in the Swedish Maiden case. At 9.30 a.m. he girded his loins – and rang Strange.

'Sir? Johnson here.'

'Well?'

'I've been sorry to read things haven't worked out at Wytham—'

'Yes?'

'It's just that if you'd be prepared to give me the chance of some men in Blenheim again—'

'*No* chance. Don't you realize that while you've been lying bare-arsed on the beaches we've had all these bloody joy-riders—'

'I've read all about it, sir. All I was thinking—'

'Forget it! *Morse* is in charge now, not you. All right, he's probably making a bloody mess of it. But so did *you*! And until I give the say-so, he's staying fully in charge. So if you'll excuse me, I've got a train to catch.'

*

Morse also had a train to catch and left on the ten o'clock for London, where Lewis had arranged for him to meet a representative of the Swedish Embassy (for lunch), and the supervisor of the King's Cross YWCA (for tea).

For Lewis himself, after seeing Morse off at Oxford railway station, there were a great many things still to be done. Preliminary enquiries the previous day had strongly suggested – confirmed really – that Morse's analysis of the case (to which Lewis, and Lewis alone, was hitherto privy) was substantially correct in most respects. Often in the past Morse had similarly been six or so furlongs ahead of the field only later to find himself running on the wrong racecourse. This time, though, it really did look as if the old boy was right; and from Lewis's point of view it was as if he'd dreamed of the winner the night before and was now just going along to the bookmaker's to stick a few quid on a horse that had already passed the winning post.

Fortunately the pressure was temporarily off the troubles at Broadmoor Lea, and it was no difficulty for Lewis to enlist some extra help. Two DCs were assigned to him for the rest of the day; and this pair were soon off to investigate both the City and the County records of car thefts, car break-ins, car vandalism, etc., in the few days immediately following the last sighting of the Swedish Maiden. Carter and Helpston had seemed to Lewis a pretty competent couple; and so, later that Wednesday, it would prove to be the case.

In mid-morning, Lewis rang *The Oxford Mail* and spoke to the editor. He'd like to fax some copy – copy which Morse had earlier drafted – for that evening's edition. All right? No problem, it appeared.

NEW DEVELOPMENTS IN SWEDISH MAIDEN MYSTERY

DETECTIVE Chief Inspector Morse of the Thames Valley CID is confident that recently unearthed evidence has thrown a completely new light on the baffling case of Karin Eriksson, who disappeared in Oxford more than a year ago, and whose rucksack was discovered soon afterwards in a hedgerow-bottom at Begbroke. A body found after a search of Wytham Woods has proved not to be that of the Swedish student, and the chief inspector told our reporter that further searches of the area there have now been called off. Murder enquiries continue, however, and it is understood that the focus of police activity is now once again centred on the Blenheim Estate in Woodstock – the scene of the first phase of intensive enquiries just over a year ago.

The police are also asking anyone to come forward who has any information concerning Dr Alasdair McBryde, until very recently living at Seckham Villa, Park Town, Oxford. Telephone 0865 846000, or your nearest police station

Later in the day both Chief Superintendent Strange and Chief Inspector Johnson were to read this article: the former with considerable puzzlement, the latter with apparently justifiable exasperation.

And someone else had read the article.

The slim Selina had been more than a little worried ever since Morse had called at the agency. Not worried about any sin of commission; but about one of omission, since she'd been almost certain, when Morse had asked for anything on McBryde, that there *had* been a photograph somewhere. Each Christmas the agency had given a modest little canapé-and-claret do; and later that afternoon in Abingdon Road, and temporarily minus the mighty Michelle, she had decided where, if anywhere, the photograph might be. She looked in the files under 'Parties, Promotions etc.', and there it was: a black and white six- by four-inch photograph of about a dozen of them, party hats perched on their heads, wine glasses held high in their hands – a festive, liberally lubricated crew. And there, in the middle, the bearded McBryde, his arms round two female co-revellers.

Morse had bought a copy of *The Times* in Menzies bookstall at Oxford railway station. In the context of the case as a whole, the two Letters to the Editor which he read just after Didcot (the crossword finished all but one clue) were not of any great importance. Yet the first was, for Morse, the most memorable letter of them all, recalling a couplet he'd long been carrying around in his mental baggage.

From Mr Gordon Potter

Sir, My interest in the Swedish Maiden verses is minimal; my conviction is that the whole business is a time-consuming hoax. Yet it is time that someone added a brief gloss to the admirable letter printed in your columns (July 24). If we are to seek a priest of Roman Catholic persuasions as the instigator of the verses, let me suggest that he will also almost certainly be an admirer of the greatest poet-scholar of our own century. I refer to A. E. Housman. How else do we explain line 3 of the printed verses ('Dry the azured skylit water')? Let me quote Norman Marlow in his critical commentary, *A. E. Housman*, page 145:

'Two of the most beautiful lines in Housman's work are surely these:

And like a skylit water stood
The bluebells in the azured wood.

Here again is a reflection in water, and this time the magic effect is produced by repeating the syllable "like" inside the word "skylit" but inverted as a reflection in water is inverted.'

Yours faithfully
J. GORDON POTTER,
'Arlington',
Leckhampton Road,
Cheltenham,
Glos.

And the second, the sweetest:

From Miss Sally Monroe

Sir, 'Hunt' (l. 18)? 'kiss' (l. 20)? And so far I only know one poem by heart. 'Jenny kissed me when we met', by Leigh Hunt (1784–1859).

Yours faithfully
SALLY MONROE (aged 9 years)
22 Kingfisher Road,
Bicester,
Oxon.

CHAPTER FORTY-SEVEN

> Yonder, lightening other loads,
> The seasons range the country roads,
> But here in London streets I ken
> No such helpmates. only men
> (A. E. Housman, A Shropshire Lad)

MORSE'S day was satisfactory – but little more.

He had arrived a quarter of an hour late, with the diesel limping the last two miles into Paddington at walking-pace, for reasons (Morse suspected) not wholly known even to the engine-driver. But he still arrived in good time at the Swedish Embassy in Montague Place for his meeting with Ingmar Engström, a slim, blond fellow in his forties, who seemed to Morse to exude a sort of antiseptic cleanliness, yet who proved competent and helpful, and willing to instigate immediate enquiries into the matter which Morse (with the greatest care) explained to him.

Lunch was brought into Engström's office, and Morse looked down unenthusiastically at the thin, pale slice of white-pastried quiche, the half jacket potato, and the large separate bowl of undressed salad.

'Very good for the waist-line,' commented the good-humoured Swede. 'And no sugar in *this* either.

Guaranteed genuine!' he added, pouring two glasses of chilled orange juice.

Morse escaped from Montague Place as soon as good manners allowed, professing profuse gratitude but refusing further offers of cottage-cheese, low-fat yoghurt, or fresh fruit, and was quite soon to be heard complimenting the landlord of a Holborn pub on keeping his Ruddles County Bitter in such good nick.

Seldom had tea as a meal, never had tea as a beverage, assumed any great importance in Morse's life. Although relieved therefore not to be faced with the choice of China or Indian, he could well have done without the large plastic cup of weak-looking luke-warm tea which he poured for himself from the communal urn in the virtually deserted canteen of the YWCA premises. For a while they chatted amiably, if aimlessly: Morse discovering that Mrs Audrey Morris had married a Welshman, was still married to the same Welshman, had no children, just the one sister – the one in Oxford – and, well, that was that. She'd been trained as a social worker in the East End, and taken the job of superintendent of the YWCA four years since. She enjoyed the job well enough, but the situation in London was getting desperate. All right, the hostel might be two rungs up from the cardboard-box brigade, but all the old categories were gradually merging now into a sort of communal misery: women whose homes had been repossessed; wives who had been battered; youngish girls who were unemployed or improvident or penniless – or usually all three; birds of passage; and druggies, and potential suicides, and of course quite frequently foreign students who'd miscalculated their monies – students like Miss Karin Eriksson.

Morse went through the main points of the statement she had made the previous summer, but there was, it seemed, nothing further she could add. Like her younger sister she was considerably overweight, with a plump, attractive face in which her smile, as she spoke, appeared guileless and co-operative. So Morse decided he was wasting his time, and sought answers to some other questions: questions about what Karin was *like*, how she behaved, how she'd got on with the others there.

Was it that Morse had expected a litany of seductive charms – the charms of a young lady with full breasts ever bouncing beneath her low-cut blouse, with an almost indecently short skirt tight-fitting over her bottom, and her long, bronzed legs crossed provocatively as she sat sipping a Diet Coke . . . or a Cognac? Only *half* expected though, for his knowledge of Karin Eriksson was slowly growing all the time; was growing now as Mrs Morris rather gently recalled a girl who was always going to catch men's eyes, who was certainly aware of her attraction, and who clearly enjoyed the attention which it always brought. But whether she was the sort of young woman whose legs would swiftly – or even slowly – ease apart upon the application of a little pressure, well, Audrey Morris was much more doubtful. She'd given the impression of being able to keep herself, and others, pretty much under control. Oh yes!

'But she – she might lead men on a bit, perhaps?' asked Morse.

'Yes.'

'But maybe' – Morse was having some difficulty – 'not go much further?'

'Much further than what?'

'What I'm saying is, well, we used to have a word for girls like that – when I was at school, I mean.'

'Yes?'

'Yes.'

'"Prick-teaser"? Is that the word you're looking for?'

'Something like that,' said Morse, smiling in some embarrassment as he stood up and prepared to leave; just as Karin Eriksson must have stood up to take her leave from these very premises, with ten pounds in her purse and the firm resolve (if Mrs Morris could be believed) of hitch-hiking her way not only to Oxford, but very much further out along the A40 – to Llandovery, the home of the red kite.

Audrey Morris saw him out, watching his back as he walked briskly towards the underground station at King's Cross, before returning to her office and phoning her sister in Oxford.

'I've just had your inspector here!'

'No problems, I hope?'

'No! Quite dishy though, isn't he?'

'Is he?'

'Come off it! *You* said he was.'

'Did you give him a glass of that malt?'

'What?'

'You didn't give him a *drink*?'

269

'It's only just gone four now.'

'A-u-d-r-e-y!'

'How was *I* to know?'

'Didn't you smell his *breath*?'

'Wasn't near enough, was I?'

'You didn't manage things at all well, did you, sis!'

'Don't laugh but – I gave him a cup of *tea*.'

In spite of the injunction, the senior partner of Elite Booking Services laughed long and loud at the other end of the line.

Morse arrived back in Oxford at 6.25 p.m., and as he crossed over the bridge from Platform 2 he found himself quietly humming one of the best-known songs from *The Mikado*:

> My object all sublime
> I shall achieve in time
> To let the punishment fit the crime,
> The punishment fit the crime...

CHAPTER FORTY-EIGHT

Players, Sir! I look on them as no better than creatures
set upon tables and joint stools to make faces and
produce laughter, like dancing dogs

> (Samuel Johnson, *The Life of Samuel Johnson*)

FOR SEVERAL persons either closely or loosely connected with the case being reported in these pages, the
evening of Thursday, 30 July, was of considerable
importance, although few of the persons involved were
aware at the time that the tide of events was now
approaching its flood.

7.25 p.m.

One of the three little maids peered out from one
side of the tatty, ill-running stage-curtain and saw that
the hall was already packed, 112 of them, the maximum
number stipulated by the fire regulations; saw her
husband David – bless him! – there on the back row.
He had insisted on buying himself a ticket for each of
the three performances, and that had made her very
happy. Did he look just a little forlorn though, contributing nothing to the animated hum of conversation all
around? He'd be fine though; and she – *she* felt shining
and excited, as she stepped back from the curtain and
rejoined her fellow performers. All right, there were
only a few square yards 'backstage'; such a little *stage*

too; such an inadequate, amateurish orchestra; such a pathetic apology for lighting and effects. And yet ... and yet the magic was all around, somehow: some competent singers; excellent make-up, especially for the ladies; lovely costumes; super support from the village and the neighbourhood; and a brilliant young pianist, an undergraduate from Keble, who wore a large earring, who could sing the counter-tenor parts from the Handel operas like an angel, and who spent most of his free time on lonely nocturnal vigils watching badgers in the nearby woods.

Yes, for Cathy Michaels the adrenaline was flowing freely, and any worries her husband might be harbouring for her – or she for *him*! – were wholly forgotten as with a few sharp taps of the conductor's baton there fell a hush upon the hall; and with the first few bars of the overture, *The Mikado* had begun. Quickly she looked again in one of the mirrors there at the white-faced, black-haired, pillar-box-red-lipped Japanese lady who was herself; and knew why David found her so attractive. David ... a good deal older than she was, of course, and with a past of which she knew so very little. But she loved him, and would do anything for him.

7.50 p.m.

The four youths, aged twelve, fourteen, seventeen, and seventeen, were still being held in police custody in St Aldate's. Whereas collectively on the East Oxford estates they had, by all accounts, appeared a most intimidating bunch, individually they now looked unremarkable. Quite quickly after their arrest had the bravado of this particular quartet disintegrated, and as Sergeant Joseph Rawlinson now looked again at one of the seventeen-year-olds, he saw only a nervous, surly, not particularly articulate lad. Gone was the bluster and aggression displayed in the back of the police car when they had picked him up from home – and now they were taking him back.

'These things all you had on you, son?'

'S'pose so, yeah.'

Rawlinson picked them up carefully, one by one, and handed them across. 'Fiver, £1, £1, 50p, 10p, 5p, 5p, 5p, 2p, 2p, 1p, OK? Comb; Marlboro cigarettes; disposable lighter; packet of condoms, Featherlite – only one left; half a packet of Polos; two bus tickets, one blue Biro. OK?'

The youth stared sullenly, but said nothing.

'And *this*!' Rawlinson picked up a red-covered diary and flicked quickly through the narrow-ruled pages before putting it in his own jacket pocket. 'We're going to keep this, son. Now I want you to sign *there*.' He handed over a typed sheet and pointed to the bottom of it.

Ten minutes later Philip Daley was once more in the back of a police car, this time heading out to his home in Begbroke, Oxon.

'Makes you wonder, Sarge!' ventured one of the constables as Rawlinson ordered a coffee in the canteen.

'Mm.' Joe Rawlinson was unhappy about committing

himself too strongly on the point: his own lad, aged fifteen, had become so bolshie these last six months that his mum was getting very worried about him.

'Still, with this – what's it? – Aggravated Vehicle-taking Bill. Unlimited fines! Might make 'em think a bit harder.'

'Got sod-all to start with though, some of 'em.'

'You're not going soft, Sarge?'

'Oh no! I think I'm getting harder,' said Rawlinson quietly, as he picked up his coffee, and walked over to an empty table at the far corner of the canteen.

He hadn't recognized the lad. But he'd recognized the *name* immediately – from that time the previous summer when he'd been working under Chief Inspector Johnson out at Blenheim. It could, of course, have just been one of those minor coincidences that were always cropping up in life – had it not been for the diary: a bit disturbing, some of the things written in *that*. In fact he'd almost expected to meet his old chief Johnson out on the estates at the weekend, amid the half-bricks and the broken bottles. But someone had said he was off on holiday – lucky bugger! Still, Rawlinson decided to get in touch if he could; try to ring him up tomorrow.

8.15 p.m.

Anders Fastén, a very junior official at the Swedish Embassy, had at last found what he was looking for. It had been a long search, and he realized that if only the files had been kept in a more systematized fashion he would have saved himself many, many hours. He would mention this fact to his boss; and – who knows? – the next tricky passport query might be answered in minutes. But he was pleased to have found it: it was *important*, he'd been informed. In any case, his boss would be pleased. And he much wanted to please his boss, for she was very beautiful.

9 p.m.

Sergeant Lewis had arrived home from HQ half an hour earlier, had a meal of eggs (two), sausages (six), and chips (legion), and now sat back in his favourite chair, turned on the BBC news, and reviewed his day with considerable satisfaction . . .

Especially, of course, had Morse been delighted with the photograph of Alasdair McBryde; and even more delighted with the fact that, on his own initiative, Lewis had given instructions for police leaflets to be printed, and for adverts to be placed in the following day's *Oxford Mail*, Friday's edition of *The Oxford Times* – and the *Evening Standard*.

'Masterstroke, that is!' Morse had exclaimed. 'What made you think of the *Evening Standard*?'

'You said you were sure he'd gone to London, sir.'

'Ah!'

'Didn't meet him by any chance?' Lewis had asked happily . . .

After the weather forecast – another fine sunny day, with temperatures ranging from 22 degrees Celsius in the south – Lewis put out the regular two milk-tokens, locked and bolted the front door, and decided on an early night. He heard his wife humming some Welsh melody as she washed up the plates and he went through to the kitchen and put his arms round her.

'I'm off to bed – bit weary.'

''appy too, by the sound of you. 'ad a good day?'

'Pretty good.'

'That because bloody Morse beggared off and left you on your own?'

'No! Not really.'

She dried her hands and turned to him. 'You enjoy workin' for 'im, don't you?'

'Sometimes,' agreed her husband. 'It's just that he sort of – *lifts* me a bit, if you know what I mean.'

Mrs Lewis nodded, and draped the dish-cloth over the tap. 'Yes, I do,' she replied.

10.30 p.m.

It was half an hour since Dr Alan Hardinge had decided it was time to walk along to St Giles' and take a taxi out to his home on Cumnor Hill. But still he sat sipping Scotch in the White Horse, the narrow pub separating the two wings of Blackwell's bookshop in the Broad. The second of his two lectures had not been an unqualified success, and he was aware that his subject-matter had been somewhat under-rehearsed, his delivery little more than perfunctory. And only one glass of wine to accompany a mediocre menu!

Still, £100 was £100 . . .

He was finding that however hard he tried, it was

becoming progressively more difficult for him to get drunk. He hadn't read any decent literature for months, yet Kipling had been a hero in his youth and vaguely he recalled some words in one of the short stories: something about knowing the truth of being in hell 'where the liquor no longer takes hold, and the soul of a man is rotten within him'. He knew though that he was becoming increasingly maudlin, and he opened his wallet to look again at the young girl . . . He remembered the agonies of anxiety they had both experienced, he and his wife, the first time she was *really* late back home; and then that terrible night when she had not come back at all; and now the almost unbearable emptiness ahead of him when she would never come home again, never again . . .

He took out too the photograph of Claire Osborne from amongst his membership and credit cards: a small passport photograph, she staring po-faced at the wall of a kiosk somewhere – not a good photograph, but not a bad likeness. He put it away and drained his glass; it was ridiculous going on with the affair really. But how could he help himself? He was in love with the woman, and he was lately re-acquainted with all the symptoms of love; could so easily spot it in *others* too – or rather the lack of it. He knew perfectly well, for example, that his wife was no longer in love with him, but that she would never let him go; knew too that Claire had never been in love with him, and would end their relationship tomorrow if it suited her.

One other thing was worrying him that night – had been worrying him increasingly since the visit of Chief

Inspector Morse. He wouldn't do anything immediately, but he was fairly sure that before long he would be compelled to disclose the truth about what had occurred a year ago . . .

10.30 p.m.

After watching the weather forecast, Claire Osborne turned off the ITN *News at Ten* – another half-hour of death, destruction, disease, and disaster. She was almost getting anaesthetized to it, she felt, as she poured herself a gin and dry Martini, and studied one of the typed sheets that Morse had sent her:

MOZART: Requiem (K626)

Helmuth Rilling (Master Works)
H. von Karajan (Deutsche Grammophon)
Schmidt-Gaden (Pro Arte)
Victor de Sabata (Everest)
Karl Richter (Telefunken)

In two days' time she would have her fortieth birthday and she was going to buy a tape or a record of the *Requiem*. All Morse's versions, he'd said, were records: 'But they're not going to be pressing any more records soon, and some of these are museum-pieces anyway.' Yet for some reason she wanted to buy one of the ones *he'd* got, although she realized it would probably be far more sensible to invest in a CD player. Herbert von Karajan was the only one of the five conductors she'd heard of, and 'Deutsche Grammophon' looked and sounded so impressive . . . Yes, she'd try to get that one. Again she looked down at the sheet, trying to get the correct spelling of that awkward word 'Deutsche' into her head, with its tricky 't', 's', 'c', 'h', 'e' sequence.

Ten minutes later she had finished her drink, and put down the empty glass. She felt very lonely. And thought of Morse. And poured herself another drink, this time putting a little more ice in it.

'*God Almighty!*' she whispered to herself.

4.30 a.m.

Morse woke in the soundless dark. From his youth he had been no stranger to a few semi-erotic day-dreams, yet seldom at night did he find himself actually dreaming of beautiful women. But just now – oddly! – he dreamed a very vivid dream. It had not been of any of the beautiful women he'd so far met in the case – not of Claire Osborne, nor of the curly-headed dietitian, nor of Laura Hobson – but of Margaret Daley, the woman with those blondish-grey streaks in her hair; hair which had prompted Lewis to ask his cardinal question: 'Why do you think people want to make themselves look older than they are, sir? Seems all the wrong way round to me.' But Margaret Daley had appeared quite young in Morse's dream. And there had been a letter somewhere in that dream: 'I thought of you so much after you were gone. I think of you still and ask you to think of me occasionally – perhaps even come to visit me again. In the hope that I don't upset you, I send you my love . . .' But there *was* no letter of course; just the words that someone had spoken in his mind. He got up and made himself a cup of instant coffee, noting on the kitchen calendar that the sun would be rising at 05.19. So he went back to bed and lay on his back, his hands behind his head, and waited patiently for the dawn.

CHAPTER FORTY-NINE

An association of men who will not quarrel with one
another is a thing which never yet existed, from the
greatest confederacy of nations down to a town-meeting
or a vestry

(Thomas Jefferson, *Letters*)

DR LAURA HOBSON, one of those who had not been
invited across the threshold of Morse's dreams, entered
his office the following morning just before nine
o'clock, where after being introduced to Sergeant Lewis
she took a seat and said her say.

It didn't, she admitted, boil down to very much
really, and it was all in the report in any case. But her
guess was that the man whose bones were found in
Pasticks was about thirty years of age, of medium height,
had been dead for at least nine or ten months, might
well have been murdered – with a knife-wound to the
heart, and that perhaps delivered by a right-handed
assailant. The traces of blood found beside and beneath
the body were of group O; and although the blood
could have been the result of other injuries, or of other
agencies, well, she thought it rather doubtful. So that
was it. The body had most probably 'exited' (Morse
winced) on the spot where the bones were found; not
likely to have been carried or dragged there after death.

There *were* other tests that could be carried out, but (in Dr Hobson's view at least) there remained little more to be discovered.

Morse had been watching her carefully as she spoke. At their first meeting he'd found her north-country accent (Newcastle, was it? Durham City?) just slightly off-putting; but he was beginning to wonder if after a little while it wasn't just a little *on*-putting. He noticed again, too, the high cheek-bones, and the rather breathless manner of her speaking. Was she *nervous* of him?

Morse was not the only one who looked at the new pathologist with some quiet admiration; and when she handed him the four typed sheets of her report, Lewis asked the question he'd wanted to put for the last ten minutes.

'You from Newcástle?'

'Good to hear it pronounced correctly! Just outside, actually.'

Morse listened none too patiently as the two of them swapped a few local reminiscences before standing up and moving to the door.

'Anyway,' said Lewis, 'good to meet you.' Then, waving the report: 'And thanks for this, luv!'

Suddenly her shoulders tightened, and she sighed audibly. 'Look! I'm not your "luv", Sergeant. You mustn't mind me being so blunt, but I'm no one's "luv" or—'

But suddenly she stopped, as she saw Morse grinning hugely beside the door, and Lewis standing somewhat discomfited beside the desk.

'I'm sorry, it's just that—'

'Please forgive my sergeant, Dr Hobson. He means well – don't you, Lewis?'

Morse watched the slim curves of her legs as she left the office, the colour still risen in her cheeks.

'What was all that about?' began Lewis.

'Bit touchy about what people call her, that's all.'

'Bit like *you*, sir?'

'She's nice, don't you think?' asked Morse, ignoring the gentle gibe.

'To be truthful, sir, I think she's a smasher.'

Somehow this plain statement of fact, made by an honest and honourable man, caught Morse somewhat off his guard. It was as if the simple enunciation of something extremely obvious had made him appreciate, for the first time, its *truth*. And for a few seconds he found himself hoping that Dr Laura Hobson would return to collect something she'd forgotten. But she was a neatly organized young woman, and had forgotten nothing.

Just before Morse and Lewis were leaving for a cup of coffee in the canteen, a call came through from PC Pollard. This rather less-than-dedicated vigilante of Pasticks had been one of four uniformed constables detailed to the compass-point entrances of Blenheim Park; and he was now ringing, with some excitement in his voice, to report that the Wytham Woods Land-rover, driven by David Michaels (whom he'd immediately recognized), had just gone down to the garden centre there. Should he try to see what was happening? Should he – *investigate?*

Morse took the portable phone from Lewis. 'Good man! Yes, try to see what's going on. But don't make it too obvious, all right?'

'How the hell's he going to do that?' asked Lewis when Morse had finished. 'He's in *uniform.*'

'Is he? Oh.' Morse appeared to have no real interest in the matter. 'Make him feel important though, don't you think?'

Chief Inspector Johnson was on his second cup of coffee when Morse and Lewis walked into the canteen. Raising a hand he beckoned Morse over: he'd welcome a brief word, if that was all right? Just the two of them though, just himself and Morse.

Ten minutes later, in Johnson's small office on the second floor, Morse learned of the red diary found the previous day on the person of Philip Daley. But before the two detectives discussed this matter, it was Johnson who'd proffered the olive-branch.

'Look. If there's been a bit of bad feeling – well, let's forget it, shall we? What do you say?'

'No bad feeling on my side,' claimed Morse.

'Well, there was on mine,' said Johnson quietly.

'Yeah! Mine, too,' admitted Morse.

'OK then?'

'OK.'

The two men shook hands firmly, if unsmilingly, and Johnson now stated his case. There'd been a flood of information over the past few days, and one sting was now pretty certain: Daley Junior had been one of the four youths – though not the driver – in the stolen BMW that had killed Marion Bridewell. From all accounts, the back wheels had slewed round in an uncontrollable skid and knocked the poor little lass through a shop window.

'Bit of an odd coincidence, certainly – the boy being involved in both cases,' commented Morse.

'But coincidences never worried you much, did they?'

Morse shrugged. 'I don't reckon he had much to do with the Eriksson case, though.'

'Except he had the camera,' said Johnson slowly.

'Ye-es.' Morse nodded, and frowned. Something was troubling him a little; like a speck of grit in a smoothly oiled mechanism; like a small piece of shell in a soft-boiled egg.

Since the tragedy, Mrs Lynne Hardinge, a slim, well-groomed, grey-haired woman of fifty, had thrown herself with almost frenetic energy into her voluntary activities: Meals on Wheels, Cruse, Help the Aged, Victim Support . . . Everyone was saying what a wonderful woman she was; everyone commented on how well she was coping.

At the time that Morse and Johnson were talking together, she got out of the passenger seat in the eight-windowed Volvo, and taking with her two tin-foiled cartons, main course and sweet, knocked firmly on a door in the Osney Mead estate.

Most of those who received their Meals on Wheels four times a week were grateful and gracious enough. But not quite all.

'It's open!'

'Here we are then, Mrs Gruby.'

'Hope it's not that fish again!'

'Lamb casserole, and lemon pudding.'

'Tuesday's was cold – did you know that?'

'Oh dear!'

The wonderfully well-coping voluntary worker said no more, but her lips moved fiercely as she closed the door behind her. Why didn't you stick it in the fucking oven then, you miserable old bitch? Sometimes she felt she could go quite, *quite* mad. Just recently too she'd felt she could easily *shoot* somebody – certainly that pathetic two-timing husband of hers.

CHAPTER FIFTY

There is but one truly serious philosophical problem,
and that is suicide. Judging whether life is or is not
worth living amounts to answering the fundamental
question of philosophy

(Albert Camus, *The Myth of Sisyphus*)

IT WAS immediately following Morse's almost unprecedentedly alcohol-free lunch (cheese sandwich and
coffee) that the crucial break in the case occurred. And
it was Lewis's good fortune to convey the tidings to the
canteen, where Morse sat reading the *Daily Mirror*.

When earlier in the week Morse had argued that a
car would have been required, that a car would have
been essential, that a car would have to be disposed of
– when earlier Morse had argued these points, the
firing plugs in Lewis's practical mind had sputtered
into life: cars lost, cars stolen, cars vandalized, cars
burned, cars abandoned, cars found on the streets, cars
towed away – Lewis had straightway gauged the possibilities; and drawing a vaguely twenty-mile radius round
Oxford, after consultation with the Traffic Unit, he had
been able to set in motion a programme of fairly simple
checks, with attention focused on the few days following
the very last sighting of Karin Eriksson.

The key evidence would have been difficult to *miss*,

really, once the dates were specified, since Lt. Col. Basil
Villiers, MC, had rung the police on no less than twelve
occasions during the period concerned, complaining
that the car found abandoned and vandalized, and
thereafter further vandalized and finally fired, was a blot
on the beautiful landscape – a disgrace, an eyesore, and
an ugliness; that he (the aforesaid Colonel) had not
fought against despotism, dictatorship, totalitarianism,
and tyranny to be fobbed off with petty excuses concerning insurance, liability, obligation, and availability
of personnel. But it had only been after considerable
difficulty (number plates now gone, though registration
markings still on the windows) that the owner of the
vehicle had been traced, and the offending 'eyesore'
towed away from the neighbourhood of the Colonel's
bungalow to some vehicular Valhalla – with a coloured
photograph the only memento now of what once had
been a newborn, sleek, and shining offspring of some
Japanese assembly line.

The keying-in of the registration number now (as
presumably a year earlier?) had produced, within a few
seconds, the name and address of the owner: James
Myton, of 24 Hickson Drive, Ealing; or rather *formerly*
of 24 Hickson Drive, Ealing, since immediate enquiries
at this address had confirmed only that James Myton
had not lived there for more than a year. Swansea
DVLC had sent three letters to the said address, but
without reply. LMJ 594E was a lapsed registration,
though still not deleted, it appeared, from the official
records kept in South Wales.

As for Myton himself, his name had appeared on

Scotland Yard's missing-persons list for the second half of 1991. But in that year over 30,000 persons were registered as 'missing' in London alone; and a recent report, wholly backed by Sir Peter Imbert himself, suggested that the index was becoming so inaccurate that it should be restarted from scratch, with a completely fresh re-check on each of the legion names listed. As Morse saw things though, it was going to take considerably more than a 're-check' to revive any hopes of the missing Mr James Myton ever being found alive again.

By mid-afternoon there was firm corroboration from Ealing that the body found in Pasticks was that of James William Myton, who as a boy had first been taken 'into care' by the local authority; later looked after by an ageing couple (now deceased) in Brighton; and thereafter supervised for a time by HM Borstal Service on the Isle of Wight. But the young man had always shown a bit of practical talent; and in 1989, aged twenty-six, he had emerged into the outside world with a reputation for adequate competence in carpentry, interior design, and photography. For eighteen months he had worked in the TV studios at Bristol. A physical description from a woman living two doors away from him in Ealing suggested 'a weakish sort of mouth in which the lower teeth were set small and evenly spaced, like the crenellations of a young boy's toy fort'.

'She should have been a novelist!' said Morse.

'She *is* a novelist,' said Lewis.

At all events Myton was not now to be found; and unlikely to be found. Frequently in the past he had been a man of no permanent address; but in the present Morse was sure that he was a permanent dweller in the abode of the dead – as the lady novelist might have phrased it in one of her purplier passages.

Yet things were going very well on the whole – going very much as Morse had predicted. And for the rest of the afternoon the case developed quietly: no surprises; no set-backs. At 5.45 p.m. Morse called it a day and drove down to his flat in North Oxford.

For about two hours that afternoon, as on every week-day afternoon, the grossly overweight wife of Luigi Bertolese sat at the receipt of custom in the Prince William Hotel, whilst her husband conducted his daily dealings with Mr Ladbroke, Turf Accountant. The early edition of the *Evening Standard* lay beside her, and she fixed her pair of half-lenses on to her small nose as she began reading through. At such times she might have reminded some of her paying guests of an owl seated quietly on a branch after a substantial meal – half dopey as the eyelids slowly descended, and then more than commonly wise as they rose ... as they rose again *now* when number 8 came in, after his lunch. And after his drink – by the smell of him.

The photograph was on the front page, bottom left: just a smallish photograph and taken when he'd had a beard, the beard he'd shaved off the day after his arrival at the hotel. Although Maria Bertolese's English was fairly poor, she could easily follow the copy beneath:

'The police are anxious to interview this man, Alasdair McBryde . . .'

She gave him the room-key, handed over two twenty-pound notes, and nodded briefly to the newspaper.

'I doan wanna no trouble for Luigi. His heart is not good – is bad.'

The man nodded, put one of the twenties in his wallet, and gave her back the other: 'For the breakfast girl, please.'

When Luigi Bertolese returned from the betting shop at four o'clock, number 8, cum luggage, had disappeared.

At the ticket office in the mainline Paddington terminus, McBryde asked for a single to Oxford. The 16.20, calling at Reading, Didcot Parkway, and Oxford, was already standing at Platform 9; but there was ten minutes to spare, and from a British Telecom booth just outside the Menzies bookshop there he rang a number (direct line) in Lonsdale College, Oxford.

Dr Alan Hardinge put the phone down slowly. A fluke he'd been in his rooms really. But he supposed McBryde would have caught up with him somewhere, sometime; there would have been a morning or an afternoon or an evening when there had to come a rendering of accounts, a payment of the bill, *eine Rechnung*, as the Germans said. He'd agreed to meet the man of course. What option had he? And he *would* see him; and they would have a distanced drink together, and talk of many things: of what was to be done, and what was not to be done.

And then?

Oh God! What then?

He put his head in his hands and jerked despairingly at the roots of his thick hair. It was the *cumulative* nature of all these bloody things that was so terrible. Several times over the last few days he'd thought of ending it all. But, strangely perhaps, it had not been any fear concerning death itself that had deterred him; rather his own inability to cope with the *practical* aspects of any suicide. He was one of those people against whom all machinery, all gadgetry, would ever wage perpetual war, and never in his life had he managed to come to terms with wires and switches and fuses and screws. There was that way of ending things in the garage, for example – with closed doors and exhaust fumes; but Hardinge suspected he'd cock that up completely. Yet he'd have to do something, for life was becoming intolerable: the failure of his marriage; his rejection by the only woman he'd really grown to love; the futility of academic preferment; his pathetic addiction to pornography; the death of his daughter; and now, just a few minutes ago, the reminder of perhaps the most terrible thing of all . . .

The second performance of *The Mikado*, as Morse recalled, was scheduled, like the first, for 7.30 p.m. Still plenty of time to get ready and go, really. But that evening too he decided against it.

The first night had been all right, yes – but all a bit nervy, a bit 'collywobbly', as the other girls had said. They'd be in really good form that second night, though. David had said she'd been fine the first night – *fine*! But she'd be better now; she'd show him!

With five minutes to go, she peeped round the curtain again and scanned the packed audience. David's ticket for each of the three nights had been on the back row, and she could see one empty seat there now, next to the narrow gangway. But she could see no David. He must, she thought, be standing just outside the hall, talking to somebody before the show began. But seat K5 was destined to remain unoccupied that evening until, during the last forty minutes, one of the programme-sellers decided she might as well give her aching feet a welcome rest.

CHAPTER FIFTY-ONE

> He that is down needs fear no fall,
> He that is low, no pride
> (John Bunyan, *The Pilgrim's Progress*)

WHETHER Morse had been expecting something of the kind, Lewis wasn't at all sure. But certain it was that the Chief Inspector appeared less than surprised when the telephone call came through from Dr Alan Hardinge the following morning. Could he see Morse, please? It wasn't desperately urgent – but well, yes it *was* desperately urgent really, at least for him.

Morse was apparently perfectly content for Lewis to interject one or two obvious questions, just to keep things flowing – the meanwhile himself listening carefully, though with a hint of cynicism around his lips. Perhaps, as Lewis saw things, it had been the preliminary niceties that had soured his chief a little:

MORSE: I was very sorry to learn of your daughter's accident, Dr Hardinge. Must have been a – a terrible—
HARDINGE: How would you know? You've no children of your own.

Morse: How did you know that?
Hardinge: I thought we had a mutual friend, Inspector.

No, it hadn't been a very happy start, though it had finished far more amicably. Hardinge had readily agreed to have his statement recorded on tape; and the admirably qualified WPC Wright was later to make a very crisp and clean transcription, pleasingly free from the multi-Tipp-Exed alterations that usually characterized Lewis's struggles with the typewriter:

On Sunday, 7 July 1991, I joined four other men
in Seckham Villa, Park Town, Oxford. I am more
embarrassed than ashamed about the shared
interest that brought us together. Those present
were: Alasdair McBryde, George Daley, David
Michaels, James Myton, and myself. McBryde
informed us that we might be in for an
interesting afternoon since a young Swedish
student would be coming to sit for what was
euphemistically termed a photographic session.
We learned she was a beautiful girl, and
desperately in need of money. If we wished to
watch, that would be an extra £50: £100 in toto.
I agreed. So did Daley. So did Michaels. I myself
had arrived first. Daley and Michaels arrived
together a little later, and I had the impression
that the one had probably picked the other up. I
knew next to nothing about these two men except
that they were both in the same line of business -
forestry, that sort of thing. I had met each of

them two or three times before, I had never met
them together before.

The fifth man was Myton, whom I'd known earlier,
I'm ashamed to say, as the editor of a series of
sex magazines whose particular slants ranged
from bestiality to paedophilia. He was a
smallish, slimly built man, with a weasel-like
look about him – sharp nose and fierce little
eyes. He often boasted about his time with the
ITV Zodiac Production team; and however he may
have exaggerated, one thing was perfectly clear:
whatever he filmed for videotapes, whatever he
photographed for 'stills', Myton had the magical
touch of the born artist.

The first part of the afternoon I can remember
only vaguely. The room in which we were seated,
the basement room, had a largish, erectile
screen, and we were there (all except Myton)
watching some imported hard-porn Danish videos
when we were aware that the eagerly awaited
Swedish star had arrived. The doorbell had been
rung; McBryde had left us; and soon we were to
hear voices just above us, in the garden outside
– the voices of Myton and the young woman I now
know to have been Karin Eriksson. I remember at
that point feeling very excited. But things
didn't work out. It soon transpired that the girl
had misunderstood the nature of her engagement;
that she was happy enough to do a series of nude
stills – but only behind a closed door, with a
camera, and with one cameraman. No argument.

It was about half an hour later that we heard
the awful commotion in the room immediately
above us, and we followed McBryde up the stairs.
The young woman (we never knew her name until
days later) lay on the bed. She lay motionless
there, with blood all over the white sheets –
vividly red blood, fresh blood. Yet it was not
her blood – but Myton's! He sat there crumpled up
on the floor, clutching his left side and gasping
desperately, his eyes widely dilated with pain –
and fear. But for the moment it was the naked girl
who compelled our attention. There were horridly
bright-red marks around her throat, and her
mouth seemed oddly swollen, with a trickle of
blood slowly seeping down her cheek. Yes, her
cheek. For it was the angle of her head that was
so startling – craned back, as though she were
trying so hard to peer over her forehead to the
headboard of the bed behind her. Then, not
immediately perhaps but so very soon, we knew
that she was dead.

If ever my heart sank in fear and froze in panic
– it was then! Often in the past I had been in some
sex cinema somewhere, and wondered what would
happen if there were a sudden fire and the exits
were blocked with panic-stricken men. The same
sort of thoughts engulfed me now: and then,
behind me – terrifying noises! – I heard a sound
like a kitchen sink clearing itself, and I turned
to see the vomit of dark-red blood suddenly
spurting from Myton's mouth and spilling in a

great gush over the carpet. Six or seven times
his body heaved in mighty spasms – before he too,
like the girl on the bed, lay still.

Of the sequence of events which had led up to
this double tragedy, it is impossible to be
certain. I can't know what the others there
thought; I don't really know what I thought. I
suppose I envisaged Myton filming her as she took
up her various poses; then lusting after her and
trying to assault her there. But she'd fought him
off, with some partial success. More than
partial success.

What was clear to us all was that she'd stabbed
him with a knife, the sort of multi-purpose knife
scouts and guides carry around with them, for she
still clutched the knife even then in her right
hand as if she'd thought he might make for her
again. How she came to have such a weapon beside
her – as I say, she was completely naked – I can't
explain.

My next clear recollection is of sitting with
the other three in the downstairs room drinking
neat whisky and wondering what on earth to do,
trying to devise some plan! Something! Anything!
All of us – certainly three of us – had the same
dread fear in mind, I'm sure of it: of being
exposed to society, to our friends, families,
children, everyone – exposed for what we really
were – cheap, dirty-minded perverts. Scandal,
shame, ruin – never had I known such panic and
despair.

I now come to the most difficult part of my
statement, and I can't vouch for the precise
motives of all of us, or indeed for some specific
details. But the main points of that day are
fairly clear to me still – albeit they seem in
retrospect to have taken place in a sort of blur
of unreality. Let me put it simply. We decided to
cover up the whole ghastly tragedy. It must seem
almost incredible that we took such enormous
trouble to cover ourselves, yet that is what we
did. McBryde told us that the only others who
knew of the Swedish girl's visit were the model
agency, and he said he would see to it that there
was no trouble from that quarter. That left – how
terrible it all now sounds! – two bodies, two
dead bodies. There could be no thought of their
being disposed of before the hours of darkness,
and so it was agreed that the four of us should
reassemble at Seckham Villa at 9.45 p.m.

For the last few months Myton had been living
out of suitcases – out of two large, battered
looking brown suitcases. And in fact had been
staying with McBryde, on and off, for several of
the previous weeks. But McBryde was still
cursing himself for letting the two of them,
Myton and the girl, go out into the back garden,
since if any of the neighbours had seen Karin
Eriksson they would quite certainly have
remembered her clearly. His fears on this score
however seem to have been groundless. As far as
Myton's suitcases and personal effects were

concerned, McBryde himself would be putting them
into the back of his van and carting them off to
the Redbridge Waste Reception Centre early the
following morning. Myton's car was a much bigger
headache but the enormous rise in the number of
car-related crimes in Oxford that year suggested
a reasonably simple solution. It was decided
that I should drive the Honda out to the edge of
Otmoor at 10.45 p.m. that same night, kick in all
the panels, smash all the windows, and take a
hammer to the engine. And this was done. McBryde
had followed me in his van – and indeed assisted
me in my vandalism before driving me back to
Oxford.

That was my rôle. But there was the other huge
problem – the disposal of two bodies, also the
ditching somewhere of the girl's rucksack. Why
we didn't decide to dump the rucksack with
Myton's suitcases, I just don't know. And what
a tragic mistake that proved! The bodies were
eventually loaded into the back of McBryde's van
which drove off under the darkness of that night
– this is what I understand – first to Wytham,
where after Michaels had unlocked the gate
leading to the woods the two foresters had
transferred Myton's body to the Land-rover,
and then driven out to dispose of the body in
the heart of the woods somewhere – I never knew
where.

Then the same men drove out to Blenheim where
Daley, naturally, had easy access to any part of

the Great Park, and where Karin Eriksson's body, wrapped in a blanket and weighed down with stones, was pushed into the lake there – again I never knew where.

Looking back, the whole thing seems so very crude and cruel. But some people act strangely when they are under stress – and we were all under tremendous stress that terrible day. Whether the others involved will be willing to corroborate this sequence of events, I don't know. What is to be believed is that this statement has been made of my own free will with no coercion or promptings, and that it is true.

The statement was dated I.viii.1992, and signed by Dr Alan Hardinge, Fellow of Lonsdale College, Oxford, in the presence of Detective Chief Inspector Morse, Detective Sergeant Lewis, and WPC Wright – no solicitor being present, at Dr Hardinge's request.

Whilst Hardinge was still only some halfway through his statement, George Daley, eager as ever to take advantage of overtime, was boxing some petunias in the walled garden at Blenheim Garden Centre. He had not heard the footsteps; but he felt the touch of a hand on his shoulder, and jerked nervously.

'Christ! You got 'ere quick.'

'You said it was urgent.'

'It *is* bloody urgent.'

'What is?'

'Now look—!'

'No, *you* look! The police'll have that statement some time this morning – probably got it already. And we've agreed – you've agreed – remember that!'

Daley took off the ever-present hat, and wiped the back of his right wrist across his sweaty forehead.

'Not any longer I haven't bloody agreed, mate. Look at this!' Daley took a letter from his pocket. 'Came in the post this morning, dinnit? That's why I rang. See what I could get done for? Me! Just for that fuckin' twerp o' mine. No, mate! What we agreed's no good no longer. We double it – or else no deal. Four, that's what I want. Not two. Four!'

'*Four?* Where the hell do you reckon that's coming from?'

'Your problem, innit?'

'If I could find it,' said the other slowly, 'how do I know you're not going—'

'You don't. Trust, innit? I shan't ask nothin' more never though – not if we make it four.'

'I can't get anything, you know that – not till the bank opens Monday.'

There was a silence between them.

'You won't regret it, mate,' said Daley finally.

'*You* will, though, if you ever come this sort of thing again.'

'Don't you threaten me!'

'I'm not just threatening you, Daley – I'll bloody *kill* you if you try it on again.' There was a menace and a power now in his quiet voice, and he turned to go. 'Better if you come to me – fewer people about.'

'Don't mind.'
'About ten – no good any earlier. In my office, OK?'
'Make it *outside* your office.'
The other shrugged. 'Makes no difference to me.'

CHAPTER FIFTY-TWO

Everything comes if a man will only wait
(Benjamin Disraeli, *Tancred*)

AN HOUR after Hardinge had left – had been allowed to leave – Lewis came back into Morse's office with three photocopies of the document.

Morse picked up one set of the sheets and looked fairly cursorily, it appeared, at the transcript of Hardinge's statement. 'What did you make of things?'

'One or two things a bit odd, sir.'

'Only one or two?'

'Well, there's two things, really. I mean, there's this fellow Daley, isn't there? He's at Park Town that afternoon and that night he shoves the girl's body into the lake at Blenheim.'

'Yes?'

'Well, then he leaves the girl's rucksack in a hedge-bottom at Begbroke. I mean—'

'I wish you'd stop saying "I mean", Lewis.'

'Well, you'd think he'd have left it miles away, wouldn't you? He could easily have dumped it out at Burford or Bicester or somewhere. I me—'

'Why not put it in the blanket? With the body?'

'Well, yes. Anywhere – except where he left it.'

'I think you're right.'

'Why don't we ask him then?'

'All in good time, Lewis! You just said *two* things, didn't you?'

'Ah, well. It's the same sort of thing, really. They decided to put Myton's body in Wytham Woods, agreed? And they *did* put it there, because we've found it. What I can't understand is why Michaels told you where it *was*. I mean – Sorry, sir!'

'But he didn't, did he? He didn't exactly give us a six-figure grid-reference.'

'He told you about Pasticks, though.'

'Among other places, yes.' For a while Morse looked out across the tarmac yard, unseeing it seemed, though nodding gravely. 'Ye-es! Very good, Lewis! You've put your finger – two fingers – on the parts of that statement that would worry anyone; anyone even *half* as intelligent as you are.'

Lewis was unsure whether this was exactly the compliment that Morse had intended; but the master was beginning his own analysis:

'You see – ask yourself this. Why did Daley have to dump the rucksack, and then find it *himself*? As you rightly say, why so close to the place they'd just dumped her body? What's the reason? What *could* be the reason? Any reason? Then, again just as you say, why was Michaels prepared to be so helpful to us? Crackers, isn't it – if he didn't want anyone to find the body? So why? Why give us *any* chance of finding it? Why not give us a duff list of utterly improbable sites? God! Wytham's as big as . . .' (Morse had difficulty with the simile) 'as the pond out at Blenheim.'

'"Lake", sir – about two hundred acres of it. Take a bit of dragging, that.'

'Take a *lot* of dragging.'

'Forget it, then?'

'Yes, forget it! I think so. As I told you yesterday, Lewis . . .'

'You still think you were right about that?'

'Oh, yes! No doubt about it. All we've got to do is to sit back and wait. We're going to have people come to *us*, Lewis. We're losing nothing. You can take it from me there'll be no more casualties in this case unless . . . unless it's that silly young sod, Philip Daley.'

'We might as well take a bit of a breather then, sir.'

'Why not? Just one thing you can do on your way home, though. Look in at Lonsdale, will you? See who was on duty at the Porters' Lodge last night, and try to find out if our friend Hardinge had any visitors in his rooms. And if so, how many, and who they were.'

For the moment, however, Lewis seemed reluctant to leave.

'You sure you don't want me to go and pick up Daley and Michaels?'

'I just told you. They'll be coming to *us*. One of 'em will, anyway, unless I'm very much mistaken.'

'Which you seldom are.'

'Which I seldom am.'

'You don't want to tell me which one?'

'Why *shouldn't* I want to tell you which one?'

'Well?'

'All right. I'll bet you a fiver to a cracked piss-pot that the Head Warden, the Lone Ranger, or whatever his name is, will call here – in person or on the phone – before you sit watching the six o'clock news on the telly.'

'Earlier than that, sir – on a Saturday – the TV news.'

'Oh, and before you go, leave these on Johnson's desk, will you? He won't be in till Monday, I shouldn't think, but I promised to keep him fully informed.' He handed over the third set of photocopied pages, and Lewis rose to depart.

'Do you want me to ring you if I find anything?'

'If it's interesting, yes,' said Morse, with apparent indifference.

Earlier that day, Lewis thought he'd had a pretty clear idea of what the case was all about; or what Morse had told him the case was all about. But now on leaving Kidlington HQ his mind was far more confused, as if whatever else had been the purpose of Hardinge's statement it had certainly muddled the waters of *his*, Lewis's, mind, though apparently not that of his chief's.

As it happened (had he remembered it) Morse would have lost any bet that might have been made, for no one, either in person or on the telephone, was to call on him that afternoon. In fact he did nothing after Lewis left. At one point he almost decided to attend the last night of *The Mikado* at Wytham. But he hadn't got a ticket, and it would probably be a sell-out; and in any case he'd bought a CD of Mozart's *Requiem.*

*

Cathy saw him there that final evening, ten minutes before the curtain was scheduled to rise: the bearded, thick-set, independent soul she'd been so happy to marry in spite of the difference in their ages. He was talking quite animatedly to an attractive woman on the row in front of him, doubtless flirting with her just a little, with that dry, easy, confidential tone he could so easily assume. Yet Cathy felt not the slightest spasm of jealousy – for she knew that it was she who meant almost everything to him.

She let the drape fall back across her line of vision, and went back to the ladies' dressing room where, over her left shoulder, she surveyed herself in the full-length mirror. The simple, short black dresses, with their white collars and red belts, and the suspender-held black stockings, had proved one of the greatest attractions of the show; and each of the three perhaps not-so-little maids, if truth were known, was enjoying the slightly titillating exhibitionism of it all. Cathy had omitted to ask David if he really approved; or if he might be just a teeny bit jealous. She hoped he *was*, of course; but, no, he needn't be. Oh no, he needn't ever be.

Like most amateur and indeed professional productions, *The Mikado* had been put together in disparate bits, with almost all chronological sequencing impossible until the dress rehearsal. Thus it was that David Michaels, though attending a good many practices during the previous month, had little idea of what, perhaps rather grandly, was sometimes called the opera's 'plot'.

Nor had his understanding been much forwarded as a result of the first night's performance, for his mind was dwelling then on more important matters. And now, on this final night, his mind was even further distanced, while he watched the on-stage action as if through some semi-opaque gauze; while he listened to the squeaky orchestra as if his ears were stuffed with cotton wool . . .

He recalled that phone call the previous evening, after which he'd driven down to Oxford, had luckily found a parking place just beside Blackwell's bookshop in the Broad, and then walked through Radcliffe Square and across the cobbles into Lonsdale College, where he'd followed his instructions, walked straight past the Porters' Lodge as if on some high behest, and then into Hardinge's rooms in the front quad, where McBryde had already arrived, and where Daley was to appear within minutes.

Over a year it had been since they'd last met – a year in which virtually nothing had occurred; a year during which the police files had been kept open (he assumed); but a year in which he and the others, the quartet of them, would have assumed with ever-growing relief and confidence that no one would, or ever could, now discover the truth about that hot and distant sunny day.

It was that bloody letter in the paper that had stirred it all up again – as well as that man Morse. What a shock it had been when they'd found the body – since he, Michaels, had no idea whatsoever it had been *there* at all. Bad luck, certainly. What a slice of *good* luck though that he'd found the antler-handled knife, because no one was ever going to find *that* again, lying deep as it was in the lake at Blenheim Park. Yes, the last vestige of evidence was at last obliterated, and the situation was beginning to right itself again; or rather *had* been so beginning . . . until he'd taken the second phone call, early that very morning; the call from that cesspit of a specimen out at Begbroke. But Daley could wait for a while; Daley would play along with them for a little longer yet. The one thing Michaels was quite unable to understand was why *Morse* was waiting. And that made him very uneasy. Perhaps everybody was waiting . . .

Suddenly he was conscious of the applause all around him, as the curtain moved jerkily across to mark the end of Act 1 of *The Mikado*.

CHAPTER FIFTY-THREE

As we passed through the entrance archway, Randolph
said with pardonable pride, 'This is the finest view in
England'
(Lady Randolph Churchill, on her first visit to Blenheim)

ON MONDAY, 3 August, Chief Inspector Harold Johnson had spent much of the morning with his City
colleagues in St Aldate's, and it was not until just gone
11 a.m. that he was in his own office back at Kidlington
HQ – where he immediately read the transcript of
Hardinge's evidence. Then re-read it. It was all new to
him, except the bits about the rucksack, of course.
Naturally he had to admit that since Morse had been
on the case the whole complexion of things had
changed dramatically: clues, cars, corpses – why hadn't
he found any of them? Odd really, though: Morse's
obsession had been with Wytham; and his, Johnson's,
with Blenheim. And according to the statement Hardinge had made, *both* of them had been right all along.
He rang through on the internal extension to Morse's
office, but learned that he had just left, with Lewis –
destination undisclosed.

Blenheim! He found the glossy brochure on Blenheim Palace still on his shelves, and he turned to the
map of the House and Grounds. There it was – the

lake! The River Glyme flowed into the estate from the east, first into the Queen Pool, then under Vanbrugh's Grand Bridge into the lake beyond: some two hundred odd acres in extent, so they'd told him, when first he'd mooted the suggestion of dragging the waters. Too vast an undertaking, though; still was. The Queen Pool was fairly shallow, certainly, and there had been a very thorough search of the ground at its periphery. But nothing had been found, and Johnson had always suspected (rightly, it seemed!) that if Karin Eriksson's body had been disposed of in any stretch of Blenheim there, it had to be in the far deeper, far more extensive waters of the lake; had to be well weighted down too, so the locals had told him, since otherwise it would pretty certainly have surfaced soon after immersion, and floated down to the Grand Cascade, at the southern end of the lake, where the waters resume their narrow flow within the banks of the Glyme.

Johnson flicked through the brochure's lavish illustrations and promised himself he would soon take his new wife to visit the splendid house and grounds built by Queen Anne and her grateful parliament for the mighty Duke. What was that mnemonic they'd learned at school? BROM – yes, that was it: Blenheim, Ramilles, Oudenarde, Malplaquet – that musical quartet of victories. Then, quite suddenly, he had the urge to go and look again at that wonderful sight which bursts upon the visitor after passing through the Triumphal Gate.

He drove out to Woodstock, past the Bear and the church on his left, then across a quadrangle and up to the gate where a keeper sat in his box, and where Johnson (to his delight) was recognized.

'You going through, sir?'

Johnson nodded. 'I thought we had one of our lads at each of the gates?'

'Right. You did, sir. But you took 'em off.'

'When was that?'

'Saturday. The fellow who was on duty here just said he wouldn't be back – that's all I know. Reckon as he thought the case was finished, like.'

'Really?'

Johnson drove on through, and there it was again, bringing back so many memories: in the middle distance the towers and finials of the Palace itself; and there, immediately to his right, the lake with the Grand Bridge and Capability Brown's beechwood landscape beyond it. Breathtaking!

Johnson accepted the fact that he was a man of somewhat limited sensitivity; yet he thought he was a competent police officer, and he was far from happy about the statement he'd just read. If this Hardinge fellow could be believed, the evidence Daley had given a year earlier had been decidedly uneconomical with the truth; and that, to Johnson, was irksome – very irksome. At the time, he'd spent a good while with Daley, going over that wretched rucksack business; and he wanted to have another word with Daley. Now!

He drove down past the Palace to the garden centre; but no one there had seen Daley that morning. He might be out at the mill, perhaps? So Johnson drove out of the estate, through Eagle Lodge, and out on to the A4095, where he turned right through Bladon and Long Hanborough, then right again and in towards the western boundary of the estate, parking beside the piles of newly cut stakes in the yard of the Blenheim Estate Saw-Mill. Only once had he been there when earlier he'd been the big white chief, and he was suddenly aware that it would have been considerably quicker for him to have driven across the park instead of round the villages. Not that it much mattered, though.

No one recognized him here. But he soon learned that Daley's van wasn't there; hadn't been there since Friday afternoon in fact, when he'd been looking after some new plantation, by the lake, and when he'd called at the saw-mill for some stakes for supporting saplings. One of the workers suggested that Daley would prob-ably have taken the van home with him for the weekend – certainly so if he'd been working overtime that weekend; and the odds were that Daley was back planting trees that morning.

Johnson thanked the man and drove to the edge of the estate, only just along the road really; then right along a lane that proclaimed 'No Thoroughfare', till he reached Combe Lodge where, Johnson had been told, the gate would probably be locked. But, well, he *was* a policeman, he'd said.

Johnson read the notice on the tall, wooden, green-painted gate:

ACCESS FOR KEYHOLDERS ONLY.

ALL OTHER VEHICLES MUST USE THE GATE IN WOODSTOCK.

DO NOT DISTURB THE RESIDENTS IN THE LODGE.

But there was no need for him to disturb the (single) resident, since a tractor-cum-trailer was just being admitted, and in its wake the police car was waved through without challenge. A little lax perhaps, as Johnson wondered. Immediately in front of him the road divided sharply; and as a lone, overweight lady, jogging at roughly walking pace, took the fork to the right, Johnson took the fork to the left, past tall oak trees towards the northern tip of the lake. Very soon, some two or three hundred yards ahead on his left, he saw the clump of trees, and immediately realized his luck – for a Blenheim Estate van stood there, pulled in beside an old, felt-roofed hut, its wooden slats green with mildew. He drew in alongside and got out of the car to look through a small side-window of glass.

Nothing. Well, virtually nothing: only a wooden shelf on which rested two unopened bags of food for the pheasants. Walking round to the front of the hut, he tried the top and bottom of the stable-type door: both locked. Then, as he stepped further round, something caught the right-hand edge of his vision, and he looked down at the ground just beyond and behind the hut – his mouth suddenly opening in horror, his body held momentarily in the freezing grip of fear.

CHAPTER FIFTY-FOUR

Michael Stich (W. Germany) beat Boris Becker
(W. Germany) 6–4, 7–6, 6–4
(Result of the Men's Singles Championship at
Wimbledon, 1991)

AT THE time that Chief Inspector Johnson had set out
for Woodstock, Lewis was driving, at slightly above the
national speed limit, along the A40 to Cheltenham. It
appeared to have been a late, impulsive decision on
Morse's part:

'You realize, Lewis, that the only person we've not
bothered about in this case so far is auntie whatever-
her-name-is from Llandovery.'

'Not an "auntie" exactly, sir. You know, it's like when
little girls sometimes call women their aunties—'

'No. I don't know, Lewis.'

'Well, it seems Karin called her Auntie Dot or Doss
– this Mrs Evans. "Dorothy", I seem to remember her
Christian name was.'

'You've profited from your weekend's rest, Lewis!'

'Don't you think we ought to get Daley and Michaels
in first though, sir? I mean, if they're prepared to back
up what Dr Hardinge says—'

'No! If I'm right about this case – which I am! – we'll
be in a far better position to deal with those two

gentlemen once we've seen the Lady of Llandovery. Remember that sign at the Woodstock Road roundabout? Left to Wytham; right to Woodstock; straight over for the A40 to West Wales, right? So we can be there in . . .? How far is it?'

'Hundred and thirty? Hundred and forty miles? But don't you think we should give her a ring just in case—'

'Get the car out, Lewis. The way you drive we'll be there in three hours.'

'Try for two and a half, if you say so,' replied Lewis with a radiant smile.

It had been after Cheltenham, after Gloucester and Ross-on-Wye, after Monmouth and the stretch of beautiful countryside between Brecon and Llandovery, that Morse had come to life again. Never, in Lewis's experience, had he been any sort of conversationalist in a car; but that day's silence had broken all records. And when finally he did speak, Lewis was once again conscious of the unsuspected processes of Morse's mind. For the great man, almost always so ignorant of routes and directions and distances, suddenly jerked up in his passenger seat:

'The right turn in a couple of miles, Lewis – the A483 towards Builth Wells.'

'You don't want to stop for a quick pint, sir?'

'I most certainly *do*. But if you don't mind, we'll skip it, all right?'

'I still think it would've been sensible to ring her, sir.

You know, she might be off for a fortnight in Tenerife or something.'

Morse sighed deeply. 'Aren't you enjoying the journey?' Then, after a pause: 'I rang her yesterday afternoon, anyway. She'll be there, Lewis. She'll be there.'

Lewis remained silent, and it was Morse who resumed the conversation:

'That statement – that statement Hardinge made. They obviously got together the four of them – Hardinge, Daley, Michaels, and McBryde – got together and cooked up a story between them. Your porter couldn't give us any names, you say; but he was pretty sure there were at least three, probably four, of 'em in Hardinge's rooms on Friday night. And if they all stick to saying the same – well, we shall have little option but to believe them.'

'Not that *you* will, sir.'

'Certainly not. *Some* of it might be true, though; some of it might be absolutely crucial. And the best way of finding that out is seeing Auntie Gladys here.'

'Dorothy.'

'You see, there was only *one* really important clue in this case: the fact that the Swedish girl's rucksack was found so quickly – *had* to be found – left beside the road-side – *sure* to be found.'

'I think I'm beginning to see that,' said Lewis, unseeing, as he turned left now at Llanwrtyd Wells, and headed out across the Cambrian Hills.

But not for long. After only a couple of miles, on the left, they came to a granite-built guest-house, 'B & B: Birdwatchers Welcome'. Perhaps it was destined to do a fairly decent trade. Was *certainly* so destined, if there were any birdwatchers around, since there was not another house to be espied anywhere in the deeply wooded landscape.

Mrs Evans, a smallish, dark, sprightly woman in her late forties, showed them into the 'parlour'; and was soon telling them something of herself. She and her husband had lived in East Anglia for the first fifteen years of their (childless) marriage; it was there that she'd met Karin for the first time eight or nine years ago. She, Mrs Evans, was no blood relation at all, but had become friendly with the Eriksson family when they had stayed in the guest-house in Aldeburgh. The family had stayed the next year too, though minus Daddy that time; and thereafter the two women had corresponded off and on fairly regularly: birthday cards, Christmas cards, holiday postcards, and so on. And to the three young Eriksson girls she had become 'Auntie Doss'. When Karin had decided to come to England in 1991, Mrs Evans had known about it; and not having seen the girl for six years or so, had suggested to her mother that if Karin was going to get over towards Wales at all there would always be a welcome for her – and a bed. *And* some wonderful birdwatching, since the beautiful red kites were becoming an increasingly common sight there. What *sort* of girl was Karin? Of course, she'd only been thirteen or fourteen when she'd seen her last but, well – lovely, really. Lovely girl. Attractive – very *proper*, though.

As the conversation between them developed, Lewis found himself looking idly round the room: armchairs, horse-hair settee, mahogany furniture, a coffee table piled high with country magazines, and on the wall above the fireplace a large map of Dyffed and the Cambrian Mountains. It seemed to him a rather bleak and sunless room, and he thought that had she reached this far, the young Karin Eriksson would not have felt too happy there . . .

Morse had now got the good lady talking more rapidly and easily, her voice rising and falling in her native Welsh lilt; talking about why they'd moved back to Wales, how the recession was hitting them, how they advertised for guests – in which magazines and newspapers. On and on. And in the middle of it:

'Oh! Would you both like a cup of tea?'

'Very kind – but no,' said Morse, even as Lewis's lips were framing a grateful 'yes'.

'Tell me more about Karin,' continued Morse. ' "Proper" you said. Do you mean "prim and proper" – that sort of thing? You know, a bit prudish; a bit . . . straightlaced?'

'Nor, I dorn't mean *that.* As I say it's five or six years back, isn't it? But she was . . . well, her mother said she'd always got plenty of boyfriends, like, but she knew, well . . . she knew where to draw the line – let's put it like that.'

'She didn't keep a packet of condoms under her pillow?'

'I dorn't think so.' Mrs Evans seemed far from shocked by the blunt enquiry.

'Was she a virgin, do you think?'

'Things change, dorn't they? Not *many* gels these days who ought to walk up the aisle in white, if you ask me.'

Morse nodded slowly as if assimilating the woman's wisdom, before switching direction again. What was Karin like at school – had Mrs Evans ever learned that? Had she been in the – what was it? – Flikscouten, the Swedish Girl Guides? Interested in sport, was she? Skiing, skating, tennis, basketball?

Mrs Evans was visibly more relaxed again as she replied: 'She was always good at sport, yes. Irma – Mrs Eriksson – she used to write and tell me when her daughters had won things; you know, cups and medals, certificates and all that.'

'What was Karin best at, would you say?'

'Dorn't know really. As I say it's a few years since —'

'I do realize that, Mrs Evans. It's just that you've been so helpful so far – and if you could just cast your mind back and try – try to remember.'

'Well, morst games, as I say, but—'

'Skiing?'

'I dorn't think so.'

'Tennis?'

'Oh, she loved tennis. Yes, I think tennis was her favourite game, really.'

'Amazing, aren't they – these Swedes! They've only got about seven million people there, is that right? But they tell me about four or five in the world's top-twenty come from Sweden.'

Lewis blinked. Neither tennis nor any other sport,

he knew, was of the slightest interest to Morse who didn't know the difference between side-lines and touch-lines. Yet he understood exactly the trap that Morse was digging; the trap that Mrs Evans tumbled into straightaway.

'Edberg!' she said. 'Stefan Edberg. He's her great hero.'

'She must have been very disappointed about Wimbledon last year, I should think, then?'

'She was, yes. She told me she—'

Suddenly Mrs Evans's left hand shot up to her mouth, and for many seconds she sat immobile in her chair as if she'd caught a glimpse of the Gorgon.

'Don't worry,' said Morse quietly. 'Sergeant Lewis will take it all down. Don't talk too fast for him, though: he failed his forty words per minute shorthand test, didn't you, Sergeant?'

Lewis was wholly prepared. 'Don't worry about what he says, Mrs Evans. You can talk just how you like. It's not as if' – turning to Morse – 'she's done much wrong, is it, sir?'

'Not very much,' said Morse gently; 'not very much at all, have you, Mrs Evans?'

'How on earth did you guess *that* one?' asked Lewis an hour later as the car accelerated down the A483 to Llandovery.

'She'd've slipped up sooner or later. Just a matter of time.'

'But all that tennis stuff. You don't follow tennis.'

'In my youth, I'll have you know, I had quite a reliable backhand.'

'But how did you—'

'Prayer and fasting, Lewis. Prayer and fasting.'

Lewis gave it up. 'Talking of fasting, sir, aren't you getting a bit peckish?'

'Yes, I am. Hungry *and* thirsty. So perhaps if we can find one of those open-all-day places . . .'

But they got little further. The car-telephone rang and Morse himself picked it up. Lewis could make out none of the words at the other end of the line – just Morse's syncopated rôle:

'*What?*'

'You *sure?*'

'Bloody 'ell!'

'*Who?*'

'*Bloody* 'ell!'

'Yes.'

'Yes!'

'Two and a half hours, I should think.'

'No! Leave things exactly as they are.'

Morse put down the phone and stared ahead of him like some despondent zombie.

'Something to do with the case?' ventured an apprehensively hesitant Lewis.

'They've found a body.'

'Who?'

'George Daley. Shot. Shot through the heart.'

'Where?'

'Blenheim. Blenheim Park.'

'Whew! That's where Johnson—'

'It was Johnson who found him.'

Suddenly Lewis felt the need for a pint of beer almost as much as Morse; but as the car sped nearer and nearer to Oxford, Morse himself said nothing more at all.

CHAPTER FIFTY-FIVE

Thanatophobia (n): a morbid dread of death, or (sometimes) of the sight of death: a poignant sense of human mortality, almost universal except amongst those living on Olympus

(Small's English Dictionary)

DR LAURA HOBSON knelt again beside the body, this time her bright hazel eyes looking up at a different chief inspector: not at Johnson – but at Morse.

'You reckon he was killed instantly?' asked the latter.

She nodded. 'I'm no expert on ballistics but it was possibly one of those seven-millimetre bullets – the sort that expand on contact.'

'The sort they kill deer with,' added Morse quietly.

'It's' – she fingered the corpse – 'er, sometimes difficult to find the entry-hole. Not in this case, though. Look!'

She pointed a slim finger to a small, blood-encrusted hole, of little more than the diameter of a pencil, just below the left shoulder blade of the man who lay prone on the ground between them. 'But you'll see there's never much of a problem with the *exit* hole.' Gently she eased the body over and away from her, pushing it on to its right side, and pointing to a larger hole that had been blasted just below the heart, a hole almost the size of a mandarin orange.

This time, however, Morse was not looking. He was used to death of course; but accident, and terrible injury, and the sight of much blood – such things he could never stomach. So he turned his eyes away, and for a few moments stood staring around him in that quiet woodland glade, where so very recently someone had shot George Daley in the back, and no doubt watched him fall and lie quite still beneath the giant oak tree there. And the owners of seven-millimetre rifles? Morse knew two of them: David Michaels and George Daley. And whatever else might be in doubt, George Daley would have found it utterly impossible to have shot himself with the rifle that was his.

'Any ideas how long?' asked Morse.

Dr Hobson smiled. 'That's the very first question you always asked Max.'

'He told you?'

'Yes.'

'Well, he never told me the answer – never told me how long, I mean.'

'Shall I tell you?'

'Please do!' Morse smiled back at her, and for a moment or two he found her very attractive.

'Ten, twelve hours. No longer than twelve, I don't think. I'll plump for ten.'

Morse, oblivious of the time for most of the day, now looked at his wrist-watch: 8.25 p.m. That would put the murder at about 10 a.m., say? 10.30 a.m.? Yes ... that sort of time would figure reasonably well if Morse's thinking was correct. Perhaps he *wasn't* right, though! He'd been so bloody certain in his own mind that the case was drawing gently if sombrely towards a conclusion: no more murder, no more deaths. Huh! That's exactly what he'd told Lewis, wasn't it? Just wait! – that's what he'd said. Things'll work out if only we're prepared to wait. Why, only that day he'd waited, before driving off to Wales, without the slightest premonition of impending tragedy.

And he'd been wrong.

There would be greater tragedies in life, of course, than the murder of the mean and unattractive Daley. No one was going to miss the man dramatically much . . . except of course for Mrs Daley, Margaret Daley – of whom for some reason Morse had so recently dreamed. But perhaps even she might not miss him all that much, as time gradually cured her heart of any residual tenderness. After a decent burial. After a few months. After a few years.

Yet there was always the possibility that Morse was wrong again.

Lewis was suddenly at his side, bending down and picking up the khaki-green pork-pie hat Daley invariably wore on freezing winter mornings and sweltering summer days alike.

'There's not *much* shooting here, it seems, sir – not like Wytham – not at this time of year, anyway. Some of the tenants have got shot-gun rights – for a bit of pigeon-shooting, or rabbits, and pheasants a bit later on. Not much, though. That's why Mr Williams, the keeper there' – Lewis pointed back in the direction of

Combe Lodge – 'says he *thinks* he may remember a bit of a pop some time this morning. He can't pin it down much closer than that.'

'Bloody marvellous!' said Morse.

'He says there were quite a lot he let through the gate – there's always quite a lot on Mondays. He *thinks* he remembers Daley going through, some time in the morning, but there's always quite a few estate vans.'

'He thinks a lot, your keeper, doesn't he?'

'And one or two joggers, he says.'

'*Literally* one or two?'

'Dunno.'

'Promise me you'll never take up jogging, Lewis!'

'Can we move him?' asked Dr Hobson.

'As far as I'm concerned,' said Morse.

'Anything else, Inspector?'

'Yes. I'd like to ask you along to the Bear and have a few quiet drinks together – a few *noisy* drinks, if you'd prefer it. But we shall have to go and look round Daley's house, I'm afraid. Shan't we, Lewis?'

Behind the spectacles her eyes twinkled with humour and potential interest: 'Anuther tame, mebby?'

She left.

'Anuther tame, please, Dr Hobson!' said Chief Inspector Morse, but to himself.

CHAPTER FIFTY-SIX

The west yet glimmers with some streaks of day:
Now spurs the lated traveller apace
To gain the timely inn

(Shakespeare, *Macbeth*)

THE HOUSE in which the Daleys had lived for the past eighteen years was deserted. Margaret Daley, so the neighbours said, had been away since the previous Thursday, visiting her sister in Beaconsfield; whilst the boy, Philip, had scarcely been seen since being brought back home by the St Aldate's police. But no forcible entry was needed, for the immediate neighbour held a spare front-door key, and a preliminary search of the murdered man's house was begun at 9.15 p.m.

Two important pieces of evidence were found immediately, both on the red formica-topped kitchen table. The first was a letter from the Oxford Magistrates' Court dated 31 July – most probably received on Saturday, 1 August? – informing Mr G. Daley of the charges to be preferred against his son, Philip, and of the various legal liabilities which he, the father, would now incur under the new Aggravated Vehicle Theft Act. The letter went on to specify the provisions of legal aid, and to request Daley senior's attendance at the Oxford Crown Court on the following Thursday when the hearing of his son's case would be held. The second piece of evidence was half a page of writing from a temporarily departed son (as it appeared) to a now permanently departed father, conveying only the simple message that he was 'off to try and sort something out': a curiously flat, impersonal note, except for the one *post-scriptum* plea: 'Tell Mum she needn't wurry'.

A copy of *The Oxford Mail* for Friday, 31 July, lay on top of the microwave, and a preoccupied Morse scanned its front page briefly:

JOY-RIDERS GET NEW WARNING

THE DRIVER and co-passenger of a stolen car which had rammed a newsagent's shop on the Broadmoor Lea estate were both jailed for six months and each fined £1,500 at Oxford Crown Court yesterday. Sentencing father-of-three Paul Curtis, 25, and John Terence Bowden, 19, Judge Geoffrey Stephens warned:

'Those who drive recklessly and dangerously and criminally around estates in Oxford can now normally expect custodial sentences – and not short ones. Heavier fines too will be imposed as everything in our power is done to end this spate of criminal vandalism.'

(**continued: page 3**)

But Morse read no further, now wandering rather aimlessly around the ground-floor rooms. In the lounge, Lewis pointed to the row of black video-cassettes.

'I should think we know what's on some of *them*, sir.'

Morse nodded. 'Yes. I'd pinch one or two for the

night if I had a video.' But his voice lacked any enthusiasm.

'Upstairs, sir? The boy's room . . .?'

'No. I think we've done enough for one night. And I'd like a warrant really for the boy's room. I think Mrs Daley would appreciate that.'

'But we don't really need—'

'C'mon, Lewis! We'll leave a couple of PCs here overnight.' Morse had reached another of his impulsive decisions, and Lewis made no further comment. As they left the house, both detectives noticed again – for it was the first thing they'd noticed as they'd entered – that the seven-millimetre rifle which had earlier stood on its butt by the entrance had now disappeared.

'I reckon it's about time we had a quick word with Michaels,' said Morse as in the thickening light they got into the car.

Lewis refrained from any recrimination. So easily could he have said he'd regularly been advocating exactly such a procedure that day, but he didn't.

At 10.30 p.m., with only half an hour's drinking time remaining, the police car drove up to the White Hart, where Morse's face beamed happily: 'My lucky night. Look!' But Lewis had already spotted the forester's Land-rover parked outside the front of the pub.

David Michaels, seated on a stool in the downstairs bar, with Bobbie curled up happily at his feet, was just finishing a pint of beer as Lewis put a hand on his shoulder.

'Could we have a word with you, sir?'

Michaels turned on his stool and eyed them both without apparent surprise. 'Only if you join me in a drink, all right?'

'Very kind of you,' said Morse. 'The Best Bitter in decent shape?'

'Excellent.'

'Pint for me then, and, er – orange juice is it for you, Sergeant?'

'What do you want a word about?' asked Michaels.

The three of them moved over to the far corner of the flagstoned bar, with Bobbie padding along behind.

'Just one thing, really,' replied Morse. 'You've heard about Daley's murder?'

'Yes.'

'Well . . . I want to take a look in your rifle-cabinet, that's all.'

'When we've finished the drinks?'

'No! Er, I'd like Sergeant Lewis to go up and—'

'Fine! I'd better just give Cathy a ring, though. She'll have the place bolted.'

Morse saw little objection, it seemed, and he and Lewis listened as Michaels used the phone by the side of the bar-counter and quickly told his wife that the police would be coming up – please let them in – they wanted to look in the rifle-cabinet – she knew where the key was – let them take what they wanted – he'd be home in half an hour – see her soon – nothing to worry about – ciao!

'Am I a suspect?' asked Michaels with a wan smile, after Lewis had left.

'Yes,' said Morse simply, draining his beer. 'Another?'

'Why not? I'd better make the most of things.'

'And I want you to come up to Kidlington HQ in the morning. About – about ten o'clock, if that's all right.'

'I'm not dreaming, am I?' asked Michaels, as Morse picked up the two empty glasses.

'I'm afraid not,' said Morse. 'And, er, I think it'll be better if we send a car for you, Mr Michaels . . .'

A very clean and shining Mrs Michaels, smelling of shampoo and bath-salts, a crimson bath-robe round her body, a white towel round her head, let Sergeant Lewis in immediately, handed him the cabinet key, and stood aside as very carefully he lifted the rifle from its stand – one finger on the end of the barrel and one finger under the butt – and placed it in a transparent plastic container. On the shelf above the stand were two gun-smiths' catalogues; but no sign whatever of any cartridges.

Holding the rifle now by the middle of the barrel, Lewis thanked Mrs Michaels, and left – hearing the rattle of the chain and the thud of the bolts behind him as the head forester's wife awaited the return of her husband. For a while he wondered what she must be thinking at that moment. Puzzlement, perhaps? Or panic? It had been difficult to gauge anything from the eyes behind those black-rimmed spectacles. Not much

of a communicator at all, in fact, for Lewis suddenly
realized that whilst he was there she had spoken not a
single word.

It was completely dark now, and the sergeant found
himself feeling slightly nervous as he flicked the head-
lights to full beam along the silent lane.

CHAPTER FIFTY-SEVEN

FALSTAFF: We have heard the chimes at midnight,
Master Shallow.

SHALLOW: That we have, that we have, that we have; in
faith, Sir John, we have

(Shakespeare, *Henry IV, Part 2*)

OF THE four men who had agreed to concoct (as Morse now believed) a joint statement about the murder of Karin Eriksson, only McBryde had ranged free in the city of Oxford that night. At 6.30 p.m. he had called in at the Eagle and Child, carrying his few overnight possessions in a canvas hold-all, eaten a cheese sandwich, drunk two pints of splendidly conditioned Burton Ale, and begun thinking about a bed for the night. At 7.45 p.m. he had caught a number 20 Kidlington bus outside St Giles' Church and gone up the Banbury Road as far as Squitchey Lane, where he tried the Cotswold House (recommended to him by Hardinge) but found the oblong, white notice fixed across the front door's leaded glass: NO VACANCIES. Just across the way however was the Casa Villa, and here one double room was still available (the last); which McBryde took, considering as many men had done before him that the purchase of an extra two square yards of bed space was something of a waste – and something of a sadness.

At about the time that McBryde was unpacking his pyjamas and sticking his toothbrush into one of the two glasses in his *en suite* bathroom, Philip Daley stood up and counted the coins.

He had caught the coach from Gloucester Green at 2.30 p.m. Good value, the coach – only £4 return for adults. Disappointing though to learn that a single fare was virtually the same price as a return, and sickening that the driver refused to accept his only marginally dishonest assertion that he was still at school. At 6.30 p.m. he had been seated against the wall of an office building next to the Bonnington Hotel in Southampton Row, with a grey and orange scarf arranged in front of him to receive the coins of a stream (as he trusted) of compassionate passers-by; and with a notice, black Biro on cardboard, beside him: UNEMPLOYED HOMELESS HUNGRY. One of the Oxford boys had told him that COLD AND HUNGRY was best, but the early summer evening was balmy and warm, and anyway it didn't matter much, not that first night. He had £45 in his pocket, and certainly had no intention of letting himself get too hungry. It was just that he wanted to see how things would work out – that was all.

Not very well, though, seemed the answer to that experiment: for he was stiff and even (yes!) a little cold; and the coins amounted to only 83p. He must look too well dressed still, too well fed, too little in need. At nine o'clock he walked down to a pub in Holborn and ordered a pint of beer and two packets of crisps: £2.70. Bloody robbery! Nor were things made easier when a shaven-headed youth with multi-tattooed arms and multi-ringed ears moved in beside him, and asked him if he was the prick who'd been staking out his pitch in the Row; because if so he'd be well advised to fuck off smartish – if he knew what was best for him.

Cathy Michaels repeatedly bent forwards, sideways, backwards, as the heat from the dryer penetrated her thick, raven-black hair, specially cut for *The Mikado* in a horizontal bob, the original blonde just beginning to show again, even if only a few millimetres or so at the roots. For a moment she felt sure she'd heard the Land-rover just outside, and she turned off the dryer. False alarm, though. Usually she experienced little or no nervousness when left alone in the cottage, even at night; and never when Bobbie was with her. But Bobbie was not with her: he was down at the pub with his master ... and with the policemen. Suddenly she felt fear almost palpably creeping across her skin, like some soft-footed, menacing insect.

Midnight was chiming, and Morse was pouring himself a nightcap from the green, triangular-columned bottle of Glenfiddich – when the phone went: Dr Hobson. She had agreed to ring him if she discovered anything further before the end of that long, long day. Not that there *was* anything startlingly new, and she realized it could easily wait till morning. But no, it couldn't wait till morning, Morse had insisted.

The bullet that had killed Daley had fairly certainly been fired from a seven-millimetre or a .243 rifle, or something very similar; the bullet had entered the back about 2 inches below the left scapula, had exited (no wince this time from Morse) about 1 inch above the heart, and (this certain now) had been instantly fatal. Time? Between 10 a.m. and 11 a.m. – with just a little leeway either side? – 9.30 a.m. and 11.30 a.m., say? Most probably Daley had been shot from a distance of about 50–80 yards: ballistics might just amend this last finding, but she doubted it.

He'd seemed pleased, and she knew she wanted to please him. There was some music playing in the background, but she failed to recognize it.

'You're not in bed yet?' she ventured.

'Soon shall be.'

'What are you doing?'

'Drinking Scotch.'

'And listening to music.'

'Yes, that too.'

'You're a very civilized copper, aren't you?'

'Only half the time.'

'Well, I'd better gor.'

'Yes.'

'Goodnate, then.'

'Goodnight, and thank you,' said Morse quietly.

*

After putting down the phone Laura Hobson sat perfectly still and wondered what was happening to her. Why, he was twenty-five years older than she was!

At least.

Blast him!

She acknowledged to herself the ludicrous truth of the matter, but she could barely bring herself to smile.

CHAPTER FIFTY-EIGHT

He who asks the questions cannot avoid the answers
(Cameroonian proverb)

THERE WAS little evidence of strain or undue apprehension on David Michaels' face the following morning when he was shown into Interview Room 2, where Sergeant Lewis was already seated at a trestle table, a tape recorder at his right elbow. He was being held for questioning (Lewis informed him) about two matters: first, about the statement made to the police by Dr Alan Hardinge, a copy of which was now handed to him; second, about the murder of George Daley.

Lewis pointed to the tape recorder. 'Just to make sure we don't misrepresent anything, Mr Michaels. We've been getting a bit of stick recently, haven't we, about the way some interviews have been conducted?'

Michaels shrugged indifferently.

'And you're aware of your legal rights? Should you want to be legally represented—'

But Michaels shook his head; and began reading Hardinge's statement . . .

He had little legal knowledge, but had assumed in this instance that he could be guilty only of some small-scale conspiracy to pervert the strict course of truth – certainly not of justice. It was the criminal 'intention', the *mens rea*, that really mattered (so he'd read), and no one could ever maintain that his own intention had been criminal that afternoon a year ago . . .

'Well?' asked Lewis when Michaels put the last sheet down.

'That's about the size of it, yes.'

'You're quite happy to corroborate it?'

'Why not? One or two little things I wouldn't have remembered but – yes, I'll sign it.'

'We're not asking for a signature. We'll have to ask you to make your *own* statement.'

'Can't I just copy this one out?'

Lewis grinned weakly, but shook his head. He thought he liked Michaels. 'Now, last time you pretended – *pretended* – you'd not got the faintest idea where any body might be found, right?'

'Yes,' lied Michaels.

'And then, this time round, you *still* pretended you didn't really know?'

'Yes,' lied Michaels.

'So why did you nudge Chief Inspector Morse in the right direction?'

'Double bluff, wasn't it? If I was vague enough, and they *found* it, well, no one was going to think I'd had anything to do with the murder.'

'Who told you it was *murder*?'

'The chap standing there on guard in Pasticks: big chap, in a dark blue uniform and checked cap – policeman, I think he was.'

The constable standing wide-legged across the door of the interview room took advantage of the fact that Lewis had his back towards him, and smiled serenely.

'Why didn't you dump the rucksack in the lake as well?' continued Lewis.

For the first time Michaels hesitated: 'Should've done, I agree.'

'Was it because Daley had his eye on the camera – and the binoculars?'

'Well, one thing's for sure: *he* won't be able to tell you, will he?'

'You don't sound as if you liked him much.'

'He was a filthy, mean-minded little swine!'

'But you didn't know him very well, surely?'

'No. I hardly knew him at all.'

'What about last Friday night?'

'What *about* last Friday night?'

Lewis let it go. 'You'd never met him previously – at your little rendezvous in Park Town?'

'No! I'd only just joined,' lied Michaels. 'Look, Sergeant, I'm not proud of that. But haven't you ever wanted to watch a sex film?'

'I've seen plenty. We pick up quite a few of 'em here and there. But I'd rather have a plate of egg and chips, myself. What about you, Constable Watson?' asked Lewis, turning in his chair.

'Me?' said the man by the door. 'I'd much rather watch a sex film.'

'You wouldn't want your wife to know, though?'

'No, Sarge.'

'Nor would you, would you, Mr Michaels?'

'No. I wouldn't want her to know about anything like that,' said Michaels quietly.

'I wonder if Mrs Daley knew – about her husband, I mean?'

'I dunno. As I say, I knew nothing about the man, really.'

'Last night you knew he'd been murdered.'

'A lot of people knew.'

'And a lot of people *didn't* know.'

Michaels remained silent.

'He was killed with a seven-millimetre gun, like as not.'

'Rifle, you mean.'

'Sorry. I'm not an expert on guns and things – not like you, Mr Michaels.'

'And that's why you took my rifle last night?'

'We'd've taken *anyone*'s rifle. That's our job, isn't it?'

'Every forester's got a rifle that sort of calibre – very effective they are too.'

'So where were you between, say, ten o'clock and eleven o'clock yesterday morning?'

'Not much of a problem there. About ten – no – just *after* ten it must have been – I was with a couple of fellows from the RSPB. We – they – were checking on the nesting boxes along the Singing Way. You know, keeping records on first or second broods, weighing 'em, taking samples of droppings – that sort of thing. They do it all the time.'

'You were helping them?'

'Carrying the bloody ladder most of the time.'

'What about *after* that?'

343

'Well, we all nipped down to the White Hart – about twelve, quarter-past? – and had a couple of pints. Warm work, it was! Hot day, too!'

'You've got the addresses of these fellows?'

'Not on me, no. I can get 'em for you easy enough.'

'And the barman there at the pub? He knows you?'

'Rather too well, Sergeant!'

Lewis looked at his wrist-watch, feeling puzzled and, yes, a little bit lost.

'Can I go now?' asked Michaels.

'Not yet, sir, no. As I say we need some sort of statement from you about what happened last July . . . then we shall just have to get this little lot typed up' – Lewis nodded to the tape recorder – 'then we shall have to get you to read it and sign it . . . and, er, I should think we're not going to get through all that till . . .' Again Lewis looked at his watch, still wondering exactly where things stood. Then, turning round: 'We'd better see Mr Michaels has some lunch with us, Watson. What's on the menu today?'

'Always mince on Tuesdays, Sarge.'

'Most people'd prefer a sex film,' said Michaels, almost cheerfully.

Lewis rose to his feet, nodded to Watson, and made to leave. 'One other thing, sir. I can't let you go before the chief inspector gets back, I'm afraid. He said he particularly wanted to see you again.'

'And where's he supposed to be this morning?'

'To tell you the truth, I'm not at all sure.'

*

As he walked back to his office, Lewis reflected on what he had just learned. Morse had been correct on virtually everything so far – right up until this last point. For now surely Morse must be dramatically wrong in his belief that Michaels had murdered Daley? In due course they would have to check up on his alibi; but it was wholly inconceivable that a pair of dedicated ornithologists had conspired with a barman from the local pub in seeking to pervert the course of natural justice. Surely so!

At 12.30 p.m., Dr Hobson rang through from South Parks Road to say that, whilst she was an amateur in the byways of ballistics, she would be astounded if Michaels' gun had been fired at any time within the previous few weeks.

'"Rifle",' muttered Lewis, *sotto voce.*

'Is he, er, there?' the pathologist had asked tentatively.

'Back this afternoon some time.'

'Oh.'

It was beginning to look as if everyone wanted to see Morse.

Especially Lewis.

CHAPTER FIFTY-NINE

This is the reason why mothers are more devoted to their children than fathers: it is that they suffer more in giving them birth and are more certain that they are their own

(Aristotle, *Nicomachean Ethics*)

THE NOON-DAY sun shone on the pale-cinnamon stone of the colleges, and the spires of Oxford looked down on a scene of apparent tranquillity as the marked police car drove down Headington Hill towards the Plain, then over Magdalen Bridge and into the High. In the back sat Morse, sombre, and now silent, for he had talked sufficiently to the rather faded woman in her mid-forties who sat beside him, her eyes red from recent weeping, her mouth still tremulous, but her small chin firm and somehow courageous in the face of the terrible events she had only learned about two hours before – when the front doorbell had rung in her sister's council house in Beaconsfield. Yet the news that her husband had been murdered and that her only son had run away from home had left her not so much devastated as dumbfounded, as though a separate layer of emotions and reactions had formed itself between what she knew to be herself, and the external reality of what had occurred.

It had helped a bit too – talking with the chief inspector, who seemed to understand a good deal of what she was suffering. Not that she'd bared her soul *too* much to him about the increasing repugnance she'd felt for the man she'd married; the man who had slowly yet inevitably revealed over the years of their lives together the shallow, devious, occasionally cruel, nature of his character. There had been Philip, though; and for so long the little lad had compensated in manifold ways for the declining love and respect she was feeling for her husband. In nursery school, in primary school, even at the beginning of secondary school, certainly until he was about twelve, Philip had almost always turned to her, his mother; confided in her; had (so preciously!) hugged her when he was grateful or happy. She had been very proud that she was the loved and favoured parent.

Whether it was of deliberate, vindictive intent or not, she couldn't honestly say, but soon after Philip had started at secondary school, George had begun to assert his influence over the boy and in some ways to steal his affection away from her; and this by the simple expedient of encouraging in him the idea of growing up, of becoming 'a man', and doing mannish things. At weekends he would take the boy fishing; often he would return from the Royal Sun in the evening bringing a few cans of light ale with him, regularly offering one to his young son. Then the air-gun! For Philip's thirteenth birthday George had bought him an air-gun; and very soon afterwards Philip had shot a sparrow at the bottom of the garden as it was pecking at some bird-seed she herself had thrown down. What a terrible evening that had been between them, husband and wife, when she had accused him of turning their son into a philistine! Progressively too there had been the coarsening of Philip's speech, and of his attitudes; the brittle laughter between father and son about jokes to which she was never privy; reports from school which grew worse and worse; and the friendship with some of the odious classmates he occasionally brought home to listen to pop music in the locked bedroom.

Then, over a year ago, that almighty row between father and son about the rucksack, which had resulted in an atmosphere of twisted bitterness. Exactly what had happened then, she was still uncertain; but she knew that her husband had lied about the time and place he had found the rucksack. How? Because neither George nor Philip had taken the dog for its walk along the dual-carriageway that morning: *she* had. Philip had gone off to Oxford very early to join a coach party the school had organized; and, on waking, her husband had been so crippled with lumbago that he couldn't even make it to the loo, let alone any lay-by on the dual-carriageway. But she knew George *had* found the rucksack, somewhere – or that someone had given it to him – on that very Sunday when the Swedish girl had gone missing; that Sunday when George had been out all afternoon; and then out again later in the evening, drinking heavily, as she recalled. It must have been that Sunday evening too when Philip had found the rucksack, probably at the back of the garage where, as she knew, he'd been looking for his climbing boots for the school trip to the Peak District – and where, as she suspected, he'd found the camera and the binoculars. Oh yes! She was on very firm ground there – because *she too had found them,* in Philip's room. Only later did she learn that Philip had removed the spool of film from the camera and almost certainly developed it himself at school, where there was a flourishing photographic society (of which Philip was a member) with dark-room facilities readily available.

A good deal of this information Morse had known already, she sensed that. But appearances were that she'd held his attention as tearfully and fitfully she'd covered most of the ground again. He'd not asked her how she knew about the photographs; yet he surely must have guessed. But he would never know about those other photographs, the pornographic ones, the ones of the Swedish girl whom she had recognized from the passport picture printed, albeit so badly, in *The Oxford Times*. No! She would tell Morse nothing about that. Nor about the joy-riding – and her mental turmoil when first she'd read those words in Philip's diary; words which conjured up for her the confused images of squealing tyres and the anguished shrieks of a small girl lying in a pool of her own blood . . . No, it would belittle her son even further if she spoke of things like that, and she would never do it. Wherever he was and whatever he'd done, *Philip would always be her son.*

As the car turned left at Carfax, down towards St Aldate's police station, she saw a dozen or more headjerking pigeons pecking at the pavement; and then fluttering with sudden loud clapping of wings up to the tower above them. Taking flight. Free! And Margaret Daley, her head now throbbing wildly, wondered if she would ever herself feel free again . . .

'Milk and sugar?'

Margaret Daley had been miles away, but she'd heard his words, and now looked up into the chief inspector's face, his eyes piercingly blue, but kindly, and almost vulnerable themselves, she thought.

'No sugar. Just milk, please.'

Morse laid his hand lightly on her shoulder. 'You're a brave woman,' he said quietly.

Suddenly the flood-gates were totally swept away, and she turned from him and wept quite uncontrollably.

'You heard what the lady said,' snarled Morse, as the constable at the door watched the two of them, hesitantly. 'No bloody sugar!'

CHAPTER SIXTY

Music and women I cannot but give way to, whatever
my business is

(Samuel Pepys, *Diary*)

JUST AFTER lunch-time Morse was back in his office at
HQ listening to the tape of Michaels' interview.

'What do you think, sir?'

'I suppose some of it's true,' admitted Morse.

'About not killing Daley, you mean?'

'I don't see how he could have done it – no time was
there?'

'Who did kill him, do you think?'

'Well, there are three things missing from his house,
aren't there? Daley himself, the rifle – and the boy.'

'The son? Philip? You think *he* killed him? Killed his
father? Like Oedipus?'

'The things I've taught you, Lewis, since you've been
my sergeant!'

'Did he love his mum as well?'

'Very much so, I think. Anyway you'll be interested
in hearing what she's got to say.'

'But – but you can't just walk into Blenheim Park
with a rifle on your shoulder—'

'His mum says he used to go fishing there; says his
dad bought him all the gear.'

'Ah. See what you mean. Those long canvas things, you know – for your rods and things.'

'Something like that. Ten minutes on a bike—'

'Has he *got* a bike?'

'Dunno.'

'But *why*? Why do you think—?'

'Must have been that letter, I suppose – from the Crown Court . . .'

'And his dad refused to help?'

'Probably. Told his son to clear off, like as not; told him to bugger off and leave his parents out of it. Anyway, I've got a feeling the lad's not going to last long in the big city. The Met'll bring him in soon, you see.'

'You said it was *Michaels*, though. You said you were pretty sure it must have been Michaels.'

'Did I?'

'Yes, you did! But you didn't seem *too* surprised when you just heard the tape?'

'Didn't I?'

Lewis let it go. 'Where do we go from here, then?'

'Nowhere, for a bit. I've got a meeting with Strange first. Three o'clock.'

'What about Michaels? Let him go?'

'Why should we do that?'

'Well, like you say – he just couldn't have done it in the time. Impossible! Even with a helicopter.'

'So?'

Suddenly Lewis was feeling more than a little irritated. 'So what do I tell him?'

'You tell him,' said Morse slowly, 'that we're keeping him here overnight – for further questioning.'

'On what charge? We just can't—'

'I don't think he'll argue too loudly,' said Morse.

Just before Morse was to knock on Chief Superintendent Strange's door that Tuesday afternoon, two men were preparing to leave the Trout Inn at Wolvercote. Most of the customers who had spent their lunch-time out of doors, seated on the paved terrace alongside the river there, were now gone; it was almost closing time.

'You promise to write it down?'

'I promise,' replied Alasdair McBryde.

'Where are you going now?'

'Back to London.'

'Can I give you a lift to the station?'

'I'd be glad of that.'

The two walked up the shallow steps and out across the narrow road to the car park: PATRONS ONLY. NO PARKING FOR FISHERMEN.

'What about you, Alan?' asked McBryde, as Hardinge drove the Sierra left towards Wolvercote.

'I don't know. And I don't really care.'

'Don't say that!' McBryde laid his right hand lightly on the driver's arm. But Hardinge dismissed the gesture with his own right hand as if he were flicking a fly from his sleeve, and the journey down to Oxford station was made in embarrassed silence.

Back in Radcliffe Square, Hardinge parked on double yellow lines in Catte Street, and went straight up to his rooms in Lonsdale. He knew her number off by heart. Of course he did.

'Claire? It's me, Alan.'

'I know it's you. Nothing wrong with my ears.'

'I was just wondering . . . just hoping . . .'

'No! And we're not going to go over all *that* again.'

'You mean you're not even going to *see* me again?'

'That's it!'

'Not *ever*?' His throat was suddenly very dry.

'You know, for a university don, you don't pick some things up very quickly, do you?'

For a while Hardinge said nothing. He could hear music playing in the background; he knew the piece well.

'If you'd told me you enjoyed Mozart—'

'Look – for the last time! – it's finished. Please accept that! *Finished*!'

'Have you got someone else?'

'What?' He heard her bitter laughter. 'My life's been full of "someone elses". You always knew that.'

'But what if I divorced—'

'For Christ's *sake*! Won't you *ever* understand? It's *over*!'

The line was dead, and Hardinge found himself looking down at the receiver as if someone had given him a frozen fillet of fish for which for the moment he could find no convenient receptacle.

Claire Osborne sat by the phone for several minutes after she had rung off, the wonderful trombone passage from the *Tuba Mirum Spargens Sonum* registering only vaguely in her mind. Had she been too cruel to Alan? But sometimes it was necessary to be cruel to be kind – wasn't that what they said? Or was that just a meaningless cliché like the rest of them? 'Someone else?' Alan had asked.

Huh!

The poorly typed letter (no salutation, no subscription) she had received with the cassette that morning was lying on the coffee table, and already she'd read it twenty-odd times:

I enjoyed so much our foreshortened time together, you and the music. One day of the great lost days, one face of all the faces (Ernest Dowson – not me!). A memento herewith. The *Recordare* is my favourite bit – if I'm pushed to a choice. 'Recordare' by the way is the 2nd person singular of the present imperative of the verb 'recordor': it means 'Remember!'

CHAPTER SIXTY-ONE

A reasonable probability is the only certainty
(Edgar Watson Howe, *County Town Sayings*)

'YOU'RE *sure* about all this, Morse?' Strange's voice was sharp, with an edge of scepticism to it.

'Completely sure.'

'You said that about Michaels.'

'No! I only said I was ninety per cent sure on that.'

'OK.' Strange shrugged his shoulders, tilted his head, and opened his palms in a gesture of acquiescence. 'There are just one or two little things—'

But the phone went on Strange's desk: 'Ah! Ah! Yes! Want to speak to him?'

He handed the phone over to Morse: Dr Hobson. Quite certainly, she said, Michaels' rifle hadn't been fired for weeks. That was all.

Strange had heard the pathologist, just. 'Looks as if you're right about *that*, anyway. We'll give the Met a call. Certain to have scarpered to the capital, don't you reckon, the lad?'

'Ninety per cent sure, sir – and we've already given the Met his description.'

'Oh!'

Morse rose to go, but Strange was not quite finished: 'What first put you on to it?'

For a few moments Morse paused dubiously. 'Several things, I suppose. For example, I once heard someone claim that all three types of British woodpeckers could be found in Wytham Woods. I think I heard it in a pub. Or perhaps I just read it on a beer mat.'

'Useful things, pubs!'

'Then' – Morse ignored the sarcasm – 'I thought if Johnson had opted for Blenheim, it'd pretty certainly turn out to be Wytham.'

'That's grossly unfair.'

'I agree.' Morse got up and walked to the door. 'You know, it's a bit surprising no one ever noticed her accent, isn't it? She must *have* a bit of an accent. I bet you I'll notice it!'

'You're a lucky bugger to hear as well as you do. The wife says I'm getting deafer all the time.'

'Get a hearing aid, sir. They probably wouldn't let you stay in the force, and they'd have to give you a few years' enhancement on the pension.'

'You *think* so? Really?'

'Ninety per cent sure,' said Morse, closing the door behind him and walking thoughtfully back through the maze of corridors to his office.

He'd omitted to acquaint Strange with the biggest clue of all, but it would have taken a little while to explain and it was all a bit nebulous – especially for a man of such matter-of-fact hardheadedness as Strange. But it *had* formed, for him, Morse, the focal point of all the mystery. The normal murderer (if such a person may be posited) would seek to cover up all traces of his victim. And if his victim were someone like Karin

Eriksson, he would burn the clothes, chuck her jewellery and trinkets into the canal, dispose of the body – sink it in some bottomless ocean or cut it up in little bits and take it to the nearest waste-disposal site; even pack it up in those black plastic bags for the dustmen to cart off, since in Morse's experience the only things they *wouldn't* take were bags containing garden waste. So! So if our murderer wanted to rid the earth of every trace of his victim, why, *why*, had he been so anxious for the rucksack and associated possessions to be found? All right, it hadn't worked out all that well, with accidental factors, as almost always, playing their part. But the rucksack *was* found, very soon; the police *were* informed, very soon; the hunt for Karin's murderer *was* under way, very soon. Now if a young Swedish student goes missing *sans everything*, then there is always *less* than certitude that she is dead: thousands of young persons from all parts of Europe, all parts of the world, disappear regularly; get listed as 'missing persons'. But if a young girl goes missing, and at the same time her possessions are discovered in a hedgerow somewhere nearby, then the implications are all too painfully obvious, the conclusions all too readily drawn: the conclusions that Johnson and almost every other policeman in the Thames Valley had drawn a year ago.

Though not Morse.

Perhaps he could, on reflexion, have explained his thinking to Strange without too much difficulty? After all, the key question could be posed very simply, really: why was the murderer so anxious for the police to pursue a murder enquiry? To that strange question

Morse now knew the answer; of that he was quite sure. Well, ninety-nine per cent sure: because the police would be looking for a body, *not for someone who was still alive.*

Ten minutes later, Lewis was ready for him, and together the two detectives drove out to Wytham Woods once more.

CHAPTER SIXTY-TWO

The one charm of marriage is that it makes a life of
deception absolutely necessary for both parties
(Oscar Wilde, *The Picture of Dorian Gray*)

THERE WERE four of them in the living room of the
low-ceilinged cottage: Morse and Lewis seated side by
side on the leather settee, Mrs Michaels opposite them
in an armchair, and the small attractive figure of the
uniformed WPC Wright standing by the door.

'Why haven't you brought David?' asked Mrs
Michaels.

'Isn't he still making a statement, Sergeant?' Morse's
eyebrows rose quizzically as if the matter were of minor
import.

'What are you here for then?' She lifted her eyes
and cocked her head slightly to Morse as if she were
owed some immediate and convincing explanation.

'We're here about your marriage. There's something
slightly, ah, irregular about it.'

'Really? You'll have to check that up with the Registry
Office, not me.'

'Regist*er* Office, Mrs Michaels. It's important to be
accurate about things. So let *me* be accurate. David
Michaels discovered that the District Office for anyone
living in Wytham was at Abingdon, and he went there

and answered all the usual questions about when and where you wanted to marry, how old you both were, where you were both born, whether either of you had been married before, whether you were related. And that was that. Two days later you were married.'

'So?'

'Well, everything is really based on *trust* in things like that. If you want to, you can tell a pack of lies. There's one Registrar in Oxford who married the same fellow three times in the same year – one in Reading who managed to marry a couple of sailors!'

Morse looked across at her as if expecting a dutiful smile, but Mrs Michaels sat perfectly still, her mouth tight, her hair framing the clear-skinned features in a semi-circle of the darkest black, the blonde roots so very recently re-dyed.

'Take any reasonably fluent liar – even a fairly clumsy liar,' continued Morse, 'and he'll get away with murder – if you see what I mean, Mrs Michaels. For example, some proof of age is required for anyone under twenty-three, did you know that? But if your fiancé says you're twenty-*four*? Well, he'll almost certainly get away with it. And if you've been married before? Well, if you say you *haven't*, it's going to be virtually impossible to prove, then and there, that you have. Oh yes! It's easy to get married by licence if you're willing to abuse the system.'

'You are saying that I – that we, David and I – we abused the system?'

'You know most English people would have settled for "me and David", Mrs Michaels.' (WPC Wright was aware of that nuance of stress on the word 'English'.)

'I asked you—'

But Morse interrupted her brusquely: 'There was only one thing that couldn't be fiddled in your case: date of birth. You see, some documentation is statutory in that respect – *if the person concerned is a foreign national.*'

A silence now hung over the small room; a palpably tense silence, during which a strange, indefinable look flitted across Mrs Michaels' features as she crossed one leg over the other and clasped her hands round her left knee.

'What's that got to do with me?' she asked.

'You're a foreign national,' said Morse simply, looking across unblinkingly at the lovely girl seated opposite him.

'Do you realize how absurd all this is, Inspector?'

'Did you have to show your passport to the Registrar at Abingdon?'

'There was no *need* for that: I'm *not* a foreign national!'

'No?'

'*No!* My name is – *was* Catharine Adams. I was born in Uppingham, in Rutland – what *used* to be Rutland; I'm twenty-four years old—'

'Can *I* see your passport?' asked Morse quietly.

'As a matter of fact you can't. It's in the post to Swansea – it needs renewing. We are going – me and David! – to Italy in September.' (Lewis could pick up the hint of the accent now, in that word 'Eetaly'.)

'Don't worry! We've already got a copy, you see. The Swedish Embassy sent us one.'

For several moments she looked down at the carpet, the one expensive item in the rather mundane living room in which she'd spent so many hours of her days: a small, rectangular oriental carpet, woven perhaps in some obscure tent in Turkestan. Then, rising, she took a few steps over to a desk, took out her passport, and handed it to Morse.

But Morse knew it all anyway; had already studied the details carefully: the headings, printed in both Swedish and English; the details required, handwritten in Swedish. Underneath the photograph, he read again:

Surname ....

Christian name(s) ....

Height in cms (without shoes) ....

Sex ....

Date of birth ....

Place of birth ....

Civic Reg. No. ....

Date issued ....

How long valid ....

Signature ....

Remarks ....

Katarina Adams (it appeared), height 168 cms in her stockinged feet, of the female sex, had been born on the 29 September 1968, in Uppsala, Sweden.

'Clever touch that, Uppingham for Úppsala,' commented Morse.

'Uppsála – if we must be accurate, Inspector.'

'"Adams" was your married name – your first

married name. And when your husband was killed in a car crash, you kept it. Why not? So . . .'

'So, what else do you want from me?' she asked quietly.

'Just tell me the truth, please! We shall get there in the end, you know.'

She took a deep breath, and spoke quickly and briefly. 'When my sister Karin was murdered, I was in Spain – in Barcelona, as it happened. I got here as soon as I could – my mother had rung me from Sweden. But I could do nothing, I soon realized that. I met David. We fell in love. We were married. I was frightened about work permits and visas and that sort of thing, and David said it would be better if I lied – if *he* lied – about my earlier marriage. Easier and quicker. So? For a start I only went out of the house here a very few times. I wore glasses and I had my hair cut fairly short and dyed black. That's why they asked me to sing in the opera, yes? I looked like the part before they started the auditions.'

Lewis glanced briefly sideways, and thought he saw a look of slight puzzlement on Morse's face.

'Didn't the Registrar *tell* you – tell your husband – that it was all above board anyway?'

'No, I'm sure he didn't. You see we said nothing about this . . . you know. Can't you understand? It was all very strange – all very unsettling and sort of, sort of nervy, somehow. David understood, though—'

'Did you enjoy your holiday in Spain?'

'Very much. Why—?'

'Which airport did you fly from to England?'

364

'Barcelona.'

'Lots of muggings, they tell me, at Barcelona airport.'

'What's that got to do—?'

'Ever lost *your* handbag? You know, with your keys and passport and credit cards?'

'No. I'm glad to say I haven't.'

'What would you *do* if you lost your passport, say?'

She shrugged. 'I don't know. I'd apply to the Swedish Embassy, I suppose. They'd probably give me a temporary document . . . or something . . .'

'But do you think it would be possible to *fiddle* things, Mrs Michaels? Like it's possible to fiddle a marriage licence?'

'I wish you'd tell me exactly what you're getting at.'

'All right. Let me ask you a simple question. Would it be possible for anyone to apply for someone *else's* passport?'

'Almost impossible, surely? There are all sorts of checks in Sweden: Civic Registration Number – that's what we use in Sweden instead of a birth certificate – details of all the information on the passport that would have to be checked – photograph? No! I don't think it would.'

'I agree with you, I think. *Almost* impossible – though not quite; not for a very clever woman.'

'But I'm *not* a very clever woman, Inspector.'

'No! Again I agree with you.' (Lewis wondered if he'd spotted the slightest trace of disappointment in her eyes.) 'But let's agree it is impossible, right. There is another way, though, a very much easier way of acquiring a passport. A childishly easy way. Someone *gives* you one, Mrs Michaels. Someone *sends* you one through the post.'

'You are leaving me many miles behind, Inspector.'

'No, I'm not,' replied Morse, with a quiet factuality that brooked no argument. 'No one – *no one* – lost any passport at Barcelona, or anywhere else. But you and your elder sister are very much alike, aren't you? My sergeant here brought me a photograph of the three of you from Stockholm. You're all blonde and blue-eyed and high-cheekboned and long-legged and everything else people here expect from the Nordic type. Even your younger sister – the shortest of the three of you – she looks very much like Karin too, at least from her photograph.'

Forcibly she interrupted him: 'Listen! Just *one* moment, please! Have *you* ever felt completely confused – like I feel now?'

'Oh, yes! Quite frequently, believe me. But not now. Not now, Mrs Michaels. And you're not confused either. Because that passport there isn't yours. It belongs to your sister Katarina – Katarina Adams. Your sister who still lives in Uppsála. Your sister who told the Swedish authorities that she'd had her passport stolen, and then applied for another. Simple! You see, your name isn't Katarina Adams at all, is it, Mrs Michaels? It's *Karin Eriksson*.'

Her shoulders suddenly sagged, as if she felt that, in spite of any innocent protestations she might make, she was not going to be believed by anyone; as if on that score at least she would perhaps be well advised to leave her case to the testimony of others.

But Morse was pressing home his advantage; and WPC Wright (though not Lewis) found his further questioning embarrassing and tasteless.

'You've got beautiful legs – would you agree?'

'What?' Instinctively she sought to pull the hem of her knee-length skirt an inch or two lower over her elegant legs; but with little effect.

'You know,' continued Morse, 'when I was talking just now about the Nordic type, I was thinking of the films we used to see of all those sexy Swedish starlets. I used to go to the pictures a lot in those days—'

'Do you want me to do a streep-tease for you?'

'You see, my sergeant here and me – and I – we've got quite a big advantage really, because we've had a chance to study your passport – if it *is* yours—'

She was almost at the end of her tether. 'What *is* it?' she shrieked. 'Please! Please *tell* me! What are you *accusing* me of? All of you?'

Resignedly Morse gestured with his right hand to Lewis; and Lewis, in a flat and melancholy voice, intoned the charge:

'Mrs Karin Michaels – Miss Karin Eriksson – I have to inform you that you are under police arrest on suspicion of murdering one James Myton, on the afternoon of Sunday, July seventh, 1991. It is my duty to warn you that anything you may now say in the presence of the three police officers here may be used in evidence in any future proceedings.'

Morse got up, and now stood above her.

'There's no need for you to say anything, not for the time being.'

'You mean you are accusing me – *me* – of being Karin, my sister? The sister who was *murdered*?'

'You're still denying it?' queried Morse quietly.

'Of course! Of *course*, I am!'

'You can prove it, you know. The Swedish authorities tell us they don't use that "Remarks" section very much at all on the passport – only really if there's some obvious distinguishing mark that can help in establishing identity. On the passport though – the one you say is yours – that section's filled in, in Swedish. And it says, so they tell me, "Pronounced diagonal scar, inner thigh above left knee-cap, eight and a half centimetres in length, result of motoring accident".'

'Yes?' She looked up at the chief inspector as if she almost willed him, dared him, *wanted* him, to prove his accusation.

'So if you *do* have a scar there, it won't necessarily prove *who* you are, will it? But if you haven't . . . if you *haven't*, then you're not now, and never were, the woman described on that passport.'

Karin Eriksson, the murderer of James Myton, now sat completely still for many agonizing seconds. Then slowly, tantalizingly, as if she were some upper-class artiste in a strip-tease parlour, centimetre by centimetre her left hand lifted the hem of the beige velvet skirt above her left knee to reveal the naked flesh upon her inner thigh.

Did she rejoice in the gaze of the two detectives

there? Had she secretly always thrilled to the admiration of the young boys in her high school class at Uppsala – of the tutors on her course? Even perhaps, for a short while, to the lust of the crude and ratty-faced Myton, who had sought to rape her out in Wytham Woods, and whom she had then so deliberately murdered?

And as Morse looked down at the smooth and unscarred flesh above her knee, he found himself wondering for a little while whether he too, like Myton, might not at some point on a hot and sultry summer afternoon have found this girl so very beautiful and necessary.

Lewis drove carefully down the road that led along the edge of the woods towards Wytham village. Beside him was WPC Wright; and in the back sat Karin Eriksson and Chief Inspector Morse.

Almost always, at such a stage in any case, Morse felt himself saddened – with the thrill of the chase now over, with the guilty left to face the appropriate retribution. Often had he pondered on the eternal problem of justice; and he knew as did most men of civilized values that the function of law was to provide that framework of order within which men and women could be protected as they went about their legitimate business. Yes, the criminal must be punished for his misdeeds, for that was the law. And Morse was an upholder of the law. Yet he debated now again, as he felt the body of Karin Eriksson close beside him, that fine distinction between the law and justice. Justice was one of those big words that was so often spelled with a capital 'J'; but really it was so much harder to define than Law. Karin would have to face the law; and he turned to look at her – to look at those beautiful blue eyes of hers, moistened now with the quiet film of tears. For a few seconds, at that moment, there seemed almost a bond between them – between Morse and the young woman who had murdered James Myton.

Suddenly, unexpectedly, she whispered something in his right ear.

'Did you ever have sex with a girl in the back of a car?'

'Not in the back,' whispered Morse. 'In the front, of course. Often!'

'Are you telling me the truth?'

'No,' said Morse.

He was conscious of a brimming reservoir of tears somewhere behind his own eyes as the police car came up to the main road and turned left, down past Wytham towards the police HQ. And for a second or two he thought he felt Karin's left leg pressing gently against him, and so very much he hoped that this was so.

CHAPTER SIXTY-THREE

All that's left to happen
Is some deaths (my own included).
Their order, and their manner,
Remain to be learnt
(Philip Larkin, *Collected Poems*)

THE STATEMENT made by Karin Eriksson added little to Lewis's knowledge of the case. Unprecedentedly, Morse had kept him informed, in key respects, from fairly early on of his suspicions surrounding the Swedish Maiden and, eventually, of his virtual certainties. There were one or two significant discrepancies – particularly concerning the amount of money Karin had with her on her arrival in Oxford, and concerning the number of voyeurs who witnessed her photographic session in Seckham Villa. But from the combined statements of Karin herself and of her (wholly legitimate) husband David, it was a straightforward matter to stitch together the sequence of events that occurred on Sunday, 7 July 1991.

Out on the M40 Karin had almost immediately been picked up by a van en route for the Rover Car Plant at Cowley, in Oxford. Dropped off at the Headington roundabout, she had been picked up, again almost immediately, by a BMW and dropped at the Banbury Road roundabout on the Northern Ring Road. Walking a few hundred yards down the Banbury Road (buses on Sunday seemed infrequent) she had noticed the Cotswold House, and on impulse felt how wonderful it would be to spend at least one night in such attractive-looking B & B accommodation. She had knocked and enquired the rates; had been told that there was one single room vacancy; but on learning the tariff had decided to find something a little cheaper, a little later. From a phone-box in Wentworth Road, just opposite the Cotswold House, she had phoned the model agency, and fairly soon been collected and driven down to Abingdon Road, where a telephone arrangement was made with McBryde for Karin to present herself at Seckham Villa, at about 2 p.m., for an hour or so's photographic session – the fee suggested, £80–£120, causing her eyebrows to lift in pleasurable surprise. She had declined further help from the agency, and walked up to St Giles', where she had a ham sandwich and half a glass of lager in the Eagle and Child.

At Seckham Villa she had been admitted by McBryde, and soon introduced to Myton. No hard pornography! – she'd immediately made her position clear on that; but, yes, she was willing to pose for a series of nude and semi-nude studies. And for an extra £20 she'd agreed that two other men there could sit in the 'studio' and watch her. Myton, she learned, was a freelance cinematographer in the sex-video world, and almost straightaway she had felt his eyes stripping off her skimpy summer clothing. But he'd seemed all right. Whilst he was preparing his paraphernalia of tripods, umbrellas, backcloths, reflectors, light-meters, and the rest, she had wandered out briefly into the back garden; and when he had come out a little while later she had found him amusing and good fun. He was a smallish, slim man, with a day's growth of darkish beard, but with much lighter-coloured hair, worn quite long with an absurd short pony-tail held in an elastic band. She had teased him a little about this, and indeed asked him to stand by the wall there while *she* could take a couple of snaps. Soon though McBryde had hurriedly ushered them inside, where she was introduced, perfunctorily, to a man in a lightweight summer-suit, and another man in grey slacks and sports jacket, incongruously (as she remembered on that hot day) holding a green pork-pie hat.

Then the 'session'. She had, she confessed, experienced some flush of excitement as the two silent men (McBryde had only come in later) ogled her as she stripped and posed and donned the see-through lingerie provided, and lay there on the bed in gaping gowns and skimpy negligées. Myton had punctuated her posturings with crude encouragements as gradually she'd felt herself relaxing: 'Christ, that's marvellous! Yeah! Ye-eah! Just hold it there, baby! Keep that hand under your tits and sort of, yes, sort of push 'em at me!' Such manner of talk had excited her and, if she were honest with herself, she'd felt a sort of orgasm of sexual vanity.

Afterwards, when she and Myton were alone, she had asked him to take one or two snaps of her with her own camera – just as a reminder really – and he'd readily done so. He'd still not so much as touched her physically, not yet; but he'd asked her where she was going and said he had his car outside if she wanted a lift anywhere. Before leaving McBryde had given her £100, all in ten-pound notes, which she had placed in her money-wallet; and then Myton had driven her back up to the top of the Banbury Road. She told him that she was thinking of going to the charity pop concert at Blenheim the next evening, 8 July, and then – suddenly – as they were passing the Cotswold House she asked him to stop: she *would* stay there now. But a white notice – NO VACANCIES – was across the door, and the lady of the house confirmed sadly that the remaining room had just been taken. As she was getting back into the car, she thought she saw a sparrow-hawk flying over towards the huge trees behind her, and she stopped and sought to focus her binoculars upon it. Fatal moment! Myton asked her if she was interested in birdwatching; and she had shown him her list of hoped-for spottings. Well, *he* knew exactly where she could see the woodpecker – probably see *all* the woodpeckers. In Wytham! He was interested himself in birds: was a member of the RSPB (this later proving untrue) and had a permit for walking in Wytham Woods (also proving to be untrue).

That was the beginning of all her woe.

Setting off from the semi-circular parking area just before the Great Wood, they had walked diagonally across a field and then along some leafy woodland pathway into a thickly forested area, where she remem-

374

bered the brittle crackling of dead twigs and branches beneath her feet; and then Myton's hands upon her body. At first perhaps she might have been prepared for some limited petting; but very soon he had grown rough and insistent, and told her that he needed her – urgently. Would *have* her! He'd stripped off her thin blouse and pulled her to the floor; but she was herself strong and determined in fighting him off. The pocket of the rucksack in which she kept her binoculars – and her knife – was still open; and she managed to struggle away from him and open the blade of the knife – and plunge it into him . . . It had entered his flesh so easily, like pushing a knife through soft cheese, she said; but a fountain of blood had spurted across the top of her semi-naked body. Unlike the blood though, *he* lay still, utterly still – his eyes wide open and glaring up at her.

She hurled the knife into the trees, picked up her scarlet rucksack, and dressed only in a blood-bespattered skirt she fled the spot in panic – emerging finally into a clearing where, panting and jabbering and whimpering, she ran and ran – she could have no idea how long, how far – before collapsing, and remembering nothing more until she looked up to see a dog, a black and white Welsh Border Collie, and a thick-set, bearded man behind the dog, his face anxious and kindly, looking down at her. A Land-rover was parked a few yards away.

In his cottage David Michaels at first had found it scarcely possible to believe the young woman's extraordinary account of what had occurred. It all seemed like some terrible *nightmare*, she'd pleaded: of a frenetic struggle and of a sudden death, if death it were; or of a man lying in the *agony* of death somewhere out there, somewhere in the woods. Indeed were it not for the blood all over her body, it *must* have been a nightmare surely! The mention of the word 'police' had driven her to hysterical tears; and clearly distressing too was the thought of the *car*, the car that from his cottage window Michaels could see even then across the lane. But *he* would deal with things, he'd promised her that – not knowing what he promised. He learned from her of Seckham Villa, and he made his decision. He got her to bath herself, to swallow half a dozen Disprin; and very soon, so suddenly, so miraculously almost, she had fallen deeply asleep, quite naked between the white sheets of his own double bed. And he realized at that moment that he was just as bad as the rest of them, for he lusted after her, just as other men had lusted after her that afternoon.

At Seckham Villa, Michaels had met the three of them – still there: McBryde, Daley, and Hardinge; and he had begun then to appreciate the complexity of the situation in which they all – including Michaels himself – now found themselves. A plan was conceived. And later executed. Just one detail that was new. Karin's intended visit to the pop concert at Blenheim could be used to their ready advantage, since the discovery of the rucksack and other personal possessions somewhere *near* Blenheim, the day *after* the concert, would throw everyone on to the wrong scent, and would promote dark suspicions of a young lady missing, presumed dead somewhere, doubtless murdered by some drug-crazed, sex-hyped youth whom she'd met at the jamboree. Fear of exposure and financial ruin was more than sufficient motivation for McBryde; fear of exposure and scandal more than sufficient for Hardinge; and a cheque (neither Karin nor David Michaels knew for how much) sufficient to ensure the co-operation of the mercenary Daley.

That night, back in the cottage on the edge of the woods, Karin had become terrifyingly distraught; he had slept with her, for she wished it so; she had sought throughout that night the reassurance of his embrace, and of his love; and gladly, gloriously, he had met her needs.

It had been *her* plan, *her* plea, to go to Wales – away, away somewhere, away anywhere; and the next morning, setting out from Wytham just after 6 o'clock, he had driven there, leaving her in the hands of a kindly woman who must fairly soon (surely, he'd felt) have been in possession of most of the facts herself. The only thing from her rucksack she had taken was £60 – leaving the rest inside her money-wallet: it seemed to them all a convincing detail. From Wales, she had phoned David frequently – sometimes several times each evening. She it was, Karin, who had phoned her mother, together with whom, and with her sisters, the next phase of the plan was conceived: the simple substitution of Katarina's passport, sent to Karin in a plain brown envelope from Barcelona.

Finally, there had been the return to Oxford – and to David Michaels, the man she was learning increasingly to love, and whose solicitude for her, in turn, seemed now to know no bounds. With her hair cut and dyed black, with a pair of black-framed spectacles, she had lived in the cottage in an idyllic state of happiness with David and Bobbie – until a gradual integration into life again: a drink at the village pub, badminton at the village hall, membership of the local operatic society. And marriage! Strange, really, that she could live so happily so near the murder. Yet she could. The nightmare had passed. It was as if a partition existed, a sort of mesh between her and the whole of her life before she'd met David – a mesh like the network of twigs and branches in the spot where the blood had spurted over her.

For the first six months or so David had daily expected to discover the body, especially so as the trees grew bare in that late autumn; or expected others to discover it, as they roamed the ridings and observed the birds, badgers, foxes, squirrels, deer ... But no. And when Morse had asked him where he himself might think of hiding a body, it had never occurred to him that Karin could have run so far, so very far from Pasticks out along by the Singing Way.

Just one more thing. Uncommonly for Swedish people, the Eriksson family were all Roman Catholic (something Lewis had suspected when he had seen the two crucifixes but, sadly, something he hadn't mentioned to Morse) and Karin had discovered the little church in the Woodstock Road. She had passed her driving test earlier that year, and was in the habit of going to Mass on Sunday mornings when David didn't require the Land-rover; and sometimes, when he did, waiting for him to pick her up after the service. Twice a month or so. Then to confession, about which she hadn't told her husband quite everything – certainly holding back from him her slowly formulating fear that her lack of contrition at having killed Myton was almost a greater sin than the killing itself had been; her fear that she might kill again, kill wildly and regardlessly if anyone came to threaten her own and David's happiness. Yet at the same time, an oddly contradictory wish was gradually growing too: the wish that someone would discover the truth of what she'd done; even that someone would *divulge* that truth . . .

But Father Richards could never do that, he'd said, as he'd comforted her, and prayed with her, and forgiven her in the name of the Almighty Father.

CHAPTER SIXTY-FOUR

The lips frequently parted with a murmur of words.
She seemed to belong rightly to a madrigal
(Thomas Hardy, *The Return of the Native*)

ON THE evening of the day following these events, Wednesday 5 August, Morse, Lewis, and Dr Laura Hobson had enjoyed a little celebration in Morse's office; and at 8.30 p.m. a sober Lewis had driven the other two down to Morse's flat in North Oxford.

'You won't want another drink?' Morse had asked of Lewis, as if the question were introduced by *num*, the Latin interrogative particle expecting the answer 'no'.

'What elegant equipment!' enthused Laura Hobson as she admired Morse's new CD player.

Ten minutes later the pair of them were sitting together, drinking in a diet of Glenfiddich and the finale of *Götterdämmerung*.

'Nothing quite like it in the whole history of music,' announced Morse magisterially, after Brünnhilde had ridden into the flames and the waves of the Rhine had finally rippled into silence.

'You think so?'

'Don't *you?*'

'I prefer Elizabethan madrigals, really.'

For a few moments Morse said nothing, saddened by her lack of sensitivity, it seemed.

'Oh.'

'I *loved* it. Don't be silly!' she said. 'But I've got to be on my way.'

'Can I walk you home?'

'I live too far away. I'm in a temporary flat – in Jericho.'

'I'll drive you home, then.'

'You've had far too much to drink.'

'You can stay here, if you like? I've got a spare pair of pyjamas.'

'I don't usually *wear* pyjamas.'

'No?'

'How many bedrooms do you have?'

'Two.'

'And bedroom number two is free?'

'Just like bedroom number one.'

'No secret passage between them?'

'I could get the builders in.'

She smiled happily, and rose to her feet. 'If there ever *is* going to be anything between us, Chief Inspector, it'll have to be when we're borth a bit more sorber. Better that way. I think *you'd* prefer it that way too, if you're honest.' She laid a hand on his shoulder. 'C'mon. Ring for a taxi.'

Ten minutes later she kissed him lightly on the lips, her own lips dry and soft and slightly opened.

Then she was gone.

*

An hour later Morse lay awake on his back. It was still hot in the bedroom and he had only a light cotton sheet over him. Many varied thoughts were crowding in upon his mind, his eyes ever darting around in the darkness. First it had been the lovely woman who had been there with him that evening; then the case of the Swedish Maiden, with only those last few lines of the complex equation to be completed now; then his failure thus far to locate the bullet that had killed George Daley – this last problem gradually assuming a dominance in his brain . . .

The bullet had been fired from about sixty or so yards – that seemed a firm assumption. So . . . So why hadn't it been found? And why could no one in Blenheim be far more definite about *hearing* it being fired: shooting in Blenheim was not the common occurrence it was in other areas . . . in Wytham, for example. The rifle itself concerned him to a lesser extent: after all, it was far easier to get rid of a rifle than to get rid of a bullet that could have landed up anywhere . . . Morse got out of bed and went to find the Blenheim Park brochure – just as Johnson had done so recently before him. The place where Daley's body had been found could be only – what? – four hundred yards or so from that narrow north-westerly tip of the lake, shaped like the head of one of those cormorants he'd seen in Lyme Regis not all that long ago . . . Yes! He would double the men on the search – on *both* searches, rather. There could be little doubt that Philip Daley must have dumped his father's rifle there somewhere – in the lake itself, like as not. And once they'd found either of them, either the rifle or the bullet—

The phone rang, and Morse grabbed at it.

'That was quick, sir.'

'What do *you* want?'

'The Met, sir. They rang HQ, and Sergeant Dixon thought he ought to let me know—'

'Let *you* know, Lewis? Who the hell's in charge of this bloody case? Just wait till I see Dixon!'

'They thought you'd be asleep, sir.'

'Well, I wasn't, was I?'

'And, well—'

'Well, what?'

'Doesn't matter, sir.'

'It bloody *does* matter! They thought I was in bed with a woman! That's what they thought.'

'I don't know,' admitted the honest and honourable Lewis.

'Or pretty much the worse for booze!'

'Perhaps they thought both,' said Lewis simply.

'Well?'

'Young Philip Daley, sir. Just over an hour ago. Threw himself under a westbound train on the Central Line, it seems – train coming into Marble Arch from Bond Street – driver had no chance, just as he came out of the tunnel.'

Morse said nothing.

'Police knew a bit about the boy. He'd been picked up for shoplifting from a wine store in the Edgware Road and taken in; but the manager decided not to prosecute – he got away with a right dressing-down—'

'That's not *all* you've got to tell me, is it?' said Morse quietly.

'No, sir. You've guessed, I suppose. That was Monday morning, half an hour after the store opened.'

'You're telling me he couldn't have shot his dad, is that it?'

'Not even if he'd been the one to hire that helicopter, sir.'

'Does Mrs Daley know?'

'Not yet.'

'Leave her, Lewis. Leave her. Let her sleep.'

An hour later Morse still lay awake, though now his mind was far more relaxed. It had been like puzzling over a crossword clue and finding a possible answer, but being dissatisfied with that answer, lacking as it did any satisfying inevitability; and then being given an erratum slip, telling him that the *clue* had been wrong in the first place; then being given the *correct* clue; and then . . .

Oh yes!

All along he'd been aware of his dissatisfaction with the *motivation* of Philip Daley for the death of his father. It *could* have happened that way, of course – far odder things in life occurred than that. But the sequence of sudden hatred and carefully plotted murder rang far from true; and Morse considered once more the original facts: the scene of George Daley's murder, beside the little coppice in Blenheim Park, still cordoned off, with nothing but the corpse removed, and even now some weary PC standing guard, or sitting guard ... Odd really, that! Morse had asked for an almost unprecedentedly large number of men in this case; what's more he'd given them all a quite specific task. Yet no one had come up with anything.

And suddenly he knew why!

He jerked up in the bed, as though crudely galvanized, and considered the erratum slip, smiling now serenely to himself. It could be. It *had* to be! And the new answer to the clue was shining and wholly fitting; an answer that 'filled the eye', as the judges said of the champion dogs at Crufts.

It was 2.40 a.m., and Morse knew that he would have to do something if he were ever to get to sleep. So he made himself a rare cup of Ovaltine, and sat for a while at the kitchen table: impatient, as ever, yet content. What exactly made him remember Heisenberg's Uncertainty Principle, he was by no means sure. Physics had long been a closed science to him, ever since at school he had once tried, without success, to take some readings from an incomprehensible piece of equipment called the Wheatstone Bridge. But Heisenberg was a splendid name and Morse looked him up in his encyclopaedia: 'There is always an uncertainty in the values obtained if simultaneous observation is made of *position* ...' Morse nodded to himself. *Time* too, as doubtless old Heisenberg had known.

Morse was soon asleep.

When he awoke, at 7 a.m., he thought he might

perhaps have dreamed of a choir of beautiful women singing Elizabethan madrigals. But it was all a bit vague in his mind; about as vague as exactly what, as a principle, 'Werner Karl Heisenberg (1901–76)' had had in mind.

CHAPTER SIXTY-FIVE

How strange are the tricks of memory, which, often
hazy as a dream about the most important events,
religiously preserve the merest trifles

(Sir Richard Burton, *Sind Revisited*)

'YOU APPRECIATE therefore, Lewis' – the two of them
stood on the scene of Daley's murder the following
morning – 'the paramount importance of leaving everything exactly as it was here.'

'But we've had everybody trampling all over the
place.'

Morse beamed. 'Ah, but we've got this, haven't we?' He
patted the roof of the Blenheim Estate van affectionately.

'Unless one of the lads's been sitting in there having
a smoke.'

'If he has, I'll sever his scrotum!'

'By the way, did you have a word with Dixon this
morning?'

'Dixon? What the 'ell's Dixon got to do with
anything?'

'Nothing,' murmured Lewis, as he turned away to
have a final word with the two men standing by the
recovery truck.

'Without getting inside at all, you say?' asked the
elder of the two.

'That's what the chief inspector wants, yes.'

'We can't do it without *touching* the bloody thing though, can we, Charlie?'

Morse himself was standing beside the van, deep in thought, it seemed. Then he walked slowly round it, peering with apparently earnest attention at the ground. But the soil was rock-hard there, after weeks of cloudless weather, and after a little while he lost interest and walked back to the police car.

'That's enough here, Lewis. Let's get over to the lodge: it's time we had another word with Mr Williams.'

As before, Williams' evidence, in specific terms, was perhaps unsatisfactory; but, in general outline, it did serve to establish a working framework for the murder – the only one really the police had. Certainly the crucial point – that Daley had driven through Combe Lodge Gate on the morning of his murder – could be pretty confidently re-affirmed. There had been a good deal of to-ing and fro-ing of two blue tractors, with their trailers, that morning, each of them making three trips from the saw-mill down to the area near the Grand Bridge to load up with recently felled timber. Williams had checked up (he said) with the drivers, and the ferrying had not begun until about 9.45 a.m., or a little later perhaps; and if there was one thing he could feel reasonably confident about it was the fact that Daley had come through the gate at the same time as one of the tractors – because although the gate was opened quite frequently that morning, it had not been *specifically* opened (Williams was *almost* sure) for the estate van. He did remember the van though – quite definite he was about that. He hadn't known Daley well; spoken to him a few times of course, and Daley had often come through the lodge, to and from the saw-mill. Usually, between those working at Blenheim, there would be a hand raised in acknowledgement or greeting. And there was another thing: Daley almost always wore his hat, even in the summer; and, yes, Daley had been wearing his hat that Monday morning.

Morse had pressed him on the point. 'You're *sure* about that?'

Williams breathed out noisily. He felt he was sure, yes. But it was a frightening business, this being questioned and giving evidence, and he was now far less sure than he had been about one or two of the things he'd said earlier. That shot he thought he'd heard, for example: he was less and less sure now that he'd heard it at *all*. So it was better, fairer too, to play it a bit more on the cautious side . . . that's what he thought.

'Well, I think so. Trouble is really about the time. You see, it might have been a bit *later*, I think.'

But Morse appeared no longer interested in the time – or in the shot, for that matter.

'Mr Williams! I'm sorry to keep on about this but it's very important. I know that Mr Daley always wore his hat around the park, and I believe you when you say you *saw* his hat. But let's put it another way: are you sure it was *Mr Daley* who was wearing the hat on Monday morning?'

'You mean,' said Williams slowly, 'you mean it mightn't have been him – driving the van?'

'Exactly.'

Oh dear! Williams didn't know . . . hadn't even

considered ... Two women joggers appeared at the
lodge, twisted through the kissing-gate and continued
their way into the park itself, their breasts bouncing,
their legs (as viewed from the rear) betraying the slightly
splay-footed run of the fairer sex. Morse followed them
briefly with his eyes, and asked his last question:

'Did you notice any jogger coming *this* way, *out* of
the park, on Monday morning? About, let's say, half-
past ten? Eleven?'

Williams pondered the question. While everything
else seemed to be getting more and more muddled in
his mind, the chief inspector had just sparked off a
fairly vivid recollection. He thought he *had* noticed
someone, yes – a woman. There were always lots of
joggers at weekends, but not many in the week; not
many at all; and certainly not in the middle of the
morning. He thought he *could* remember the woman
though; could almost see her now, with the nipples of
her breasts erect and pushing through the thin material
of her T-shirt. Was that Monday *morning*, though? The
simple truth was that he just couldn't be certain and
again he was unwilling to commit himself too positively.

'I may have done, yes.'

'Thank you very much, sir.'

What exactly he was being thanked for, Mr Williams
was not quite clear, and he was aware that he must have
appeared a less-than-satisfactory witness. Yet the chief
inspector had looked mightily pleased with himself as
he'd left; and he'd said 'very much', hadn't he? It was
all a bit beyond the gate-keeper of Combe Lodge in
Blenheim Park.

CHAPTER SIXTY-SIX

As when that divelish yron engin, wrought
In deepest hell, and framd by furies skill,
With windy nitre and quick sulphur fraught,
And ramd with bollett rowed, ordaind to kill,
Conceiveth fyre

(Edmund Spenser, *The Faerie Queene*)

THE SEMI-CIRCULAR area where birdwatchers and the occasional loving couple were wont to park was packed with police cars and vans when, half an hour after leaving Blenheim, Lewis drove through the perimeter gate ('The woods are closed to Permit Holders until 10.00 a.m. every day except Sunday') and into the compound, on his left, marked off with its horizontal four-barred, black-creosoted fencing. Here, under the direction of Chief Inspector Johnson, some fifty or so policemen – some uniformed, some not – were systematically conducting their search.

'No luck yet?' asked Morse.

'Give us a chance!' said Johnson. 'Lot of ground to cover, isn't there?'

The large wooden sheds, the stacks of logs and fencing-posts, the occasional clump of trees, the rank growth of untended bushes – all precluded any wholly scientific search-pattern. But there was plenty of time;

there were plenty of men; they would find it, Johnson was confident of that.

Morse led the way up the curving track towards the furthest point from the compound entrance, towards the hut where David Michaels had his office, right up against the recently erected deer-fence. To the left of this track was a line of forty or so fir trees, about thirty feet high; and to the right, the hut itself, the main door standing padlocked now. On the wooden sides of this extensive hut, at the top, were six large bird-boxes, numbered 9–14; and at the bottom there grew rank clumps of nettles. Morse looked back down the sloping track; retraced his steps, counting as he went; then stopped at a smaller open-sided shed in which stood a large red tractor with a timber-lifting device fixed to it. For a minute or two he stood beside the tractor, behind the shed wall, and then, as if he were a young boy with an imaginary rifle, lifted both his arms, curled his right index-finger round an imaginary trigger, closed his left eye, and slowly turned the rifle in an arc from right to left, as if some imaginary vehicle were being driven past – the rifle finally remaining stationary as the vehicle's imaginary driver dismounted, in front of the head forester's hut.

'You reckon?' asked Lewis quietly.

Morse nodded.

'That means we probably ought to be concentrating the search up there, sir.' Lewis pointed back towards Michaels' office.

'Give him a chance! He's not so bright as you,' whispered Morse.

'About fifty, fifty-five yards. I paced it too, sir.'

Again Morse nodded, and the two of them rejoined Johnson.

'Know much about rifles?' asked Morse.

'Enough.'

'Could you use a silencer on a seven-millimetre?'

'"Sound-moderator" – that's the word these days. No, not much good. It'd suppress the noise of the explosion, but it couldn't stop the noise of the bullet going through the sound-barrier. And incidentally, Morse, it might be a .243 – don't forget that!'

'Oh!'

'You were thinking it might be around here, weren't you?' Johnson kicked aside a few nettles along the bottom of the shed, and looked at Morse shrewdly, if a little sadly.

Morse shrugged. 'I'd be guessing, of course.'

Johnson looked down at the flattened nettles. 'You never did have much faith in me, did you?'

Morse didn't know what to say, and as Johnson walked away, he too looked down at the flattened nettles.

'You're quite wrong, you know, sir. He's a whole lot brighter than me, is Johnson.'

But again Morse made no reply, and the pair of them walked down to the low, stone-built cottage where until very lately Michaels and his Swedish wife had lived so happily together.

Just as they were entering, they heard a shot from fairly far off. But they paid little attention to it. As Michaels had informed them, no one was ever going to be too disturbed about hearing a gun-shot in Wytham: game-keepers shooting squirrels or rabbits, perhaps; farmworkers taking a pot at the pestilential pigeons.

Inside the cottage, just beside the main entrance, stood the steel security cabinet from which Michaels' rifle had been taken for forensic examination. But there was no longer any legal requirement for the cabinet to be locked, and it now stood open – and empty. Lewis bent down and looked carefully at the groove in which the rifle had stood, noting the scratches where the butt had rested; and beside it a second groove – with equally tell-tale signs.

'I'm sure you're right,' said Lewis.

'If you remember,' said Morse, 'he told us *himself*, Michaels did. When you told him you'd seen no rifles in the hut he said . . . he said "Oh, I couldn't keep 'em *there*" – those were his exact words, I think.'

'You're still certain he did it, sir?'

'Yes.'

'What about that "Uncertainty Principle" you were on about this morning?'

'What about it?' asked Morse. Infuriatingly.

'Forget it.'

'What's the time?'

'Nearly twelve.'

'Ah, the prick of noon!'

'Pardon?'

'Forget it.'

'We can walk down if you like, sir. A nice little ten-minute walk – do us good. We can work up a thirst.'

'Nonsense!'

'Don't you enjoy walking – occasionally?'
'Occasionally, yes.'
'So?'
'So drive me down to the White Hart, Lewis! What's the problem?'

CHAPTER SIXTY-SEVEN

Scire volunt secreta domus, atque inde timeri
(They watch for household secrets hour by hour
And feed therefrom their appetite for power)
(Juvenal, *Satire III*)

'WHAT PUT you on it this time?' asked Lewis as they sat opposite each other in the small upstairs bar, Morse with a pint of real ale, Lewis himself with a much-iced orangeade.

'I think it wasn't so much finding Daley like he was – out at Blenheim. It was the photographs they took of him there. I don't think it hit me at the time; but when I looked at the photographs I got the idea somehow that he'd just been dumped there – that he hadn't been shot there at all.'

'You mean you just – well, sort of had a *feeling* about it?'

'No. I don't mean that. You may think I work that way, Lewis, but I don't. I don't believe in some unaccountable intuition that just happens occasionally to turn out right. There's got to be *something* there, however vague. And here we had the hat, didn't we? The hat Daley wore wherever he was, whatever the weather. Same bloody hat! He never took it *off*, Lewis!'

'Probably took it off in bed?'

'We don't even know that, do we?' Morse drained his beer. 'Plenty of time for another.'

Lewis nodded. 'Plenty of time! Your round though, sir. I'll have another orange. Lovely. Lots of ice, please!'

'You see,' resumed Morse, a couple of minutes later, 'he was almost certainly wearing his hat when he was shot, and I very much doubt myself that it would have fallen *off.* I'd seen the tight sweat-mark round his forehead when we met him earlier. And even if it *had* fallen off – when he dropped dead – I just had the feeling . . .'

Lewis lifted his eyebrows.

'. . . it wouldn't have fallen *far.*'

'So?'

'So, I reckon it was put down there deliberately, just beside his head – *after* he was shot. Remember where it was? Three or four feet *away* from his head. So the conclusion's firm and satisfactory, as I see it. He was wearing his hat when he was shot, and like as not it stayed on his head. Then when he was moved, and finally dumped, it had come off; and it was placed there beside him.'

'What a palaver!'

Morse nodded. 'But they had to do it. They had to establish an alibi—'

'For David Michaels, you mean?'

'Yes. It was Michaels who shot Daley – I've no doubts on that score. There was the agreement Hardinge told us about, wasn't there, the agreement the four of them made – a statement by the way that contains quite as much truth as falsehood, Lewis. Then something comes

397

along and buggers it all up. Daley got a letter spelling out his financial responsibilities for his boy, and Daley knew that he was the one who had a hold over – well, over *all* the others, really. But particularly over David Michaels! I reckon Daley probably rang him and said he couldn't afford to stick by the agreement; said he was sorry – but he needed more money. And if he didn't get more money pretty soon . . .'

'Blackmail!'

'Exactly. And there may well have been a bit more of *that* than we think.'

'Quite a hold over Michaels, though, when you think of it: knowing he was married to . . . a murderess.'

'Quite a hold. So Michaels agrees – *pretends* he agrees – to go along with it. They'll meet at Wytham earlyish on Monday – quarter to ten, say. No one around much at that time. No birdwatchers allowed in the woods till ten – remember the notice?'

'The RSPB people were there.'

'They turned out to be a blessing in disguise, though.'

'Take it a bit slower, please!'

'Right. Let's just go back a minute. The rendezvous's settled. Daley drives up to Wytham. Michaels has said he'll have some money ready – in notes, no doubt – just after the bank's opened. He's ready. He waits for Daley to drive up to his office. He waits for a clear view of him as he gets out of his estate van. I don't know *exactly* where he was waiting, of course; what I *do* know is that someone as experienced as Michaels, with a telescopic sight, could hit *this*' – Morse picked up his empty glass

– 'no problem! – from a hundred, let alone from fifty yards.'

But any further reconstruction of Daley's murder was temporarily curtailed, since Johnson had walked in, and now sat down beside them.

'What'll you have?' asked Morse. 'Lewis here is in the chair.'

'Nothing for me, thank you, er, Lewis. Look! There's this call for you from forensics about the van. I told 'em I wasn't *quite* sure where you were—'

'What'd they say?'

'They found prints all over the shop – mostly Daley's, of course. But like you said, they found other prints – on the tail-board, on the steering wheel.'

'And I was right about them?'

Johnson nodded. 'Yes. They're Karin Eriksson's.'

At lunch-time that same day, Alasdair McBryde came out of the tube station at Manor House and walked briskly down the Seven Sisters Road – finally turning into one of the parking-and-garage areas of a high-rise block of flats that flanks the Bethune Road. He had spotted the unmarked car immediately: the two men seated in the front, one of them reading the *Sun*. It was quite customary for him to spot danger a mile or so off; and he did so now. Number 14 was the garage he was interested in; but softly whistling the Prelude to Act Three of *Lohengrin*, he walked boldly into the nearest open garage (number 9), picked up a half-filled can of Mobiloil, before nonchalantly retracing his steps to the main road; where, still clutching the dirty can, he walked quietly and confidently away in the direction of Stamford Hill.

'False alarm!' said the policeman with the *Sun*, as he resumed his reading of various illicit liaisons among the glitterati.

At 3.25 p.m., no more than four or five yards from the spot where Chief Inspector Johnson had earlier stood, there amongst the nettles and the cow-parsley and other less readily recognizable plants and weeds, Constable Roy Wilks made his discovery: a .243 bullet – the bullet (surely!) for which the party had been searching. Never, in his life hitherto, had Wilks been the focus of such attention; and never again (as he duly recognized) would he be likely to experience such felicitous congratulations.

Most particularly from Morse.

CHAPTER SIXTY-EIGHT

The Light of Lights
Looks always on the motive, not the deed,
The Shadow of Shadows on the deed alone
(W. B. Yeats, *The Countess Cathleen*)

'JUST simply, Morse! Just simply! I don't want to know what a clever sod you are. Just a straightforward – brief! – account. If you can manage it.'

Following the final discoveries, new statements had been taken from both David Michaels and Karin Eriksson; and now, the following morning, as he sat in Strange's office, Morse was able to confirm in nearly every respect the pattern of events he'd outlined to Lewis in the White Hart.

Daley had been to the office in Wytham Woods on more than one occasion before, and a meeting had been arranged for 9.45 a.m. on Monday, 3 August. At that time there would, with any luck, be virtually no one around; but only if no one *was* around, would the deed take place. And the deed *did* take place. When Daley got out of the van, Michaels shot him dead with his .243 rifle – the latter buried later out on the Singing Way. To Michaels himself the report had sounded terrifyingly loud; but following it a strangely eerie silence had reasserted itself, and no one had come rushing into the compound there demanding explanation, seeking causes. Nothing. A newly still, clear morning in early August. And a body – which Michaels had swiftly wrapped in black plastic sheeting and lifted into the back of Daley's own van. Only two or three minutes after the murder, this same van was being driven out through Wolvercote, over to the A44 towards Woodstock, left at Bladon, and then into Long Hanborough – and finally up to Combe Lodge, on the western side of the Blenheim Estate. The keys to the lodge gate would doubtless have been somewhere on the body, but the van-driver waited a while and was very quickly rewarded when the gate was opened for a tractor and trailer; and when the van driver, pulling Daley's khaki-green hat down over her short, black hair, moved into the trailer's wake, raising a hand in acknowledgement to any anonymous observer as she drove gratefully through. A few hundred yards along she had spotted an ideal location in which to leave a van, and a body, and a hat. Daley had not been a heavy man, and she herself was a strong young woman; yet she had been unable to lift the corpse – just to pull it over the tailboard, whence it fell with a thud to the hard soil. The plastic sheet was messily sticky with blood, and she had taken it with her as she ran off, across the road, to the tip of the lake, where she washed the blood from her hands and wedged the sheet beneath some reeds. Then, following the arranged plan, she'd jogged her way back – though not, she claimed, through Combe Lodge, as Morse had suggested (and Williams could have sworn) – but down by the western side of the lake, across the small bridge that spans the River Glyme below the Grand Cascade, and out of the park via Eagle Lodge.

'Helluva long way, whichever route she took,' mumbled Strange.

'Some people are fitter than others, sir.'

'Not thinking of *yourself*, are you?'

'No!'

'Bit lucky, though – the fellow at the lodge remembering the van going through.'

'With all respect, sir, I don't think that's true. In fact, it led us all to believe that Daley was alive until after ten o'clock – when David Michaels was miles away with his RSPB pals round the bird-boxes. But Michaels could *never* have done it himself – not by himself – that morning. There was no way at all that *he* could have got out to Blenheim and somehow – somehow – got back to Wytham.'

'But his wife could. That's what you're saying.'

'His wife did.'

'She was a brave girl.'

'She *is* a brave girl, sir.'

'You know, if they'd only have played it straight up and down the wicket from the start – either of them – they'd probably have got away with justifiable homicide, self-defence, take your pick.'

'Perhaps.'

'You don't sound very convinced.'

'I think she's a rather more complex woman than that. Perhaps ... perhaps she couldn't quite persuade herself that killing Myton had been purely in self-defence.'

'You mean – you mean she might have enjoyed it?'

'I didn't say that, sir.'

Strange shook his head. 'I see what you're getting at, though. Prepared – wasn't she? – to drive Daley's body out to Blenheim and . . .'

'She's a complex woman, as I say, sir. I'm not sure I understand her at all really.'

'Perhaps she's a bit of a mystery even to herself.'

Morse got up to leave. 'Same thing in most cases, isn't it? We never really understand people's motives. In all these things it's as if there's a manifestation – but there's always a bit of a mystery too.'

'Now don't you start going all religious on *me*, Morse!'

'No chance of that.'

'I don't suppose anyone'll miss Daley all that much.'

'No. He was a *small* man—'

'Was he? How tall was he?'

'No. I didn't mean small in that sense. But he *was* physically small, yes. Only weighed eight stone, four pounds.'

'How do you know that?'

'They weighed him, sir – *post mortem*.'

CHAPTER SIXTY-NINE

Just as every person has his idiosyncrasies, so has every typewriter

(*Handbook of Office Maintenance*, 9th edition)

THE FOLLOWING day, Friday, 8 August, Morse's attention was early drawn to the correspondence columns of *The Times*.

From Lt. Colonel Reginald Postill

Sir, Over these past years we have all become aware of the increasing influence of trial (and retrial) by TV. We have seen, for example, the collapse of cases brought against the Birmingham Six and the Guildford Four; and doubtless in the years ahead we may confidently anticipate the acquittal of the Towcester Two and the Winchester One.

Are we now to become similarly conditioned to pol-ice enquiries conducted in the nation's quality daily newspapers (including, of course, your own, sir)? I learn that the Thames Valley Police has now been able to prefer charges against persons in the 'Swedish Maiden' case – and this in considerable measure thanks to the original verses published in your correspondence columns. Clearly we should be grateful for such an outcome. But am I alone in being troubled by such a precedent? Am I alone in believing that such affairs,

both judicial and investiga-	Yours faithfully,
tive, are better left in the	REGINALD POSTILL,
hands of those men and	6 Baker Lane,
women suitably trained in	Shanklin,
their respective specialisms?	Isle of Wight.

Lewis had come into his office as Morse was reading this; and duly read it himself.

'Bit hard that, isn't it? I'd have thought it all helped us quite a bit. I can't myself really see what's wrong with getting a bit of public co-operation and interest.'

'Oh, I agree,' said Morse.

'Perhaps we shouldn't be too much worried about some retired old colonel from the Isle of Wight, sir.'

Morse smiled knowingly across at his old friend. 'What makes you think he's retired?' he asked very quietly.

That same evening, Morse's celebratory mood was undiminished; and he had walked down to Summertown immediately after *The Archers* and carried back up to his flat four bottles of champagne: not the dearest, it must be admitted – yet not the cheapest either. Strange, Johnson, Lewis – and himself. Four of them. Just for a congratulatory glass or two. Dr Laura Hobson had been invited too (how otherwise?); but she had phoned earlier in the evening to make her apologies – an emergency; sorry, she'd've loved to have been there; but these things couldn't be helped, could they?

Harold Johnson was the first to leave, at 9.15 p.m.

One glass of bubbly, and the plea that the wife would be awaiting him. Yet of all of them it was probably Johnson who was the most grateful soul there that evening: the procedures surrounding the prosecutions of two suspected murderers – David Michaels and Mrs Michaels – would be entrusted now to him, to Johnson and his team, since Morse had announced his intention of resuming immediately his truncated furlough which had begun (so long ago it seemed) in the Bay Hotel at Lyme Regis.

Three glasses of bubbly and ten minutes later, Strange had struggled to his feet and announced his imminent departure.

'Thanks! And enjoy your holiday!'

'If you'll let me.'

'Where are you going this time?'

'I was thinking of Salisbury, sir.'

'Why Salisbury?'

Morse hesitated. 'They've just tarted up the cathedral there, and I thought—'

'You *sure* you're not going religious on me, Morse?'

Two of the champagne bottles were finished, and Morse picked up a third, starting to twist open the wire round its neck.

'No more for me,' said Lewis.

Morse put the bottle back on the sideboard. 'Would you prefer a Newcastle Brown?'

'I think I would, to be honest, sir.'

'C'mon, then!'

Morse led the way through to the cluttered kitchen.

'You trying for *my* job, sir?' Lewis pointed to the ancient portable typewriter that stood at one end of the kitchen table.

'Ah! That! I was just writing a brief line to *The Times*.' He handed Lewis his effort, a messy, ill-typed, xxxx-infested missive.

'Would you like me to re-type it for you, sir? It's a bit . . .'

'Yes, please. I'd be grateful for that.'

So Lewis sat there, at the kitchen table, and retyped the brief letter. That it took him rather longer than it should have done was occasioned by two factors: first, that Lewis himself could boast only semi-competence in the keyboard-skills; second, that he had found himself looking, with increasingly puzzled interest, at the very first line he'd typed. And then at the second. And then at the third . . . Especially did he find himself examining the worn top segment of the lower-case 'e', and the slight curtailment of the cross-bar in the lower-case 't' . . . For the moment, however, he said nothing. Then, when his reasonably clean copy was completed, he wound it from the ancient machine and handed it to Morse.

'Much better! Good man!'

'You remember, sir, that original article in *The Times*? When they said the typewriter could pretty easily be identified if it was ever found? From the "e"s and the "t"s . . .?'

'Yes?'

'You wrote those verses about the girl yourself, didn't you, sir?'

Morse nodded slowly.

'Bloody hell!' Lewis shook his head incredulously.

Morse poured himself a can of beer. 'Champagne's a lovely drink, but it makes you thirsty, doesn't it?'

'Think anyone *else* suspected?' asked Lewis, grinning down at the typewriter.

'Just the one person. Someone from Salisbury.'

'Didn't you say you would be going there, though? To Salisbury?'

'*Might* be, Lewis. Depends.'

Half an hour after Lewis had left, Morse was listening to Lipatti playing the slow movement of the Mozart piano concerto No. 21, when the doorbell rang.

'It's a bit late I know but . . .'

What had been a semi-scowl on Morse's face now suddenly burgeoned into a wholly ecstatic smile.

'Nonsense! It just so happens I've got a couple of bottles of bubbly . . .'

'Will that be enough, do you think?'

'Come in! I'll just turn this off—'

'Please not! I love it. K 467? Right?'

'Where've you parked?'

'I didn't come by car. I thought you'd probably try to get me drunk.'

Morse closed the door behind them. 'I *will* turn it off, if you don't mind. I've never been able to cope with two beautiful things at the same time.'

She followed Morse into the lounge where once more he picked up bottle number three.

'What time will you have to go, my love?'

'Who said anything about going, Chief Inspector?'

Morse put down the bottle and swiftly retraced his steps to the front door, where he turned the key, and shot the bolts, both top and bottom.

EPILOGUE

Life never presents us with anything which may not be
looked upon as a fresh starting point, no less than as a
termination

(André Gide, *The Counterfeiters*)

THE CORRESPONDENCE columns of *The Times* carried
the following letter on Monday, 10 August 1992:

---

*From Detective Chief
Inspector E. Morse*

Sir, On behalf of the Thames
Valley Police, I wish to
record the gratitude of myself and of my fellow officers
for the co-operation and assistance of *The Times* newspaper. As a direct result
of lines of investigation
suggested by some of its
correspondents about the
'Swedish Maiden' verses, per-

sons now being held in custody will be duly brought to
face trial in accordance with
the law's demands.

I am, sir,

Yours,
E. MORSE,
Thames Valley Police HQ,
Kidlington,
Oxon.

[This correspondence is now
closed. Ed.]

Like the rest of his staff, the editor had been
fascinated by the crop of ideas that sprang from the

Swedish Maiden verses; and although the case was now finished he felt he should reply briefly to Morse's letter. In mid-afternoon therefore he dictated a few lines of reciprocal gratitude.

'Do we have a private address for him?' asked his personal secretary.

'No. Just address it to Kidlington HQ – that'll be fine.'

'What about the initial – do we know what that stands for?'

'The "E"?' The editor considered the question for a second or two. 'Er, no. No, I don't think we do.'

COLIN DEXTER

Service of all the Dead

£6.99 Pan Books

'*The sweet countenance of Reason greeted Morse serenely when he woke, and told him that it would be no bad idea to have a quiet look at the problem itself before galloping off to a solution . . .*'

Chief Inspector Morse was alone among the congregation in suspecting continued unrest in the quiet parish of St Frideswide's.

Most people could still remember the churchwarden's murder. A few could still recall the murderer's suicide. Now even the police had closed the case.

Until a chance meeting among the tombstones reveals startling new evidence of a conspiracy to deceive . . .

WINNER OF THE CWA SILVER DAGGER AWARD

COLIN DEXTER

The Daughters of Cain

£6.99 Pan Books

'Bizarre and bewildering – that's what so many murder investigations in the past had proved to be . . . In this respect, at least, Lewis was correct in his thinking. What he could not have known was what unprecedented anguish the present case would cause to Morse's soul.'

Chief Superintendent Strange's opinion was that too little progress had been made since the discovery of a corpse in a North Oxford flat. The victim had been killed by a single stab wound to the stomach. Yet the police had no weapon, no suspect, no motive.

Within days of taking over the case Chief Inspector Morse and Sergeant Lewis uncover startling new information about the life and death of Dr Felix McClure. When another body is discovered Morse suddenly finds himself with rather too many suspects. For once, he can see no solution. But then he receives a letter containing a declaration of love . . .

COLIN DEXTER

The Silent World of Nicholas Quinn

£6.99 Pan Books

'*Morse had never ceased to wonder why, with the staggering advances in medical science, all pronouncements concerning times of death seemed so disconcertingly vague.*'

The newly appointed member of the Oxford Examinations Syndicate was deaf, provincial and gifted. Now he is dead . . .

And his murder, in his North Oxford home, proves to be the start of a formidably labyrinthine case for Chief Inspector Morse, as he tries to track down the killer through the insular and bitchy world of the Oxford colleges . . .

COLIN DEXTER

The Dead of Jericho

£6.99 Pan Books

'*Morse switched on the gramophone to "play", and sought to switch his mind away from all the terrestrial troubles. Sometimes, this way, he almost managed to forget. But not tonight . . .*'

Anne Scott's address was scribbled on a crumpled note in the pocket of Morse's smartest suit.

He turned the corner of Canal Street, Jericho, on the afternoon of Wednesday, 3rd October.

He hadn't planned a second visit. But he was back later the same day – as the officer in charge of a suicide investigation . . .

WINNER OF THE CWA SILVER DAGGER AWARD